Alice Through the Looking-Glass

Genre Fiction and Film Companions

Series Editor: Simon Bacon

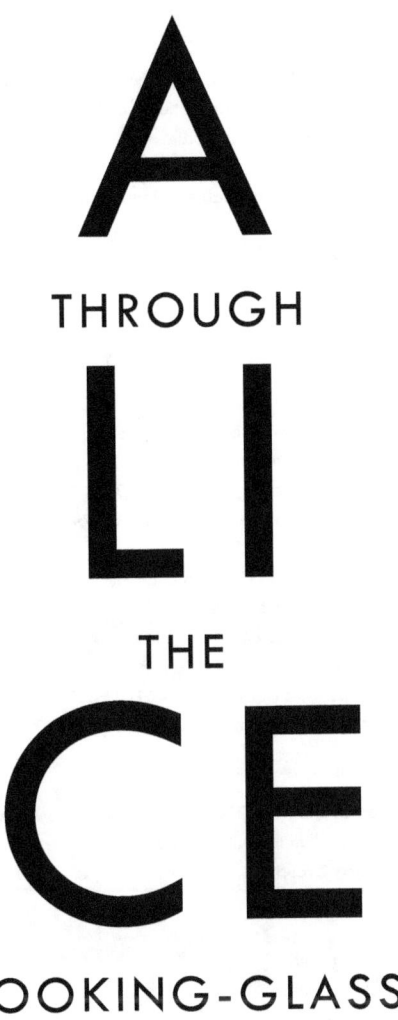

A
THROUGH
LI
THE
CE
LOOKING-GLASS

A Companion

Edited by Franziska E. Kohlt and
Justine Houyaux

PETER LANG

Oxford - Berlin - Bruxelles - Chennai - Lausanne - New York

Bibliographic information published by the Deutsche Nationalbibliothek. The German National Library lists this publication in the German National Bibliography; detailed bibliographic data is available on the Internet at http://dnb.d-nb.de.

A catalogue record for this book is available from the British Library.

Library of Congress Cataloging-in-Publication Data

Names: Kohlt, Franziska, editor. | Houyaux, Justine, editor.
Title: Alice through the looking-glass : a companion / Franziska E. Kohlt, Justine Houyaux.
Description: Berlin ; New York : Peter Lang Publishing, 2024. | Series: Genre fiction and film companions, 2631-8725 ; volume no. 13 | Includes bibliographical references and index.
Identifiers: LCCN 2024010126 (print) | LCCN 2024010127 (ebook) | ISBN 9781800799844 (paperback) | ISBN 9781800799851 (ebook) | ISBN 9781800799868 (epub)
Subjects: LCSH: Carroll, Lewis, 1832-1898. Through the looking-glass—Criticism and interpretation.
Classification: LCC PR4612 .A75 2024 (print) | LCC PR4612 (ebook) | DDC 823/.8—dc23/eng/20240521
LC record available at https://lccn.loc.gov/2024010126
LC ebook record available at https://lccn.loc.gov/2024010127

Cover images: Adobe Stock image 612160641. Standard license. Alice stepping through the Looking-Glass, by John Tenniel. In the public domain.
Cover design by Peter Lang Group AG

ISSN 2631-8725
ISBN 978-1-80079-984-4 (print)
ISBN 978-1-80079-985-1 (ePDF)
ISBN 978-1-80079-986-8 (ePUB)
DOI 10.3726/b20155

In memory of Tom McLeish (1962–2023)

Contents

Contents

Acknowledgements

The editors are indebted, in the first place, to all the contributors, organizers, and supporters of the 2021 *Through the Looking-Glass Sesquicentenary Conference*, and all contributors to this book. Notably, we would like to thank for funding the Templeton Religion Trust, the University of York's ECLAS project, and its Humanities Research Centre for its IT support without which it would have been significantly more challenging to facilitate a global conference during the Covid-19 pandemic.

The editors would also like to thank the University of Southern California Libraries, Linda and George Cassady, whose award of a Carrollian Fellowship to Franziska Kohlt supported the completion of this book. For the provision of high-resolution scans of John Tenniel's *Alice* illustrations, and the libretto material for Chapter 18, we are also grateful to Matthew Demakos. We thank all artists, including those whose work is featured in this collection, for kindly giving permission to reprint their artwork.

We would especially like to acknowledge the unwavering support from the first minute for this project of Prof Tom McLeish, to whose memory we dedicate this volume. We also note the passing, during the final stages of completing this volume, of Edward Wakeling, whose pioneering scholarship, and editorship has made much of the work of our authors accessible, if not, possible, in the first place, and of George Cassady.

Franziska E. Kohlt and Justine Houyaux

Introduction

'Alice in Wonderland' is, unquestionably, one of the most popular books ever written. However, what is popularly referred to as 'Alice in Wonderland' is really two books: *Alice's Adventures in Wonderland* and *Through the Looking-Glass and What Alice Found There*.[1] The distinction between the two has often become blurred, and, as a result, so have discussions of the works. When the prolific amounts of literary criticism discuss 'Alice', they more often focus on *Wonderland* than *Looking-Glass*; and when *Looking-Glass* is treated separately, it is not infrequently with bewilderment, or unfavourably. That the two books are somehow different has been implicitly accepted. As a poll by the Lewis Carroll Society of North America indicated, Carrollians seem to fall into two categories: #TeamLookingGlass or #TeamWonderland, in almost equal proportions[2] (as, indeed, do the two editors of the present collection[3]).

Notably, the same sense of bewilderment at the 'difference' between *Wonderland* and *Looking-Glass* is replicated and progressively made more pronounced in the discussion of works of the author following the *Alice* books, such as *Sylvie and Bruno* and *Sylvie and Bruno Concluded*. The matter of 'difference' also arises in response to Carroll's non-literary writing, from mathematics, science, theology, or on the theatre, which are – like

---

1   We will be referring to the two books as *Wonderland* and *Looking-Glass*, respectively, in this publication, and as *Alice*, when both books are meant; see below for the 'two books' notation.

2   'The Great Debate: Wonderland vs Looking-Glass', *Lewis Carroll Society of North America*, 24 July 2021, <https://www.lewiscarroll.org/event/the-great-debate-wonderland-vs-looking-glass/>.

3   Houyaux: *Wonderland*; Kohlt: *Looking-Glass*.

Looking-Glass – often called '*too* serious', and thus unlike 'Alice' – 'Alice' meaning *Wonderland*. Granting *Through the Looking-Glass* a dedicated volume, a fuller re-appreciation as a work in its own right in this context sheds new light on this 'difference': as one of degree, rather than one of kind. *Looking-Glass* now appears as a significant stepping stone in the development of 'Lewis Carroll', his ideas, and his way of presenting them in literary form, as it reflects more candidly the many strands of inquiry that preoccupied the polymathic mind of its creator – no longer a self-funded first-time author, but that of a best-selling, budding franchise. What exactly shaped this mind, and influenced the narrative choices that ultimately came to constitute this so-often neglected 'Alice sequel', is what this volume aims to explore through a like-mindedly polymathic approach.

This book is the result of an invitation to continue many fertile discussions of the international, online *Through the Looking-Glass Sesquicentenary* conference that had sought to revisit in 2021 the 'second Alice book' in this spirit. The conference called for re-approaching the work from traditional angles, such as through Victorian and children's literature studies, but also new directions in scholarship and newly prominent interdisciplinary fields of study, such as the Environmental and Medical Humanities and posthumanism. Most of all, it aimed to address the historical and intellectual contexts from which the work emerged from as many as possible of the array of fields in which its author was interested, and to which he contributed, both as Lewis Carroll and Charles Lutwidge Dodgson: the mathematician, clergyman, amateur scientist, theatre, music and art enthusiast, deep thinker, and vocal participant in Victorian intellectual and social discourse. This would illuminate whether and how these fields and the debates within them found representation in his texts, and whether that had any connection to the way they have been read and adapted across the past 150 years. Ultimately, the conference was curious to investigate when, and for what reasons, we had arrived at the situation we set out from: how it was that *Looking-Glass* started blending into 'Alice in Wonderland', but also appeared as so different. As a result, the chapters in this collection open up a fresh and kaleidoscopic perspective into a book deliberately different in nature and approach to its predecessor, with a distinct impact within the afterlife of *Alice*, facilitating fresh ways to rethink the latter in turn.

Through the Looking-Glass followed the publication of *Alice's Adventures in Wonderland* in 1871, and is, strictly speaking, the third of the *Alice* books. 'Alice' was originally told as a series of extemporized fairy-tale episodes, most famously on a boat trip in Oxford on 4 July 1862, by mathematical tutor Charles Lutwidge Dodgson, in the company of his colleague, the Reverend Robinson Duckworth, and three of the daughters of Henry George Liddell: Lorina, Edith, and Alice. Although a prolific storyteller, 'Lewis Carroll'[4] had never written down a story of this length before and did so only after Alice made this request of him. The manuscript of *Alice's Adventures Under-Ground* was gifted to her two years later. The publication followed only after a number of endorsements and encouragement, amongst others by Greville MacDonald, son of Scottish author, educator, clergyman, and scientist George MacDonald. After *Wonderland* proved a success, its publisher Alexander Macmillan, who had already been responsible for the publication of an earlier fantastic fairy tale about a child conversing with animals and fantastic creatures – Charles Kingsley's *The Water-Babies* (1862–1863) – encouraged Carroll to write a sequel. Not only did this result in an 'Alice sequel' but, with Carroll continuing to publish with Macmillan for the rest of his life, also a 'fourth' *Alice* – *The Nursery Alice* (1890), as well as a reprint of the manuscript of 'Alice's Adventures Under-Ground'.

This potted publication history is significant for the present reconsideration of *Looking-Glass*. Even the difference between that earliest manuscript version of *Alice* – a much shorter and simpler story, missing many of the now-famous scenes, such as the Mad Tea-Party – highlights, amongst others, the differences between Dodgson as a private and public storyteller.

---

4   Charles Lutwidge Dodgson had first used the pseudonym 'Lewis Carroll' in 1856
     when publishing in Edmund Yates's periodical *The Train: A First Class Magazine*.

It marks also another oft-neglected history of *Alice*, responsible for many of the later books' features: the beginning of *Alice*'s commercialization.

Through the Looking-Glass was, after some uncertainty, illustrated once more by John Tenniel, with whom dealings were at times tense – so much so that Carroll had compiled a list of possible other illustrators, should Tenniel decline (these included William Schwenck Gilbert, of Gilbert and Sullivan fame). It is in such mundane practicalities of the publication process we find clues as to the rich and often-mystified history of the book and its writer. The Tenniel-Carroll relationship was notably to blame for the omission of an entire chapter – 'The Wasp in a Wig'. The link to Gilbert hints at Carroll's connectedness, both personally and intellectually, to Victorian culture in ways that bust the myth of the shy and isolated Oxford don, and cast *Alice* as the product of, and in correspondence with, many facets of Victorian culture, in the context of which the works have yet to be more fully explored. It was thus not only Gilbert but also Sullivan with whom Carroll had corresponded about having his books set to music for the stage. As his diaries show, Carroll was an admirer of both Sullivan's comedic and religious compositions. This reveals Carroll, perhaps unsurprisingly, as a connoisseur of Victorian comedy and visual culture, but perhaps more surprisingly to some, of Anglican religious culture – and a type of stage entertainment frowned upon by segments of it, with which biography could quickly otherwise affiliate him.[5]

Such nuances illuminate, firstly, the multiform influences upon Carroll and, secondly, about where, in the much larger picture, he would sit within this discourse – a picture much more complex than the label of 'children's literature' and its often retrospectively imposed limits presume. But it is these complex contexts that connect the *Alice* books to a wide range of fields within Victorian culture, their concerns and internal debates, and situate its author and works within them, in such a way as to shine a light

---

5   Charles Lutwidge Dodgson, later a deacon in the Anglican Church, was the son of Archdeacon Charles Dodgson, who was, like many of Carroll's Christ Church circles at the University of Oxford, and indeed the younger Dodgson's ordaining Bishop Samuel Wilberforce, a member of the Oxford Movement that opposed theatre attendance.

on where content was not only determined by ideas and ideals but also practical audience and marketing-oriented considerations.

Carroll had at this point in life formed influential friendships, notably, for instance, with many artists of the Pre-Raphaelite Brotherhood. He had developed a love of theatre and music: well-documented (cf. Lovett 1989; Foulkes 2019; Wakeling 2015), but only recently the focus of historicist literary scholarship (cf. Wakeling 2015; Vaclavik 2020; Richards 2023), again, however, with a lesser focus on *Looking-Glass*. Recent work of this kind has also focused on hitherto even less-discussed topics of paramount importance to Carroll himself, such as his religion (Lovett 2022; Gardiner 2020), and his interest in the sciences (Shuttleworth 2014; Kohlt 2016; Beer 2016), which had been regarded as antithesis to his religion (White 2019). A more integrated view of *Alice*'s portrayals of the natural world and its inhabitants has shed new light on Carroll's fairy-tale settings (Talairach 2014; Bown 2001; Keene 2015). Focusing, however, again largely on *Wonderland*, these have nonetheless succeeded in indicating how intimately linked Science and Religion were in Victorian publishing (see Lightman 2007; Secord 1885; Fyfe 2000; Topham 2007) and the much richer environments as part of which they invite us to discuss Carroll, *Looking-Glass* and their afterlives – a part of them, not apart from them.

This edited collection thus undertakes the significant attempt of reconstructing the intellectual environment from which *Looking-Glass* emerged – straddling also how that factors into *Looking-Glass*'s reception history, as both distinct from and intermingled with that of *Wonderland*, or 'Alice'.

It will make a significant intervention into the study of one of the world's most popular books and pop culture phenomena by ambitiously reframing the nature and territories of the scholarly discussion around 'Alice' through a re-exploration of its less-explored sequel. It places *Looking-Glass* centre-stage and illuminates through Carroll's multifaceted interests and areas of impact in Victorian culture the book's intellectual scope, and scope of social and societal concerns, which have hitherto not been comprehensively explored. It invites scholars and practitioners from these fields of Carroll's interests to enrich the discussion of the literary subject with knowledge from their respective disciplines. Investigating thus also *Looking-Glass*'s history of adaptation and commercialization, beginning in Carroll's lifetime, and spanning to the present, it will draw out hitherto glanced-over connections between the concerns of the books and their adaptations. This will shed new light on the reasons for 'Alice's' seemingly perpetual and universal popularity, and why the books seem so uniquely suited for adaptation in such a wide range of media, expressing an even wider range of issues refracted through these adaptations (this book will cover it as an engagement with subjects as diverse as AI, ontology, and sexual abuse). This will be enhanced by juxtaposing some of these scholarly analyses with some artists' own reflections on their engagements with the work.

Our book will thus fulfil two purposes: it is, firstly, a re-appreciation of *Through the Looking-Glass*, and through it one of the most popular books and franchises of all time, and the first comprehensive interdisciplinary exploration of its kind in Carroll studies. As such, it marks a departure from the psychoanalytic methods that have dominated many of the efforts of past edited collections of literary analyses of *Alice*. It will, secondly, showcase an array of state-of-the-field methodologies and put into dialogue scholars and discourses, the public and practitioners, writers and audiences, breaking down frequently assumed boundaries, rivalries, or mutual exclusivity of fields. Mirroring the circumstances of *Alice*'s genesis, this book thus hopes to model the possibilities of transdisciplinary humanities studies, aspiring to be not only a *Companion* to the rediscovery of *Alice* but also other literary works, and the central place still occupied by popular narrative in public discourse. It thus hopes to appeal to scholars, practitioners, and teachers, alike: breaking new ground as a concise case study mapping scholarly paradigm shifts in interdisciplinary and applied literary studies, knowledge exchange, and public engagement.

The book is structured by the different disciplinary fields it explores. Part I sets the scene, beginning with Alice's 'environment', reconsidered through Victorian Natural History.

Talairach draws links between *Looking-Glass*'s portrayal of Nature, as both familiar and unfamiliar, to the culture of Victorian menageries, zoological gardens, and museums as sites of renegotiation of taxonomies, and through them, social and biological hierarchies. As Natural History was a foremost vehicle of learning and education, and one often involving, perhaps counter-intuitively today, fairies, Allen re-assesses if *Alice* is really merely 'delicious nonsense', or if, and if so what, Alice learns on her journey. Fagan and Witen re-approach *Looking-Glass* as a proto-post-humanist work, taking seriously the potentially behaviour-changing impact Carroll may have foreseen for his work and how it is modelled in his narrative play and subversion of conventional child–animal and child–plant encounters.

Such considerations firmly position Carroll and Alice at the heart of Victorian scientific and moral discourse, of which *Alice* has often been claimed to be morally and otherwise agnostic. Engaging with scientific references in *Looking-Glass* in their historical and cultural context, however, reveals a different, more nuanced picture of a socially and morally engaged author. That this squares with both, the 'serious' dedicated anti-vivisectionist Charles Dodgson, and children's entertainer, the clergyman-logician, and fairy-tale author will be illuminated, in Part II, which focuses on Natural Philosophy.

Kohlt documents how Carroll grew up immersed in Victorian optical culture, which, with its 'philosophical toys' and their accompanying literature, aimed to be edifying and entertaining, and consciously modelled his narratives on it, mirroring its themes and images – in *Looking-Glass* and already in *Wonderland*. McLeish considers Carroll in comparison to his friend and polymathically minded kindred spirit, George MacDonald, and their reflections upon the imagination. How it was these polymathic roots of *Looking-Glass* that made it a medium through which to consider complex scientific and mathematical problems is examined by Schilero. He shows how Carroll's polymathically informed literary writing provided a language for Einstein and Gödel's discussions of paradoxical, unimaginable science, illuminating the work's reception history beyond the literary. The chapters of this section, collectively, challenge not only the Carroll-Dodgson 'split personality' theories, but also complicate 'two cultures' and 'conflict theory' approaches – of science and humanities, science and fantasy, or science and religion.

This prepares the discussion of the topic most important to Carroll, his life and thought: the subject of religion. Consciously positioned alongside the science chapters, the authors in Part III will approach them not as opposites, but, as understood by Carroll and many others, as complementary paths to truth (cf. Dixon 2008; McGrath 2007; Ungureanu 2019). Picking up the thread from the Natural History, Gardiner considers, once more, the Looking-Glass Insects and their naming from a theological perspective, and thus also the postcolonial dimension of the re-naming of 'exotic' fauna. Considering, once more, alongside Carroll and MacDonald, and the use of mirrors in *Looking-Glass* and *Lilith*, Rawleigh gets to the heart of Carroll's literary use of the Looking-Glass, the mirror, as Biblical: as an instrument facilitating reflection upon questions of knowledge in discourses as complex as that of science, nature, and moral thought and action within, and in relation to them.

Both Gardiner and Rawleigh shed light on what ultimately alienated Dodgson from the established churches of his time, driving him from high to broad Church affiliation (Lovett 2022), and abandoning a primary clerical career. Alongside Gabelman, whose *Theology of Nonsense* (2016) laid the foundations for much of the debate around the faith of (so-called) children's writers, and the 'serious' use of 'nonsense' within it, they reposition Carroll's *Alice* as a contribution to this literature – an alternative pursuit of his clerical endeavour. How spiritual and religious literature outside the High Church Anglican canon contributed to the formation of this is further illuminated by Brown. Her discussion of Carroll's interest in the spiritualism of John Dee and Francis Bacon also notes how references to it in *Looking-Glass*, in turn, made it a medium for contemporary writers wishing to explore such questions further.

Closing in on the ultimately psychological function of the mirror, Part IV moves from Carroll's own interest in the mind and the history of the mind-mirror metaphor, as pertaining to the soul and its health, to how Carroll's literary adaptation of it could encapsulate it in such ways as to be applicable beyond its literary confines. Flynn discusses how Carroll's investment in the nascent science of psychology and fascination with dreaming was shaped especially by the newly flourishing periodical market. Schaefer-Salins, tantalizingly, juxtaposes this historical account with a survey of *Looking-Glass*'s afterlife in the literature of psychological theory, in which it has been, unusually, more prevalent than its predecessor. Coates and Coalville carry us across the threshold of history and theory, illustrating how in marketing psychology 'Looking-Glass thinking' practically assists innovators in thinking up 'six impossible things before breakfast' to productively displace them mentally beyond the constraints of time, space, language, science, and other inconvenient practicalities.

As language is Carroll's main vehicle to convey the aims he envisaged for his work, it becomes necessary to reframe Carroll's reading and own work on logic and language in Part V. Further strengthening the connection between *Alice* and Carroll's pedagogic writing and practice, Gerlach analyses the narrative progression of *Looking-Glass* as a mirroring of the stages of Aristotle's Logic and Carroll's novel as a mnemonic: a teaching tool, pre-dating his later Logic teaching works for children, such as the *Game of Logic*. Where such mediations of truth via language placed Carroll in relation to his contemporaries is the subject of Savenije, who, focusing on Humpty Dumpty's attitudes on language, situates Carroll among linguist-logicians of his time, and those he later influenced, uncovering another of *Looking-Glass*'s distinct afterlives.

The following sections now shift their gaze more firmly on the afterlives of *Looking-Glass* through considering various forms of its adaptation. Once more considering the practical dimensions of publishing and marketing, Part VI begins to map, and thus locate, the history of the blurring of *Wonderland* and *Looking-Glass* in this context. Offering a translation of an unpublished essay on Lewis Carroll by surrealist Louis Aragon, Houyaux illuminates frictions between text, translation, and artistic license in the practice of translation as a form of popularization. How artistic and marketing choices deprioritize text and meanings is mapped in detail by Amanda Lastoria, who traces the history of repackaging *Looking-Glass* as a *Wonderland* sequel in multi-volume or combined editions. In the first comprehensive history of *Looking-Glass*'s stage adaptations, Richards and Imholtz illustrate further the extent to which textual accuracy and fidelity to the text gave way to income-generating spectacle. Newly devised songs, dances, and additional scenes for extending the stage time of celebrity actors pre-empt what would half a century later become a commonplace in such adaptations as Disney's 'Alice in Wonderland', in which the two books become one.

Taking a step back in Part VII, de Nobriga deconstructs the text into its building blocks through the theme of choices. Theorizing the insights of earlier chapters through the methods of data visualization, she shows how *Looking-Glass* can become adaptable in different contexts – offering a unique perspective into the intersections of categories otherwise considered separately. A creative engagement with the infinity loop of childhood engagement with Humpty Dumpty, his popular culture variations, and his own creative contribution, Paxman's visual essay reflects on the building blocks and choices in the process of one such path of creative adaptation.

Recapturing the theme of the earlier chapter, of *Looking-Glass*'s more mature notes, Part VIII considers the legacy of illustrating *Looking-Glass*. Dillon shows how Benjamin Lacombe's illustrations re-interpret it as an exploration of pubescent female identity and Mitchell's photography as a transgression of female boundaries, to offer a more specific take on *Looking-Glass* both *being* more mature and conveying *the process of* maturing. Pereira's comparative analysis of international illustrators' takes on the moment Alice steps through the mirror and further draws out varying interpretations of the work as commentary on becoming and transcendence to examine what beliefs, choices, and historical contexts are reflected in these images. This is, finally, viewed through the eyes of an illustrator, as Peliano reflects on the philosophical and professional preoccupations of fellow *Looking-Glass* illustrators, from Švankmajer to Kusama, and herself.

Having considered the historical and philosophical contexts, the marketing and visual culture dimensions of *Looking-Glass* prepare a different framework to the subsequent literary engagements with it – in Part IX, 'Before Carroll', and Part X, 'Beyond Carroll'. Arnavas's history of the mirror as fairy tale symbol and its Victorian remediations resonates with psychological considerations of earlier essays when, considering Alice's actions in relation to female agency in such earlier texts. Khan further draws out concerns of female agency by juxtaposing *Looking-Glass* with mirror-themed works of Tennyson, whom Carroll admired. Together, these chapters tease out the satirical and wish-fulfilling potential of the dream-mirror that becomes crucial in the age of modernism and Freud, discussed in Part X, where Martin, Magri da Rocha and Rapucci, and Yin cast their gaze beyond Carroll, at postmodern adaptations in UK, US, and Chinese-American literature. Through similarly contextual, biographical, and historical readings, the works of Virginia Woolf, Gertrude Stein and Grace Lin become the product of their cultural contexts, but also co-production of childhood cultures and their authors' participation in it. Martin recapturing the earlier theme of optical apparatus determining literary form and narrative in Dorothy Sayers in a way parallel to Carroll's *Looking Glass* as product of optical culture – Carroll emerges, here, as proto-modernist in the way he envisaged his books' practical materiality, their application in society, as more-than-a-book.

This prefaces, penultimately, the reconsideration of the global, multi- and transmedial setting of pop culture, film and graphic novel, video games, and fashion, in which *Alice*'s overwhelming presence has been widely acknowledged (Brooker 2004; Kohlt 2012; Vaclavik 2018). Is it possible to discern a distinct role for *Looking-Glass* in this afterlife? Bevington, Cherry, and Gibson examine three intriguing subjects through which to address this question. Bevington sheds light on the *Looking-Glass* references in Garland's AI thriller *Ex Machina* (2013) and its themes of individual, human choice, the possibility of free will, and ambiguity of moral ideals within certain cultural contexts. Her discussion gains richness through prior chapters' discussions of science, religion, and colonialism, exemplifying how this book can be put into dialogue with historical contexts and contemporary applications, to shed new light on how *Alice* can function so effectively in such apparently unrelated settings. The semiotic flexibility of *Looking-Glass*'s mirror, as relating to the theme of maturity and maturing, is instrumental in its addressing of psychologically traumatic childhood abuse and its impact on identity in Cherry's chapter on *Lost Girls* (2006). That *Looking-Glass* has been read as, and thus attracts, more 'serious' philosophical discussions, becomes even clearer when Gibson turns to the prolific, and only apparently non-distinct use of *Alice* references in the *Matrix* franchise, where she identifies *Looking-Glass* imagery as 'doing the heavy lifting'.

As has been the case with 'Alice', overall, one part of *Looking-Glass* in particular has developed a life of its own, to which the book's final two sections turn, by addressing its poems and paramount poetic achievement: 'Jabberwocky'.

Kelen interrogates 'Jabberwocky' as Carrollian synecdoche and as a text impossible to translate, decipher, and understand, and yet endlessly tempting translators to do so, as emblematic of Carroll's writing. Kérchy contextualizes this struggle for semiosis, alongside the Jabberwock's kindred Carrollian cryptid, the Snark: an embodiment of vanishing, nothingness, and elusiveness, yet pursued for infinity, whose echoes in the global history of translations are surveyed by Sundmark.

The relevance of those questions of translation and transmediation is made palpable from the perspective of the translator and that of the poet, as La Mura and Roberts walk readers through the thought processes behind their original pieces presented here: a new Italian translation of 'Jabberwocky', and four new parodies of it – a rare insight into their minds at work.

In keeping with the theme of poetry, and coming full circle by returning to the shores of the natural world from which this book set off, the final two chapters of Part XI reflect on the distinct legacy of *Looking-Glass*'s poetry. Both focus on 'fishy' subjects, that is, seaside-themed poetry, and reinterrogate the function of this site as one of moral transformation from which these poems derive their political, satirical sharpness, and their potential for didactic and moral commentary. Demakos and Susina reframe Carroll's nonsense poetry, his humour, as instrumental, not contradictory to his 'serious' interest in Logic and Truth. As an exercise in sense-making by the logician Lewis Carroll, ever seeking to hold the mirror up to society and individuals, to confront them with the deceptions of realities, these poems, ultimately, encapsulate what *Looking-Glass* enacted and facilitated: a 'seeing through' what lies beyond its appearances.

The book comes full circle in more than one way. It will have reinvestigated *Looking-Glass* in its own right, but also provided a stepping stone to Carroll's later works – a key to his life, work, and thought. It will have circled through Carroll's preoccupations with the numerous aspects of contemporary intellectual discourse, his remediations of them, and those adaptations, which, through Carroll's imagery, navigate kindred concerns in their own times. By having honed in on elements that have previously unsettled or inhibited criticism of *Looking-Glass*, and by acknowledging and contextualizing them through historical perspectives, facilitated by transdisciplinary modes of scholarship, this book discerns ways in which Carroll's texts were truly innovative, even radical, interventions into Victorian children's literature intellectual discourse, while at the same time keenly aware of their conventions.

This approach aids in situating where *Alice* – and Carroll – saw themselves, and where they were seen by others to be situated. It unlocks, in turn, how the *Alice* books could capture the minds of Victorians, and minds across time, making them at once familiar, and yet facilitating through that familiarity, novel ways of seeing, seeing through, and knowing. In this light, *Looking-Glass*, finally, extends an invitation to 'seriously' consider 'unserious', or 'too serious' 'unserious' literature, ways of recontextualizing children's literature and children's authors, and authors and literature similarly bracketed, that may have thus been short-changed, compared to what they originally envisaged as their aims and areas of impact, and how, despite, or because of that, they were received, at their time, and beyond their time, and why.

Part I

Natural History

Laurence Talairach

1 Fabulous 'creetures': Lewis Carroll's Fantastic Zoo in *Through the Looking-Glass and What Alice Found There*

> Of course the first thing to do was to make a grand survey of the country she was going to travel through. 'It's something very like learning geography,' thought Alice, as she stood on tiptoe in hopes of being able to see a little further. 'Principal rivers – there *are* none. Principal mountains – I'm on the only one, but I don't think it's got any name. Principal towns – why, what *are* those creatures, making honey down there? They can't be bees – nobody ever saw bees a mile off, you know –' and for some time she stood silent, watching one of them that was bustling about among the flowers, poking its proboscis into them, 'just as if it was a regular bee', thought Alice.
>
> However, this was anything but a regular bee: in fact, it was an elephant – as Alice soon found out, though the idea quite took her breath away at first. (46–47)

As Alice explores her new environment with the aim of making a 'grand survey of the country she was going to travel through', the town she notices only reveals strange creatures making honey: bee-like elephants she has never seen before. Like *Alice's Adventures in Wonderland*, Lewis Carroll's sequel narrates the journey of a little girl fallen into a fantastic world peopled with unfamiliar animals. But whether fantastic, mythical, or nonsensical Wonderland and Looking-Glass creatures are informed by contemporary knowledge about the natural world. Alice's adventures recall the world of Victorian explorations, collections, and exhibitions of strange and unfamiliar animals. In *Through the Looking-Glass; and What Alice Found There*, Alice starts off pretending she is 'a hungry hyæna' (*TTLG*: 8) before she finds herself in the 'wilderness' (*TTLG*: 37), and, like many a Victorian naturalist exploring unknown lands, the little girl then needs to walk, fly, or take the train to study looking-glass fauna and flora.

Natural History

Carroll's creatures reflect the scientific context of the time. As Rose Lovell-Smith has shown, several animals encountered by the little girl in *Alice's Adventures in Wonderland* strongly recall Charles Darwin's own research, such as the pigeon – 'a Darwinian bird' (Lovell-Smith 2007: 41).[1] Similarly, for U. C. Knoepflmacher, 'the Dodo, the Caterpillar, [and] the Pigeon [...] are imports from a Darwinian world of aggression, voracity, and sexual selection' (1998: 167). In both fantasies, the numerous references to eating or being eaten add to the evolutionary threat which permeates Alice's adventures. Her constant misclassification rewrites her position as a human being among animals, illuminating in so doing 'the dislodging of humanity from its confident "overseeing" of nature' (Lovell-Smith 2007: 28).

As this article argues,[2] the way in which Carroll's fantasy reverses 'the usual direction of the natural history gaze' and 'bring[s] Alice under nature's gaze' can be read in the context of Victorian museum culture (Lovell-Smith 2007: 28). As Laura White notes, Carroll 'liked to take children to exhibits of animals, living animals as at aquariums and zoos and stuffed or skeletonized ones as at museums of natural history' (2017: 190). Carroll's acquaintance with Henry Acland, who initiated the establishment of Oxford's Museum of Natural History, suggests the writer's familiarity with many of the natural history specimens then exhibited at Oxford, some of which he had taken photographs of in 1857.[3]

It is tempting, in this context, to imagine that the Lobster Quadrille in *Alice's Adventures in Wonderland* was intended as a variant of the Hippopotamus Quadrille (or Polka), inspired by the 'hippomania', a craze ignited by the first hippopotamus seen in Britain, Obaysh, which arrived at the London Zoo on 25 May 1850 (Simmons 2012: 114). Alice believes that

---

1   Darwin studied the domestic pigeon in *The Origin of Species* (in the chapter 'Variation Under Domestication').

2   This article sums up several ideas developed in my *Animals, Museum Culture and Children's Literature in Nineteenth-Century Britain: Curious Beasties* (Palgrave Macmillan, 2021).

3   As recorded in his diary, Carroll took six photographs of the museum specimens for Henry Acland on 16 June 1857. Among the animals were skeletons of a brown kiwi, an anteater, a cod's head and shoulders, a cobra, a sunfish, a tunny-fish (bluefin tuna), a platypus, and possibly a squirrel.

she sees 'a walrus or hippopotamus' (*AAIW*: 41) when she is in the pool of tears, although the animal turns out to be a mouse. The 'Lobster Quadrille' was seen by Carroll as resembling some of the wild animals at the Zoological Gardens: 'Did you ever see the Rhinoceros, and the Hippopotamus, at the Zoological Gardens, trying to dance a minuet together?' (Qtd. by Gardner in Carroll 1970: 131). The Lobster is later humorously presented as a species already seen by Alice at 'Dinn' (*AAIW*: 135). The change from 'dinner' to 'Dinn' – a place where animals may be seen – matches the changing function of the zoo in the second half of the nineteenth century, as Jed Mayer explains, shifting 'from one mode of consumption to another: from the acclimatization of foreign species to be consumed as meat and leather, to the display of exotic animals to be consumed by avid spectators' (Mayer 2017: 215). Furthermore, Alice's fear that the flamingo might bite recalls the many accidents which occurred daily in Victorian menageries, whilst John Simons argues that the hedgehogs which roll themselves into balls may have been inspired by the armadillos found at Jamrach's shop in London (Simons 2008: 102).[4]

As soon as she tumbles down the rabbit hole, however, Carroll's little girl is turned into an object which *Wonderland* animals examine, trying to classify *her*, thus inverting the dynamics of Victorian animal-human relationships displayed in natural history museums and zoos. Alice's shift from subject to object needs to be seen, as Jed Mayer argues, as part of 'a shift in her understanding of the place of the animals in Victorian society, and the complicity of spectatorship in rendering animals as objects of contemplation, whether for amusement, study, or experimentation' (Mayer 2017: 221).[5]

4   It has also been suggested that Carroll's dormouse may have been modelled on Dante Gabriel Rossetti's wombat, purchased at Jamrach's as well, alongside other creatures, like kangaroos, wallabies, armadillos, and a zebu. This idea is suggested by Martin Gardner, but as Simons explains, *Alice's Adventures in Wonderland* was written in 1864, thus before Rossetti's wombat, Top, had arrived. However, Carroll did visit Rossetti and his family, took photographs of them and Rossetti had several dormice, alongside owls, armadillos, a raccoon, kangaroos, wallabies, jackasses, peacocks, parakeets, and a Japanese salamander (Simons 2008: 113).

5   Mayer analyses Christina Rossetti's 'Goblin Market' (1862), a poem certainly influenced by Dante Gabriel Rossetti's own collection of exotic animals, as well as the numerous creatures he enjoyed viewing at the London Zoological Gardens.

In the Looking-Glass world, likewise, the curious 'beasties' (as exotic or fantastic creatures) look back, deconstructing their own objectification in (sometimes) humorous and satirical ways. They not only denounce the commodification of animals but also blur the divide between humans and animals. The bee-like elephants, 'bustling among the flowers' and poking their proboscis into them, foreshadow many other looking-glass 'creatures,' including Alice, who may be 'animal – or vegetable – or mineral' (*AAIW*: 288). This blurring of species is at the heart of Carroll's 'zoological' nonsense that tackles 'predator-prey relationships' and hints at 'reversals in hierarchy' (2017: 120; 122). But it also owes much to the museum culture Carroll humorously derides: Alice believes, for instance, that she 'may visit the elephants later on,' like in zoological gardens; the Tiger-lily[6] in the garden of live flowers, protected from danger by a tree that can bark, is another of the many allusions to the exhibition of curious species imported into Britain in the nineteenth century, often brought together under one roof.[7]

Although White reads such references to large animals as characteristic of Carroll's 'comedy of scale' (2017: 132), it is important to note that Alice's attention is immediately captured by the 'creatures' that inhabit the Looking-Glass world, which she attempts to place according to her knowledge of Victorian menageries. Among the curious Looking-Glass 'beasties' she encounters are the already mentioned honey-making elephants, creatures which 'look [–] like kangaroos' (*TTLG*: 209), and imaginary lions or

6   Tiger-lilies (*Lilium lancifolium*) were an Asian species of lily, hence as much associated with exoticism as other animals imported into Britain. The first tiger-lilies arrived at Kew Gardens around the beginning of the nineteenth century.

7   In *Alice's Adventures in Wonderland*, the possible presence of the old Surrey Zoological Gardens in Tenniel's illustration of the Queen's croquet-ground, with a domed glasshouse in the background of the picture (Lovell-Smith 2003: 388), evokes as well the simultaneous display of plants for flower shows and exotic animals, since the site merged the animal and the vegetable behind its glass panels. The conservatory of the old Surrey Zoological Gardens (300 ft in circumference and more and 6,000 ft) was the largest glass building in England in the 1830s, hosting both plants and the cages for the exotic animals then kept at the Royal Surrey Gardens. The place anticipated the public's attraction for the Crystal Palace in 1851.

tigers which sound like steam trains (*TTLG*: 79). Yet, these often do not match the shape and size of the creatures generally exhibited in zoos and museums, proposing a literary world much wilder than that of Victorian menageries. Indeed, like in *Wonderland*, *Looking-Glass* constantly destabilizes species typologies and categorization. When Alice encounters the unicorn – the nursery rhyme (and legendary) creature, suddenly made 'real' – it instantly turns the little girl into a 'fabulous monster':

> 'This is a child!' Haigha replied eagerly, coming in front of Alice to introduce her, and spreading out both his hands towards her in an Anglo-Saxon attitude. 'We only found it to-day. It's as large as life, and twice as natural!'
>
> 'I always thought they were fabulous monsters!' said the Unicorn. 'Is it alive?'. (*TTLG*: 151)

Just like the Gryphon in *Alice's Adventures in Wonderland* (Reichertz 1997: 47),[8] the portrayal of the unicorn reframes Carroll's sequel as another travel narrative, in which Alice is turned into a specimen worthy of (scientific) interest, a wonder to be displayed in a cabinet of curiosities. Evoking Charles Kingsley's water-baby that tries to avoid being collected and named, the scene forcefully conveys Carroll's commentary on the Victorian museum as a place where, ironically, categories are never fixed but always potentially evolving.

In *Looking-Glass*, the discourse on species is further foregrounded when the Lion asks Alice, playing the traditional guessing game, whether she is 'animal – or vegetable – or mineral' (*TTLG*: 153). As a 'fabulous monster', the little girl evades all attempts at classifying or naming. The unicorn's remark recalls an earlier scene in which Alice loses her own name in the wood in which 'things have no name' (*TTLG*: 61), where she fears she might be given another one, having to track the 'creature' which has been given hers in due course. Taxonomy appears as an unstable concept.

8　Reichertz also adds that the Gryphon is 'especially associated with antipodes … Mandeville included a report on griffins in his account of his voyages, griffins so enormous that humans used their talons for drinking cups' (Reichertz 1997: 47). This link with travel literature supports the view of Carroll's narrative as a rewriting of tales of exploration.

Natural History

The word 'creature' itself gradually becomes a mere series of uncertain signs, and is applied as much to Alice as to the other characters she encounters, as the White King makes explicit:

> … 'I'll make a memorandum about her, if you like – She's a dear good creature,' he repeated softly to himself, as he opened his memorandum-book. 'Do you spell "creature" with a double "e"?'. (*TTLG*: 150)

Looking-Glass 'creetures' and 'creatures' deceive the ear as much as the eye, hence Alice's recurrent belief that she has been deluded by 'a conjuring trick' (*TTLG*: 206) as she faces creatures which change shape, melt away, like the Goat's beard (54) or turn into other species: the sheep 'gets more and more like a porcupine' (104), the Gnat is 'about the size of a chicken' (54) and elephants make honey like bees. The human child, however, observed and objectified through a telescope, microscope, and opera-glass (50),[9] and eventually named a 'fabulous monster', indicates the collapse of species categorization (the monster) and the annihilation of the boundary between myth and reality ('fabulous'). Alice becomes, therefore, a taxonomic anomaly.

Throughout the fantasy, the failure of the classification system mocks the Victorians' obsession with taxonomies and finds echoes in the various embeddings and reversals that punctuate the fantasy. The Rocking-horse-fly, which 'lives on sap and sawdust', the Snap-dragon-fly, which lives on 'frumenty and mince-pie', or the Bread-and-Butterfly, which lives on 'weak tea with cream in it' (59), which Alice encounters at the beginning of her journey (as *Looking-Glass* versions of the horsefly, the dragonfly and the butterfly), all embody Carroll's nonsensical discourse on naming. If, as White contends, their description matches the expectations of natural history, since 'each is described in terms of structure, habitat, means of locomotion, and diet', and if Tenniel's illustrations 'show each insect as a natural history exhibit' since the insects 'are displayed in order of their threat' (2017: 197), Looking-Glass insects, nonetheless, point out the arbitrariness of the link between signifier and signified.[10]

---

9   For more on 'magic glasses' and scientific optical devices see Chapter 4 in this collection.

10 For more on the Looking-Glass Insects, see Chapters 3 and 7.

The breakdown in the relationship between signifier and signified is further magnified by the Jabberwocky poem, where invented words give life to imaginary creatures that turn the whole natural system on its head:

> Twas brillig, and the slithy toves
> Did gyre and gimble in the wabe:
> All mimsy were the borogoves,
> And the mome raths outgrabe (126).

The poem, first printed in mirror writing, needing to be deciphered, constructs classification as a complex, mysterious – and almost alchemical – activity. The use of portmanteau words, compounds of different words, which just as the imaginary compound creatures, unsettle types of diet as much as species categories, lay bare Carroll's nonsense-commentary on taxonomy. These species include toves, a species of badger with short horns like a stag, 'something like lizards – and [...] something like corkscrews' (128), which makes nests and lives on cheese; borogoves, an extinct kind of parrot without wings, 'something like a live mop' (129) which lives on veal; and raths, a species of land turtle with a mouth like a shark, simultaneously 'a sort of green pig' (129). Embedded in the main narrative, the Jabberwocky poem does not, however, function as a reflecting device to help Alice and the reader understand the mystery of species classification. On the contrary, it mystifies classification even more through its use of portmanteau words and imaginary creatures, making it even more puzzling as it is printed in reverse. The text-within-the-text, crowded as it is with 'curious-looking creatures' (128), is thus a literal (reversed) mirror image of Looking-Glass creatures, whose species categories are as insecure as they are changeable.

Finally, the poem hosts at its heart a 'monster' – the Jabberwock.[11] Both the Jabberwock and Alice, as another 'fabulous monster', evoke the inherent and inevitable failure of the taxonomic systems so central to Victorian Natural History culture, in their attempt to accommodate all possible species. By epitomizing instead mystification, the monstrous Jabberwock

---

11   For more on 'Jabberwocky', see the penultimate section of this collection, and Chapter 33 on unstable categories.

displays Carroll's mad cabinet of curiosities, presenting the creatures who inhabit *Looking-Glass* as mere literary creations – associations of signifiers and of literary pieces themselves being capable even of engendering ever new creatures (literary and otherwise). Thus, by evading classification, the Jabberwock, like many of the *Wonderland* and *Looking-Glass* 'creetures', also resists capture. The Looking-Glass beasties thus offer a satirical journey, virtually as well as figuratively, through the mirror which effectively challenges the imperial appropriation of animals which the *Alice* books recurrently allude to. As a result, Looking-Glass species, foreshadowing Carroll's Snark, or Boojum, just like some of Edward Lear's nonsensical beasties, such as Clangle-Wangles, show how Victorian nonsense enabled writers to turn the mirror back on naturalists' attempts at mastering non-human animals, with a vengeance.

Brittani Allen

2 *Through the Looking-Glass* and 'Bruno's Revenge': Language, Nonhumans, and the Environment

Alice is a protagonist who grows and matures by learning in the Looking-Glass world, whereas Carroll is the child-at-heart character who witnesses the animals and fairies receive an education in 'Bruno's Revenge' and is himself educated by it. Although current scholarship from Laurence Talairach, Caroline Sumpter, Franziska Kohlt, and Jason Marc Harris address fairies as an educational tool in Victorian literature, there are few pieces addressing the educational implications in Carroll's *Through the Looking-Glass* and 'Bruno's Revenge', especially in the context of the important role of animals and fairies.

This essay will juxtapose the role the main characters serve as educators or learners in these works and examine the ways in which Carroll invites readers to explore how the natural elements of each world, along with the inhabitants, alter the presentation of and experiences in each world. It will thus address the involvement of animals and fairies and the implementation of simple language, as opposed to overly elaborate or technical jargon, to gain insights into Victorian society and ideologies. It will discuss how the differences and similarities amongst Looking-Glass world, Fairyland, and Victorian England, and how linguistic choices and the presence of fairies and animals are responsible for, and reinforce, the lessons across *Through the Looking-Glass* and in 'Bruno's Revenge'.

Through the Looking-Glass

The peculiar phenomenon of how language operates within *Through the Looking-Glass* is first highlighted by Alice's misunderstandings in the Looking-Glass world. In addition to the importance of interpersonal behaviour, it is also important for her to mind her linguistic behaviour, especially in relation to pragmatics, the study of naturally occurring verbal and non-verbal utterances exchanged during communication. The nonsense Alice encounters is new to her at first. She tries to make sense of the differences between the worlds based on what she could see and what she is now immersed in, though she is still taken by surprise with each new discovery. However, once she begins to understand that these occurrences will keep happening as long as she is in the Looking-Glass world, she attempts to learn about them and participate in the conversations by adhering to the Cooperative and Politeness principles, as outlined by Geoffrey Leech in *The Principles of Pragmatics*. The Cooperative Principle encourages a speaker to evaluate the social encounter and say what needs to be said, as well as when and in the manner the information needs to be said. The Politeness Principle emphasizes polite communication, which is responsible for regulating a person's social demeanour when engaging in conversation.

Although Alice is reminded to mind her manners, as she was taught in her Victorian upper-middle-class upbringing, she embraces the fantastical and nonsensical, as she becomes gradually more willing to participate in and use her imagination in conjunction with her understanding of logic and reasoning to adapt to and function within the new world. Her manners, some of which constitute unspoken communication, can have as much of an impact on her interactions with the fantastical creatures as what is spoken.

As Alice learns to navigate Looking-Glass world, she becomes more assertive and moves from wanting to learn and understand to wanting to be a learner and a teacher, something she demonstrates as she makes her wishes quite apparent.

Many critics, such as Per Aage Brandt, James R. Kincaid, Jean-Jacques Lecercle, Linda M. Shires, and Marina Yaguello, have explored the language use and interactions that occur in *Looking-Glass*, but repeatedly scrutinize only specific passages and excerpts, when the novel as a whole lacked the attention it deserves, as a linguistic revelation within Victorian children's literature.

Robert Polhemus writes, '[L]anguage is anything but a neutral, transparent medium that simply reflects an existing reality,' which is what Looking-Glass world represents (Polhemus 1994: 341). Language is also not something that can be understood as concrete or proper, but rather something that is constantly evolving in response to ever-changing experiences and encounters. There is the ability for nonsense to create meaning, because, as Alice discovers in Looking-Glass world, nonsense may have meaning of its own.

Although language is abstract and nonsense can be meaningful, Polhemus does not recognize this, because nonsense is 'nonsense', and it does 'not refer to the real world' (Polhemus 1994: 602). Shires, however, explains how fantasy, nonsense, and language can be interpreted in a realistic manner. A main concept within this is the connection between uncertainty, instability, and nonsense. All three qualities are evident when Alice is confronted by the White Queen and Red Queen about Alice's dinner party. Alice is startled to think that the party was being held on her behalf and she was not even allowed to invite the guests, which leads to a discussion that brings into question Alice's manners. The White Queen then, abruptly, asks about Alice's ability to do addition, something Alice excelled at when in Humpty Dumpty's presence. However, in the presence of the White and Red Queens, Alice is flustered, confused, and unsettled. The Queens shift from addition to subtraction to asking her, 'Take a bone from a dog: what remains' (*TTLG*: 190)? Alice is faced with uncertainty and instability during this conversation and declares: 'What dreadful nonsense we *are* talking about' (*TTLG*: 191). The uncertainty, instability, and nonsense of language place limitations on one's life, much like Alice experiences as she interacts with the creatures in Looking-Glass world.

Limits may be defined by the individual, but they are also placed by society. Alice illustrates Polhemus's idea that 'there may be a wild and brave child struggling to get out and mock the withering realities that govern life,' because it is 'through the child, he [Carroll] strips away both personal and social conventions and prejudice' (Polhemus 1994: 343). To escape her governing society, Alice must recognize that there are positive qualities to the nonsense she encounters. She embraces the nonsense that is capable of occurring in the Looking-Glass world when she exclaims that she will shake the Red Queen into a kitten as if it would have been a normal occurrence to shake a shrunken human-like creature to morph it into a different species; this is the epitome of participating in and applying the nonsense Alice learned during her time in the Looking-Glass world (*TTLG*: 215).[1]

Michael Holquist defines nonsense as 'a collection of words or events which in their arrangement do not fit into some recognized system,' an especially beneficial concept to understand Alice's social and linguistic journey, created to escape her life and enter a new environment – a new world, even (Holquist 1999: 104). Alice socializes with the creatures in the Looking-Glass world, where she learns how words, phrases, and happenings differ in a world that parallels Victorian England.

Using a familiar article to conduct mathematics, another familiar and logical concept for Alice, she cautiously accepts the often-nonsensical word choices, phrasing, and actions that take place around her. This wavering sense of fear when encountering the unfamiliar promotes further conversational exchanges and reiterates the existence of a power hierarchy, which, as described by Lecercle, is necessary for anyone to understand any environment or world, as that is how order is maintained (81).

Alice's linguistic choices and her ability to rationalize positively contribute to the understanding of her place as an educated child in a nonsensical world, for instance, when conversing with the Gnat. The concept of civility and where one is from is expressed when Alice and the Gnat discuss her preference for insects that speak, which only occurs in Looking-Glass world. Therefore, she does not like the insects 'where *I* come from,' yet she 'can tell you the names of some of them' (*TTLG*: 55). However, knowing the 'name' of an insect holds a different meaning in Looking-Glass world than Alice alludes to during her conversation with the Gnat. Instead of Alice being able to identify an insect by its scientific name, the Gnat is assuming

---

1   On unstable human-animal boundaries, see Chapter 1 of this collection.

'name' during their conversation means the insect's conversational name, like Alice's name is Alice and not girl or human – an episode that serves to interrogate how hierarchies are constructed through language.

Beatrice Turner illustrates this importance by emphasizing one of the first scenes in the novel in which Alice does not recognize the language in a book she opens, but soon realizes that 'it's a Looking-Glass book, of course! and if I hold it up to a glass, the words will go all the right way again' (*TTLG*: 21). Turner explains how Alice relies on the characters to go into detail about what each unfamiliar word or phrase means, and when one word has multiple meanings, as defined by the character, Alice becomes confused and requires a further explanation: 'To wield language in these texts, be it intelligible, "normal," or otherwise, is to have the power to define, to create, to destroy' (Turner 2010: 244). This kind of power promotes an environment in literature, like Carroll's, where characters can create their own meaning and context for language use amongst each other. Turner also insinuates that the language use in the novel provides a context for power dynamics among Alice and the creatures.

Alice's own place within Victorian hierarchies becomes more evident in the use of language in *Looking-Glass*, where her language use has become influenced by her imaginative encounters. Alice thus learns to appreciate the power of language in social and natural hierarchies. Not only does she use her speech in an authoritative manner when she speaks to Dinah's kittens at the beginning of the novel, but she also makes her wants and wishes clearer. When Alice encounters an outwardly human figure, the Red Queen, she is reminded of her own society. The Red Queen asserts her hierarchical superiority over Alice and ensures she addresses the Queen properly and eloquently. Alice learned how to use her words to respectfully contradict the person in a role of authority, which is apparent when she tests her own authority by calling out 'Waiter! Bring back the pudding' shortly after the Red Queen requested it to be removed from the table (*TTLG*: 206). This suggests that the rules and propriety of Alice's world and the Looking-Glass world are parallel. Although Alice continues to curtsy and carry out the actions, her conversational style implies that she is assuming a more assertive role.

Alice, accordingly, wishes to actually play the chess game through which Looking-Glass is conceptualized, and become a Queen in it. To become a Queen, the Red Queen lists the rules of the game as enacted in Looking-Glass world, which include Alice adhering to them and using both English and French, reinforcing that rigid rule systems exist in Looking-Glass world, mirroring those of Victorian Britain. Now Alice must use the many forms of English used by the inhabitants of the Looking-Glass world, and manipulate and master it, to win their game. Minding her manners, Alice agrees to play the game, respecting its rules, because she would gain the power role of Queen at the end, which is her goal. The expectation to use two types of languages, or modes of engagement – that of her own waking reality, and its mirror image in Looking-Glass world – is a concept that Alice is becoming more accustomed. Her willingness to adapt to the language rules demonstrates her ability to abide by various roles within the new world as well as the ever-changing rules surrounding language use. This suggests that Alice is beginning to grow as she embraces and appreciates differentiated linguistic rules for each world she is in, even if she does not fully understand them in either.

Without her encounters with the fantastical creatures and their conversations, Alice would not have been able to learn as much as she did, and thus this learning enhances other forms of education and exposes diverse language use situations that she would otherwise perhaps not have experienced, but which aid in her development as a maturing young girl.

'Bruno's Revenge'

Looking-Glass constitutes a development in Carroll's literary writing, and its increasingly clearly articulated educational intent, which becomes even more evident when examining another post-Wonderland text, 'Bruno's Revenge'. While it is expected that a new environment with new creatures and new conversational exchanges would pose a learning experience for a girl of Alice's age, one might assume the narrator of 'Bruno's Revenge' from *Sylvie and Bruno*,[2] Lewis Carroll, would be the only educator in the chapter, especially as the oldest character in the story. Instead, Carroll recognizes that 'fairies' often teach those who interact with them, before acknowledging his ability to offer the fairies an education:

> I want to know why fairies should always be teaching *us* to do our duty, and lecturing *us* when we go wrong, and we should never teach *them* anything? You can't mean to say that fairies are never greedy, or selfish, or cross, or deceitful, because that would be nonsense. (Carroll 1868: 65)

The entire first page of 'Bruno's Revenge,' the short story for *Aunt Judy's Magazine*, that would eventually become expanded into the two *Sylvie and Bruno* novels, is directed towards the reader, and offers a sense of direction, while also providing instructions for how to locate a fairy, and how to interact with it once one appears. In the preface of *Sylvie and Bruno*, Carroll articulates his intentions for the story in the form of an apology, as he hopes for it to be 'acceptable nonsense for children' while dealing with 'some of the graver thoughts of human life'. His dedication to using simple language, in addition to making the work accessible to young children, to convey a story within a story invites readers to participate in Carroll's educational interactions with animals and fairies in a new environment, Fairyland.

After Carroll instructs readers as to the right conditions for locating a fairy and introducing the story's creatures – beetles, moths, spiders, frogs, toads, crickets, leaf-cutter bees, and a 'little creature' (Carroll 1868: 68) – he provides an account of his interactions with the animals, suggesting that he could be of help to the poor, overturned beetle. Instead, however, a small fairy appears and talks to the beetle, 'half scolding and half comforting, as a nurse might do with a child that had fallen down' (Carroll 1868: 66). This is demonstrative of the role a governess might take on if this scenario had taken place in Victorian England rather than Fairyland. A governess would not have instructed her pupil to turn over a beetle, but if readers consider the role of a governess and her pupil and view the fairy as a governess-like figure for the beetle, we can conclude that the beetle

---

2   For more on 'Bruno's Revenge' see Chapter 4 in this collection.

was receiving assistance from the fairy about conducting oneself properly, especially when the fairy Sylvie instructs the beetle to 'be a good beetle, and don't keep your chin in the air' (Carroll 1889: 195).

Metaphorically child readers, for whom Carroll intended this work, can learn how to treat others and how to behave properly from the interactions of the characters. The creature Carroll refers to in the beetle scene is eventually identified as the female fairy. The balance between inquiry-based lessons from Sylvie to the beetle during their conversation suggests that she is teaching the beetle a lesson, and by Carroll conveying the lesson, as the narrator, he is educating the reader. Laurence Talairach reinforces the idea that these tales offer educational value for readers. With attention to Charles Kingsley's 'emphasis on the role of imagination in children's education' about depicting how 'fairies and fairy tales were given a didactic role to convey scientific lessons' and 'elicit emotional responses in their readers', Talairach writes: '[T]he wonders of this natural fairy tale lie in the mystery of the natural world, leading the naturalist and the amateur to investigate the "form of plants, shells, and animalcules"' (Talairach 2014: 26). Thus, readers of 'Bruno's Revenge' can easily access a story where the creatures who are immersed in natural environments demonstrate lessons of how to properly navigate the world in which they live.

Unlike in *Looking-Glass*, there is an understanding of the social hierarchy in Fairyland. Carroll states that 'a fairy's a kind of queen over them', referring to the other animals (Carroll 1868: 68). By using the term 'queen', it is clear to readers that there are rules and consequences. Thus, one must learn what constitutes appropriate and inappropriate behaviours to avoid being scolded like the beetle. One rule that Carroll shares is that crickets are to stop chirping when a fairy is present. Though he senses an 'eerie feeling' as he learned it meant a fairy was present, he later observes that 'no crickets were chirping; so I felt quite sure that "Bruno" was a fairy, and that he was somewhere very near' (ibid.). This demonstrates that those lower in hierarchical status intuitively abide by the rules and the behaviours of those animals in others, like Carroll, being alerted to a fairy's presence. The rules and consequences in Looking-Glass world are much more pronounced, as the characters vocalize what is expected of others through conversations, questioning, and other utterances rather than an aura that a creature, like the fairies in 'Bruno's Revenge' emit.

While there are characteristics of the nonsense, imaginative, and fantastic, it is important to note that Fairyland can be viewed as a parallel to Victorian England. Even though 'imagination and civilization were poles apart' initially, the genre of 'children's literature as highly visual rather than instructive' was emerging to provide "tales figuring animals, birds, or insects, anthropomorphized [...] humorously" ' (Talairach 2015: 23, 25). There are no talking animals, insects, or flowers, as in the Looking-Glass world, and the only characters who speak in 'Bruno's Revenge' are Carroll, who is a human, and Sylvie and Bruno, who have human-like features. Carroll also does not fall into a new world or enter through a mirror like Alice willingly does to access the Looking-Glass world. Instead, he curiously believes in the fairies and seeks them out. The parallel to Victorian England accounts for the distinctness of 'right' and 'wrong' in the story in which Victorian ideologies are clearly present and enacted by Sylvie and Bruno, as well as Carroll during his interactions with the creatures.

Paul Fagan and Michelle Witen

3 Live Flowers and Fabulous Monsters: Nonhuman Life and Extinction in *Through the Looking-Glass*

In this chapter, we explore how the principle of nonhuman life in *Through the Looking-Glass* extends beyond anthropomorphized animals and objects and into the novel's vibrant ecology. Flowers, trees, rushes, fields, rivers, brooks, snow, rain, wind, *etc.* are presented as agentic subjects, and thus the novel's environments, when read through theories of nonhuman studies, present matter as a vital and fluid assemblage. By calling attention to the life and material agency of nonhuman things, Carroll's novel critiques taxonomical categorizations as not only enforcing hierarchies of power onto nature but also concealing the continuity of human and nonhuman life. Similarly, Alice's role within the hierarchy is often that of a predator, continually placing the ecosystem of *Looking-Glass* under threat of violence or extinction.[1] Thus, we claim that the novel's challenge to anthropocentrism by representing not only zoocentric but also ecocentric perspectives and experiences cannot be disentangled from the power dynamic staged between Alice and her environment.

---

[1]   In Chapter 1, Laurence Talairach explores this theme through an imperialist and
        Darwinian lens.

Vibrant Matter

Jane Bennett's *Vibrant Matter: A Political Ecology of Things* theorizes a 'vital materiality' that exists in 'the capacity of things – edibles, commodities, storms, metals – not only to impede or block the will and design of humans but also to act as quasi agents or forces with trajectories, propensities or tendencies of their own' (Bennett 2010: viii). Thus conceived, matter is inherently agentic, 'a source of action that can be either human or nonhuman; it is that which has efficacy, can do things, has sufficient coherence to make a difference, produce effects, alter the course of events' (ibid.). This conceptualization of what Bennett calls 'thing-power' is in opposition to the anthropocentric worldview associated with Enlightenment rationalism and humanism, which discursively constructs 'the human' as the master interpreter and organizer of its environment – apart from, even master over, 'nature,' which is constructed, in turn, as inanimate dead matter, a supposedly endless source of knowledge, industry, profit. This humanist 'parsing [of] the world into dull matter (it, things) and vibrant life (us, beings)' (Idem: vii) has, in Pippa Marland's determination, 'impeded our ability to recognize the generative dynamism of matter, often with devastating consequences for both human and nonhuman life and for the earth's ecosystems' (Marland 2020: 3). Beyond its use of anthropomorphized animals, objects, and ecologies for the purposes of nonsense and satire, this clash between humanist and vitalist worldviews is both thematically and formally generative of the action that is staged in *Looking-Glass*.

In Chapter 1, Alice anthropomorphizes the environment outside her window in a fantasy of the elements of nature held in a romantic embrace:

> 'Do you hear the snow against the window-panes, Kitty? How nice and soft it sounds! Just as if some one was kissing the window all over outside. I wonder if the snow *loves* the trees and fields, that it kisses them so gently? And then it covers them up snug, you know, with a white quilt; and perhaps it says, "Go to sleep, darlings, till the summer comes again." And when they wake up in the summer, Kitty, they dress themselves all in green, and dance about – whenever the wind blows – oh, that's very pretty!' cried Alice […]. 'And I do so *wish* it was true!' (*TTLG*: 6)

The language here is filled with verbs that portray nature not only as anthropomorphized but also as agentic and active (kisses, loves, covers, says, dress themselves, dance, etc.) – yet Alice dismisses such a view of nonhuman matter as little more than a wishful fantasy. However, once in the Looking-Glass world, Alice is confronted everywhere by a distinctly vibrant ecology. Examples are legion, but perhaps the most immediately striking is the Garden of Living Flowers.

Coming upon a flowerbed bordered by daisies, Alice immediately addresses the Tiger-lily with the same fantasy:

> 'O Tiger-lily,' said Alice, addressing herself to one that was waving gracefully about in the wind, 'I *wish* you could talk!'
>
> 'We *can* talk,' said the Tiger-lily: 'when there's anybody worth talking to.'
>
> Alice was so astonished that she could not speak for a minute: it quite seemed to take her breath away. [...] 'And can *all* the flowers talk?'
>
> 'As well as *you* can,' said the Tiger-lily. 'And a great deal louder.' (*TTLG*: 28)

Although her wish is granted, Alice nevertheless seeks to control her environment. The thrill of the flowers' anthropomorphic act of talking soon pales when Alice realizes that she cannot control the content of their speech. Unhappy with 'being criticized,' Alice begins to ask questions to re-assert the human dimension onto the nonhuman: 'Aren't you sometimes frightened at being planted out here, with nobody to take care of you?' (*TTLG*: 30). When the daisies laugh at her for not understanding their language or the vibrant ecology of trees that are also caregiving, Alice escalates her attempt to re-establish the human/nonhuman power dynamic by menacingly threatening silencing and extinction: 'If you don't hold your tongues, I'll pick you!' (*TTLG*: 31).

The aliveness of the environment is indicated in non-anthropomorphized terms at other points in the text. For instance, the rain is granted agency (in Bennett's terms):

> 'But it may rain *outside*?'
> 'It may – if it chooses,' said Tweedledee. (*TTLG*: 83)

Elsewhere, Alice and the Sheep sit in a boat gently gliding 'among beds of weeds (which made the oars stick fast in the water, worse than ever), and sometimes under trees, but always with the same tall river-banks frowning over their heads' (*TTLG*: 106). In this vibrant ecology, Alice once again enacts violence upon the plants. Her automatic response upon seeing them is to roll up her sleeves and 'get hold of the rushes a good long way down before breaking them off [catching] at one bunch after another' (*TTLG*: 107). Alice's momentary gratification, in effect, carelessly kills them:

> What mattered it to her just then that the rushes had begun to fade, and to lose all their scent and beauty, from the very moment that she picked them? Even real scented rushes, you know, last only a very little while – and these, being dream-rushes, melted away almost like snow, as they lay in heaps at her feet – but Alice hardly noticed this, there were so many other curious things to think about.

In this act of plucking, we see Alice's humanist instinct to separate 'dull matter' from 'vibrant life,' thus illustrating the clash between her anthropocentric worldview and the trans-corporeal vitality of the Looking-Glass world.

Looking-Glass Taxonomies

The ecology that Alice encounters beyond the looking-glass is perhaps an inversion but still a reflection of our own. As Gillian Beer observes, Alice enters 'not so much the carnivalesque "world upside down" as the world sideways on, an egalitarian zone in which everything becomes possible and nothing is unlikely because all forms of being have presence and can argue: doors, time, eggs, queens, caterpillars, cats and hatters, oysters, gnats, and little girls – all have their say' (Beer 2016: 4). The introduction of these zoocentric and ecocentric perspectives reveals the subjectivity and agency of nonhuman life[2] and challenges the hegemonic

---

2   For a discussion of contemporary references to how Carroll constructs these interactions, see Chapters 1 and 4.

subjectivity of the human scientific gaze that sees but is not seen by the animal. However, this aspect of the text can also be challenged as mere anthropomorphism that ultimately maps onto human social categories (for instance, the gendered depiction of the Living Flowers).

When she arrives in the Looking-Glass world, Alice attempts to make sense of her surroundings through the application of an anthropocentric system of categorization. Chapter 2 begins with the privileging of the human subjective gaze on the objectified surroundings: 'I should see the garden far better,' said Alice to herself, 'if I could get to the top of that hill' (*TTLG*: 26). Chapter 3 starts, similarly, with Alice standing 'on tiptoe in hopes of being able to see a little further' in order 'to make a grand survey of the country' (46):

> 'It's something very like learning geography,' thought Alice [...]. 'Principal rivers – there *are* none. Principal mountains – I'm on the only one, but I don't think it's got any name. Principal towns – why, what *are* those creatures, making honey down there? They can't be bees – nobody ever saw bees a mile off, you know –' and for some time she stood silent, watching one of them that was bustling about among the flowers, poking its proboscis into them, 'just as if it was a regular bee,' thought Alice. (*TTLG*: 46)

The anthropocentric scientific gaze Alice is made to mimic in this scene is shown to be blind to the vibrant agency of the nonhuman world, rather categorizing it in hierarchical and binary terms (human/animal, culture/ nature, mind/body, animate/inanimate, subject/object, etc.). This taxonomical drive is manifested, for instance, in Alice's compulsion to 'name' the looking-glass insects. However, in each case, her anthropocentric perspective – in which the human is always the subject who sees, the nonhuman always the object that is subjected to human sight, desire, exploitation – is challenged, as the world reveals itself to be alive, agentic, vibrant. As Koustinoudi writes, the nonhuman 'is not only given its own distinct voice, but almost total authority and agency over Alice [...]. Speaking of and for themselves, the creatures resist familiar modes of classification and categorization, perform only at their own will and not because they have been trained to do so, behaving as speaking subjects in their own right' (Koustinoudi 2020: 54).

In her encounter with the insects in Chapter 3, Alice is introduced to an ecocentric perspective in which human taxonomy and categorization are rendered 'nonsense':

> 'I don't *rejoice* in insects at all,' Alice explained, 'because I'm rather afraid of them – at least the large kinds. But I can tell you the names of some of them.'
>
> 'Of course they answer to their names?' the Gnat remarked carelessly.
>
> 'I never knew them to do it.'
>
> 'What's the use of their having names,' the Gnat said, 'if they won't answer to them?'
>
> 'No use to *them*,' said Alice; 'but it's useful to the people who name them, I suppose. If not, why do things have names at all?'
>
> 'I can't say,' the Gnat replied. 'Further on, in the wood down there, they've got no names – however, go on with your list of insects: you're wasting time.' (*TTLG*: 55)

Without the acknowledgment of insects in the naming process, Alice is confronted with the usefulness of the naming process, realizing that it benefits 'the people who name them,' but without the complicity of the named, authority, agency, and hierarchies are all called into question.[3]

When Alice, devoid of her human identity (and not just her named identity), loses her memory of categorical delineations and labels, she is able to live harmoniously with nature. At first, she is disconcerted by her inability to remember the names of things:

> She was rambling on in this way when she reached the wood: it looked very cool and shady. 'Well, at any rate it's a great comfort,' she said as she stepped under the trees, 'after being so hot, to get into the – into *what*?' she went on, rather surprised at not being able to think of the word. 'I mean to get under the – under the – under *this*, you know!' putting her hand on the trunk of the tree. (*TTLG*: 61)

However, she is soon confronted with the vitalism of the tree and its own 'thing-power': 'What *does* it call itself, I wonder? I do believe it's got no name – why, to be sure it hasn't!' In this moment of acknowledgement,

---

3   For a discussion of Lewis Carroll's view on the philosophical and theological implications of contemporary biology and naming, see Chapter 7.

Alice herself loses her name: 'And now, who am I?'(*TTLG*: 62). Once she is on equal footing with the ecosystem of the Looking-Glass world, she is able to befriend the Fawn. However, once her human agency is re-established so too is her dangerous humanity, and she once again becomes a threat: ' "I'm a Fawn!" it cried out in a voice of delight, "and, dear me! you're a human child!" A sudden look of alarm came into its beautiful brown eyes, and in another moment it had darted away at full speed' (*TTLG*: 64).

In *The Animal That Therefore I Am*, Jacques Derrida condemns fabulization as 'an anthropomorphic taming, a moralizing subjection, a domestication. Always a discourse of man, on man, indeed on the animality of man, but for and in man' (Derrida 2008: 34). Any mode of discourse in which the nonhuman 'does not give its word [...] except by means of a projection or anthropomorphic transference' (ibid., 129), ultimately, in Derrida's evaluation, doubles down on a form of logocentrism which is inseparable from a position of mastery, as 'a thesis regarding the animal, the animal deprived of the *logos*, deprived of the *can-have-the-logos*' (ibid., 27). And yet, Derrida acknowledges the debt that his thinking on 'the logic of the limit' (ibid., 29) owes to Carroll's *Alice* books (ibid., 7).

Here, we contend that while *Through the Looking-Glass* employs anthropomorphism both for comic effect and to satirize the human social sphere. It calls attention to the life and material agency of nonhuman things by deconstructing taxonomical categorizations. This not only enforces hierarchies of power onto nature but also conceals the continuity of human and nonhuman life. For example, in 'The Lion and the Unicorn,' Alice and the unicorn are confronted by the mutual deconstruction of their own categorizations, each terming the other a 'fabulous monster':

> [The Unicorn] stood for some time looking at [Alice] with an air of the deepest disgust.
>
> 'What – is – this?' he said at last.
>
> 'This is a child!' Haigha replied eagerly [...]
>
> 'I always thought they were fabulous monsters!' said the Unicorn.
>
> 'Is it alive?'

'It can talk,' said Haigha solemnly.

The Unicorn looked dreamily at Alice, and said 'Talk, child'. (*TTLG*: 151)

In response to the nonhuman denunciation of Alice's existence and nature, Alice responds with the more human fabulization of the unicorn, in an attempt to enact 'anthropomorphic taming' (Derrida 2008: 37), repeating the observation as an insult: 'Do you know, I always thought Unicorns were fabulous monsters, too?' (*TTLG*: 151). The Unicorn's question, 'Is it alive?' and the desire to give her speaking agency, is twisted by Alice into an observation of authority: 'I never saw one alive before!' (Idem).

Nevertheless, the Looking-Glass world asserts its own authority and flexibility through the creation of the new category of 'Monster':

> The Lion looked at Alice wearily. 'Are you animal – or vegetable – or mineral?' he said, yawning at every other word.
>
> 'It's a fabulous monster!' the Unicorn cried out, before Alice could reply.
>
> 'Then hand round the plum-cake, Monster,' the Lion said. (*TTLG*: 155)

Alice adjusts well to her new denomination and, by embracing of this creation of a new category that is non-categorical, challenges the arbitrary limits and dualisms of the humanist taxonomical approach. Throughout the novel, we see Alice continually confronted by vibrant matter; at points she enforces a humanist ecosystem, making her a predator or threat towards extinction. However, towards the end of the novel, Alice has embraced a new looking-glass taxonomy. This is seen through the titling of the final chapter 'Which dreamed it?' where the humanist who/ whose dream was it has been replaced by a 'thing-power' where Alice even doubts whether she or the Red King has agency over the story/dream.

Conclusion

Having gone through the looking-glass, both Alice and Carroll's reader encounter a form of matter that is vital, trans-corporeal, and agentic. The

book's acknowledgment of the vitality of animals, plants, and ecologies –
and of the threat to this existence posed by strict humanist and scientific
realist hierarchical categories and dualisms – serves to destabilize anthropocentric assumptions, which profess to map and measure both human
and nonhuman bodies.

Natural History

Part II
Natural Philosophy

Franziska E. Kohlt

4 Through Magic Glasses: Optics as Edifying Entertainment in Victorian Culture

While little, in relation to the book's predecessor, has been written about *Through the Looking-Glass*, one particular area stands out as wanting for the historicist scrutiny of the *Alice* books that has recently flourished (cf. Shuttleworth 2015; Kohlt 2016, 2019). Perhaps surprisingly, with regard to its title, the field it implies, and the extent of work on it in other corners of Victorian literary and cultural studies, sustained attention is yet to be directed at the scientific and cultural aspects of Victorian optical culture of the *Wonderland* sequel (cf. Willis 2011; Rhys Morus 2006; Wade 2004; Armstrong 2008; Crary 1991). By 'optical culture', this chapter will mean not the literary theme of mirrors, its fairy-tale and psychoanalytical dimensions, which have dominated such critical approaches that there have been, and which have directed their gaze inwards, to the individual of Alice, but an outwardly focused historicist reframing of the text. This will examine *Looking-Glass* through the culture that sprang up around a fascination with optics, optical trickery, and optical toys, and Carroll's participation in it.

This will, in turn, shed light on scientific and cultural referential frameworks of *Looking-Glass* and the literary uses to which the scientific functions of optical instruments were put, once translated into literary imagery. Embedding both *Looking-Glass* and *Wonderland* in this framework will highlight consistencies in Carroll's work that challenge the oft-purported view of the post-*Wonderland* works as uncharacteristic, or out of the ordinary for Carroll, in their objective, scope, or execution. As *Wonderland* appears more similar to them through these less-noted elements and frameworks, such a historicist framing can acknowledge and accommodate a more complex intellectual scope of Carroll's work, which 'Alice interpreted as children's literature' primarily, has thus far 'radically undercut' (Jacques 2015: 66).

Through the Looking-Glass

Mirrors – or looking-glasses – appear the most obvious starting point for such an exploration. They exerted a fascination not only on Carroll but on many contemporaries. But they did so, especially in their amalgamation in a host of other optical contraptions which enchanted, enhanced, and stretched, and supposedly even penetrated the Victorian mind, in settings of education, scientific exploration, and medical treatment, but also in entertainment, enchantment, and play. Many such contraptions occupied many, or even all of these categories, at once, teasing the imagination into considering the tantalizing possibilities of applying mirrors in any of these fields, interchangeably, transferring the specific semiotic potential they possessed in each of them.

.The culture of microscopes and telescopes exemplifies this. The much-mythologized Victorian scientific progress had relied heavily on the refinement of optical instruments, which, in turn, had become somewhat synonymous with 'science' itself. Telescopes had facilitated the discovery of hitherto unknown stars and planets, and laws of their movement, and microscopes had revealed secret populations inside a drop of river water or saliva: worlds hidden in the worlds around, or inside, us. By making visible and graspable that which lay beyond what we could see with the ordinary eye, they appeared to merely reveal latent, and thus authoritative, knowledge, from which equally indisputable guidance, such as what improved or endangered health of the individual or society, could be derived.

In the light of such an indispensable guide to life, the universe, and everything, Victorian children were encouraged by an entire genre of literature on microscopy and Natural History to take up the instrument for themselves and explore the world around them. These narratives instructed them on *how* to see – through, below, inside, and beyond – and interpret *what* had thus been made visible: what it *meant*.

That such *Magic Glasses*, as Arabella Buckley called them, were more than just a scientific instrument, but one to reveal wonders, discern truth from deception, a device facilitating revelation, is evident. The literature on them, in due course, overcame social, disciplinary, and philosophical boundaries that are nowadays often uncritically assumed.

Frequently authored by clergy, printed often cheaply, *en masse,* especially by religious presses, these children's books promoted scientific study of nature, for forming in children a *scientific* mindset (cf. Secord 1885; Fyfe 2000; Topham 2007). This would enable them to recognize the truths evident in God's creation and understand Nature as 'God's book', God's 'fairy tale', 'written upon earth': the unbiased bearer of unquestionable moral lessons that were just waiting to be 'deciphered' (Kingsley 1890 [1846]: 310).

Science acting as revealer of God, through optical instruments as its handmaiden, challenges not only science-religion conflict narratives that so often frame this period as one of 'progressive secularisation' (Lightman 2007: 42; Ungureanu and Hutchings 2021). It also unsettles other categories, now seen as fixed, but then more fluid, including that of 'children's literature' and its contribution to scientific discourse, and, in due course, the social constructedness of the latter.

Through their popularity in Victorian parlour culture, optical devices that toyed with mirrors, such as magic lanterns and phantasmagoria, zoetropes and thaumatropes, they took on many roles, and epistemologies, as they dazzled the Victorian mind in recreational settings. Where microscopes had magnified the hidden lives of bacteria to the eye, magic lanterns magnified the monstrous shapes of bacteria, unseen sea creatures, living and moving into the drawing room, and immersed audiences among them. The same mechanism that the newly styled 'scientists' had used to demonstrate irrefutable truths, also projected the fabled monsters of mythology, or what appeared to be the ghosts of the dead: a spectacle known as phantasmagoria.

The fascination of kaleidoscope inventor David Brewster with those 'mechanisms that fooled the eye' – 'accidental and deliberate' was characteristic, as they created 'illusionistic representations of reality', which could, indeed facilitate 'popular amusement' and 'experimental assistance' – even at the same time (Rhys Morus 2006: 101; O'Connor 2008: 266; Wade 2004: 102). They taught *and* deceived, they edified *and* entertained. They

Natural Philosophy

were *the* medium through which to interrogate the boundaries of knowing, what to believe, and why – a dual role in which they would consciously be employed in their literary reflections.

As the boundary between recreation and education in the worlds of Victorian optics was as blurred as a not-quite-adjusted lantern slide projection, the possibility of discovering a hidden world of truth, that changed the meaning of this world forever, appeared as likely as discovering a hidden world of trickery that unsettled one's trust in it. The experience of optical culture was a constant revisiting of the conundrum posed by the dream of the Ancient Greeks, with its gates of ivory and horn, of revelation and deception, yet with the difference that they needn't be two distinct types of experiences. And as fiction was as capable of elevating, educating, and revealing truths by the means of optical analogy, as the optical device, applied apparently scientifically, it could, equally, deliver deception disguised as truth.

'Most Conveniently Transparent'

All this was part of how Charles Lutwidge Dodgson experienced Victorian optical culture. He was introduced to microscopy and telescopy and the wonder of the study of the hidden worlds in Nature early in childhood, through such 'useful and entertaining' Christian Natural History books he continued to collect in adulthood. These included the works of Jane Marcet and Anna Barbauld, authors, respectively, of *Conversations on Chemistry* (1805) and *Evenings at Home* (1792–1796), Philip Henry Gosse's *Evenings at the Microscope* (1859), and Edwin Lankester's *Half-hours with the Microscope* (1859): a 'guide to the use of the microscope as a means of amusement and instruction'.

To the practicalities of optical instruments, Carroll became accustomed in the typical parlour setting that blurred the realms of science and leisure. He became a photographer – photographing even his aunt's attempts at microscopy (Figure 1) – and collector of microphotographs, to which he introduced Alice and her sisters the day he first told them 'the fairy-tale

of *Alice's Adventures Under-Ground*' in 1862 (*Diaries* IV: 96). He was a
visitor at the 'dissolving views' and a collector of 'very fine' microscopes,
telescopes, and scores of books on their practicalities, philosophies, applications, and fictions (Lovett 1999). He was as immersed in Victorian
optical culture as it comes.

Figure 1. Lucy Lutwigde with microscope, Charles Lutwidge Dodgson.

The feedback between Carroll's scientific, playful, inquisitive, and
morally profound literary imagination pairs with the multiform aspects
of philosophical toys and permeates *Alice* from the start. It functions on
a literal level: in references such as Alice 'shutting up like a telescope', or
being looked at 'through a telescope, then through a microscope, and then
through an opera-glass' (51). It works on a cultural level: when her journey
through a dark tunnel may as well have been led down the dark tube of
the microscope into the magnified world of wonders of Victorian Natural

History books so clear is the book in its imitation of their narrative elements and structure (Keene 2015).

It worked on a marketing level when *Alice* was reworked for the early childhood book market in the *Nursery Alice* (1890), the text rewritten to descriptively centre around the pictures – now large and colourized – as customary for the lanternists. The *Nursery Alice* was to be read as a lantern show brought to the nursery. Where episodes of *Alice* appear isolated vignettes to modern readers, their images themselves static, like single lantern slides – they then read, as synthesized through narration, thus producing meaning, like dissolving views, to contemporaries.

That it worked on a visual level, in the earlier books is clear in how Carroll explicitly draws the reader's attention to the presence of optical trickery. Where the *Nursery Alice* encourages the child to 'turn over the corner of this leaf' to experience the process of the '[Cheshire] Cat vanish[ing] quite slowly' (Carroll 1890: 36), in *Wonderland*, the first illustrations are already thus positioned (Figure 2). Early merchandise was 'on brand', as a stamp case displayed, on its envelope and inserted a pig turning into a baby (Figure 3). The turning of the page in *Looking-Glass*, which makes Alice disappear *through* it is facilitated by the illustrations positioned overleaf (Figures 4 and 5). It engages the reader physically in the story, as the illustrations function as a thaumatrope – as the *Alice* books *become* an optical, philosophical toy themselves, by its readers literally being encouraged to use them as such.

Figure 2. Cheshire Cat vanishing, John Tenniel.

Figure 3. Alice stamp case, baby turning into pig, John Tenniel.

Alice – fiction – can so work on the same philosophical level as those optical devices, something its author had already rehearsed at this point. *Wonderland* was followed, not immediately by *Looking-Glass*, but by the poetry collection *Phantasmagoria* (1869), whose title-giving poem muses what benefits the interactions with such spectral visitors as 'Pepper's Ghost' might offer. It also contained 'Hiawatha's Photographing', where an autobiographical photographer's camera exposes beyond posed moral superiority, hypocrisy, and a lack of any such morals (Kohlt 2016), enacting the Victorian belief that the camera could, analogous to the microscope, diagnose: reveal with 'unerring accuracy the external phenomena of each passion [...] as the *really certain* indication of internal derangement' (Diamond 1976 [1857]: 20).

It is little surprise that the sequel of *Wonderland* led her *through* a Magic Glass that was to perform just as the instruments, and the literature

Figures 4 and 5. Alice stepping through the Looking-Glass, John Tenniel.

it imitated, as a moral guide, mental training for children to discern truth beyond that which merely disguises itself as such.

Revisiting the language in which the young Charles Dodgson conveys his first experimentations with a microscope in his diary is thus instructive:

> We had an observation of the Moon and Jupiter last night, and afterwards live animalcules in his large microscope: this is a most interesting sight, as the creatures are most conveniently transparent, & you see all the organs jumping about like a complicated piece of machinery, & even the circulation of the blood. (*Diaries* I: 47)

In the parlour setting scientific instruments became truly 'philosophical toys', as they were then frequently referred to – playful aids to facilitating contemplation, eliciting wonder that led to questioning, and thus deeper, truer insight into Nature. It is the parlour setting in which *Through the Looking-Glass* opens, by the contemplation of life through a glass that was 'conveniently transparent' – 'like all soft like gauze, so that we can get through'; 'a sort of mist' (10).

The stage was thus set.

Enter Lewis Carroll. Enter *Alice*.

And What Alice Found There

'*Through* is just the Word you're looking for', was Alexander Macmillan's advice to Carroll for the second *Alice* book, of which he was an early encourager (Macmillan in Cohen and Gandolfo 1987: 38). On the back of the success of *Wonderland*, Carroll drew out more explicitly and confidently in *Looking-Glass* what he had written into *Wonderland*, more confidently already from when he had first written it down as *Alice's Adventures Under-Ground* (1862) – a trajectory that characterizes the *overall* trajectory of Carroll's oeuvre. As *Wonderland* had made Alice see, and recognize, what had seemed significant and serious and true, as

Natural Philosophy

ludicrous, *Looking-Glass* made her see that what had seemed insignificant as a source of truth, of revelation.

Alice's encounters with insects – in the 'Looking-Glass Insects', and 'Wasp in a Wig' chapters – recapture a common trope of microscopic instructive literature to expose immorality, and effect moral transformation.

On the surface, Alice's introduction to the 'Rocking-Horse Fly' and 'Bread-and-Butter-Fly' look like 'mere nonsense', like 'Pigglywigglia Pyramidalis' of Edward Lear's *Nonsense Botany* (1871–1877) – mere entertaining wordplay. But even Lear, really, poked fun of the newly prolific Linnean notations, thus commenting on the self-serious performance of gentlemanly science through language, how it colonized the authority of the naming of Nature – a contested area at the time – thus not free of moral content. Equally, there was more to Alice's exploration of Looking-Glass entomology, as indicated in her shifting affective relationship with it. At first Alice boldly declares that she does not 'rejoice in insects at all'; she was afraid of them, especially the 'large kinds' that 'sting' (54; 53). Once, however, her guide, the Gnat is magnified – as by a microscope or magic lantern – in narrative presence and font size alike, and 'after they had been talking together so long' (Figures 6 and 7), Alice 'couldn't feel nervous' any longer (55; 56). Next, through her study of the other insects, learning about their habits and habitat, their Natural History, sparks 'great curiosity', and thus greater care (57). The impending death of the Bread-and-Butter-Fly, for want of vital food-sources, leaves her 'pondering', 'thoughtfully', and 'in silence' (60).

The effect of the philosophical benefits of microscopic study becomes clear in the 'Wasp in a Wig' chapter (not, ultimately, included, upon the daunting pressure of its illustrator).[1] At the near-conclusion of her journey, Alice encounters a human-sized Wasp – the archetype of a 'large kind' of insect that stings. Having become accustomed to look at insects non-anthropocentrically, beyond their human convenience, Alice's words are now: 'I hope you're not in much pain', 'I'm afraid you're not well', 'Can

---

1   Tenniel and Carroll's tense relationship (Wakeling and Cohen 2003) had already led to the withdrawal of the first edition of *Alice's Adventures in Wonderland*, due to apparent flaws in the print quality of the illustrations, at the author's expense.

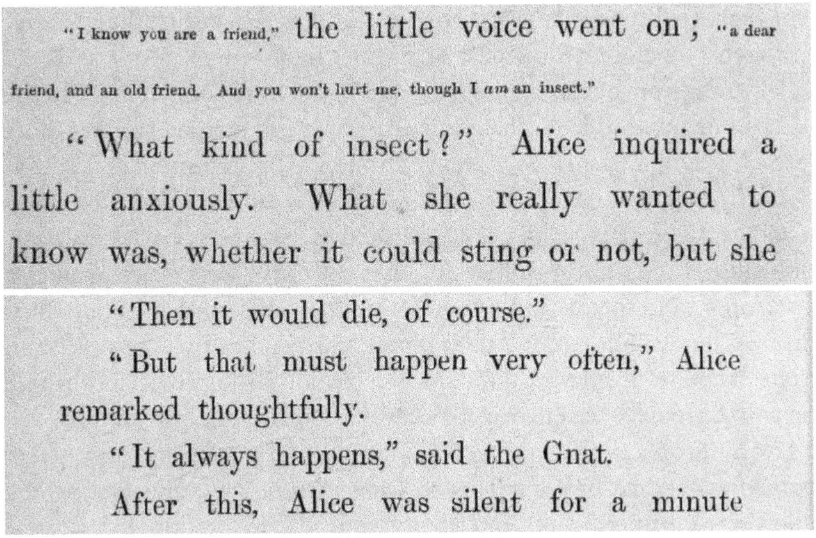

"I know you are a friend," the little voice went on ; "a dear friend, and an old friend. And you won't hurt me, though I *am* an insect."

"What kind of insect?" Alice inquired a little anxiously. What she really wanted to know was, whether it could sting or not, but she

"Then it would die, of course."

"But that must happen very often," Alice remarked thoughtfully.

"It always happens," said the Gnat.

After this, Alice was silent for a minute

Figures 6 and 7. Font size change in the Gnat's speech.

I do anything for you?' (Carroll 1973 [1871?]: 29–30). She assists the Wasp in its needs, feeling 'pleased that she had gone back to make the poor old creature comfortable' (Carroll 1973 [1871?]: 37).

Looking-Glass thus seems to pre-empt the future Carroll of 'Some Popular Fallacies on Vivisection' (1875) in its interrogation of boundaries between what life one may or may not injure, asking readers to consider 'any insect one might tread on' (Carroll 1875: 848), suggesting that 'serious concerns' were a 'later development' in his writing. Yet this plotline had already appeared prior to *Looking-Glass*, in 'Bruno's Revenge' – the predecessor of his later *Sylvie and Bruno* novels. Observing how the fairy Sylvie helps a Beetle – 'the poor thing' – 'on its feet again', the autobiographic narrator ponders in a lengthy monologue 'what an insect would *like*', and what may 'please' various other species, coming to the conclusion, that, 'if I were a beetle and had rolled over on my back, I should always be glad to be helped up again' (Carroll 1868: 66–67).

Un-masking deception, and finding moral elevation thus, was also at the heart of *Wonderland*'s iconic insect encounter, in which Alice laments she had 'tried to say "How doth the little busy bee," but it all came [out] different' – before her attempt of another moral rhyme also 'comes out [...] wrong from beginning to end'. A caterpillar lecturing a child on morals derives its humour from the knowledge of insect metamorphoses. Both are 'children', in their own species, and both 'exactly three inches high' (*AAIW*: 67). But Isaac Watts's bee-poem was exposed as a flawed insect analogy. Conceiving, as I do, of children as 'little busy bee[s]', as nothing more than uniform workers, renders the purveyors of such analogies, as expressed in the parody, as predatory Crocodiles, preying upon 'little fishes' – upon children, and their moral, spiritual health – the vulnerable state of their souls. Carroll unmasks as deception analogy that clothes itself in truth through Natural imagery, conveying, really, an understanding of it as for anthropocentric convenience. This is the very attitude *Looking-Glass* remedies in Alice, by getting her to know insects, in Nature, first hand – like the many microscopic 'entertaining and edifying' fictions of Victorian optical culture had done before it.

Conclusion

Through the Looking-Glass is thus not in principle different from *Wonderland*, but it embraces more boldly what Carroll believed it did. This was, in turn, not different from what Carroll had hoped his mathematics would achieve, as he expressed in *Game of Logic*, whose main mission it was to teach, by making a child move red and white pieces on a board of squares, the dangers of 'false analogy' (Carroll 1886: 81). Nor was that different, in principle, from *Sylvie and Bruno*, which mirrors deliberately scenes of *Wonderland*, in two different worlds, that mirror and thus interpret one another (Kohlt 2019; Wakely-Mulroney 2021).

This highlights how morals, or pedagogic purpose, were not absent in Alice, for all the entertainment it provided, that morals not 'atypical' of Carroll as the-author-of-*Alice*, or Carroll-as-children's-writer – in fact, as per the author himself. Carroll saw *Alice* as a contribution to 'those stories' of 'healthy amusement', and *Alice*'s exceptionality in its speaking of 'solemn things' through 'mixing together things grave and gay' – even if, as he noted himself, people may be astonished to hear 'such words' from the 'writer of "Alice"' in a 'book of nonsense' (Carroll 1967: 226–227). The imitation of Victorian optical devices and optical culture, and the sort of fiction Carroll produced from it reflects their typical concerns, and Carroll, unusually for the genre, applies them to a wide variety of social aspects.

That this echoes certain Christian morals, with Dodgson the deacon, and Macmillan, a devout Christian, as publisher, is only plausible, especially in a publishing environment in which fellow Christian scientists and fairy-tale writers Kingsley and MacDonald had already harnessed the Bible's most famous verse on mirrors, psyche, truth, and knowledge-making, so intimately connected to childhood and maturity:

> When I was a child, I spake as a child, I understood as a child, I thought as a child: but when I became a man, I put away childish things. For now we see through a glass, darkly; but then face to face: now I know in part; but then shall I know even as also I am known. (1 Corinthians 13)[2]

In the context of optical culture, *Alice* cannot be put away as a childish thing. It invites contemporary criticism to consider Victorian knowledge-making discourse as more heterogeneous, as established already by the rich, multidisciplinary work on Victorian optical culture, into which Carroll, and his works, are yet to be more fully integrated. This has else-where, shed much light on subjects highly relevant to Carroll's interest: on education, especially that of children, scientific culture, beyond its elite sites, and what these could tell us about Victorian knowledge production, and the place of people like Carroll, who inhabited multiple, intersect-ing spheres within it. In the case of Carroll, as cleric, amateur scientist, and 'children's' author – these were, furthermore, spheres not necessarily traditionally associated with knowledge-making – let alone that of sci-ence, such analysis therefore promising insights precisely into these

---

2   For more on this passage from Corinthians, and Carroll's relationship with moral-ity as expressed in the works of Kingsley, see Chapters 9 and 38, respectively.

Natural Philosophy

intersections. *Alice* – as is clearest through *Looking-Glass* – was meant as a philosophical toy, a thinking aid, entertaining, and edifying – and, thus perhaps unsurprisingly, this is, precisely how it still works: Alice helps us to see through, think through, and know through this process – it makes us wonder, while never ceasing to be entertaining.

Tom McLeish

5 Lewis Carroll, George MacDonald, and the Poetry, Prophecy, and Imagination of Science

A half-century before Lewis Carroll and his close friend George MacDonald wrote about science and imagination, Johann Wolfgang von Goethe had reminded his own readers, in *An die Morphologie* (1827), that 'science arose from poetry', yet had 'forgotten its provenance'. The intervening years of nineteenth-century literature added amnesic layers, including not only the disenchanting invectives of John Keats and Edgar Allan Poe but also explicit accounts of their divorce, as in Robert Hunt's *The Poetry of Science* (1850). Yet, as any scientist knows, the imagination is essential to the immense task of re-creating a shared model of nature from the scale of the cosmos, through biological complexity, to the smallest subatomic structures. This is precisely the point that MacDonald makes in his essay 'The Imagination, its Function and its Culture' (1893) – but he fills it with theological resonance:

> We yield you your facts. The laws we claim for the prophetic imagination. 'He hath set the world in man's heart', not in his understanding. (MacDonald 1893: 12)

In this chapter, I explore the layers beneath both Goethe's and MacDonald's insights into the narrative histories and human desires that thread through the prophetic, the poetic, and the scientific imaginations. I will show how examples of the mathematical imagination of Carroll construct a bridge to rare cases when scientists reveal the 'heart' processes of scientific ideation, and their link to what Jacques Monod termed 'night science'. Monod's term denoted the opposite of the 'day science' of experimental hypothesis-testing resonate with a forgotten poetic and theological tradition that characterized the early modern science of Bacon, Boyle, and Margaret Cavendish, when poetry presented as a serious candidate for the appropriate literary form of the new experimental philosophy, and when scientific imagination reflected what it means to be human, drawing on theological ideas of the purpose of creativity and the image of God – themes whose relationship Carroll negotiated through his writings throughout his life.

It is a painful paradox that the same century that saw the products of such polymathematical minds as George MacDonald and Charles Dodgson also witnessed a widening of the gap between literature and science, between *poesis* and *theoria*, which Carroll reflected upon in numerous ephemeral writings. Accusations levelled at the trajectory science had taken since its early modern turn, of its disenchantment of the world (Keats 'unweaving the rainbow' in 'Lamia') or its predation on human values (Poe's 'vulture' in 'Sonnet to Science') were not easy to answer. Even the contemporary scientist and science communicator Michael Faraday seemed unwilling to confess his marvellously inventive scientific imagination in the public light of day, writing that he was an 'imaginative person, and could believe in the *Arabian Nights* as easily as in the *Encyclopaedia*, but facts were important to me and saved me' (Jones 1870). The strong ties of 'science' with 'fact' and 'imagination' with what Coleridge had termed 'fancy' echoes more of William Blake's outrage at Newtonian reason than the experience of the mind that could conjure the field concept from elegant benchtop experiments with electric currents and magnets: 'In the grandeur of Inspiration to cast off Rational Demonstration [...] to cast off Bacon, Locke and Newton; I will not Reason and Compare – my business is to Create' (Blake 1810). The trail of divorce proceedings between science writing and the literature of imagination goes at least as far back as the early 'biography' of the early Royal Society by Thomas Spratt in its first decade (Guite 2012).

At first sight a candidate for a nineteenth-century development of Goethe's older insight is Robert Hunt's *The Poetry of Science* (1850). Hunt, like MacDonald, a contemporary of Carroll, would not, however, be sympathetic to a view that the creative processes of science and poetry are in any way comparable, or that they draw on a shared resource of imagination. On the contrary, he takes them to be antithetical:

> The fumes of the laboratory, its alkalics and acids, the mechanical appliances of the observatory, its specula and its lenses, do not appear fitted for a place in the painted bowers of the Muses. (Hunt 1850)

Rather, for Hunt, science is comparable to poetry because it shares the capacity to evoke beauty, wonder, and the sublime, through its discoveries made and shared. As Irmtraud Huber has pointed out, for Hunt, science is even capable of higher reaches into the sublime than poetry (2020). 'The phenomena of Reality are more startling than the phantoms of the Ideal,' Hunt claims; 'Truth is stranger than fiction.' He does acknowledge that science chained purely to facts fails to rise above the dust, constituting that

> [a] cheerless philosophy which clings to the earth, and reduces the mind to mechanical condition, delighting in the accumulation of facts, regardless of the great laws by which they are regulated, and the harmony of all Telluric combinations secured. (Hunt 1850)

For Hunt, it is not the factual content, but the unifying and harmonizing insights of scientific theory that reaches the poetic, and beyond the poetic.

Here, he is strongly echoing Cambridge University's deviser of the neologism 'scientist', William Whewell, who wrote in the same period that scientific facts on their own are like individual 'pearls on a string' (quoted in Huber 2020). On their own, facts might be pretty but lead to nothing except through a deeper connective framework, when an emergent object of beauty may appear. Whewell describes this process of connection through their underlying patterns the 'imposition of formal unity'. Science is never 'read off' nature, but 'written into' a picture, a narrative, or an abstract constructed representation of it. Hunt takes this extrapolation further still:

> In these studies of the effects which are continually presenting themselves to the observing eye, and of the phenomena of causes, as far as they are revealed by Science

in its search of the physical earth, it will be shown that beneath the beautiful vesture of the external world there exists, like its quickening soul, a pervading power, assuming the most varied aspects, giving the whole its life and loveliness, and linking every portion of this material mass in a common bond with some great universal principle beyond our knowledge. [...] But if admitted even to a clear perception of the theoretical Power which we regard as regulating the known forces, we must still see an unknown agency beyond us, which can only be referred to the Creator's will.

Here lies the clue to the separation of ways, for Hunt begins to privilege science, not only with the power to discern the 'phenomena of causes' but also to reveal the Creator's power. The constructed opposition of science and poetry is not unconnected with the contemporary rhetoric around the alleged opposition of science and religion.

It is also at this point that Hunt comes closest to MacDonald, who was as enamoured with the possibilities of science to see into mysteries, and to exercise the human imagination, as he was sure of its connection to the work of a Creator. MacDonald is more explicit than Hunt, however, on the quotidian role of imagination in the scientific process, so sees no necessary parting of science and poetry. His insight is remarkable: not only into the *poiesis* of great theoretical constructs but also the imaginative necessity implied by the experimental method itself. Reading on in his essay 'The Imagination, its Function and its Culture', we find in his imagined dialogue with a character strongly resembling Thomas Spratt of the Royal Society (who speaks first):

But the facts of Nature are to be discovered only by observation and experiment!

True. But how does the man of science come to think of his experiments? Does observation reach to the non-present, the possible, the yet unconceived? Even if it showed you the experiments which ought to be made, will observation reveal to you the experiments which might be made? And who can tell of which kind is the one that carries in its bosom the secret of the law you seek? We yield you your facts. The laws we claim for the prophetic imagination. 'He hath set the world in man's heart,' not in his understanding. And the heart must open the door to the understanding. It is the far-seeing imagination which beholds what might be a form of things, and says to the intellect: 'Try whether that may not be the form of these things [...] Nay, the poetic relations themselves in the phenomenon may suggest to the imagination the law that rules its scientific life. Yea, more than this: we dare to claim for the true, childlike, humble imagination, such an inward oneness with the laws of the universe that it possesses in itself an insight into the very nature of things.'

MacDonald reveals a remarkable insight into the dual connectivity of theory and experiment. It is not only the latter that 'checks' or 'refutes' the former but also the observations of the world elicited in a careful experiment that may hint at, or suggest, the form of the hypothetical theories themselves. In reciprocal creative energy, the imagined 'inward oneness' of the world will provoke the imaginative creativity necessary to devise experiments, which are by no means 'read off' the world.

At this point we arrive at a forgotten nexus of literature and science – but forgotten only because the 'scientific method' is described in the tradition of philosophy and sociology of science almost exclusively in terms of the experimental and observational testing of hypotheses. Even Kuhnian accounts buy into this modal, as it is the weight of evidence that, in a 'scientific revolution', suddenly overbalances an old hypothesis in favour of a new and previously unpopular one. Yet the process of 'conjecture and refutation' is only and at best the second half of a complete 'scientific method', which increasingly proves to be a misnomer, as the first and most significant half possesses no 'method' (Kuhn 1966). This far more significant, and primary, work in science, the work that differentiates the transformative from the trivial, the profound from the prosaic, is the imaginative work of formulating the hypotheses in the first place (McLeish 2019). Karl Popper, in *The Logic of Scientific Discovery* (2002), did admit that this stage was a necessary foundation for everything that follows, but confesses rapidly and very early in the book that he had nothing to say about the creative act by inductive formulation of what the hidden structures and dynamics of nature might be. For there is no logic to be had – this is what François Jacob (1988) termed 'night science' in contrast to the 'day science' of hypothesis testing and evaluation:

> Night science wanders blind. It hesitates, stumbles, recoils, sweats, wakes with a start. Doubting everything, it is forever trying to find itself, question itself, pull itself back together. Night science is a sort of workshop of the possible where what will become the building material of science is worked out.

Nothing could be further from the 'day science' of method, clear laboratory or computational procedures, and data. Jacob might even have allowed MacDonald his descriptive terms of the 'prophetic imagination'
and the work of the 'heart' over the head. Jacob's physiological manifestations of recoil, sweat, and questions rather than answers also suggest that
night science evokes narrative. In parallel, the 'workshop of the possible'
points to poesis. Here finally lies bare the live connection between the
sciences and the humanities, so alive indeed that science resembled, if not
becomes, a humanity (at least at night).

If MacDonald is able to lead us into the night-side narrative of the
scientific imagination, then his contemporary and friend, mathematician
Charles Dodgson ('by day' – Lewis Carroll 'by night' in our scientific
sense) can exemplify the immersive narrative of night science imagination
at work. In the light of the covert processes of scientific creation that we
are mapping, I want to suggest that the celebrated mathematical allusions
and metaphors in Carroll's fiction are more than a playful representation of
his mathematical interests breaking the surface of his literary work. More
than that, they are the manifestations of Dodgson's experience of the, often
covert, pathways of mathematical creativity. That there are strong similarities between the creation of mathematical ideas, and those of science more
broadly, is apparent from the well-known accounts of Jacques Hadamard
(1945) and Henri Poincaré (1945), who developed a notion of the atomic
agency of mathematical ideas:

> [they must be] something like the hooked atoms of Epicurus. During the complete
> repose of the mind, these atoms are motionless; they are, so to speak, hooked to the
> wall; so this complete rest may be indefinitely prolonged without the atoms meeting,
> and consequently without any combination between them. [...] After this shaking-
> up imposed upon them by our will, these atoms do not return to their primitive rest.
> They freely continue their dance.

Dodgson illustrates Poincaré's conjecture that mathematical creativity
calls on a partially subconscious generative interplay of imagined agency
imputed to ideas themselves, within a narrative 'dance'. Their repeated
occurrence within his fictional narratives provides readers with not just

a mathematically informed storyteller but also a mathematician whose stories become windows into his mathematical imagination.

Viewed from this novel perspective, they can be read not only as literary constructs alone, but also as insights into the way that Dodgson thought as a mathematician. His interests in topology furnish an almost ubiquitous exemplar theme. Topologically singular objects become explicit in his late *Sylvie and Bruno Concluded* (Carroll 1893, chapter 7); the characters discuss the 'non-orientable' forms of the Möbius Strip and the Klein Bottle (Figures 8 and 9). The first is a looped tape containing a half-twist that means that it possesses only one side and one edge, rather than two. The second represents an equivalent closed surface with no separable inside or outside, and carrying the additional force that its non-orientable three-dimensional form can only be represented without self-intersection in four-dimensional space (it is possible to construct, and indeed even to knit, in three dimensions, but requiring a self-intersection).

Figures 8 and 9. Möbius Strip (left)and Klein Bottle (right).

Carroll's characters' discussion of the objects is reminiscent of a journey of exploration. An example as the conversation passes from the strip to the bottle will suffice:

'The Ring has only one surface, and only one edge, It's very mysterious!'

'The bag is just like that, isn't it?' I suggested.

'Is not the outer surface of one side of it continuous with the inner surface of the other side?' 'So it is!' she exclaimed.

Natural Philosophy

'Only it isn't a bag, just yet. How shall we fill up this opening, Mein Herr?'

'Thus!' said the old man impressively, taking the bag from her, and rising to his feet in the excitement of the explanation.

'The edge of the opening consists of four handkerchief edges, and you can trace it continuously, round and round the opening: down the right edge of one handkerchief, up the left edge of the other, and then down the left edge of the one, and up the right edge of the other!'

'So you can!' Lady Muriel murmured thoughtfully, leaning her head on her hand, and earnestly watching the old man.

'And that proves it to be only one opening!'

She looked so strangely like a child, puzzling over a difficult lesson, and Mein Herr had become, for the moment, so strangely like the old Professor, that I felt utterly bewildered: the 'eerie' feeling was on me in its full force, and I felt almost impelled to say, 'Do you understand it, Sylvie?' (Carroll 1893: 96)

The text is tactile, haptic, sensual and emotive. The writing guides the reader's eye only the materiality of the stitched Klein bottle – the 'Purse of Fortunatus' (Kohlt 2019: 225). It resembles accounts of scientists and mathematicians deploying one of the techniques, such as they exist, for solving theoretical problems, that of entering the object of study, often with an imagined change of scale. The playful engagement with higher dimensions suggests that this must have been a conversation topic with MacDonald, whose original title for *Lilith* (in the B-manuscript) was *Anacosm: A Tale of the Seventh Dimension* (cf. MacDonald 1895(?): 1; Kohlt 2019: 236; 255).

Topological themes are present in only slightly more disguised form, in the *Alice* novels. The encounter with the Caterpillar is a good example, in that it explores, one by one, the invariances of topological relations. Alice undergoes sequentially the transformations against which topological properties (such as those of the Möbius Strip or Klein Bottle) are invariant. The first set constitutes changes of scale (Alice's height varies, depending on what potent substance she has eaten, from the giant to the microscopic). Then follows examples of continuous geometric deformation (in extreme moments of the encounter, her neck extends in a serpentine fashion). The same point is made by the transformation of a baby into a pig. That this is possible to imagine through a proto-filmic sequence of continuous deformation testifies to the topological properties that humans share with all mammals, pigs included. More to the point, this imagined scene is not as unconnected as appears on first reading with the way that mathematicians who are visual thinkers (not all are) operate in exploring the structures of their contemplation. Hadamard included the response he received from Albert Einstein among the correspondence in preparation for his book:

> The words or the language, as they are written or spoken, do not seem to play any role in my mechanism of thought. The psychic entities which seem to serve as elements in thought are certain signs and more or less clear images which can be 'voluntarily' reproduced and combined. There is, of course, a certain connection between those elements and relevant logical concepts. It is also clear that the desire to arrive finally at logically connected concepts is the emotional basis of this rather vague play with the above-mentioned elements. But taken from a psychological viewpoint, this combinatory play seems to be the essential feature in productive thought – before there is any connection with logical construction in words or other kinds of signs which can be communicated to others.

Words come later to Einstein; first is the imagined, visualized – sometimes even 'felt' as he testified elsewhere – physicality of the mathematical objects, concepts, and elements at play. Note too that these accounts of 'night science' are as emotionally entangled as they are cognitive (McLeish 2019), and what Hadamard describes here is the equivalent of the Victorian concept of 'unconscious cerebration' that Carroll establishes as the underlying principle of the *Sylvie and Bruno* novels (cf. Kohlt 2019: 227; 253).

A series of papers published in the unlikely journal *Genome Biology*, by computational biologists Itai Yanai and Martin Lercher, has given a fresh and contemporary dress and depth to the long-buried truth of the imaginative process in scientific research, and in particular on the allocation of intentionality (Yanai and Lercher 2020). These authors also devised and presented a regular blog and podcast, Night-Science, that pursues the same theme, using Jacob's metaphor for the covert and creative processes of science, in conversation with other scientists and philosophers. They defend the use of imaginative, narrative, and even agential stories that 'night science' invokes of genes, bacteria, and even electrons; the perception of agency is a powerfully developed and adaptive capacity of the human mind, akin to simulated visual thought. The absence of actual mental agency in the behaviour of these and other physical and material objects of science is beside the point, for the second half, the 'day science' of the scientific method, is always ready to apply its rigorous evaluation to any theory of material function, once that theory exists. The act of creation that brings it into existence is bound by no rules, and requires no constraint of paradigm or agreement with data.

The non-verbal science-drama of Einstein, and the visual play of mathematical forms of Dodgson and Hadamard represent one such route to ideation, but there are others that do take more direct verbal or literary form. Words do not need to follow ideas, though they may; they may also precede them. In the final stage of this discussion, we need to return to another tradition of imaginative natural philosophy, overlaid in the modern era by the same forces that precipitated Goethe's reminder – the power of poetry itself in the creative foreground of science. It is of note that there has been a quiet and continuous tradition of science and mathematics engaging with poetry, and of their proponents writing it. Carroll himself is a case in point. It is almost to wear a point too thin to point, as have many others, to 'Jabberwocky' as a brilliant near-nonsense eliciting of an experience of liminal comprehension, akin to the groping of scientific imagination up to and over the horizon of current understanding. Reading it has been compared to a first encounter with scientific literature in an unfamiliar field (Grumbine 2009); a recent fascinating example was reported by the head of a cancer research laboratory working with early career researchers on how to accommodate strange and unfamiliar concepts as they learned the new science behind the nefarious disease (Gubar 2018). Carroll furnishes a further example of articulating the scientific experience of approaching the unknown and conceptually out of reach, using the metaphor of climbing a hill whose summit remains hidden until the last few steps, in Canto VI of his poem *Phantasmagoria*. Though the mathematician's struggle is not its explicit theme, reading it alongside the accounts of searching for proofs, in Hadamard or Poincaré, and knowing Dodgson's official Oxford academic work, more than strongly suggests that he is conveying personal mental experience in poetic form. The more general confrontation of the human mind with nonhuman nature, which constitutes an implicitly theological framework (McLeish 2014) within which science is situated as a human imperative, was a topic for George MacDonald, who was a prolific poet as well as a novelist. His One with Nature echoes Carroll's liminal descriptions of crossing from the familiar to the strange, and even the transcendent, in the mental exploration of nature. Beginning with the familial encounter: 'I have a fellowship with every shade/Of changing nature: with the tempest hour/My soul goes forth to claim her early dower/, the experience passes through […] The speechless majesty of love', to an unanticipated breadth of final vision: 'And she from homely intercourse of eyes/. Hath gathered visions wider than the sky.' The poem is thoroughly Joban in its encounter of nature through storm and strangeness, towards an image of the divine. Here, the nexus of science, poetry, and theology emerges as a trinity within which the discussion between any two seems to occasion the third (Guite 2012; McLeish 2014).

Through examples such as these from our companions of Carroll and MacDonald, the formal structure of poetry reveals, once the habituated distance from science is carefully and deliberately removed, a close structural kinship with the combination of 'night' with 'day' science. The discipline of rigorous expression, of rhyming connections between lines, of thematic coherence, of the meter of chosen form – all these constraints map onto 'day science' constraint of quantitative and qualitative coherence, of mapping, between theory and observation or experiment. But poetry's form is not an inward constraint around nothing, but a shaping of an energy with outward dynamic: the imaginative, emotive, expressive content of the poem. As I have written elsewhere (McLeish 2022, chapter 5).

If poetry is the creative meeting of imaginative energies and ideas with the shaping constraint of form, then what could act as a better metaphor for the scientific imperative to describe the world in layered and connected detail as well as grand design? In other words, what could call upon greater imaginative energies than the invitation to reimagine the universe, and what could constitute a tighter constraint of form than to conform that imagination to the universe we observe? Science becomes a metaphor for poetry, or perhaps for a single, polyvocal poem, while poetry patterns science for the same reason.

So strong, indeed, is the kinship between the paired and tensioned forces of creativity and form, in both science and poetry, that it becomes less strange to recall that so much pre-modern and early modern science itself took explicitly poetic form. The century of Francis Bacon and Robert Boyle's explicitly theological (Harrison 2007) articulation of experimental method also saw the scientific poetry of Margaret Cavendish (1663) and Andrew Marvell's (1681). Cavendish's atom poems of 1663 are full of ideation and novelty, not only at the level of atomistic verse in the tradition of Lucretius, but of the explanatory power of the atomic hypothesis. For example, her 'Of Aiery Atoms' constitutes the first occurrence of an exploration of hollow atomic structure (McLeish 2022). In the case of Marvell's 'The Mower Against Gardens', there is an early and insightful subversion of gardening as a dawning Anthropocene, in which the formal structure of the verse suggests, then deconstructs, the formality of artificial gardens. The standard text on silkworms and silk-spinning technology at the start of the seventeenth century, Thomas Moffett's (1599) 'The silkewormes, and their flies', is a lengthy text entirely in octave. A case can be made that for the functionalist intervention of Spratt, Oldenburg, and the other early Royal Society functionaries who steered the literary form of early modern science towards the journal of letters, the dominant form might have continued as that of poetry for much longer than it did (Poon 2022).

The covert, nocturnal, imaginative, and creative powers of scientific ideation, long hidden from public view by a strange taboo of modern scientific institutions, become visible through the writings of MacDonald and Carroll when recognized through the eyes of scientists who experience the *poiesis* of imagination and form as part of their nightly, if not daily, work. Furthermore, a reappraisal of the literature and poetry of these writers, as well as of others before and since, suggests a re-engagement with imaginative writing, as well as of poetry, not only as media of wider communication and contemplation of scientific insight but also as generators of new scientific ideas.

Nicholas Schilero

6 Gödel, Einstein, Carroll: Parallels and Crossovers[1]

Gödel and Einstein hold a mirror to each other: eccentric personalities; dear friends later in life; giants in their respective fields, publishing fundamental results (Holt 2018: 3–14). Gödel even discovered a very Gödelian and, as Holt puts it, 'Alice in Wonderland-like' solution for Einstein's General Relativity field equations – the solution's closed time-like curves describe a possible model of the universe where backward time travel is possible at great-enough speeds (ibid., 12–13).

Logic and geometry, Carroll's mathematical specialties, join all three – a common intellectual heritage. Non-Euclidean geometry and metamathematics grew out of the independence proof of Euclid's Parallel Postulate (see Nagel, Newman 2001 [1958]). The former figures directly into General Relativity (curved warping four-dimensional spacetime). The latter ushered in modern logic, culminating in Gödel's Incompleteness Theorems (Idem).

Paradoxical Personalities: *Who Are You?*

To start, all three are eccentric, paradoxical figures in their own right, their own inverse looking-glass counterparts.

---

1   This chapter is the author's abridged version of his full, unpublished essay.

Natural Philosophy

Dodgson (*or …?*)

Carroll was a renowned children's author but weary of fame. Weary of fame but a photographer. A photographer, forgetful of faces[2] (Collingwood 1898: 135). A deacon and poet – *nonsense* poet – with a slight stutter. And he was deaf in one ear (Drupaladmin 2017). Meanwhile, *Alice*'s celebrated illustrator Tenniel was blind in one eye. But an exquisite artist, who brought Carroll's fantasy and nonsense to life.

Looking-glass duality similarly characterizes each pursuit. Magic: reality, illusion. Writing: reality, fiction; fictional worlds, fantasy worlds. Photography: the real-world subject, the photographed subject; the photograph, the unexposed negative – *literal* black-and-white duality, chesslike – well, minus Carroll's Red Army. Christian theology: body, soul; man, God; Earth, Heaven; Heaven, Hell; good, evil. Logic: truth, falsity. And geometry: Euclidean, non-Euclidean; physical space, mathematical space.

Einstein Through the Looking-Glass

Einstein established the particle-wave duality of light as well as the paradoxical equivalences of energy and mass, gravity and acceleration, and space and time. His cosmological constant is now used to help explain mysterious, Cheshire-invisible dark matter and energy: the universe through the looking-glass.

Einstein also rejected black holes, and he resisted Gödel's closed timelike curves and the de Sitter empty universe model – all contributions to General Relativity. Ditto the expanding universe, that is, the Big Bang, which he initially discounted but ultimately came to praise, abandoning his static model of the universe and the cosmological constant he introduced for it. He'd call that constant his 'greatest blunder'. But, as mentioned above,

---

2   A 'sillygism' (1889: 45)!

it was resurrected decades later to explain dark matter and energy. Even his 'blunders' are breakthroughs. Dynamic indeed. Death has not stopped Einstein from unveiling the secrets of the cosmos.

Gödel Through the Looking-Glass

Gödel *embodied* paradox, a real-life Humpty Dumpty – that literal walking, talking chicken-or-egg paradox, who was also a danger to himself. Gödel's results are counter-intuitive and paradoxical. He believed time did not exist and published a very technical argument for it (a 70th birthday present for Einstein) (Holt 2018: 12). He proved incompleteness by ingeniously incorporating the age-old Liar Paradox into number theory.

Gödel's life was paradoxical too. He was anxious and suffered from paranoid delusions. He insisted his food was being poisoned. His wife Adele would taste-test his meals for him. His delusions tragically drove him to his death: self-imposed starvation (see Holt 2018: 3–14). It is difficult to imagine how Gödel could believe these bizarre, irrational ideas. He was a genius, of logic no less, yet he starved himself to death, so as not to possibly poison himself consuming food. Self-defeating reasoning. Indeed, self-destructive. Death by paradox.

Carroll is especially prescient in pairing madness and logic: hyper-rational, extra-literal-minded thinking is taken to its logical, ultimately mad (and positively maddening) extremes. Some decades later, Chesterton advanced the thesis that logicians go mad exploring logic and infinity, the latter a staple of the field (see Chesterton, Manguel: 2014 [1908]; see Baker 2020). Chesterton wrote that the logician, forcing infinity into head, splits it in two, and that madness is not the loss of reason but the loss of everything *but* reason (Manguel 2014 [1908]). It wasn't long before the golden age of modern logic tested his thesis (see Doxiadis, Christos, Papdimitriou 2009). Proof-positive.

Madness is everywhere in the *Alice* books: Mad Hatter and Hare, the Mad Tea Party, and, of course, Cheshire's quasi Liar Paradox – 'we're all mad here' (*AAIW*: 30) – plus plenty of other otherworld absurdities.

Natural Philosophy

Madness in life too. Carroll's uncle, Skeffington Lutwidge, led an asylum reform movement. Tragically, a patient later killed him (Sellon 2013). Logic is a recurring theme throughout the books too (see Gardner 2015). Even Carroll's logical work – 'Tortoise' (1895) – is related to *Wonderland* by way of Mock Turtle. Logic and madness are interwoven for Carroll.

Moreover, fedora-clad Gödel is Mad Hatter incarnate. There are riddles, paradoxes. Undecidable propositions: 'A raven is like a writing-desk,' is an apparently true proposition in Wonderland but neither provable nor disprovable[3] (*AAIW*: 32). And Hatter is, of course, mad … well, *maybe*.

Scholars have conjectured that Hatter's madness stems from Mercury poisoning, historically associated with the hat-making process.[4] Poison makes Hatter go mad, and Gödel goes mad fretting over the same. His diet 'consisted mostly of butter, baby food, and laxatives' – not unlike Hare's inedible pocket-watch (Holt: 4; *AAIW*: 32).

Perhaps most startling is the Hatter's (delusional?) belief that the Tea Party is perpetually stuck at six o'clock (*AAIW*: 34). Like the always time-angsty White Rabbit, Gödel was preoccupied with the problem of time. He did not believe time exists and even believed he had refuted it (see Holt 2018: 3–14).

And we can't forget Alice feared consuming poisoned food, too. Her fear, however, makes good sense, given her situation. She was irrational to relax caution just because she double-checked for a warning label (*AAIW*: 5). As if poisoned foods are always as candid as the Liar Paradox. Though the self-referential 'Eat Me' currants were surprisingly suicidal (6).

---

3   Some possible solutions of my own: both–ought to be free from contradiction: writings; contravention; – have a black wing on either side of it ('a writing', 'a writing').

4   Though other theories, including tuberculosis, also common amongst textile workers have been discussed (Kohlt 2016; Davies 2010).

The *Three*-Way Mirror

Gödel, Einstein, and Carroll are looking-glass reflections of one another as well. The parallels are most pronounced in the trio's recurring and mutually reinforcing themes of madness, aberrant time, and inescapability.

Rabbit-Hole Black Holes and Looking-Glass Light-Clocks

Nowhere is Einstein more Wonderlandian than black holes. Gravity is so great that its escape-velocity exceeds the speed of light. Nothing can escape, not even light, hence *black* hole – they're Cheshire-invisible. Forget about parallel lines – spacetime becomes so warped, Alice need not bother with Longitude or Latitude (*AAIW*: 3). Time itself halts – a 'virtual eternity, gateways to Nowhen' (Holt 2018: 19). 'Time can be extinguished like a blown-out flame,' says Wheeler, the theoretical physicist who coined 'black hole' (reprinted in Overbye 2008). Physics as we know it, falls apart. At the hole's centre is the singularity, a point of infinite density where all unfortunate, horizon-crossed matter converges, crushed infinitesimally small – as if 'going out altogether', as Alice put it, worried she'd shrink away completely (*AAIW*: 5).

So again there are themes of madness, inescapability, and stopped time. The singularity, a breakdown of the laws of physics, is tantamount to the whole universe gone mad, Cheshire-style – or Chesterton-style: actual *infinity* sewn right into the fabric of reality. Escape is physically impossible – physic's breakdown notwithstanding. Gödel dispenses with time. The Tortoise captures Achilles in a loop for eternity.[5] And the black hole freezes time forever.

---

5   For further discussion of paradox in Carroll's Logic, see Chapter 14 of this collection (Editors' note).

The White-Rabbit Black Hole

Let's take a closer look through Alice's accordion-like telescope. There's plenty more black hole/rabbit-hole parallels. Both deal with death. Black holes are born out of dead stars, collapsed under their own gravity. The Rabbit races back to the hole lest he's so late they execute him – a *grave* situation, indeed! And the rabbit-hole might be time-stuck indefinitely if we're to take seriously Alice's concerns about falling forever (*AAIW*: 12).

The **Rabbit-Hole Rat-Hole** Wormhole

The rabbit-hole leads out to the Garden door, said to be about the size of a rat-hole, with a rodent – Mouse – nearby (*AAIW*: 4, 9). There are good grounds – underground – for interpreting this hole as a second rabbit-hole, or, better yet, as one end of an Earth-Wonderland wormhole with the rabbit-hole opposite. The rat-hole is quite literally part of the rabbit-hole: *rabbit-hole*. It's paradoxical enough that every w**hole** has a **hole** (not to mention that **o** in the middle) – that a hole has one too, well, that's practically a singularity (times 2) – the **rat-hole rabbit-hole** hole-in-a-hole. Small puns (pun on *small*) like these shouldn't be overlooked (easy as it is not to see a hole (inside a hole)) – wordplay is practically Gospel in Carroll's creations.[6]

The Looking-Glass – *No Mere Metaphor*

Even the portals themselves are mirrored opposites: a black hole – hence invisible – rabbit-hole versus the instrument-of-light

---

6   And his creations? – the word*play* of God!

looking-glass. At least, opposite on the surface. Let's dig deeper. The rabbit-hole goes right to Rabbit's house, Alice's first stop. Inside: another looking-glass (*AAIW*: 16). Another *portal*? – doubtful that it's just a plain-face mirror: looks apparently mean little in Rabbit's home, as seen by the Alice-housemaid mix-up (15). Down the rabbit-hole, through Rabbit's looking-glass – imagine the possibilities. And how about Special Relativity's light-clock? It's the looking-glass *through the looking-glass* – the possibilities are endless! Recursion like that goes on forever – didn't Alice wonder the same about the rabbit-hole (3)? But nothing tops the black hole, ironically the greatest mirror in the whole universe. In fact, it's a mirror *of* the whole universe – infinitely many times over (see Sutter 2021). A 'grotesque [...] fun house hall of mirrors' (Sutter 2021).

The Mad Tea Party (*Plus-Two*)

Nowhere is time more Wonderlandian than the Mad Tea Party. Time is forever stuck at 6 p.m. Carroll's calendar calculation just got easier: identity function and done! Or at least Hatter is mad enough to believe time is stuck. And if it really is, he's surely gone mad. It'd also mean that time is not absolute – Einstein's right, even in Wonderland. Though Wonderland's Time is very, *very* real – no mere illusion, as Einstein would have it, albeit just as stubborn (Holt 2018: 14).

Why not just leave? The guests appear locked into a modular game of (cacophonous) musical chairs, round and round. Stand up, scoot one seat over, sit, sip some, repeat. It's mechanical. And clocklike, even though time is halted – probably the pocket-watch too, which might explain Hare buttering it up, as if to oil its gears (*AAIW*: 32).

Looking-Glass Algebra: Numeric Wordplay

Anagrams are like looking-glass reversals, iterated over pairs of letters –
no wonder Carroll is fond of this kind of witticism.[7] Special monotonic
anagram cases include palindrome and anadrome (also called a 'semord-
nilap', the anadrome for 'palindromes'). Ambigrams are monotonic x-axis
reflections or rotations. Mirrors par excellence. Puns, another Carrollian
staple, also suggest looking-glass linguistics: one body, two referents. We
can uncover more madness, captivity, and anomalous time by applying
these operations to the Tea Party's vocabulary, its words and numerals,
riddle-like.

> TEA PARTY = TEA PAR TY (syllable spacing)
>
> = T PAR T (pun)[8]
>
> = TPART (respacing)
>
> = TRAPT (anadrome)
>
> = TRAPPED (pun)

So TEA PARTY = TRAPPED. But the Tea Party just *is* Alice and the
trio, thus, Alice and the others are in fact trapped! And what's the deal
with this tea anyhow?

> TEA = ATE (anagram)
>
> = EIGHT (pun)
>
> = 8 (definition)
>
> = ∞ (ambigram)
>
> = INFINITY (definition)

---

7   For example, 'Alice' through the Treacle Well, namely, 'Lacie'.
8   See Britannica (2016) for pronunciation.

Aha! Now we're onto something. Infinity snuck into the party – and into the partier's heads, by way of mouth, slithy and poisonous. No wonder the bunch has gone mad. The Tea Party really is an infinity trap – no doublet word ladder out of that (Danesi 2009)!
The sleepy Dormouse, of all creatures, might be catching on. Remember his capricious interest for things that start with 'M' (1865: 36)?

$m = \infty$ (x-axis reflection)

And what's more: mousetraps were first on his list (*AAIW*: 36). It's an infinity *mouse*trap – the infinity trap for mice, Dormouse included! He's caught on, indeed. And it's funny that the *Dor*mouse should speak of the mousetrap, as we previously likened the *rat*-hole *door*way to an inescapable black hole.

Price, Size, or Something Else Entirely …

What about numerals? It's time we take a closer look at that 10/6 price tag. 10/6 = 1.6 repeating. Just like time, there's no point,[9] it's 6 repeating, forever. We can even eliminate 1. 1.6 repeating is, upside down, infinitely many 9s followed by a 1. But that's impossible – there's no 1 after the 9s because those 9s never end. It's just infinite 9s, which, flipped back around, is 6 repeating. In fact, it's 666 repeating. 666 – *times infinity*.[10] Is Hatter damned for all eternity? No use turning one of those 6s into a door handle then – there's no way out of Hell.[11] It's *infinitely many* locked doors in this hallway.

The Mad Gardener and his chain of wrong keys will see to that (Carroll 1889: 30). And don't bother with a Double Rule of Three on these doors (1889: 30). You'll only get more 6s – no wonder the gatekeeper went

9   The 'point' isn't pronounced in prices.
10 The Number of the Beast – the Jabberwock Beast! Just dying to snicker-snack back – the Ol' Chesterton one-two (-three- …).
11 Money really is the root of all evil. Or at least a fraction.

mad! And definitely don't bother him with 'one-and-sixpence', that is, 1/
6, lest you're prepared to go to Hell *and back* – it's a whole other hallway
(1889: 30). An 'infinite' and 'grotesque' 'fun house hall of mirrors' – Hilbert's
haunted hotel (Sutter 2021; Freiberger 2017).

Part III

Religion and Spirituality

Karen Gardiner

7 'Must a name mean something?': Theological Evolution in *Through the Looking-Glass* Expressed through Victorian Broad Church Philology

In a letter to his sister Elizabeth on 29 November 1894, Lewis Carroll describes his theological position as 'Broad Church'. Whilst this letter was written in the last decade of Carroll's life, his reading, correspondence, and friendships indicate that despite being from a High Church background, there is ample evidence of Carroll's engagement with Broad Church interests throughout his adult life. This chapter will highlight how the Broad Church stance with which Carroll identified is intimately connected with the etymological and philological interests which the author demonstrates in the *Alice* books.

Victorian comparative philology, far from being a purely secular undertaking, was deeply rooted in a progressive theology which was in turn being influenced by new and developing evolutionary ideas. Darwin himself considered philology to be a branch of natural science and included a chapter on the development and evolution of language in *The Descent of Man*, referencing the philologist Max Müller who was at Oxford concurrently with Carroll:

> We see variability in every tongue, and new words are continually cropping up; but as there is a limit to the powers of the memory, single words, like whole languages, gradually become extinct. As Max Müller has well remarked: 'A struggle for life is constantly going on among the words and grammatical forms in each language. The better, the shorter, the easier forms are constantly gaining the upper hand, and they owe their success to their own inherent virtue.' (Darwin 1872: 69)

Broad Church theologians, then, had embraced Darwinian theories of evolution not only as a way of expressing how God's nature is progressively revealed and interpreted through history, but also as a way of understanding the development of language. They engaged with philological ideas in speculating on the origins and purposes (divine or otherwise) of language and naming, and in considering to what extent individual words and names evolve or devolve to reveal or conceal philosophical and theological truth. Mid-nineteenth-century Broad Church philologists known to, and read by, Lewis Carroll included the popular but controversial comparative philologist at Oxford, Friedrich Max Müller, as well as Broad Church theologians affiliated with Cambridge including F. D. Maurice, Frederick Farrar, and Richard Chenevix Trench. Carroll pronounced in his diary as early as 15 March 1853 that he wished to read all of Trench as part of his study of etymology, and works by Trench, Farrar, Maurice, and Max Müller are all found in Carroll's personal library. Carroll's interest in and engagement with these theologians and their philological publications justify a theologically informed philological reading of his imaginative works, and this article will point to Carroll's philological interests by considering his 'Looking-Glass Insects' chapter in *Through the Looking-Glass and What Alice Found There*. Specifically, Trench's *On the Study of Words* will be highlighted in relation to the ideas found in the insects' chapter, as Carroll reflects on who it is that has the power to name and un-name, the purpose names hold in forming our identities, and the power that words may have over our existence and destiny.

'Looking-Glass Insects' begins with Alice making a geographical survey of the area in which she finds herself. This proves to be a failure, not just because there appear to be very few identifying features in the landscape but because those that there are have not been named, and so cannot be meaningfully categorized.[1] Alice's fellow railway passengers seem to be aware of her disorientation but the gentleman opposite her pronounces, 'So young a child ought to know which way she's going even if she doesn't

---

1   See also Chapters 1, 2, 3 and 4 on naming, taxonomies, and scientific, philosophical, and Victorian cultural aspects of it with regard to the Looking-Glass Insects, and their educational purpose.

know her own name' (Carroll 1881: 50). The question of whether one can hold on to one's purpose without knowing one's name is an idea which is explored throughout Alice's experience in this chapter.

The Gnat makes his presence known to Alice during the railway journey, and he appears surprised that Alice does not already know him. He initially talks in smaller type face, identifying himself only as 'an insect' (TTLG: 53) but once he has been named by the author as 'the Gnat' (*TTLG*: 54) the type face increases and he becomes physically bigger, as well as gaining a capital letter for his name, showing that in his case, at least, being named is correlated with a more substantial existence. Once named himself, the Gnat is in a position to name others and he is eager to give Alice a philosophical natural history lesson including discussing with her the very purpose of the insects having names.

> 'I don't rejoice in insects at all,' Alice explained, 'because I'm rather afraid of them – at least the larger kinds. But I can tell you the names of some of them.'
>
> 'Of course they answer to their names?' the Gnat remarked carelessly.
>
> 'I never knew them do it.'
>
> 'What's the use of them having names,' the Gnat said, 'if they won't answer to them?'
>
> 'No use to *them*,' said Alice, 'but it's useful to the people that name them, I suppose. If not, why do things have names at all?' (*TTLG*: 55)

For the Broad Church theologian Richard Chenevix Trench, names are of use because they give us something on which to fix our feelings and thoughts which stop them from getting lost. Furthermore, Trench interprets the giving of names by God in the Bible as a means by which humanity are given identity and purpose. Thus, in *On the Study of Words*, he states,

> Thoughts of themselves are perpetually slipping out of the field of the immediate mental vision, but the name [given by God] abides with us, and the utterance of it restores them in a moment (Trench 1874: 23).

This will be Alice's experience later in the chapter when she meets the fawn. Carroll also describes this sense of things 'slipping out of the field' in the fifth chapter of *Looking-Glass*, 'Wool and Water'.

> The shop seemed to be full of all manner of curious things – but the oddest part of it all was that, whenever she looked hard at any shelf, to make out exactly what it had on it, that particular shelf was always quite empty thought the others around it were crowded as full as they could hold. (*TTLG*: 103)

Trench argues that God has put a 'seal of truth' (Trench 1874: 7) on language, and that truth is discovered through gradual revelation which takes place through the natural (i.e. God-given) development of language. God and humanity, then, for Trench, engage in naming in partnership with one another. In *Looking-Glass*, it is the Gnat who appears to possess the divine power to name. Indeed, the insects that are introduced to Alice by the Gnat only seem to come into existence (and certainly only come into Alice's consciousness) at the point at which they are named by him, though they clearly share some etymological history with the insects that Alice is familiar with from home. The horsefly/Rocking-horse-fly, it might be argued, has evolved into something altogether more interesting than its relative in our world, but the dragonfly/Snap-dragon-fly is somewhat disconcerting with its head on fire, and the Bread-and-butterfly (Figure 10) is clearly an evolutionary disaster.

> 'Crawling at your feet,' said the Gnat (Alice drew her feet back in some alarm), 'you may observe a Bread-and-butterfly. Its wings are thin slices of bread-and-butter, its body is a crust, and its head is a lump of sugar'.
>
> 'And what does it live on?'
>
> 'Weak tea with cream in it.'
>
> A new difficulty came into Alice's head. 'Supposing it couldn't find any?' she suggested.
>
> 'Then it would die of course.'
>
> 'But that must happen very often,' Alice remarked thoughtfully.
>
> 'It always happens' said the Gnat. (*TTLG*: 59)

Rather than evolving, the Bread-and-Butterfly has *de*volved from its etymological relative the butterfly. The devolution and inevitable extinction of the poor Bread-and-butterfly may be blamed on it having been poorly named at the moment it was called into existence by the Gnat. Its very name and following description reveal that not only is it impossible

Figure 10. Bread-and-butter-fly, John Tenniel.

for the Bread-and-butterfly to survive but it can never have existed in the first place.

The inevitable demise of the Bread-and-butterfly causes Alice to think about her own identity:

> After this, Alice was silent for a minute or two, pondering. The Gnat amused itself meanwhile by humming around her head: at last it settled again and remarked 'I suppose you don't want to lose your name?'
>
> 'No indeed,' said Alice, a little anxiously.
>
> 'And yet I don't know,' the Gnat went on in a careless tone: 'only think how convenient it would be if you could manage to go home without it.' (*TTLG*: 59)

Alice's decision to enter the Wood does necessitate the losing of her name, but she comforts herself by planning how she might find a way of gaining it again should it be given to someone else in her stead. It does not occur to Alice that her name might be entirely lost forever, nor does it occur to her to accept a new name; such is her identity tied up with the word 'Alice'. In the wood, neither Alice nor the fawn has language to frame and categorize their experiences and Alice's experience here provides a mirror to that of the Gnat's experience at the beginning of the chapter. Whilst he is enlarged by the giving of his name, she is diminished in agency and identity by the losing of hers.

Trench's idea that names are a means of holding on to identity and affirming meaning is something which can be found throughout both books of Alice's adventures. She is continually being asked who she is, often with the demand to provide proof whether it is to a caterpillar, a Queen or a pigeon. Although the railway passengers at the beginning of this chapter claim that Alice ought to know where she's going even if she doesn't know her own name, the reality in the wood is that having lost her name, she has also temporarily lost the sense of what it means to be Alice.

The discovery that one might lose one's old name and gain a new one is usually connected to loss in Alice (consider how keen she is not to have become Mabel in her first adventure in Wonderland), but other authors have considered the idea redemptive. Carrollians who are aware of Carroll's propensity to mark special days in his diary with a 'white stone' might be interested in George MacDonald's sermon 'A New Name' which was published in his *Unspoken Sermons* in 1867, based on the text of Revelation 2: 17:

> He that hath an ear, let him hear what the Spirit saith unto the churches; To him that overcometh will I give to eat of the hidden manna, and will give him a white stone, and in the stone a new name written, which no man knoweth saving he that receiveth it.

In this sermon, MacDonald addresses what he considers to be the true essence of a name:

> […] the giving of the white stone with the new name is the communication of what God thinks about the man to the man. In order to see this, we must first understand what is the idea of a name, – that is, what is the perfect notion of a name. The true name is one which expresses the character, the nature, the being, the _meaning_ of the person who bears it. It is the man's own symbol, – his soul's picture, in a word, – the sign which belongs to him and to no one else. Who can give a man this, his own name? God alone. (MacDonald 1887: 105)

Looking-Glass is in part an exploration of language and the power of naming, and we have seen in this article that Carroll's interest in the theological philology espoused by his contemporaries is reflected in some of the characters and scenes in *Looking-Glass*. It is hoped that this very brief introduction to Broad Church philology through the 'Looking-Glass Insects' will enable the reader to follow this theme through the book, seeing Humpty Dumpty and the White Knight not merely as figures of ridicule but also as theological and philological questioners.

For nineteenth-century Broad Church Philologists, words were living, changing, evolving things that eventually led to a clearer revelation and reflection of God; thus, for these theologians, they are much more than artificial signs, whatever Humpty Dumpty might say. Words, at their highest calling and at their most evolved, are understood to reflect an image of truth, though they are, at present, incomplete in their revelation. The Gnat, as the mirror image of a competent creator and sustainer, is demonstrated to be an inadequate name giver, who cannot ensure the survival of his creations. Alice immediately sees the flaw in his creation, and she unmakes the Bread-and-Butterfly by simply asking the right questions.

In Trench's *On the Study of Words*, he expressed the belief that children are able to comprehend the spiritual truth that lies within words much more readily than adults:

> There is a sense of reality about children which makes them rejoice to discover that there is also a reality about words, that they are not merely arbitrary signs, but living powers. (Trench 1874: 41)

Alice stands with Trench. She refuses to believe that 'words can mean anything I want them to', and both her experiences and observations demonstrate that words are in fact alive, evolving, and meaningful. Nevertheless, Alice finds herself wondering in her later conversation with Humpty Dumpty, 'Must a name mean something?' Her question reflects the concerns of theological philologists who held in tension the twin ideas that words are both meaningful and God-given, but also evolving or devolving, since they are substantive and alive.

Despite the Red Queen's injunction to 'remember who you are' in her journeys, Alice discovers that identity is not as straightforward as it might seem and that words and especially names, just like the looking-glass itself, have the power to both conceal and reveal the truth. Alice's own challenge is not to discover a new true name such as MacDonald suggests, but rather to hold on to the one she has been given. The name 'Queen Alice' does not live up to its promise and she is content to return to her home beyond the Looking-Glass minus her crown. Perhaps Alice's identity is actually a symbol of the one we are all striving for. Arguments about words and their meanings, and threats to rename or un-name her are unable, ultimately, to threaten her identity, and Alice herself, despite her many challenges, and many arguments about the meaning of words, ultimately maintains an accurate, confident, evolved reflection of herself.

Joshua Rawleigh

8 Through the Looking-Glass Darkly: The Mirror Theology of Alice's Adventures

One of the enduring oddities of Lewis Carroll's second *Alice* book is the title: *Through the Looking-Glass*. True, the looking-glass begins Alice's adventures, but by far the more substantial framing device of the novel is the chess frame. As scholars like Martin Gardner have noted, for a book so concerned with its formal and stylistic components, the foregrounding of the looking-glass over some of the more pervasive images in the novel seems incongruous. This chapter asks, however, what it might mean to take Carroll's use of the looking-glass framing as something to assist the sense of development and change which accompany the dominant chess frame. I propose that a meaningful way to understand Carroll's use of the looking-glass theme is through its theological implications, specifically the mirror theology articulated by Carroll's close friend George MacDonald. From this viewpoint, the looking-glass is not merely a means of entering another world, but a means of entering a truer world. In nineteenth-century Romantic theology, here typified by MacDonald, the looking-glass was frequently used as an image for conceptualizing the soul's capacity to change, mould, and be perfected into the divine image it is meant to be.

Reading Alice's journey in the looking-glass world through this theological lens thus enables us to see her movements in the novel's chess frame not as separate from the looking-glass theme but as intimately tied to it since both are about a sense of progress and self-development. Throughout the book, Carroll envisions his heroine as moving along a path of theological actualization that leads her to apotheosis at the novel's conclusion. Apotheosis refers to a moment of near or actual divinization by which the individual in tandem with the Holy Spirit comes to resemble God more closely. Read in this way, *Through the Looking-Glass* is not merely a work of nonsense fiction, but an expression of divine logic and its impact on the development of the soul.

The theological implications of the mirror predate Lewis Carroll and the Romantic theologies of his contemporaries. St Paul twice uses the image to describe the Christian's position in relation to divine knowledge: 'But we all, with open face beholding as in a glass the glory of the Lord, are changed into the same image from glory to glory, even as by the Spirit of the LORD' (2 Cor 3:17–18), and the sanctified self: 'For now we see through a glass, darkly; but then face to face: now I know in part; but then shall I know even as also I am known' (1 Cor 13:12).[1] Many Christian writers from St Ephrem in the fourth century to Nicholas Love's reworking of Pseudo-Bonaventure into *The Mirror of the Blessed Life of Jesus Christ* in the fifteenth century built upon Paul's imagery of the mirror to describe the Christian life as something which captures and transforms the image of the individual. This association between transformation and the mirror may seem strange to us today due to our familiarity with silvered mirrors, Newtonian optics, and a Lockean sense of the mirror as a mechanical depiction of the one who gazes into it. In the nineteenth century, however, those developments were relatively recent, and to Lewis Carroll and many in his circle, there was an effort to reclaim a more ancient and dynamic understanding of the mirror's relation to the individual.

Indeed, in his sermon on Pauline mirror imagery, 'The Mirrors of the Lord', George MacDonald foregrounds the value of this difference in understanding: 'Paul never thought of the mirror as reflecting, as throwing back the rays of light from its surface; he thought of it as receiving, taking into itself, the things presented to it – here, as filling its bosom with the glory it looks upon.' The mirror absorbs rather than reflects. This absorption, however, is not static but allows that which is being absorbed to change, morph, and grow. When Paul speaks of being 'changed into the same image' through looking at the similar-yet-different image in the mirror, he is speaking of this absorption, one where the imperfect is taken

---

1   For further thoughts on the science-theological implications of this quote within *Looking-Glass*, see Chapter 4.

into the mirror and turned into the perfected picture which one sees in it. As MacDonald says:

> The mirror and the thing mirrored are of one origin and nature, and in closest relation to each other… [God] will work until the same likeness is wrought out and perfected in us, the image, namely, of the humanity of God, in which image we were made at first, but which could never be developed in us except by the indwelling of the perfect likeness. (MacDonald 'The Mirrors of the Lord': 51)

From a Pauline perspective, the mirror draws in a person's image, bending and transforming it, and then casting that image back to the original viewer. In MacDonald's interpretation of Paul, because humanity was created in the image of God and thus shares 'one origin and nature' with him, Christ was able to draw human nature into himself, transform it, and then present that transformed image to humanity through the Incarnation (MacDonald 'The Mirrors of the Lord': 51).

In viewing the mirror as something which draws the forms and symbols of the world into itself and casts back a more real vision of those forms, MacDonald was also following a Coleridgean Romantic tradition. As Adam Walker writes, the Platonic understanding of mimesis – literally imitation – allowed Coleridgean Romantics to depict 'the mirror as an object used to transform reality […] the Romantics used the mirror as an object which makes things come alive and represents an energetic, living world' (Walker 2018: 16). According to MacDonald, Paul sees Christ drawing humanity into himself via scripture, nature, and Christian community. In each case, the work of the mirror is to revivify that which is drawn into it, allowing that which was without to be transformed within.

Similarly, in *Through the Looking-Glass*, Alice's first interactions with the looking-glass mark it as a space of spiritual and moral transformation. She holds up the black kitten to the looking-glass 'to punish it' and so that 'it might see how sulky it was' (*TTLG*: 9). Alice thus conceives of the looking-glass house as a space of moral redemption, one in which the kitten might make amends for its bullying of Dinah and Snowdrop.[2] Her perspective of the looking-glass as a morally

2   Snowdrop being another point of intersection between MacDonald and Carroll, as named after Mary MacDonald's pet cat.

transformative space emerges from the belief in the looking-glass world's supreme beauty. After all, if the looking-glass world is more perfect than the material, then surely it will cause that which enters it to likewise become more perfect, 'changed into the same image', as those things which surround it.

The operative word here is also the other substantial term in the book's title – 'through'. The word was one which Carroll and his publisher, Alexander Macmillan, laboured over before settling on 'through'. However, as Walker notes, 'The title "Into the Looking-Glass" would have been more apposite, were the looking-glass only an access point. The choice of the preposition "through" bequeaths deeper meaning as the story unfolds' (Walker 2018: 17). That the word was deliberately chosen as, according to Macmillan 'just the word' Carroll was 'looking for', underscores the deliberateness of this distinction (Macmillan in Cohen and Gandolfo 1987: 85). In Walker's understanding, the looking-glass is not just a portal to another world; it is another world, one which fulfils the Romantic ideal of enchantment wherein ordinary objects literally come to life. Moreover, the looking-glass world is not simply one in which objects are transformed, but one in which Alice herself is changed. Alice must journey *through* the looking-glass, learning lessons that eventually enable her personal and spiritual maturation.

This process of maturation comes through chess: the novel's other framing device. As Alice moves throughout the looking-glass world, she does not simply follow a linear narrative progression but finds herself in the midst of a chess game which often entails counter-intuitive movements, feints, and challenges. Alice's movements from one space to another, however, follow moments of self-development. The most powerful of these moments is when she enters the eighth square and is 'queened'. Throughout the novel, Alice has struggled to understand the rules and inhabitants of the looking-glass world. However, in her encounter with the White Knight, she develops a true fondness for him, despite his clumsiness and absurdities, and works to encourage him in his own movements across the chessboard. In the end, she is able to communicate with the White Knight in a meaningful way because she has learned something of the rules of this new world.[3] Thus, when she finally leaves the seventh square, she does so entirely of her own volition, recognizing what she is doing, saying, ' "[…] and now for the last brook, and to be a Queen! How grand it sounds!" A very few steps brought her to the edge of the brook. "The Eighth Square at last!" she cried as she bounded across' (*TTLG*: 183). No longer is she tepidly jumping from trains, unsure of what will happen to her (210) or fleeing large beasts which may or may not be able to reach her (80). Instead, she has come to understand the looking-glass world at least in part and is thus able to move in it by her own will. This, in itself, is a mirroring, of the structure of Wonderland, and its turning point, situated at the middle point of the work: the Mad Tea-Party, at which Alice, for the first time decides consciously to abandon an unsettling encounter with the Wonderland dwellers, and choose her own path (Kohlt 2016).

In the chess structure of the book, *Through the Looking-Glass* culminates with Alice ascending from an imperfect, lower being – the pawn – to the most powerful form she can attain – the queen. In the looking-glass theology, this apotheosis occurs because she has learned to live within the logic of the foreign world which she has entered as demonstrated by her effective communication with the White Knight. Thus, despite the Red Queen and the White Queen still conversing with typical Carrollian nonsense, they treat Alice as an equal, enabling her to communicate with them. Unlike at the end of *Alice's Adventures in Wonderland* where the Queen of Heart's rule is absolute and arbitrary, in *Through the Looking-Glass*, because Alice has earned her crown, she is able to exert some degree of control.

It is worth noting that some scholars, such as Gillian Beer in *Alice in Space* (2016), argue that Alice in fact resists development. Indeed, Beer situates Alice against characters from MacDonald's works who more obviously undergo moral development throughout the course of the narrative. Beer emphasizes that the changes Alice undergoes are markedly physical, not spiritual or moral, and therefore cannot be read as allegorical: 'Alice herself undergoes no transformation of the self, although her body bulges and diminishes. She learns a lot, but it is all lateral and inconsequential, not driving on toward adulthood' (Beer 2016: 18–19). However, as we have

---

3   For linguistic aspects of this education, see Chapter 2.

seen that very ability to learn to live within the logic of the looking-glass world is a sign of spiritual progression. In learning to communicate and exert authority, she transforms, perhaps not into an adult but certainly into a more spiritually actualized individual.

That she receives a crown as her reward for her progress through the looking-glass world is also telling, as crowns bear with them the connotation of spiritual achievement. The various authors of the epistles in the New Testament refer to receiving a crown of glory or righteousness as the ultimate reward for spiritual devotion (2 Tim 4:7; James 1:12; 1 Peter 5:4). In Carroll's Romantic theology, this crown is something which is both earned, in that Alice has worked her way across the board, and granted, in that, as she steps into the eighth square, the crown just appears on her head. However, Alice cannot simply remain stationary in the eighth space; she must return from the looking-glass and carry the lessons she has learned back into ordinary reality. Indeed, unlike in *Wonderland*, in *Through the Looking-Glass*, Carroll dwells on Alice's return from her adventures. The impetus for her return comes when she grows tired of the Red Queen and 'takes' her (184). In the chess match, Alice has captured the Red Queen and at the same time positions herself to checkmate the Red King. She is victorious and thus able to control and manipulate the world around her into the reality she desires it to be. Therefore, when she calls the Red Queen a kitten, the Red Queen becomes a kitten (213–214).

As she settles into the mundane world again, though, she loses some of the level of control she had in the spiritual, looking-glass world as she loses her crown. This perhaps accounts for some of the immutability Beer reads in Alice's identity since Alice physically begins and ends in the same place. However, in the logic of the looking-glass world, this return does not mean Alice has regressed. Instead, some personal sacrifice must accompany her victory. This is, of course, fundamental to chess. If the pawn-turned-queen ends the game, it is necessarily stripping itself of its authority since, at the beginning of the next game, it will return to being a pawn. The highest end of one's spiritual journey is also to relinquish whatever personal authority one has gained. In the book of Revelation, the saints who have received crowns of glory and righteousness 'cast their crowns before the throne', on which Christ reigns (Rev. 4.9–11). In the theology of Christian sanctification, the further one's progress the more one must learn to sacrifice since Christ's highest example is one of selflessness. Like Alice, Christ relinquished his divine crown in favour of entering the terrestrial world. Furthermore, just as Christ's participation in the mundane world is intended to spread the message of the Kingdom of God, so Alice tells her kittens of her adventures in the looking-glass world immediately upon returning. Much like Christ in the Gospels, Alice's message is largely ignored by her audience, but this does not stop her from continuing to try to spread her 'good news'.

While it may seem a stretch to associate Alice's preaching to the kittens with Christ's ministry in the New Testament, Alice's adventures are defined by their nonsense. Moreover, Christian theologians since Paul himself have seen the Christian faith as a form of nonsense, or 'foolishness', when viewed through the apparent logic of the mundane world (1 Cor. 1.18). As Josephine Gableman says, nonsense 'seems to be a true characterization of aspects of Christian belief' in that it highlights a rationale to the world that is differently oriented from the ordinary yet intimately tied to it (Gableman 2016: 206). This paradox is at the heart of what she defines as 'nonsense theology' or what has more traditionally been thought of as the divine logic of the apophatic. Divine logic, just like literary nonsense, 'plays with sense and this often takes the form of reversals and inversions of our fixed expectations of how the world works through doctrines like the Incarnation and the Trinity (167). In entering the looking-glass, Alice encounters a world defined by such reversals. And just as in Christian theology, these reversals are ultimately not intended to baffle but to bring understanding.

In defending nonsense theology, Gableman quotes one of the first studies of nonsense fiction, Edward Strachey's 'Nonsense as a Fine Art' (1888). Strachey writes that nonsense is 'not a mere putting forward of incongruities and absurdities but the bringing out a new and deeper harmony of life in and through its contradictions' (qtd. in Gableman 2016: 169). Such an understanding of nonsense fits MacDonald's perception of the mirror which Carroll imported into his work. In this conception, the mirror presents a world both similar to and different from the mundane, yet precisely because of that dual relationship, it is able to reorder one's notions of the world into closer accord with God's divine logic. Read in this light, *Through the Looking-Glass* is not a tale that lacks internal logic or rationality but one which engages with a different form of logic, a divine nonsense that dictates the apparently disordered elements of the novel. The eccentric characters, bizarre locations, and topsy-turvy movements all operate according to their own rationale and are ultimately able to lead Alice through her adventures to a moment of apotheosis. The reader, just like Alice, sees this logic 'through a [looking –]glass, darkly,' shaded by the formal chaos of nonsense but present in its ability to guide her towards the divine will.

Josephine Gabelman

9 Faith Through the Looking-Glass: A Postmodern Homily

The theologian is widely considered something of an interloper in the study of literary nonsense. As one theorist observes: 'God and religion' are 'absolutely forbidden grounds' (Tigges 1988: 80). The obvious exception is Carroll's (notably unpopular) *Sylvie and Bruno* stories (described as 'pious gruel' by Elizabeth Sewell [Sewell 1987: 199]) in which Carroll introduces 'some of the graver thoughts of human life' alongside the nonsense narratives (Carroll 1890: xvi). But even here, as his nephew observes, religion and nonsense are placed 'side by side [...] he used them alternately and did not blend them' (Collingwood 1899: 375). Carroll adhered scrupulously to the postulate that religion and nonsense should never mix. For example, he renamed the bad-tempered flower in *Looking-Glass*, 'Tiger-lily,' when it was pointed out that his initial choice – the passion-flower – had religious connotations (see Collingwood: 150–151). Carroll applied this principle to his life as much as his work: he was exceptionally uncomfortable with irreverent jesting,[1] and, not infrequently, wrote to friends pressing them to refrain from bringing 'sacred subjects into ridicule'. 'There is', he writes, 'no surer way of making one's beliefs *unreal* than by learning to associate them with ludicrous ideas' (Collingwood 362). Such an ardent desire to separate the realms of nonsense and faith contributed, in no small way, to the insistence that Lewis Carroll was not to be found at the address of the Reverend Charles L. Dodgson.[2]

---

1   Cf. Lewis Carroll, 'The Stage and the Spirit of Reverence'.
2   Though often repeated, this anecdote cannot be corroborated by Carroll's letters or diaries.

We might suggest that Carroll's religious faith had a vitric quality – resembling the strength and fragility of glass. G. K. Chesterton, the first commentator to offer a religious assessment of literary nonsense, describes the peculiar paradox of glass: 'to be breakable is not the same as to be perishable. Strike a glass, and it will not endure an instant; simply do not strike it, and it will endure a thousand years' (Chesterton 1909: 100). This appears to be true of Carroll's religious zeal. His hatred of religious controversy, together with his vehement prudishness could be viewed as a deficient faith that could not withstand antagonism. Yet his letters, prayer life, and reports of his sermons have an intensely earnest quality. Holiness, for Carroll, required faith to be kept out of the looking-glass, safe from association with the nonsensical and out of reach of the dialectician, for glass is oppositional by nature, forcing the viewer to confront his reverse perspective.

Nevertheless, with the onset of modernism, religion *has* been dragged through the looking-glass, and just as Carroll feared, we have learned to associate faith with ludicrous ideas, such that many reasonable modernists have found themselves applying Alice's dictum to faith: '[O]ne *can't* believe impossible things' (*TTLG*: 100). However, following the advent of postmodernity, the image of the possible has once again been reversed, and it is the stability of logocentricism that now appears on the ludicrous side of the glass.[3] From a postmodern perspective, Alice's totalizing reason and her insistence on non-parodic signification is the seductive fantasy in the mirror, while Humpty Dumpty's syntactic and semantic dislocation is the humdrum stutter of the real.

There is little need to argue the case that *Looking-Glass* can be read as anticipating central themes of postmodernity such as the problem of origins, the free play of language, the collapse of certainty, and the deferral of meaning. Indeed, as Brian McHale in *The Cambridge Introduction to Postmodernism* writes: 'So ubiquitous are allusions to *Alice* in postmodern novels in particular that the presence of *Alice* might almost be considered

---

3   Logocentricism refers to the belief that an external point of reference provides authority that guarantees meaning within a particular field such as science, philosophy or theology.

a *marker* of literary postmodernism' (McHale 2015: 53). Within philosophy, the seminal texts of Giles Deleuze (*Logique du sens*, 1969) and Jean-Jacques Lecercle (*Philosophy of Nonsense*, 1994), both offer anachronic readings of Carroll's texts by forefronting postmodern concerns. Deleuze's anti-systematic approach inverts the traditional binary of sense and nonsense, paradoxically defining the terms in apophatic relation to each other. Lecercle, informed by Deleuze and Lyotard, draws on Carroll's literature to explore 'the other side of language' – the darker side – in which the field of linguistics is shown to be riddled with paradox, corruption, anarchy, and untidiness (Lecercle 1994: 48). Accordingly, Lecercle believes 'the works of Lewis Carroll anticipate the main aspects of the current philosophical debate on language' (ibid., 2).

Given the compatibility between postmodern themes and literary nonsense, it is not surprising that Carroll's instruction to keep divinity out of the looking-glass has been assiduously followed by a century of nonsense criticism.[4] On the surface, it seems obvious that the theologian would find little to enrich their study of divine reality in looking-glass land which 'push[es] language and meaning toward dangerous limits of dissolution' (Shires 1988: 268). In fact, the aggressive severance between signifier and signified (insisted upon by Humpty Dumpty) seems fundamentally anti-theological in its demand for self-mastery and consequent elevation of the ego:

'When *I* use a word,' Humpty Dumpty said in rather a scornful tone, 'it means just what I choose it to mean – neither more nor less.'

---

4   John Caputo, whose postmodern theology is significantly informed by Deleuze, is disappointed that Deleuze fails to register the shared anarchic impulse present in Carroll's worlds and within the Kingdom of God. He writes: 'Deleuze should have suspected an event there. He should have wondered whether the zany reversals and astonishing paradoxes in the New Testament were any less than the offspring of an event that is the tale of a tardy rabbit darting down a hole' (Caputo 2007: 60). However, tracing the compatibility between Carroll's nonsense and theological concerns is not a major theme in Caputo's work. For a summary of the few theological reflections on literary nonsense see Gabelman (2016: 161–164).

For an extensive discussion of aspects of the history of linguistic implicated in Humpty Dumpty's question, see Chapter 15.

> 'The question is,' said Alice, 'whether you *can* make words mean so many different things.'
>
> 'The question is,' said Humpty Dumpty, 'which is to be master – that's all.' (*TTLG*: 124)

The instability of the sign is thus a central component uniting Carroll's world with a postmodern perspective, and as such, appears to preclude the religious. Nevertheless, this view fails to comprehend the Christian paradox of existing in the 'now and the not yet' – the spiritual awareness that 'the synthesis of the world has not been made' (Lubac 1987: 10). St Paul describes man's condition as 'groaning' after a synthesis, and one might therefore *expect* language to reflect a post-laspsarian severance from its origin (Romans 8: 22). Indeed, God appears to play something of a postmodern prank in the Tower of Babel narrative, saying: 'Come, let us go down and there confuse their language, so that they may not understand one another's speech' (Genesis 11: 7). Alice comes up against the consequence of linguistic mayhem in her exchange with the litigious Red Queen: 'I only said "if"!"' poor Alice pleaded in a piteous tone.

> The two Queens looked at each other, and the Red Queen remarked, with a little shudder, 'She *says* she only said 'if'–'
>
> 'But she said a great deal more than that!' [...]
>
> 'I'm sure I didn't mean–' Alice was beginning, but the Red Queen interrupted her impatiently.
>
> 'That's just what I complain of! You *should* have meant! What do you suppose is the use of child without any meaning?' (*TTLG*: 187–188)

Alice is forced to reckon with the impossible task of saying precisely what she intended. In Derrida's words, she has said, 'more, less, or something other than what [s]he would wish to say' – a problem, it seems, with divine design (Derrida 2016: 171).

Carroll's friend, theologian, and author of his own literary nonsense, George MacDonald, previews this aspect of Derrida's thought a century earlier in his homiletic series: *Unspoken Sermons*. 'That the thing signified transcends the sign, outreaches the figure, is no discovery; the thing figured always belongs to a higher stratum' (MacDonald 1889: 50–51).

Again, we face the suggestion that perhaps the 'disturbing [...] anarchy' of Carroll's world that we assume offends religion causes no such injury (Shires 1988: 268). Rather, the hollowed-out sign, foregrounded in literary nonsense, is not simply 'pure absence, pure gap' (ibid., 274). Rather, it is the 'gap God opens' (Caputo 2013: x) to enable mankind to register the deficiency of self-striving. Interpreted in this light, *Hélène Cixous'* post-structural rendering of fantasy as a 'rehearsal for death' could also be regarded as an overture to resurrection (Shires 1988: 274).

The slippage in meaning that secular postmodernists view as breaking apart logocentrism has already been insisted upon for centuries in the Judaeo-Christian tradition – most obviously by apophatic writers.[5] The mystical theologian Pseudo-Dionysius observes: '[T]he more it climbs [to the transcendent], the more language falters' (Pseudo-Dionysius 1987: 139). Derrida's philosophy of deconstruction, in certain ways, is a type of inverse mystical theology, or mysticism in the looking-glass; he drives language towards negativity, only to discover that negation, 'pushed to the limit [...] resembles an apophatic theology' (Coward and Foshay 1992: 4). Carroll's intention, therefore, to keep faith out of the looking-glass, is not only misplaced zeal, but futile cautiousness for, it is only 'in a mirror dimly' that God allows himself to be glimpsed, and then, only 'in part' – in a fractured sign, which always unsays itself and defers ultimate meaning (1 Corinthians 1: 12). Admittedly, for Derrida, the chain of signification is one of endless proliferation, whereas religious mysticism preserves an expectation of eschatological synthesis. Nonetheless, it is at least not inconceivable to begin to see a path for the theologian on the other side of the glass.

It is not only semiotic insecurity that makes *Looking-Glass* a fertile text for postmodern reflection, the question of dreaming also unsettles the status of the real. Again, if taken seriously, this premise appears as something of an insult to the ontological security found in the traditional belief in God as creator. But, as we will see, the mindset of faith involves a more paradoxical type of negative positing in its conception of truth.

---

5   Apophatic theology is the attempt to express something true and meaningful about the divine nature by recourse to what it is not. Such thinkers observe that positive statements fail to express the essential ineffability of God.

Alice, ever the representative of enlightenment absolutism, is frightened by the contention that she is 'only a sort of thing in his [the Red King's] dream' and eager to deny the logical conclusion that if he were to wake '[she'd] go out – bang! – Just like a candle!' (*TTLG*: 81). Carroll refuses Alice (and the reader) closure to the Cartesian problem of looking-glass land. In contrast to the first *Alice* book, in which she concludes, without diffidence: 'Oh, I've had such a curious dream!' (*TTLG*: 189), *Looking-Glass* defers such closure by raising questions without answers. The final chapter is titled: 'Which dreamed it?'; the story ends with the question, 'Which do *you* think it was?' and the last line of the concluding poem asks, 'Life, what is it but a dream?' This embedded resistance to finality, offering no promise of resolution, has led critics to emphasize the melancholic nostalgia of *Looking-Glass*, interpreting the concluding poem as a type of depressed postmodernism, which affords the last word to the 'shadow of a sigh' (*TTLG*: front matter).

However, the promotion of 'dream' as a synonym for life is not exclusive to postmodern thought but also has theological connotations. MacDonald titles the final chapter of *Lilith*, 'The "Endless Ending"' and never clarifies whether the central character, Mr Vane, is awake or asleep, alive or dead. For MacDonald, the deferral of ending allows the reader to experience a type of 'noble unrest [...] a ceaseless questioning', which, MacDonald regards as fertile territory for spiritual growth (MacDonald 1893: 1). In *Lilith* and elsewhere, MacDonald seems to advertise the aporia surrounding dream and reality, suggesting: 'You cannot perfectly distinguish between the true and the false while you are not quite yet dead' (MacDonald 1895: 324). MacDonald, unlike Alice, seems relaxed about ontological instability referencing Novalis: 'Our life is no dream, but it should and will perhaps become one' (MacDonald 1895: 351).

It is not only MacDonald who discerned profound meaning in Novalis' riddles, Michel Foucault uses Novalis to assist his postmodern elevation of the dream as 'the very centre of becoming and objectivity' (Foucault 1986: 52). In his essay, 'Dream, Imagination and Existence', Foucault obfuscates the borderline between true and false, using the category of dream to object to the traditional binary: 'The dream unveils, in its very principle, that ambiguity of the world which at one and the same time designates the existence projected into it and outlines itself objectively in experience' (Foucault 1986: 51). Carroll's whimsical parting question: 'Life, what is it but a dream?' is taken up earnestly by MacDonald, Novalis, and Foucault. Foucault discerns in the depth of man's dream his encounter with death and sees 'death as the destiny of freedom' and as 'the fulfilment of existence' (Foucault 1986: 54–55). Christian teleology, as conceived by MacDonald and Novalis, has a parallel starting point; the culmination of life is death; death is more real than life. Life therefore has the quality of a dream when conceived eschatologically. MacDonald's disciple C. S. Lewis ends his popular Narnia series with a train accident that kills the children and their parents. Aslan explains their death by telling them: 'The dream is ended: this is the morning' (Lewis 1966: 175).

Of course, this is not Foucault's intended meaning in his description of death as 'the fulfilment of existence', neither is it Carroll's hope that the theologian would follow his 'dream-child' through the looking-glass. But as Derrida has reminded us, our words always mean something more, less, or other than what we intend. The real question that Carroll would wish us to ask is whether the new meaning is edifying. Despite insisting that his stories 'didn't mean anything but nonsense', in proleptic accord with Derrida, he admits that 'words mean more than we mean to express when we use them; so a whole book ought to mean a great deal more than the writer means. So, whatever good meanings are in the book, I'm very glad to accept' (Collingwood 1899: 173). Perhaps, following the demise of religious authority in the 150 years since publication, Carroll might now be prepared to offer *Looking-Glass* as a postmodern homily. I have suggested that Carroll's cautious regard over the association of religion and nonsense leaves an impression of a fragile, vitric faith – imperishable but vulnerable. Yet the glass in the story possesses peculiar properties that renders Chesterton's characterization inapposite. Carroll's glass is 'soft like gauze', it 'melts' into a 'bright silver mist' that can be penetrated without shattering (*TTLG*: 10–11).

Perhaps this yielding, pliant glass could offer a helpful metaphor for religious faith in our contemporary age. Perhaps at the sesquicentenary of the last *Alice* novel, the secular critics of literary nonsense might relax their puritanical stance that there is not a hint of 'religion [...] even of the vaguest kind' present in the text (Lecercle 2009: 369). We have seen how theology within the bible, medieval mysticism, Victorian non-conformism, and post-secularism *expects* language to falter, absolutes to remain elusive, and death to eclipse life. Maybe God is his own iconoclast who allows Derrida, Foucault, and Deleuze to work as his mutineers. *Looking-Glass* is thus of consummate value to the theologian – not because it tells us who God is but because it reveals mankind's ordained deficiencies. Namely, that, like Alice, we are neither omniscient, inviolable nor ascendant.

Celia Brown

10 The Influence of Francis Bacon and John Dee on Carroll's *Looking-Glass and What Alice Found There*

Two figures from Elizabethan England cast long shadows into the future to play roles in the popular imagination of the Victorian era, when Carroll wrote *Through the Looking-Glass*. One was the philosopher Francis Bacon (1561–1626), Queen Elizabeth's legal adviser, who was still admired in the nineteenth century for his contributions to scientific and logical thought. The other was the mathematician John Dee (1527–1608/1609), the Renaissance queen's astrologer, who remained an inspiration at a time when the Victorians were captivated by all things magical and eerie. An interest in Bacon and Dee is in keeping with Carroll's subject of mathematics and his particular fascination with logic and codes. His own book collection provides evidence of his interest in Bacon, whose complete works in ten volumes in the 1803 edition were in his library. Given that Carroll's own mathematical treatises were largely based on Euclid, it is plausible that he would be familiar with John Dee as a predecessor of historical importance. Dee wrote the preface to the English Euclid published in 1570 (Yates 1969: 347). Another aspect of Carroll's wide-ranging interests, his curiosity about magical phenomena, is confirmed by his collection of esoteric books, including a first edition of *A System of Magic* by Daniel Defoe, with John Dee as its frontispiece (Defoe 1727),[1] and *Narratives of Sorcery and*

---

1   This history of the Black Art by Daniel Defoe (c. 1660–1731) examines how to distinguish between holy miracles witnessing to God's interventions on Earth and the workings of the Devil.

Magic by Thomas Wright, including some tales about the collaboration between John Dee and Edward Kelly (Wright 1851). An interest in astrology is underlined by Carroll's ownership of a compendium from the seventeenth century entitled *Christian Astrology* written by William Lilly (Lilly 1878 [1647]) (see also Brown 2015: Ch. 4, 5).[2] Thus, the link between Bacon, Dee, and Carroll arises historically, through Carroll's contemporary literary connections, and is also, especially in the case of Dee and Carroll, often made in popular culture to *Looking-Glass*, such as in Neil Gaiman's *Sandman* series.[3] This chapter will therefore investigate their historical, and philosophical connections and examine clues pointing to Bacon and Dee in Carroll's text.

Carroll's Mirror

'The subtlety of nature', according to Francis Bacon's aphorism X, 'is far beyond that of sense or of the understanding' (Bacon 1620: Book I. X), a lesson that Alice learned to appreciate in Carroll's wonder- and mirror-lands. Bacon went on to argue that 'all the perceptions both of the senses and the mind bear reference to man and not to the universe, and the human mind resembles those uneven mirrors which impart their own properties to different objects, from which rays are emitted and distort and disfigure them' (Bacon 1620: Book I. XLI). Could Bacon have influenced Carroll's idea of an 'uneven mirror', a doorway to a distorted reflection of the external world? The world turned around is both familiar and strange. The curious assaults on Alice's perceptions in *Through the Looking-Glass* confirm Lewis Carroll's interest in the workings of the human mind and the fickle nature of reality. Notably, instead of reflecting a person back as a reverse image like a conventional mirror, Carroll's

2   Lilly was a friend of Elias Ashmole, founder of the Ashmolean Museum in Oxford.
3   The use of mirrors in *Looking-Glass* and a variety of Graphic novels will be treated in Chapter 30.

looking-glass dissolves into a kind of mist on being approached, allowing a human being, the literary figure of Alice, to materialize in a different realm. This magical property is similar to that of an Aztec 'smoking mirror', such as that used by John Dee to scry into the future with the help of supernatural beings, who purportedly revealed themselves on his 'shew-stone'.

Like Francis Bacon, John Dee also believed in the fundamental importance of 'ubiquitous rays'. Unlike Bacon, who dissociated himself from accusations of sorcery (Yates 2008: 163), Dee was at pains to manipulate rays to make hidden phenomena visible. According to Deborah Harkness 'Dee began to lay the universal, physical foundations for his conversations with angels in the *Propaedeumata aphoristica* through a discussion of the "rays" that all things, both immanent and occult, dispersed throughout the universe. Later, Dee used his crystal "showstone" to capture and magnify the rays on which angels were said to travel into the natural world' (Harkness 1999: 72).

Carroll's looking-glass functions at first as a normal mirror reflecting the 'real' world back to Alice, but then as a means of access to a place where the unsuspecting visitor can do things that were impossible in the world they have just left behind. Alice is transformed by her entry into the room seen in the mirror: she floats downstairs like a ghostly apparition to explore the strange countryside outside. Since Carroll's misty mirror enables Alice to pass through, it seems likely that all the residents she meets *Through the Looking-Glass* could represent mirror materializations of recognizable figures from her real world, past and present. It is therefore worth speculating about the kind of mirror Carroll had in mind, in the hope of being able to recognize some of these figments of his imagination.

Figure 11. Alice through Dee's Mirror, Celia Brown.

John Dee's Mirror

The great magician John Dee lived in an era when magical mirrors were popular in Europe. John Dee's looking-glass, kept nowadays in the British Museum, is a black obsidian 'shew-stone' (Figures 11–12). Chemical analysis has recently established that the circular-shaped obsidian came from Mexico (Campbell et al. 2021). The artefact was brought to Europe soon after the Spanish conquest by the invaders. Dee would have acquired the mirror while travelling around Europe, possibly when he lived in Bohemia in the 1580s. It was associated with the deity Tezcatlipoca, whose name means Smoking Mirror in the Nahuatl language of the Aztecs. As the god of rulers, warriors, and sorcerers, he is often shown wearing a circular obsidian mirror (ibid.). Mexican priests used smoking mirrors of various sizes and shapes for conjuring up apparitions and for divination.

The John Dee mirror now in the British Museum was once owned by the historian and antiquarian Horace Walpole (1717–1797). Walpole helpfully noted its usage on its protective case, 'The Black Stone into which Dr Dee used to call his Spirits'. On the label, Walpole quotes Samuel Butler (1612–1680), who described the stone as the 'Devil's Looking-Glass' used by Edward Kelly, the conjuror who enabled Dee to decipher what the angels supposedly said:

> 'Kelly did all his feats upon
> the Devil's Looking-Glass, a stone:
> Where *playing with him at bo-peep*,
> He solv'd all Problems ne'er so deep.'
>
> (Butler 1684 v. 631–634)

These lines from Samuel Butler's satirical poem *Hudibras* are also quoted in a compilation of *Popular Rhymes* owned by Carroll with the comment 'The reader will recollect what Butler says of Sir Edward Kelly, the celebrated conjuror' (Halliwell 1849: 109). This entry confirms that Dee, Kelly, and the shew-stone were part of common knowledge in Carroll's era. Halliwell describes an ancient form of Bo-peep as a child's game 'in which the nurse conceals the head of the infant for an instant, and then removes the covering quickly' (ibid.). Playing at Bo-peep thus refers to the temporary revelation of secrets, for Butler in an esoteric tradition, but for Halliwell relegated to the category 'Game-Rhymes'.

There is a specific clue in *Through the Looking-Glass* that suggests the presence of John Dee in the form of one of the twins Alice meets in Chapter IV. According to Carroll's text, TweedleDEE has DEE embroidered on his collar, so could embody John Dee. TweedleDUM would then be Dee's untrustworthy collaborator Kelly. Thomas Wright wrote in 1851 that 'Kelly soon proved himself a very skilful skryer, and he seems to have used the greatest cunning in practising upon Dee's credulity, and insinuating himself into his confidence' (Wright 1851: 231). In the Tweedles chapter, there are several hints at implausible paranormal phenomena: branches of a tree that make music without the help of human hand, for example. Alice is threatened with going 'out – bang! – just like a candle!', which in a Victorian séance would be treated as evidence of interfering spirits.

Religion and Spirituality

Carroll's inquisitive approach to the feats that challenged the Victorians' credulity is confirmed by his being an early member of the Society for Psychical Research (SPR). An interest in the occult is more difficult to establish with certainty. Janet Oppenheim's assessment of *The Other World* of the Victorians might well apply to Carroll: 'Both spiritualists and psychical researchers insisted that their inquiries were part of the mainstream of modern thought, not remnants of magical mumbo jumbo from bygone ages' but she asserts that in practice, many had links to the occult (Oppenheim 1985: 159–160).

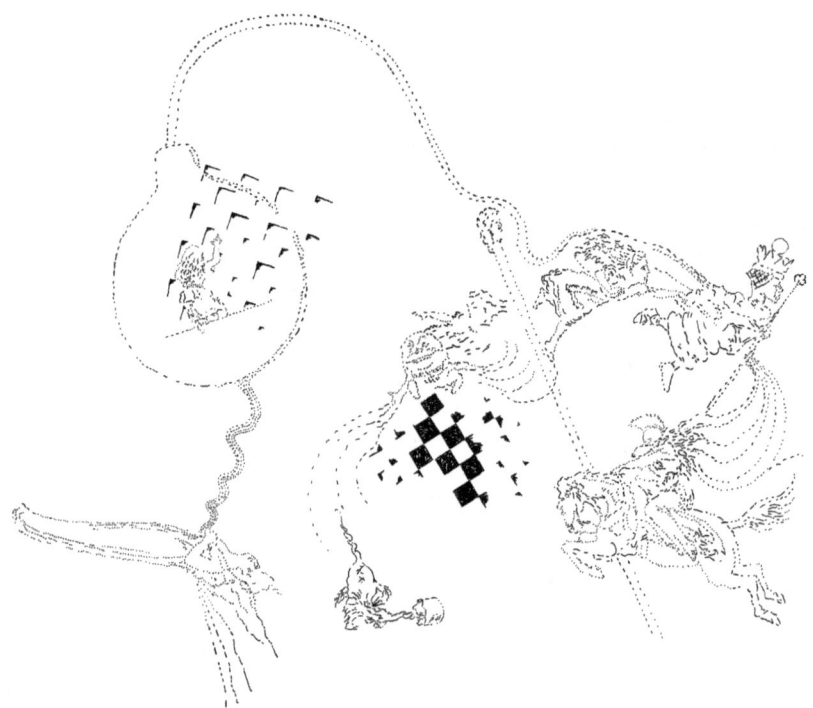

Figure 12. *Chessboard Challenges*, Celia Brown.

Fingerposts

Carroll's friend George MacDonald, who encouraged the budding author to publish the original version of *Alice's Adventures in Wonderland*, referred to Francis Bacon in 1867 in support of his argument that the imagination[4] plays a positive role in generating hypotheses, 'Lord Bacon tells us that a prudent question is the half of knowledge. Whence comes this prudent question? we repeat. And we answer, From the imagination' (MacDonald 1867). Carroll hinted that he was proud of his ability as a mathematician to write books based on imagination in a positive sense (Cohan and Green 1979: 65).[5] From the text of *Through the Looking-Glass* he appears to be especially interested in the fallacies – Bacon's 'idols' – produced by the crooked mirror of the human mind.

Like the ship on the frontispiece of the *Novum Organum*, Bacon was entering uncharted waters, whereas Carroll was at heart a traditional mathematician sending Alice from square to square in a straightforward sequence, where she tries to make sense of her encounters. Prior to meeting Tweedledum and Tweedledee, Alice is puzzled by a curious road sign that offers nonsensical directions, ' "And now, which of these finger-posts ought I to follow, I wonder?" It was not a very difficult question to answer, as there was only one road through the wood, and the two fingerposts both pointed along it. "I'll settle it," Alice said to herself, "when the road divides and they point different ways" ' (*TTLG*: 64). The term 'fingerposts' parodies the term that introduced Bacon's new experimental methodology to free the mind from 'idols' as set out in his *Novum Organum* (Bacon 1620): two or more propositions should be tested against each other on the basis of experience from the senses rather than unfounded argument. Bacon's fingerpost is an example of a 'prerogative instance' offering highly pertinent evidence concerning abstract natures: 'Among Prerogative Instances I will put in the fourteenth place Instances of the Fingerpost, borrowing the

---

4   My thanks go to Franziska Kohlt for this connection.
5   *Alice in Wonderland* 'furnishes evidence that Mathematics are not inconsistent with writing works of imagination' (Letter to Tom Taylor, 25 January 1866).

term from the fingerposts which are set up where roads part, to indicate the several directions' (Bacon 1620: xxxvi).

There is one reality – the road through the wood – that can only be probed if it is divided into alternative pathways for comparison. The testing of opposites continues as a philosophical theme throughout the following encounter with Tweedledum and Tweedledee. The nonsense dialogue of the Tweedle twins seems to echo Bacon's deliberately impenetrable style of formulation, designed to avoid the pitfalls of vernacular speech. ' "I know what you're thinking about," said Tweedledum; "but it isn't so, nohow." "Contrariwise," continued Tweedledee, "if it was so, it might be; and if it were so, it would be but as it isn't, it ain't. That's logic" ' (*TTLG*: 68). An eliminative method echoing Francis Bacon's inductive method: '[...] instances of the fingerpost show the union of one of the natures with the nature in question to be sure and indissoluble, of the other to be varied and separable; and thus the question is decided, and the former nature is admitted as the cause, while the latter is dismissed and rejected' (Bacon 1620: VI).

In Carroll's Looking-Glass world, there are constant battles between opposing hypotheses – as befits two teams on a chessboard, where one aims to eliminate the other. The alternating black and white (or, in this Victorian case, red and white) squares of the chessboard offer a metaphor for the oppositions indicated by Francis Bacon's fingerposts.[6] The opening scene of *Through the Looking-Glass,* in which Alice plays with her kittens before passing through the mirror, introduces her more analytical journey across the chessboard, and implies that Bacon's analytical method may have been one inspiration for the oppositional theme in the story as a whole. The first chapter opens with a choice between black and white: 'One thing was certain, that the white kitten had nothing to do with it – it was the black kitten's fault entirely.' Alice is trying to wind up a ball of wool – the tangled mesh of nature – which she will gradually learn to unravel as she travels from square to square, following in the footsteps of Francis Bacon, who was seeking common underlying general principles that would enable a process of working backwards from the visible symptoms to a set of probable

6   More on opposites in Carroll's Logic in Chapter 14.

causes, from the disorderly wool back to Alice's black kitten as one of a pair of contrariwise kittens.

Cryptography and Carroll's Codes

Is it admissible to try to unravel Carroll's allusions woven into the text? On reaching the eighth square of the chessboard, Alice is encouraged by the chess queens to interpret the unexpected and counter-intuitive. Significantly, a dish cover that holds 'like glue' in the White Queen's poem may point to the materialization through Carroll's 'smoking mirror' of the early alchemist Maria Prophetessa, who purportedly lived between the first and third centuries in Alexandria. She counts as the inventor of an airtight container known as a *kerotakis*, which is linked to the idea of a hermetic seal and thus to the hidden and occult. The challenge in the poem to 'un-dish-cover the fish' could be referring to the riddle of Alice's enigmatic journey. The Red Queen's advice to 'Take a minute to think about it, and then guess' would be good advice to the reader of the whole book.

The discovery of Francis Bacon and John Dee in Mirrorland is an aid to appreciating the sophistication of Carroll's code creativity. We know that Carroll loved ciphers in general, as he even compiled his own *Memoria Technica*. His 'method assigns two consonants to each number from 0 to 9, fills in vowels to make words, and sets the words in rhymed couplets that help the user to remember not just dates but almost any other body of facts' (Cohen 1996: 393–394). In the book of the History of England, mentioned by Humpty Dumpty, encrypted messages were valuable in espionage. Perhaps it is no coincidence that Humpty Dumpty becomes agitated at the thought of the King sending 'all his horses and all his men' and accuses Alice: 'You've been listening at doors – and behind trees – and down chimneys – or you couldn't have known it!' (*TTLG*: 117). Alice denies her role as an eavesdropper, but she is constantly encouraged to be one.

Codes were also sought out and deciphered in order to predict events. Dee made astrological predictions to help the Queen in decision-making by observation and interpretation of the celestial code of the planets and stars. Both Bacon and Dee held views on how to read the Book of Nature. Bacon emphasized that Nature's code was not encapsulated in human language, laying the foundation for Carroll's appreciation of the disjunction between names and things and the semiotic problem that Alice encountered in the wood where she lost her name: the lack of fit between a word, in common usage, and the thing it referred to. Bacon's sceptical rationalism, which casts doubt on words that embroil men in discussing the meaningless, presages Humpty Dumpty's presumptuous claim to be able to manage words. Bacon recognized that Nature had its own language and investigated abstract natures that are 'as the alphabet or simple letters, whereof the variety of things consisteth' (Bacon 1734: Ch. 13). When Queen Alice assures the other chess queens that she knows her ABC, she may unknowingly be making a much bigger claim: to have understood Nature's hidden code, such as Bacon's *Abecedarium Naturae* (1622). John Dee had a more mathematical approach. He expounded in his preface to Euclid on the numerical nature of God's creative process: He assigns a number to everything in the world. According to Dee, progressive deterioration of the earth since the fall of Adam could be conceived as a slowing down of God's 'Continuall Numbrying'. Should God decide to delete a number, wrote Dee in his preface to Euclid, this would mean 'that particular thing shall be Discreated' (quoted in Harkness 1999: 142). Interestingly, in the Tweedledum and Tweedledee chapter, Alice risks being 'discreated' if the Red King awakens from his dream. Was this elusive chess piece, who is luckily still asleep in Figure 13, engrossed in regal mathematics?

There is an echo here[7] of the Gryphon and the Mock Turtle's musing in *Wonderland* on the Tortoise who 'taught us', beginning with 'ten hours of lessons the first day', but reducing by an hour each subsequent day. The lessons lessen until no hours are left, which Alice interprets happily as a holiday. The Gryphon's unwillingness to explain what happens on the twelfth day thus takes on an ominous note, perhaps implying a further threat of being discreated.

7   I am grateful to Franziska Kohlt for this point.

Figure 13. *Tweedledee's Vision*, Celia Brown.

With time running backwards in the land through the Looking-Glass, the value of past inventions and beliefs is heightened, in keeping with a strand of thinking in the Victorian era which envisaged the whole world deteriorating, challenging the more optimistic expectations of constant progress. Max Müller, a colleague and friend of Carroll at Christ Church, was a proponent of the sad descent of Man from a nobler race, in contrast to the mainstream notion of ascent from savagery (see Turner 1981: 109).[8]

---

8   See also Chapters 7 and 15 for more on Carroll and Müller.

In a similar vein, a couple of centuries earlier, Francis Bacon's plan for the instauration of science aspired to a return to the pristine state of Man – Adam – before the Fall (Yates 2008: 158).

Conclusion

In view of his intricate play with ambiguous terms to puzzle and delight the readers of the Alice books Carroll deserves to be regarded as an inventor of a special kind of code. The example of Bacon's fingerposts shows how he deftly separated an ambivalent interpretation into a visual image to be read at a simple level – a signpost by the roadside – and a more sophisticated level, referring here to Bacon's philosophy. This layering of meanings applies to both *Alice* books. The different levels at which they can be interpreted depend on Carroll's ability – like Humpty Dumpty – to manage words and make them work for him. The best guesses about Carroll's trains of thought in his text are those which identify the double-meaning of a word like 'fingerposts' and find further links in the text to the same theme, in this case to Bacon's philosophy and to TweedleDEE. It is then worth asking whether these thoughts fit with what is known about Carroll's interests.

The magical and eerie aspects of the story are strengthened by this reading, but without losing sight of Carroll's scientific and mathematical inquiries. Although it is possible that the Alice books are coded to be deciphered systematically by an esoteric audience, the analysis offered in this chapter stops far short of such a claim. Carroll would rather seem to be playing irreverently with cryptic motifs to amuse the reader and himself.

Thinking of the whole *Looking-Glass* story as an adventure inspired by John Dee's looking-glass and Francis Bacon's unravelling of Nature locates the book firmly in the past, as well as the present and future. Like the head of Janus, which was the Dodgson family crest, Carroll looks in opposite directions. If the realm on the other side of the mirror is understood as a distorted reflection of this world made up of a composite of historical and contemporary allusions, it makes sense to identify figures hitherto of unsuspected relevance like Dee and Bacon. This approach invites a reconsideration of the book as a roman-à-clef. Looking for historical references, rather than being a mere undecisive game, can offer insights into the roles played by the figures on the chessboard and the philosophical conundrums of concern to Carroll with which they are associated.

Part IV

Psychology

Hayley Flynn

11 Mirrors of the Mind

When Alice enters Looking-Glass Land by passing through the physical boundary of the mirror, she enters a fantastically distorted reflection of her own world. While the same can be said of Alice's original adventure in Wonderland, this time she passes through the vertical boundary of the mirror, rather than the horizontal boundary of the world beneath her feet. Carroll addresses such mirror distortions in many of his publications, though it is only in *Through the Looking-Glass* that the fantastically distorted mirror image of the world finds such extensive literal expression. The fantastical worlds in both *Alice* books are dream worlds, so the mirror by which they are reflected and inflected is the mind. Nineteenth-century research into the mind and brain was a shifting, uncertain, and contentious subject – and dreaming was central to it. Some of the ongoing research and the uncertainty therein was a source of fear for both professionals and the public – as they were for the author of the Looking-Glass world, which, as this chapter will show, negotiates some of these concerns.

Concerns elicited by Victorian dream research revolved principally around questions about the origins of dream, what kind of forces influenced the functions of the mind, and whether it could be externally manipulated – the latter in particular remaining a source of debate in publications fictional and factual. Likewise, the question of just how similar a 'rational' mind was to an 'insane' one was prominent in these debates, and of particular interest to Carroll. Carroll's interest in dream and the importance of dream in the Alice books has been frequently commented upon, and his interest in insanity, a concept seen as related to dreams in this period, has also been noted (see Kohlt 2016, 2022). The pervasive fear which connects those two subjects was portrayed extensively in periodical literature of the time and is particularly important to *Through the Looking-Glass*.

Carroll expressed his concerns with the fine boundary between dream and insanity in his diary:

> Query: when we are dreaming and, as often happens, have a dim consciousness of the fact and try to wake, do we not say and do things which in waking life would be insane? May we not then sometimes define insanity as an inability to distinguish which is the waking and which is the sleeping life? We often dream without the least suspicion of unreality: 'Sleep hath its own world', and it is often as lifelike as the other.

Carroll's expression of this query also identifies one of the most unsettling elements of the question: how reliable is our own perception?

Carroll owned numerous books on psychology, psychiatry, and dreaming, which give further insight into what thoughts, theories, and understandings shaped the dream-based Looking-Glass world. G. H. Lewes' *Problems of Life and Mind* is one such example. Notably, the way Lewes discusses the inability to distinguish between the real and unreal in this book is the thought experiment of a 'fruit lying on the surface of the table and its reflected image on the surface of a mirror' (Lewes 1875: 40), which bears a remarkable conceptual similarity to the concept of *Through the Looking-Glass*. This highlights the common metaphorical and rhetorical conflation of mirror and mind in Victorian psychological discourse and demonstrates that this discussion was visible in a wide range of text types.

The way that new theories on the mind were disseminated to the public is an important consideration when attempting to understand how Carroll understood dreams. Academic texts, written by professionals with the intention of advancing their field, formed part of Carroll's knowledge but were not the only place he encountered dream theories or concerns about their connection to insanity. One of the most pervasive professional publications which addressed the origin of dreams, *Inquiries Concerning the Intellectual Powers and the Investigation of Truth* by physician John Abercrombie, referred to dream and insanity as 'mental phenomena [which] have a remarkable affinity to each other' (263). Originally published in 1830, the book went through many editions which were published throughout and beyond the 1860s (being in its nineteenth edition by 1871), evidencing its popularity. The theories on dream it contains were also quoted, or simply copied, frequently. The popularity of Abercrombie's work on this subject is partly due to the apparently paradoxical fact that while the subject drew wide fascination, there were not many book-length works exploring dreams, but adding to this apparent paradox, Abercrombie's theories were not even entirely new. Many can be found in David Hartley's much earlier *Observations on Man* (1749); highlighting the long-standing interest in this subject, preceding the Victorians. While there is no evidence that Carroll read Abercrombie's book, therefore, there is a very high chance that he would have come across Abercrombie's (and thus Hartley's) theories elsewhere.

Periodicals were very frequently the platform for these repetitions of scientific fact, often portrayed by their authors in a way that would appeal more to the general public (see Dawson 2010). They are, therefore, key to understanding how Victorians engaged with dream theory. The popular interest in dream is apparent from the vast number of periodical publications on the subject, particularly when considering the range of periodicals available during Carroll's time which were engaging with the subject. As Hendrika Vande Kemp discovered, while tracing publication trends between 1860 and 1910, 'dream psychology in periodical literature tended to develop independently of similar developments in books' (Kemp 1981: 91). And there were a number of significant developments relating to the function of the mind and brain in the mid-nineteenth century. For example, the 1860s saw a movement away from Romantic philosophical theories of the unconscious mind and dream, towards physiological explanations, though those Romantic influences remained very visible.

These publications also illustrate that psychology was still not an established subject, in the modern understanding of the concept, and even the language used to talk about the function of the unconscious mind and dream was uncertain. As Roger Smith (2004) has noted, 'Dream', when Carroll was writing both *Alice* books, was often used alongside terms such as 'trance', 'reverie', 'daydream', and 'mesmeric sleep'; sometimes interchangeably within the same publication (Idem). The origin of dreaming was also variously claimed to be supernatural, physiological, or divine, even within the same publications. It is unsurprising, when considering the nature of periodical publication, that it was in the dynamic, responsive, and multi-disciplinary weekly or monthly that the various associated elements of dream found the ideal space to interact and influence one another.[1] The interaction of those elements would become hugely important to the development of psychology, as can be seen in Freud's later comment that 'one day I discovered to my great astonishment that the view of dreams which came nearest to the truth was not the medical but the popular one, half involved though it still was in superstition' (Freud 1901: 634–635).

The fluidity of the discipline of psychology and its language, as well as the broad range of associations dream had, therefore made the subject of dreaming perfect for general literary periodicals, rather than simply 'scientific' periodicals. In general literary periodicals, ideas about dream could be found in fiction as well as in factual articles aimed at non-professional audiences, blurring these boundaries. It is significant that within this hybrid form, theories about mind and dream were debated and formulated. Especially for the audiences who may not otherwise have had the opportunity to engage with theories on the mind and brain, the potential for exploration of the origin and meaning of dreams expanded even further.

Charlie Lovett, in this context, highlights the importance of Carroll's relationship with periodicals, both because his writing career 'began and ended with contributions to periodicals', and because he was 'clearly a reader of papers and journals himself' (Lovett 1999: 1; 10). Periodicals, which were so important to developing theories on dream and, simultaneously, of importance to Carroll, who returned to the subject of dream throughout his career, contributed to shaping his ideas about dream and the way he portrayed them in the *Alice* books. Considering two of the periodicals we know Carroll owned, shows that these reveal a wealth of dream discussion. In just one of the volumes (ser. 2, vol. 2) of *Notes and Queries* that Carroll owned, we find the apparently true story of a prophetic dream foretelling the dreamer's own death; a short story in which it is implied that 'oft a

---

[1]   It should be noted that dream was far from the only subject to combine the concerns of science with the supernatural. This was, in fact, very common during the nineteenth century. Examples can be found in *The Victorian Supernatural* (ed. Nicola Bown, Burdett and Thurschwell 2004).

warning voice speaks to us in dreams'; and a request for recommendations of 'dream books', or dream interpretation guides, alongside a number of other dream references.[2] Volume 12 of *La Belle Assemblée*, which Carroll also owned, contains a short story in which dream is indistinguishable from reality and an extract from 'The Winter's Wreath' which bears the motto 'Dreams Come from God' (190). In the latter, a series of prophetic dreams, which are compared to 'the grotesque changes of a phantasmagoria', precede the dreamer being saved by those dreams as they cause him to rush out of a building moments before it collapses (192).

These extracts of just two periodicals Carroll owned, demonstrate the range of dream discussions in which Carroll was immersed. And, as Lovett suggests, Carroll was undoubtedly engaging with a much broader range of periodicals, including those he was published in. For example, while he did not have copies in his possession at his time of death, diaries show that Carroll clearly interacted with *All the Year Round*, in which its editor Charles Dickens, whom Carroll much admired, himself published his musings on dreams (See *The Uncommercial Traveller* 1860: 348–352). As well as submitting his own work to that periodical ('Faces in the Fire', February 1860: 369–370), Carroll mentions further dream stories in his letters. He asks his sister, Mary, for instance: '[D]o you remember that curious story of a ghost-lady (in *Household Words* or *All the Year Round*), who sat to an artist for her picture? It was called "Mr H – 's Story" ' (1979: 104). This story was, in fact, published twice in *All the Year Round*. Originally a second-hand anecdote forming part of 'Four Stories' in September 1861, a more detailed version featured the following month after Mr Heaphy himself contacted the editor, Charles Dickens.[3] *Household Words*, which had also been conducted by Dickens, had been published for the last time in May 1859 and was immediately followed by the first publication of *All the Year Round*. Considering the many similarities between the two, it is unsurprising that Carroll could not remember which the story featured in,

2   Sir Thomas Prendergast (89), 'Coming Events Cast Their Shadows Before' (283), 'Proclamations' (238), 'St. Gervais' (509).

3   Carroll slightly misremembers the title of the story, which actually appears at 'Mr H's Own Narrative'.

though it provides intriguing evidence that he was familiar enough with both to make the potential mistake.

Readers of 'Mr H's Own Narrative' would have passed an instalment of Bulwer Lytton's serialized novel *A Strange Story*, which began that issue of *All the Year Round*. Dream is central to that story, where various existing theories on its origin and meaning are discussed, though it is ultimately shown to be a tool of supernatural control. Using theories popular in Spiritualist and Mesmeric discourses, the tale implies that one mind might be controlled by another during a dream state. This was another of the fears surrounding the uncertain nature of dreaming which was raised frequently. The narrator of *A Strange Story* is particularly concerned about the potential influence of the villain over the mind of a woman who is one of those with a 'mind so predisposed' that their world 'melts away into Dreamland' (1862: 294).[4] It is easy to see this same concept in Alice's discovery that the glass separating her from the dream world in *Through the Looking-Glass* 'was beginning to melt away' (143).

The most important similarity between these two representations is the fact that no solid, discernible boundary exists between the real and dream worlds. In *A Strange Story* this becomes a frightening concept for various reasons; partly because those 'predisposed' to frequent Dreamland travel (a trait which they inherently possess) are at risk of manipulation, but also partly because the narrator is often unable to recognize when he is/was dreaming and when he is awake. When considering this in the context of contemporary fears about the similarity of dream to insanity, it is easy to see why the permeability of that boundary seemed so unsettling. Carroll explores this unsettling fear frequently by causing his reader to question their own perception of the dream-reality boundary in his fiction.

The lack of distinct boundary between the dream and real world is clearly present in both *Alice* books, as previously mentioned. It could be argued that the lack of boundary is even more obvious in Alice's original adventure, where she moves so seamlessly into her dream world that

---

4   This particular fear is very often associated with women, particularly in regard to mesmerism. See Alison Winter, *Mesmerized: Powers of Mind in Victorian Britain* (University of Chicago Press, 2000).

neither she nor the reader realizes at what point she starts dreaming. Alice announces her desire to enter Looking-Glass Land before enacting that desire in *Looking-Glass*, though her transition into and out of the mirror is similarly seamless. This kind of seamless transition is also found in the *Sylvie and Bruno* novels, where Carroll merges the dialogue of real-world and dream-world characters in a way which makes it impossible for the reader to identify, at times, which parts of the dialogue occurred within the dream. This addresses the fear at the heart of Carroll's 'Query', which wonders how easily one might slip into a non-rational state, but it also accurately represents the process of the mind of a dreamer. Carroll's representations of the function of the unconscious mind are a noteworthy element of his writing and relevant to the *Alice* books.

The conflation of optical instruments, such as the mirror, but also other Victorian contraptions that utilized it to the end of manipulating vision and perception, in analogous ways to dreams (or so they contended) was equally omnipresent in Victorian culture, as is further underlined by Jonathan Potter.[5] He notes that 'as the century progressed, the magic lantern became an increasingly common trope for describing the dream experience' (2018: 56). By projecting an image from a transparent glass slide, the lantern could be used to create fantastical, seemingly irrational scenarios. By tracking the lantern towards and away from the screen, for example, an object might appear to grow and shrink; by doubling two of the glass slides, one shape might seem to change rapidly into another; or commonly, an image could simply be projected onto a gauze screen to present the audience with a ghostly, floating figure.[6] The lanterns themselves, as they projected the fantastical into the rational world, were a way to question the reliability of perception, as well as being ideal sources of imagery to describe the sensation of dreaming. All of the lantern show techniques listed above are recognizable in Alice's dream world (see Chapter 4), though for most other authors the use of the lantern to portray dream was not so specific. In Potter's own

5   This conflation is further discussed, from a science-historical perspective in Chapter 4, and within a theological framework in Chapter 8.

6   Making it particularly noteworthy that Alice describes the looking glass as 'getting all soft like gauze' before it becomes the mist which she is able to pass through.

example, he highlights the chapter 'Mrs Flintwinch has another Dream' in Dickens' *Little Dorrit*. The dream reference is fairly brief and Dickens simply compares the shifting shadows of a scene as a character falls asleep to the shadows of a magic lantern. It is an interesting example because, as Potter points out, the 'dream' referred to is actually reality misconstrued as a dream, meaning that it perfectly represents the unreliability of vision. It is, however, quite different from Carroll's use of lantern techniques, which is more concerned with authentically portraying the transitions of an unconscious mind. While Carroll drew on the currency of this discourse, his own portrayal is quite distinct. Another example of this can be found in 'The Winter's Wreath' where the dream is described by its 'grotesque changes of a phantasmagoria', which was an early type of lantern show.[7] Again, this is different from Carroll's use of specific lantern techniques to portray the function of the mind during dream. While Carroll is in some ways using a common trope when he connects magic lantern techniques to dream, therefore, he is using it in a way that is in this context unique.

This difference may originate in Carroll's knowledge of the technology. Carroll had experienced the magic lantern as early as 1840, when he visited an exhibition at Warrington Town Hall which featured a phantasmagoria. As an adult he then bought his own magic lantern (in 1856), which he used to create his own performances.[8] This factor sets him apart from many of his contemporaries who were also associating the dream experience with that of a magic lantern show; Carroll integrates the variety of lantern techniques into his portrayal of Alice's dream world because he was so familiar with them. Ultimately, this leads to a more detailed and accurate portrayal of the mind during a dream. This was not the only way that Carroll used technology to portray the workings of a dreaming mind, he also did so in his photography. The camera, similarly to the magic lantern, was often used as a tool to question viewer's perceptions of reality, though most often

7   The early phantasmagoria was actually used to demonstrate the unreliability of perception and expose those who would attempt to trick others into belief in ghosts. See *Encyclopaedia of the Magic Lantern*.

8   *The Diaries of Lewis Carroll*, p. 99.

Psychology

through the production of ghost or spirit photography.[9] Using two separate photographs and the technique of double exposure, a ghostly, translucent figure could be produced within the original image. Rather than attempting to create a ghost, Carroll uses this technique to portray the dream of a sleeping figure on more than one occasion. In his photograph of 'Mary J. MacDonald dreaming of her father [George MacDonald] and brother Ronald' (Figure 14), for example, Carroll shows us the solid, sleeping figure of Mary on the left of the photograph, while the 'dream' figures of her father and brother appear in a faded, ghostly, form to the left of her.

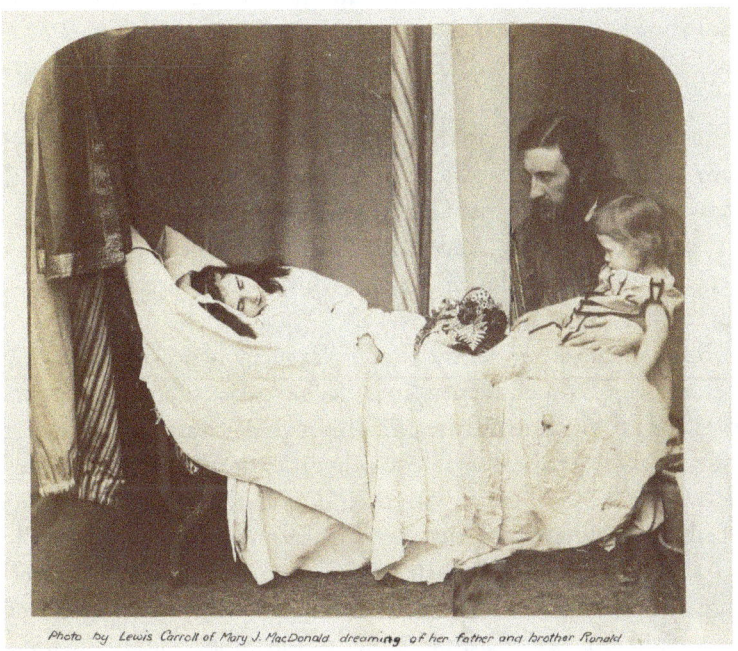

Photo by Lewis Carroll of Mary J. MacDonald dreaming of her father and brother Ronald

Figure 14.   Mary J. MacDonald dreaming of her father and brother Ronald, 1864, Charles Dodgson.

9   Shane McCorristine discusses the questioning of perceptual experience in connection to ghost-seeing in the nineteenth century in his *Spectres of the Self* (Cambridge University Press, 2010). As Carroll was interested in supernatural phenomena and using the same photographic techniques as many of these photographers, this is undoubtedly another element of questioning perception which he engaged with.

Carroll took that photograph approximately one year before the original publication of *Alice's Adventures in Wonderland* and it further demonstrates his intention to accurately portray the workings of a dreaming mind. It also provides a visual portrayal of the dream and real worlds merging, highlighting the lack of distinct boundary which is so important to the *Alice* books.

In *Through the Looking-Glass*, as suggested earlier, Alice does take a more active approach to her dream-world entrance. While her fall down the rabbit-hole seems accidental in the original adventure, in order to enter Looking-Glass Land Alice intentionally exercises her imagination, announcing 'Let's pretend that you're the red queen, Kitty!' (*TTLG*: 8) before detailing all of her ideas about the Looking-Glass House. However, if there is a greater degree of intent in Alice's entrance to the dream, the comfort of that fact is more than balanced by the scene of the Red King's dream, which highlights Alice's discomfort at the implication of these dream debates. It is here that Carroll most overtly addresses the fear which was present in his 'Query'. Alice is quite disturbed to be told that she is 'only a sort of thing in the Red King's dream' which would 'go out – bang! – just like a candle!' (81) if he were to wake.

This presents the reader with a complex metaphysical question. Within her dream world, which elements of Alice's experience and identity belong to the real and which to the dream? Although Alice attempts to assert the fact that 'I *am* real!', she is unable to prove it to the doubting Tweedledum and Tweedledee (82). Faced with their doubt, her fear and frustration at her inability to differentiate between the real and unreal distresses Alice so much that she begins to cry.[10] This moment in the book is fairly brief and Alice swiftly brushes away her tears and the 'nonsense' idea that they are also not real. However, Carroll highlights the importance of the moment by returning to it at the end of the book. The title of the final chapter itself

---

10   Wrongful confinement as a result of the inability to demonstrate one's own sanity is another recurring fear which stems from the unnervingly fine boundary between rationality and insanity. It formed a key part of Wilkie Collins' *The Woman in White*, which was serialized in *All the Year Round*.

poses the question 'Which Dreamed It?'. Within that final chapter, Alice requests the consideration of the 'very serious question' of 'who it was that dreamed it all'. Emphasized by the italicized repetition of the question '*was it the Red King Kitty?*', the final line of the book then turns the question to the reader: '[W]ho do *you* think it was?' It might be argued that the direct address to the reader in the final line of the book indicates the answer to the question by drawing our attention to the authorial voice – it was, in fact, Carroll himself who 'dreamed' it all. If the Red King is a product of Alice's mind, then Alice is a product of Carroll's.

It is in *Through the Looking-Glass*, therefore, where Carroll fully delves into the questions and fears he was considering when he noted his 'Query' decades before. While Alice's second adventure continues to explore the dream experience and the ease of transition between dream and real worlds in the same way as the previous book, it also develops those ideas in new ways. The more literal distorted reflection of the world, for example, provides the dreamland with a distinct theme, one which is reminiscent of the optical technologies which were being used to question the reliability of perception in the same way that dream was. The fears and theories about dream and the unconscious mind were discussed nowhere in more detail and with more frequency than in the periodical. Reading *Looking-Glass* through the lens of Carroll's engagement with the broader debates around dreams reveals more about their context as well as highlighting the ways in which his approach to the frightening uncertainty of dreaming minds was unique.

Ellen Schaefer-Salins

12 The *Looking-Glass* Self and Other *Looking-Glass* Inspired Psychological and Sociological Theories

The best-known writings of Lewis Carroll – *Through the Looking-Glass,* and *Alice's Adventures in Wonderland* – have influenced the development of several psychological and sociological theories. These include The Looking-Glass Self by Charles Horton Cooley, whose theory, in turn, led to the development of George Herbert Mead's Symbolic Interactionism. Both theories are being used prominently by mental health professionals, and continue to be taught in psychology, sociology, and social work classes today. Other theories inspired by Carroll's writings include the Dodo Effect, the Alice in Wonderland Syndrome, the Mad Hatter Syndrome, the White Rabbit Syndrome, the Snark Syndrome, and the Red Queen Effect.

Lewis Carroll was brilliant in writing about the psychology of his characters, and this shows in the number of theories and syndromes that are influenced by and named after the titles and the characters of these famous children's stories. This chapter will explore, focusing on the impact of *Through the Looking-Glass* on psychological and sociological theories.

In *Looking-Glass* and *Wonderland,* Alice is continually wondering who she is and what her identity is. She is a strong character who does not seem bothered by the opinions, thoughts, and interactions of others as she is mistaken numerous times, for 'Mary-Ann' in *Wonderland,* or when she becomes a Queen in *Looking-Glass.* While she is teased, bullied, and questioned, she ultimately stands her ground and is confident with strangers and strange animals talking to her. She does not seem to wonder what others think about her during her adventures and wonders more about the thoughts of those around her. These characteristics of *Looking-Glass* Alice are crucial to the way in which she has influenced psychological and sociological theory.

George Horton Cooley (1964–1929) used the title of *Through the Looking-Glass,* for the name of his theory, the Looking-Glass Self. This theory was first discussed by Cooley in a manuscript called *Human Nature and the Social Order* published in 1902. In this manuscript, Cooley talks of the self and how a person learns to view and understand who they are. A person cannot understand who they are without the opinions and interactions of others (Cooley 1902: 139). The theory was first discussed just a few years after the death of Lewis Carroll in 1898, which was widely publicized in England, the United States, and worldwide. Cooley was born in the town of Ann Arbor, Michigan in the United States, and as an adult he became a professor of sociology at the University of Michigan in the same city of his birth (American Sociological Association 2021: 251).

Much of what Cooley writes about in the Looking-Glass Self appears to have connections to *Through the Looking-Glass*. He states in his famous 1902 writing:

> Each to each a looking-glass
> Reflect the other that doth pass. (Cooley 1902: 139)

Cooley used the following example for his theory in later writings in 1927. Interesting that Alice and her hat is the example that he chose.

> Two friends walk toward each other; one, Alice, sporting a new hat and the other, Angela, wearing a recently purchased dress. Alice sees Angela and while walking toward her thinks, 'I look great in this hat.' Angela waves, and in the distance Alice can see Angela gesturing toward her own hatless head and Alice thinks, 'She's noticed my hat and she thinks it looks great on me too!' In recognition of Angela's seeming compliment to Alice's hat, Alice first excitedly 'vogues' her hands around her new hat while exaggerating an open-mouthed smile and rolling her eyes toward the sky, as if the image of her face has been captured on a glossy fashion magazine, and thinks, 'Angela knows that I know I look great in this hat' and then decides to return the compliment by gesturing up and down her own body, acknowledging her friend's new dress. As they are almost within proximity to exchange physical greetings, Angela

sucks in her cheeks and does a quick mocking model catwalk twirl and thinks, 'Alice really thinks she looks wonderful in that hat,' all the time going through the exact steps of herself and her dress as Alice did with her hat Although both are only really known to their possible maker(s), both momentarily feel wonderful about who they are. (Cooley 1927: 200; Stonebanks and Stonebanks 2010: 230)

The Alice and Angela examples show the three main points of Cooley's theory. The Looking-Glass Self is a theory of self in which we learn who we are through interactions with others. Cooley theorized that a person understands how they see themselves through the following:

1. The imagination of our appearance to the other person;
2. The imagination of his or her judgement of that appearance; and
3. Some sort of feeling derived from this action, such as pride or mortification (Cooley 1902; Siljanovska and Stojcevska 2018: 63).

As can be seen in the Alice interaction above, good thoughts came from the interaction with Angela. After their exchange, both felt positive about their hat and their dress. Interactions with others can cause people to feel positive or negative about his or her looks, intelligence, personality, and more. And the whole theory is based on assumptions. A person's sense of self comes from what they think that others think of them, and is not based on facts, meaning what another person really does think about them (Cooley 1902: 189; Siljanovska and Stojcevska, 2018: 63).

Cooley wrote another way to think of this theory. The theory says that a person sees oneself in this way:

I am who you think I am;
I am not who I think I am:
I am who I think you think I am. (Cooley 1927: 201)

In *Wonderland*, Lewis Carroll's Alice famously says, 'I knew who I was this morning, but I've changed a few times since then.' Alice changes many times throughout both *Wonderland* and *Looking-Glass*. It is not clear how Alice views herself during her many changes such as becoming a Queen in *Through the Looking-Glass* but many characters comment on her changes.

Psychology

Cooley's theory of the Looking-Glass Self was the basis for Symbolic Interactionism which is a theory developed by George Herbert Mead (1861–1931) and Herbert Blummer (1900–1987). Symbolic Interactionism is a theoretical framework or paradigm based on the assumption that social reality is created and recreated (continuously) through human interactions through the use of symbols. It emphasizes the roles that symbols, language, and thought play in society (Quist-Adade 2019: 23). An example is the symbol of an engagement ring. What is the meaning of this symbol and of the words 'engagement ring'? Our society places a great deal of meaning on this term and most of the time it is a positive symbol. But suppose one person proposes to a second person who does not want to get married. In that case the engagement ring that was offered in the proposal becomes a negative symbol to both people involved.

Symbolic Interactionism looks at the meaning of language and how it impacts people. How does a person feel to be told they are smart? Does this mean they are intelligent or that they are dressed smartly? And is this always positive or can it carry negative connotations for some? Lewis Carroll loved to play with words and symbols, so it is an appropriate starting point for that theory. Consider Humpty Dumpty playing with symbols/words while talking to Alice:

> 'It is a – most – provoking – thing,' he said at last, when a person doesn't know a cravat from a belt!'
>
> 'I know it's very ignorant of me,' Alice said, in so humble a tone that Humpty Dumpty relented.
>
> 'It's a cravat, child, and a beautiful one, as you say. It's a present from the White King and Queen. There now!'
>
> 'When I use a word,' Humpty Dumpty said, in rather a scornful tone, 'it means just what I choose it to mean – neither more nor less.' 'The question is,' said Alice, 'whether you can make words mean so many different things.' 'The question is,' said Humpty Dumpty, 'which is to be master – that's all. (*TTLG*: 124)

Lewis Carroll was looking at the meaning and impact of words before Mead and Blummer developed Symbolic Interactionism. Carroll also invented such words as brillig, snark (people now say things are snarky), chortle, and frabjous, leaving one to figure out the definitions and meaning of these words. Though some decide on the definitions such as when Humpty Dumpty defines the meanings of the words in the poem 'Jabberwocky' that Alice reads at the beginning of *Through the Looking-Glass* (*TTLG*: 22). Martin Gardner (1960), explains in *The Annotated Alice,* the meanings of words and symbols in the two Alice books. The meanings of words have an impact on how people interact with one another within society and that again is the basis of Symbolic Interactionism (Quist-Adade 2019: 23).

Through the Looking-Glass was also used to name another theory called the Red Queen Effect. The theory was named after the following quote by the Red Queen to Alice as they are running as fast as they could, but their surroundings were not changing:

> Now, here you see, it takes all the running you can do, to keep in the same place. If you want to get somewhere else, you must run at least twice as fast as that! (*TTLG*: 42)

This theory was originally coined by the biologist van Valen to talk about a biological evolutionary theory of organisms that must keep evolving to survive (Derfus, Maggitti, Grimm, and Smith 2008: 61). It has since been used in other contexts such as military arms races or competition between rival business firms. The theory means you must 'run' twice as fast as your competition or as yourself to get ahead of others, or ahead of something such as evolution (Derfus et al. 2008: 61).

Looking-Glass has also influenced the development of the Alice in Wonderland Syndrome – which may have been misnamed. It was first alluded to by Caro Lippman in 1952 in the *Journal of Nervous and Mental Diseases.* The article discussed people having migraines which caused a 'Tweedledum and Tweedledee' feeling where people feel short and fat (Lippman 1952: 347). Dr John Todd coined the term Alice in Wonderland Syndrome in a 1955 *Canadian Medical Association Journal.* This article discussed migraines again that caused people to have a variety of symptoms where people felt alterations of their body image. People felt short and fat, or very tall or very small, or the sizes of external objects are perceived incorrectly (Burstein 1994; Larner 2005; Todd 1955). Since Tweedledee and Tweedledum are *Looking-Glass* characters, and the Looking-Glass can distort body image, it seems that both books influenced the name of this syndrome. Maybe it should be called the 'Alice in Wonderland and Through the Looking-Glass Syndrome'?

Looking-Glass is the lesser-known book, compared to *Wonderland*. Even so, it is *Looking-Glass* that has had a great influence on the development of the Looking-Glass Self and Symbolic Interactionism, well-known psychological and sociological theories that are still in use today. Carroll's writings and ideas have stood the test of time as his books are still popular 150 years after their first publications. It is a tribute to Lewis Carroll that the Looking-Glass Self, the Red Queen Effect, and the 'Wonderland/ Looking-Glass' Syndrome are still being studied and applied today. The famous ideas and theories of how one understands and analyses oneself through the eyes of another, or in their own reflection, were born in the writings of *Looking-Glass* and its strong main character, Alice. *Looking-Glass*, therefore, has had a great, and distinct impact on our social and psychological concept of self.

Nick Coates and Ned Colville

13 The Alice Code: Looking-Glass Thinking for Innovators

What unites Harry Potter and Uber?[1] How do you shrink an ice-cream that's famous for being big (Magnum)?[2] How do you invent a new category, like Belvita or *Cirque du Soleil*?

The answers to these riddles – world-swapping, scale-switching, perspective framing – are all commonplaces of innovation that should also ring bells for even the most casual *Alice*-fan. We're surprised that the connection remains faint in the literature since, in our own commercial practice over 15+ years, *Alice* has been a constant source of inspiration.

Why? Because in our field – consumer psychology, insight, and co-creation – we're trying to do two things:

- access the emotional and irrational dimensions of behaviour ('thick' not 'thin' data, humans as messy not neat);
- engage the imagination and a childlike sense of possibility (to encourage ideation without rules, pre-conceptions, or constraints).

Because our co-creators (consumers and clients) both have embedded assumptions about what's permissible (to share) and what's possible (to change), we need tools, techniques, and 'thinking spaces' that facilitate dreaming, wonder, and imagination.

Enter Alice. Her journey is a trippy tale that challenges and reframes rationality. In *Wonderland,* things swap places, words become unstable,

---

1   Answer: 'product magic' (ridehailing UI = Marauder's Map in feel).
2   Answer: reframe Magnum as intensity, not size, and focus Magnum Mini on 'crunch'.

people and objects shrink and grow, and mirrors abound. In *Through the Looking-Glass,* normal rules are suspended, challenged, or subverted, and alternate realities glimpsed, albeit fleetingly.

It's obvious that our inner (imaginary) worlds are a lot like this: feelings are rarely reasonable or rational, we're just taught how to channel and conceal them. And then there are dreams, those manifestations of desire and delirium. Tapping into both, we'd argue, is a wellspring of both understanding and inspiration. A kaleidoscope of future experiences.

And this matters because human risk aversion is deep-seated and, in the case of businesses, often structurally enshrined through processes, structures, incentives, and culture. Businesses are organized to prioritize short-term survival. They are often primarily inward-looking. They see customers as captives and consumers as 'targets' (Tannir et al. 2022). To stay relevant requires foresight, yet short-term myopia blinds them to disruption, and what's happening at the edges.

So this isn't fantasy so much as a healthy approach to anticipating societal, economic, and technological changes (where today's reality is an unhelpful starting point). It's an important corrective to the short-term logic of markets and management – a way of 'seeing around corners' (McGrath 2019).

Towards a New Framework: The Alice Code

For us the people and places in the Alice books constitute a grammar of imagining/reimagining. A way to systematically deconstruct and reconstruct ideas for new products, services, and experiences. A generative tool for turning banal working into wonderland.

A. Method

The overall arc of *Alice's Adventures* (the journey of katabasis/anabasis) is a helpful metaphor for innovators because we think, at its heart, it reflects the creative problem-solving process: a succession of 'divergent' and 'convergent' waves.[3]

And for us the boundary of the business is the equivalent of the looking-glass. Piercing that boundary, entering a new space, helps us to diverge: to defamiliarize the familiar, disassemble the bonds of meaning and current logic so that we can reassemble them, to glimpse new 'adjacent possibilities'.[4] To avoid the 'black hat' mode of thinking (see De Bono 2016). The journey back allows us to take stock, reflect, and rebuild, so we can then put the black hat back on.

If this all sounds a bit theoretical, let's take a real-world example. Imagine you've been tasked with reinventing Christmas for a major UK retailer in the middle of July. While most people are leaving for holidays in the sun, enjoying alfresco dining in the park, and thinking about suncream (not Santa), coming up with Christmassy products and retail ideas could feel like hard work.

This was the challenge we faced back in 2018. So we hired a professional Santa, got the company Christmas tree and tinsel out of storage, built a fireplace, cranked up 'jingle bells', and turned our team into elves. We needed a play space and it needed to feel different from the moment you walked in. We needed a day through the looking-glass: method mixed with madness, a game-like process of exploration that suspended normal rules for long enough to envisage the new. And on Day 2 we got to make sense of it all, to sift, sort and structure.

B. Mindset

Carrollian characters exemplify many of the best innovation mindsets, lessons in how to correct the narratives, beliefs, and behaviours that, in corporate life, can suffocate creativity. From Carroll's pantheon of playfulness, we've selected three.

3   In divergent thinking we explore, widen our aperture, and seek volume, diversity, and bravery; we ask, '[W]hat are *all* the ways …?' In convergent thinking we select the best ideas, we judge logically against measurable objectives. This duality acts like 'lungs' for the creative process, it lets ideas breathe. See Guilford (1967).
4   Stuart Kauffman's term (see Johnson 2010: 25–42).

Open to Curious Connections (Like the Gnat)

Starting as a small voice in Alice's ear, by the fourth square, the Gnat has – improbably – become the size of a chicken. The conversation that ensues explores naming puns for the 'looking-glass insects', creatures that echo, and subvert, 'normal' insects. Enter the Rocking-horse-fly, Snap-dragon-fly and Bread-and-butter-fly.

As the Gnat reminds us, in ideation and improvisation alike, improbable connections and combinations must be treated as entirely natural. Embracing synectics is the hallmark of a confident lateral thinker; it's a repeatable way of reframing and rewiring existing realities.

The ability to ask, 'what if ?'.

Up for Serious Play (Like Humpty Dumpty)

What can feel wilfully obtuse in the conversation between Alice and Humpty Dumpty, is actually common sense in the innovation process. We need to be open to possibility, embrace the 'slow hunch', and view failure as an opportunity, repurpose, and reframe.

After all what began at 3M as a failed glue gradually found a new application as a peelable paper solution, the humble post-it note. Increasing our chances of letting seedling ideas grow means playing the game to its logical conclusion, asking, 'Why not!'

Comfortable with Impossible Thoughts (Like the Red Queen)

Possibility, realism, caution, problem-spotting … all fantastic attributes of sensible living. They keep us safe, prevent us from overthinking, and help us anticipate future stumbling blocks. But being reasonable is a terrible starting point if our goal is to create the new, break rules, think big.

The notion of 'impossible thoughts before breakfast', a barb hurled at Alice by the Red Queen, is an excellent divergent thinking practice. In divergent mode we need to be comfortable to decouple 'as is' and 'could be' for as long as needed. In fact, we need to luxuriate in ambiguity and counterfactuals. It's about being fluent in 'let's see!'

C. Moves

The looking-glass is a very particular kind of image: mirrors don't just reflect, they invert, they distort, they allow us to play with ideas, to translate and to transform them. In our work this shows up most tangibly in the exercises and frameworks we deploy, a practical toolkit of innovation techniques called 'The C Space Way'. What began forming in a portable prototype of cards carried in trains, planes, and taxis, first saw the light of day in 2017 (Figure 15).

Figure 15. The Magic Box.
Source: C Space Way 'Magic Box' toolkit.

In what follows we'll unpack some of the techniques that particularly embody 'looking-glass thinking', and try to show how they apply not just to product and service innovation but also to culture more widely.

We've grouped them under five 'mirrored' headings in Figure 16.

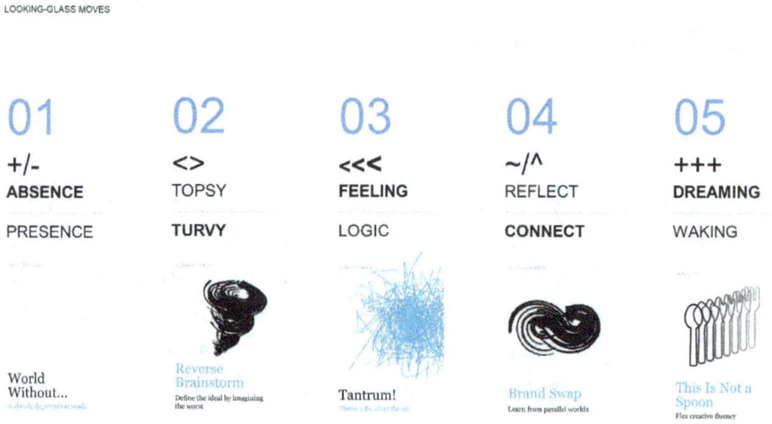

LOOKING-GLASS MOVES

01	02	03	04	05
+/-	<>	<<<	~/^	+++
ABSENCE	TOPSY	**FEELING**	REFLECT	**DREAMING**
PRESENCE	**TURVY**	LOGIC	**CONNECT**	WAKING

World Without... | Reverse Brainstorm | Tantrum! | Brand Swap | This Is Not a Spoon

Figure 16. Magic Box Cards.

01 *Absence/Presence*

Alice is constantly confronted by absence: familiar anchors slip away; objects, characters, and places appear and disappear; and the Cheshire Cat fades to a smile. The looking-glass is a cipher for the liminal, the in-between of here and there, and of erasure. It invites us to think about what to keep and what to lose. It helps us overcome loss aversion.

Prince's breakthrough achievement on 'When Doves Cry' was what he took away: the bass. George Perec's *La Disparition* is a tale about the disappearance of the letter 'E', which (self-referentially) is also totally absent from the text. Apple's original iPod removed keys in favour of a new (old) interaction method, a wheel. Products like Coke Zero or Burt's Bees base their entire proposition on what's NOT in the product.

World Without (a deprivation experiment) is one manifestation of this kind of move. To understand the potential for Samsung to attract iPhone users, we created a process called 'Phone Swap', a deep (five-week) experiment where consumers were forced to give up their phones (with all their data) and switch platforms. It was painful and people got frustrated. Outcome? A new app called Samsung Smartswitch that makes platform-switching child's play.

02 Topsy/Turvy

Contrary logic is a defining feature through the looking-glass. The chessboard itself is the narrative stage on which pairings, opposites, reversals, and inversions are dramatized. The Red and White queen already represent opposites, but when Alice reaches the end of the board and becomes queen, an unlikely transformation – that overturns the power structures that *Alice in Wonderland* has built up – is complete.[5]

In culture, we might look to Bach's crab canons – mirrored musical palindromes – or even Harold Pinter's *Betrayal* – a relationship drama where each subsequent scene takes place before the previous one. But the same patterns exist in commerce too. Consider the Dyson Airblade, a hand-dryer that works by blowing, not heating. Or Polo Holes, a kind of confectionary joke, a round mini-mint that conceptually fills the holes that are Polo's signature shape. Or perhaps IKEA, whose entire business model is based on an inversion – you (the customer) assemble, not us.

We love a good *Reverse Brainstorm*. The game's simple: pick a rule and invert it, and then build that opposite reality. It's one of the ways we helped transform travel loyalty, which a decade ago had become stale and predictable. Where travel was exciting, points were boring. Working with GHA (the Global Hotel Alliance) we took that norm and turned it on its head. Instead of points, we built Discovery out of unique local experiences. No points in sight! And ten years later, Discovery has just relaunched, with

---

5   Opposites in Carroll's Logic, in relation to *Looking-Glass* and its narrative structure, are discussed in Chapter 14.

a new inversion: rewards as good *when you're not travelling* as when you are (the 'Live Local' programme).

03 *Feeling/Logic*

Society tends to reward emotional containment. But looking-glass feelings are less grown-up, less continent. In looking-glass world, characters express their feelings without adult 'lids'. We need to look no further than Tweedledum and Tweedledee for an example of how contrariwise feelings can be. In our world, of consumer feelings, what psychologist Roy Langmaid calls the 'background conversation'[6] knows no moderation, no 'reasonableness'.

Jacob Collier's reharmonization of Moon River[7] is an extraordinary, microtonal, exercise in sketching 'between the lines' of traditional tuning to create almost imperceptible, yet highly palpable, emotional shifts. Spotify's Mood Search (based on the insight we developed that music is a psychotropic technology of the self) broke the paradigm of searching by genre. Luxury goods – say Prada trainers – often trade largely on emotion, far beyond their rational economic value. Secret Cinema amplifies the core emotions inherent in the movies they celebrate by creating an immersive world around the screening itself.

In business, research and 'stage-gates' are typically rational constructs. As a corrective we seek to create space for open questions and emotional extremes – the gateway to solving the *real* issues. In our process, we encourage *Tantrums* (and the odd broken rattle …). On the way to thinking about the future of flying, we weren't expecting to stumble upon Happy Socks, but frequent flyers found standard socks laughable. So Virgin Atlantic made them standard for their Upper Class customers.[8]

6   Roy used this term frequently when we worked together.
7   www.youtube.com/watch?v=VPLCk-FTVvw. See also Jacob's Logic session breakdown of the song: www.youtube.com/watch?v=9d4-URyWEJQ.
8   <https://apex.aero/articles/virgin-atlantic-steps-amenities-game-happy-socks>

04 Reflect/Connect

Mirrors reflect, but they also distort and create strange new kaleidoscopic patterns. In looking-glass world, objects, places, people, and body parts connect in new and unexpected combinations, but often via the lateral logic of puns, portmanteaus, and other linguistic games. In addition to the looking-glass insects we've referenced, 'Jabberwocky' is full of neologisms: 'slithy', 'galumphing', and 'chortle' just for starters (*TTLG*: 22).

Star Wars is a cultural remix (WWII movies + Flash Gordon + Japanese Samurai culture – specifically Kurosawa's *The Hidden Fortress).* Brian Eno's *Oblique Strategies* cards helped shape Bowie's Berlin period. Innovation also loves combinatory approaches. When the brand Belvita launched, it created an entirely new category – the breakfast biscuit. Apple has created the most lucrative retail space on the planet by switching up the codes of tech retail: from indoor trees signifying a social 'town square' to giant farmhouse-style tables. And the Genius Bar? A transplanted hotel concierge in an Apple t-shirt!

We are constantly surprised and delighted at the outcomes we derived from synectic approaches, including techniques like *Brand Swap*, where we imagine that one brand (e.g. Disney) is now running another brand (e.g. Google), or vice versa. When working on the future of oral care for Colgate, we collaborated with sex toy designers to understand what brushing pleasure might look like. Redefine by borrowing.

05 Dreaming/Waking

In dreams rules are suspended. New realities become possible. The looking-glass represents a mental gateway: between the conscious and unconscious. We know during REM sleep creative brain activity is high. Taking the Red Queen's idea of thinking impossible thoughts before breakfast seriously isn't just provocative, it's supported by neuroscience.[9] Embracing the dream state is fuel for problem-solving.

9   See Johnson 2010 – Chapter 4, 'Serendipity' – on REM sleep and acetylcholine-releasing cells. Sleep is no longer viewed as a liberation from forms of Freudian repression, instead sleep is a process of creative exploration.

Literary experiments, from *Finnegan's Wake* to *On the Road* (written on a 120 ft roll of paper in one twenty-day burst of activity), were attempts to capture subjectivity and spontaneity. Business often wants quick answers, 'efficient' decisions, and evidenced business cases, and rightly so. But creating enough space to dream, follow the thread of unlikely thinking, take random ideas seriously, is essential to the ideation process.

Because we know this isn't easy in our waking day-to-day, we need to view all ideas as gifts. A game like *This Is Not a Spoon* (pass an object round the circle, giving alternative uses)[10] helps collaborators to embrace alternative meanings, to decouple existing assumptions and linkages so they can reassemble them. *Creative Visualization* meanwhile (a guided meditation) helps customers dream about the future: visions of trees and rivers that this conjured up inspired Tesco to create a more natural feel in new stores.

Outro

Through the Looking-Glass is 150. Born in an age of discovery, invention, and wonderment, Alice still shapes culture today. Can the Alice Code inspire better innovation too? We hope so. Happy un-birthday!

10   An obvious reference to Magritte's *Ceci n'est pas une pipe*; surrealism owes a debt to Carroll of course.

Part V

Logic and Language

Eric Gerlach

14 Aristotle, Alice, and a Pair of Queens: The Looking-Glass, Opposites, and Aristotle's Logic

At the end of Alice's dream in *Through the Looking-Glass*, she is seated between opposite queens, a confused child and a strict governess like an angel and devil on her shoulders. I have argued (Gerlach, 2020) that a great deal of evidence suggests Lewis Carroll, a logician who studied, and taught Aristotle's logic to children and adults, plotted out the characters of *Wonderland*, *The Looking-Glass*, and 'The Hunting of the Snark' as illustrations of basic lessons in Aristotle's logic and ethics, serving as a mnemonic device, what Carroll calls a 'Memoria Technica', for Aristotle's ten logical categories, four forms of proposition, and balance between extremes. In sum, *Wonderland* can be read as mnemonic device for teaching basic lessons of Aristotle, as a walk through Aristotle's ten logical categories, ruled by the four forms of proposition. Each is illustrated and symbolized by a memorable character such that Alice and other child readers in due course learn and remember to balance the inclusive passion of childhood and exclusive substance of adulthood with lessons in patience, perspective, and character to make logical choices for themselves, taking heroic action while attending patiently to others. *Looking-Glass*, which follows *Wonderland*, mirrors these forms, and, parallel to *Wonderland*, numerical chapter by chapter, Aristotelian category by category, and the *Snark* can be read as a logic problem solved with clues found in Alice's two adventures.

Figure 17. Alice between Queens.

Figure 18. Carroll's Characters as Aristotle's Categories.

Why would Carroll go to such lengths, and compose such serious but humorous stories that illustrate and repeat such elementary forms of classical education, ethics, and logic? The real-life Alice (1852–1934), for whom Carroll composed *Wonderland*, was the daughter of Henry Liddell (1811–1898), composer of *Liddell & Scott Greek-English Lexicon* (1843), classics scholar of great repute, and the dean of Christ Church, Carroll's college at Oxford. Carroll was himself an educator as well as an entertainer, who wanted children to learn forms of logic, lessons from history, play games, sing songs, and listen to stories, in an informing and entertaining way. In Carroll's earliest diaries we find references to composing lessons that teach forms of logic and mathematics to children and adults with concern for effectiveness. At the time he met the Liddell sisters, including Alice (1855, 4th and 6th September), he was lecturing in mathematics at Oxford and taught at a boys' school (1856, 28th and 29th January). Crucial for our interests, this is also the time he developed his own *Memoria Technica* (1856, 1857, 1875, 1876, 1878) following Grey's *Memoria Technica* (1857), in which Carroll, firstly, encodes forms into symbols, and then, secondly, weaves the symbols into memorable, silly stories such that Carroll himself can remember them easily. The conception of Carroll's *Memoria Technica* thus happened concurrently to, as, and after Carroll invented, wrote, and published *Wonderland* (1865), *Looking-Glass* (1872), and *The Hunting of the Snark* (1876). In his diaries, as Carroll worked on each 'Fit' of 'The Hunting of the Snark', and sent each to his publisher following the great success of *Alice's Adventures* (1865), he completed his quantitative 'Memoria Technica' and hoped to publish it as *Logarithms By Lightning: A Mathematical Curiosity*.

Here is Carroll's device, found in *Rediscovered Lewis Carroll Puzzles* (1995), and diary entries that explain the two steps of, firstly, encoding forms and, secondly, illustrating them with amusements:

> 1 June 1877: My 'Memoria Technica' is a modification of Gray's; but, whereas he used both consonants and vowels to represent digits, and had to content himself with a syllable of gibberish to represent the date or whatever other number was required, I use only consonants, and fill in with vowels ad liberitum, and thus can always manage to make a real world of whatever has to be represented.

1	2	3	4	5	6	7	8	9	0
b	d	t	f	l	s	p	h	n	z
c	w	j	q	v	x	m	k	g	r

Figure 19. Carroll's Memoria Technica.

When a word has been found, whose last consonants represent the number required, the best plan is to put it as the last word of a rhymed couplet, so that, whatever other words in it are forgotten, the rhyme will secure the only really important word.

Now suppose you wish to remember the date of the discovery of America, which is 1492; the '1' may be left out as obvious; all we need is '492'. Write it thus: 4 9 2, f n d … The poetic faculty must now be brought into play, and the following couplet will soon be evolved: Columbus sailed the world around, Until America was FOUND.

1 Nov, 1875: Wrote anecdotal accompaniments for the words, making most of them into one continuous story. My system differs from Grey's in having the words all real – no gibberish to remember. This I manage by having a larger choice of symbols. With the addition of similar words for useful statistics, such as the dates of the Kings of England, it might make a popular little pamphlet.

Wonderland and Aristotle's Categories

In his *Categories*, traditionally bound in one volume with Aristotle's work on logic as the introductory text, Aristotle lists ten types of truth that can be stated about things: (1) *substance*, the material being of this or that thing, such as soup or tarts, (2) *quantity*, the number or amount of a thing, such as two or seven, (3) *quality*, an aspect of a thing, such as rude or best, (4) *relations*, the interaction of a thing with others, such as ruler or servant, (5) *space*, the place a thing is in, such as a house or garden, (6) *time*, the duration of a thing, such as short or forever, (7) *position*, the situation of a thing with other things, such as outside or inside, (8) *state*, the status of a thing, such as circling or dead, (9) *action*, what a thing does, such as cry or swim, and (10) *passion*, what moves a living thing to this or that action, such as delight or despair.

Aristotle starts with noble *substance*, of truth and being itself, and proceeds only somewhat systematically to illustrate many, but not all of the ten, leaving the last few, such as lowly bestial *passion* largely unillustrated, saying we could each easily illustrate these with examples from our lives. If we turn Aristotle's own list of ten categories *backwards*, starting from the lowest rather than the highest, like a text in a mirror, we have *passion*,

action, state, position, time, space, relations, quality, quantity, and *substance.*
This inverted list fits the order of events and characters Alice encounters in
both of her adventures incredibly well, chapter by chapter. It makes sense
of many puzzling moments and jokes, and gives the overall moral and
message a path from low to high, from the passion of beasts and children
to the formalities of adults and royalty.

Thus, the White Rabbit in the first chapter of *Wonderland* illustrates
passion, which Aristotle argues we share with lowly beasts and irrational
children. Alice is, accordingly, frustrated by the dry, unillustrated text of
her elder sister, unlike her own passionate, illustrated adventures to follow,
and Alice is bored as she sees the worried Rabbit rush by which is why she
follows him down the Rabbit Hole. Aristotle said that *we,* humanity, are
the rational animals, which is why a rabbit worried about time, making an
appointment, and wearing a watch is absurd and interests Alice. The White
Rabbit contradicts Aristotle's words with his own words, which makes him
a fantastic, counterfactual creature, an absurd, memorable example which
Alice can use to learn by counterexample. He rushes to please others, she
rushes after him, 'burning with curiosity', and falls without time to think
of past forms, sadly empty of substance, such as a jar without marmalade.
Alice worries about killing someone, what opposite others think and that
her cat will miss her, follows the Rabbit into a frustrating hall of locked
doors and cannot solve the problem of the golden key no matter how she
grows or shrinks, having little rational control over how she negotiates
space and perspective. She cries and demands that she herself stop crying
this minute, impatient with herself and too passionate to follow her own
advice to herself.

There are several sets of characters that are bestial as well as stately in
Alice's dreams, starting with the White Rabbit, the first fantastic character, illustrating Aristotelian passion and form as opposed to and comple-
menting each other, together in the dream, imagination, and thought. At
the Mad Tea Party, the passionate March Hare and logical Mad Hatter
lean on both sides of the dreaming Dormouse, much as the queen's nap
on Alice's shoulders at the end of *Looking-Glass,* and the Hare and Hatter
appear bestial and rude in the first dream, but over-acting and stately in
the second, where they re-appear as Royal messenger Hatta and Haigha.

The Walrus and Carpenter are passionate beasts and form-building men, terribly consuming childlike oysters between them. The Lion and Unicorn are a similar pair, ferocious beasts of the jungle and mythical form, sharing pudding between them and everyone, all over town after battling. The walk through Aristotle's *Categories* balances innocent, inclusive childhood, and assertive, exclusive adulthood, minding the extremes.

The White Rabbit is not a villain, but proud of his house and position, and so he is no hero, but a servile coward who does what he can for good, but should be somewhat better. Consider alongside what Carroll writes in his diary:

> 1856, Jan 7th: I think that the character of most that I meet with is *merely refined animal*, viewing life either as life apostolic merely, or intellectually. How few seem to care for the only subjects of real interest in life. – What am I, to say so? Am I a deep philosopher, or a great genius? I think neither. What talents I have, I desire to devote to His service, and may He purify me, and take away my pride and selfishness.

This clearly indicates that Carroll saw behaviour such as the Rabbits situated clearly in relation to passion and virtue.

After the White Rabbit and *passion* lead Alice *Down the Rabbit Hole* (Chapter 1), Alice's untempered, passionate action results in inaction, and the *Pool of Tears* (Chapter 2), which leads to further, successful action by imitating others, after Alice follows the Mouse, with everyone else following after, swimming to the 'steady state on the shore'. The Mouse in the second chapter illustrates *action*, which Aristotle argues is the result of the passion that drives it. Alice considers the useless act of sending presents to her feet, can't remember who she is, and so she tries to act as others can't, but instead of reciting a piece about a busy bee storing up activity the poem warps into a crocodile welcoming fish swimming into its jaws. She sees a mouse acting, swimming in her own passionate tears and hopeless situation, and she speaks to him of cats and dogs, expressing her passion but not thinking of his, so he reacts and swims away, then turns and swims back to her. They agree to swim to shore together, and many others follow them, swimming in their wake.

The Dodo in the third chapter illustrates *state*, playing on the use of the word for government. In the first words of the chapter we are told that they reach a *steady state* on the shore, the *party assembles,* and Alice feels she has *known them all her life.*

The White Rabbit again in the fourth chapter illustrates *position*, with the Rabbit mistaking Alice for his own subordinate and ordering her into his own house. She accepts the order and fills his entire house, occupying the entire position available. Aristotle's examples of position in his *Categories* include sitting and lying down, and Alice does both uncomfortably.

The Caterpillar in the fifth chapter illustrates *time*, which teaches Alice patient temperance, which allows her to attend to the interests of others. The Caterpillar and Alice look at each other *for some time* in silence, he asks her who she is, and she says she knew this morning but has *changed so much since then.* All statements circle around time: Alice's failed recitation of the poem is phrased in this spirit: that it is wrong *from beginning to end,* the entire duration.

The Cheshire Cat in the sixth chapter illustrates *space* and shares its space and a chapter with the Duchess, who illustrates *relations*, poorly like the Pigeon. Alice watches *space* intertangle with *relations* as the Queen's Fish-Footman tangles wigs with the Duchess' Frog-Footman.

In the following chapters, the Cat teaches Alice perspective, which opens the tree to grant her the golden key. Wisdom *in time* gives inclusive attendance, but wisdom *in space* gives exclusive position, which balanced Alice will take against the court that unjustly accuses her in the end, ending her dream.

The Mad Hatter and party in the seventh chapter illustrate *quality*, poor again in examples like the Pigeon and Duchess. Explaining the category *quality*, Aristotle's first *poor* examples are rudeness and madness, both on display at the Mad Tea Party. The Hare and Hatter offer her non-existent wine, suggest a haircut, and ask her a riddle with no answer; the Hare uses the *best* butter to absurdly fix the Hatter's watch; and Alice leaves what she says is the *stupidest, worst* tea party ever.

The Queen of Hearts in the eighth chapter illustrates *quantity*, and in the opening words Alice finds the two, five, and seven of spades painting white roses red, and then all the rest of the deck parade by in order.

Carroll and other logicians of his day were seeking rules and foundations for mathematics and logic, like a lawless croquet game where the equipment doesn't behave and there are no orderly turns.

There are four remaining chapters and all illustrate substance, but first *lack of it*, much as the Duchess is poor in relations and the Hatter and Hare in quality. The Mock Turtle sings of 'beautiful soup' we should buy with no account of what goes into it.

The King of Hearts, illustrating substance, holds a trial to gather evidence over who stole the recovered tarts, and he admits all testimony whether or not it is important or unimportant. Alice grows into the largest substance and body of evidence in the room, and just as she says they haven't had any solid, substantive evidence or testimony yet she is called to the stand. Alice assures herself the Royal court are all cardboard, which causes her to rise up, say they're *all a pack of cards*, ending the trial and her dream.

Looking-Glass and Aristotle's Categories

Carroll followed *Wonderland* with the sequel *Through the Looking-Glass*, and in both books the first chapters and characters illustrate *passion* without the satisfaction of *action*, the second *action* without a *state* of destination, the third *state* with confused *positions*, and the fourth *positions* that lack *relations*, wisened by patience and perspective. The fifth and sixth chapters illustrate *time*, *space*, and *relations*, confusing and interwoven. The seventh chapters illustrate *quality* of *relations*, the eighth *quantity* and *relations*, and the remaining chapters illustrate *substance*, or lack thereof.

If so, the Black Kitten in the first chapter of *Looking-Glass* illustrates *passion*, who attacks the yarn. We hear Alice pretend she is a hyena, she moves the pen of the King, and we hear the story of the horrible, unexplained Jabberwock. The Red Queen in the second chapter illustrates *action*, which is much like a corkscrew, circling while pushing forward. The corkscrew path keeps turning Alice back, but she pushes on to flowers that can't move or act, and a tree that can only bark. The Queen and Alice run as fast as they can to stay in place.

The Train and Gnat in the third chapter illustrate *state*. The Gnat tells Alice of the rich Snap-dragon-fly, and the poor Bread-and-Butterfly, who 'always' fails to find food enough and dies. Tweedle Dum and Dee in the fourth chapter illustrate *position* poorly, offering Alice opposed *positions* in logic contrariwise.

The White Queen in the fifth chapter illustrates *time*, then changes into the Sheep and illustrates *space*, and remembers whatever happens both ways. She acts like a child, says her shawl is out of *temper*, doesn't see a problem with jam days other than today (punning on Latin *iam*, used in future and past tense), tells Alice to consider how she's grown over her life, how long she's come this day, and what time it is right now to distract herself, as nobody can do two things *at the same time*.

She runs ahead of Alice into the next space, turns into the Sheep, and tells Alice she can look this way or that but can't look all around herself at once, teaching her perspective after begging her attendance like a child. The shop turns into a river and back into a shop, space changing locations. The White Queen can't put things in people's hands herself, as place doesn't *place* things in our hands.

Humpty Dumpty in the sixth chapter is *relations*, as he perches dangerously on a wall, expecting all the King's men to save him if he falls; The Lion and Unicorn in the seventh chapter illustrate *quality*, but unlike most so far in Alice's dreams they do too much rather than too little. The White King sends far too many horses and men, and praises Alice's eyes when she sees nobody. Unlike Hare and Hatter at the Tea Party, Haigha and Hatta overextend themselves for others and overact with Anglo-Saxon attitudes. The Lion and Unicorn over-fight, knocking each other down eighty-seven times each, but share pudding and the Unicorn and Alice agree to believe in each other, with *quality* redeeming *relations*.

The White Knight in the eighth chapter similarly over-invents, illustrating *quantity*, with an endless *quantity* of impractical ideas, has a hive with no bees, a mouse trap without mice, and constantly falls off the horse he rides entirely this way or that. The pair of Red and White Queens in the remaining chapters, from the sums to the banquet, illustrate substance, first sums without substance and then substances changing places at the banquet.

Alice shakes the Red Queen, just as she disrupts the King's Court, saying both are mere form, and then the Red Queen changes form. At first, Carroll did not know what form she should change into, but then, the Red Queen turns into the Black Kitten, such that the Red and White Queens parallel the black and white kittens. In both instances, Alice is frustrated at the adult world of forms, trials and banquets, and shakes herself and others out of it, waking from her dream. Victorian Chess sets were often red and white, instead of black and white, so that the Red Queen indeed would be the equivalent of the Black Queen.

Figure 20. Carroll's Courts as Aristotle's Four Forms of Proposition.

The Four Forms of Proposition and the Rulers of Alice's Dreams

In his *Categories*, Aristotle uses white, pale alarm, and red, blushing shame, as his examples of passive qualities, saying they arise from passions and bodily elements. Carroll pairs the colour white with childhood and life, and the colour red with adulthood and death several times in *Wonderland*. When she reaches the royal rose-garden Alice sees white roses being painted red. In the *Looking-Glass*, the colours white and red take even more prominent places as the two sides of the royal chessboard, with the White Queen a timid child and the Red Queen a governess.

In his published works on Logic, Carroll tells us clearly that a thing can be symbolized with a symbol, just as a symbol can stand for a thing.

The White Rabbit can illustrate *passion* and then *position*, just as *passion* in turn is illustrated by the White Rabbit and then the Black Kitten. *ALL*, *SOME*, *NONE*, and *SOME-NOT* form what logicians called *the Square of Opposition*, and Carroll studied these forms and the modern logic based on them as he wrote *Wonderland*. Carroll's own system of logic uses only *ALL, SOME*, and *NONE*, and he argues that you only need these three of Aristotle's four.

The four royal characters in each of Alice's dreams stand for Aristotle's four forms of proposition, *All, Some, None*, and *Some-Not*, and the character who stands for *SOME-NOT* in each is either silent or disappears, such as the Baker, *some* and *substance*, in the Snark Hunt. In *Wonderland*, the White Rabbit is a royal court character who has his own house and is *some* of this and that, timid and servile but also assertive and demanding depending on his position. The Duchess in the following house is unhelpful and unattendant, *some-not*, unlike the Rabbit and absent in court at the end. The Queen of Hearts, known for screaming *Off with their heads* is *Not*, subtraction personified, and the King of Hearts, who admits all evidence and hates cross-examination is *All*. The King and Rabbit are overly inclusive, and the Queen and Duchess are overly exclusive.

Following *Wonderland*, in the *Looking-Glass* we have four royal court characters, the pair of kings and queens, white and red. The Red Queen like the Queen of Hearts illustrates *Not* as absurdly exclusive, says *all ways are hers*, so *none* are anyone else's, contradicts Alice consistently, shows Alice the distance to travel, but travels no distance herself, *none* as she runs. She tells Alice '*Queens never make bargains*, which suggests it is the queens who are *All* and *None*, with the kings some and some. In the *Looking-Glass*, Alice meets and knows each King following their queen, which illustrates Aristotle's *subalternation*: If we *know NONE*, we *know SOME-NOT*, and if we *know ALL*, then we *know SOME*, *meeting each* in turn. If so, the silent Red King illustrates *Some-Not*, sleeping in the woods, absent from the royal banquet at the end like the Duchess at the court of *Wonderland*.

The White Queen, illustrates *All*, is absurdly inclusive like the King of Hearts, living time both ways, thinking impossible things before breakfast, incapable of *subtraction* under any circumstances, and dashes the full distance of the board. The White King following his queen is, like the

Red King, absent from the royal banquet at the end, out in the common town sharing pudding after cautiously presiding over the lion and unicorn, illustrating *Some* like the cautious White Rabbit. Thus at the end of her adventures, Alice finds herself much like the White Rabbit at the beginning, between *All* and *None* as *Some*, making choices for herself.

Bas Savenije

15 'Which is to be master?' Humpty Dumpty and the Philosophy of Language

One of the extraordinary aspects of *Through the Looking-Glass* is the character of Humpty Dumpty, and his statements about the meaning of words. They have brought him some fame but also qualifications as pedant and authoritarian. However, it would be too easy to discard all his statements about language. I will focus on one of them which has often been cited (*TTLG*: 124–125).

> 'When *I* use a word, it means just what I choose it to mean – neither more nor less.'
>
> 'The question is,' said Alice, 'whether you *can* make words mean so many different things.'
>
> 'The question is,' said Humpty Dumpty, 'which is to be master – that's all.'
>
> To confirm that he is really the master, he adds: 'When I make a word do a lot of work […], I always pay it extra.'

This fragment shows a remarkable resemblance with a statement by Lewis Carroll, formulated some years later: 'Any writer of a book is fully authorized in attaching any meaning he likes to any word or phrase he intends to use' (Carroll 1897: 166).

In this article I will place these statements in the context of the study of language in nineteenth-century England and analyse the framing of Humpty Dumpty in more recent discussions about language.

Historical Background

Ever since Plato's dialogue 'Cratylus', the question of how words acquire their meaning has been debated. And, more specifically, is language natural or conventional? Put another way: do words label with an inherent meaning, mirroring things and concepts, that exist prior to language, or do they get their meaning from conventions, introduced by the *usage* of language?

During the late antiquity and Middle Ages, Aristotle's view remained dominant: names of things differ from language to language but refer to concepts in the mind which are universal to all languages and existed prior to language. If this view is correct, the analysis of a language should be the best source for knowledge about reality. But in the seventeenth century, this view was questioned by the rise of experimental science, when it appeared that things existed which had no name in any language. Philosophers like Bacon (*Novum Organum*, 1620), Locke (*An Essay Concerning Human Understanding, 1689*), Leibniz (*Nouveaux essays sur l'entendement humain*, 1680) and Vico (*Idea d'una grammatica filosofica*, 1740) shared the view that languages are not transcriptions of universally equal, predefined concepts and that each language forms its own patterns. This resulted in a growing interest in the history and comparison of different languages.

Yet, especially in France, the Aristotelian view gained new authority through Descartes and the rationalists, who believed that languages must share a basic structure reflecting universal characteristics of human thought. Efforts to build a new theory of language to replace Aristotelian theories were not followed up. Combined with the relative disinterest of philosophers in language and meaning, this implied that the study of language was back at Aristotle (De Mauro 1967).

The interest in the comparison of languages, however, did not disappear, nor the historical interest. Due to the resulting focus on the origin of language, linguistic studies now began concentrating on the reconstruction of 'mother languages'. Under the name 'philology', a broad range of subjects was combined: etymology, language family trees, and historical and comparative language studies. But there was no interest for syntax and semantics; for these areas one still relied on Aristotle.

In England, Herder's Romantic philology (from 1772) had gained popularity: language as the voice of the people, which was also related to national identity (Dowling 1986). A special year in England was 1786 when two influential but entirely different books on language were published.

The first was *Diversions of Purley* (1805) by John Horne Tooke. Horne Tooke was not interested in the origin of language. According to him all languages share a common underlying structure, consisting of small numbers of names for simple sensations. Other words are so-called abbreviations, incorporated by a historical process, outside the influence of men. 'The business of the mind [...] extends no further than to receive impressions, that is, to have sensations or feelings, what are called its operations, are merely operations of language. A consideration of ideas, or of the mind, or of things (relative to the part of speech) will lead us no further than to nouns; i.e. the signs of those impressions, or names of ideas' (Tooke 1805: 25). The system of language is independent of the mind and it is perfect; it is our understanding of language that is defective. He deduced his detailed theory from a number of *a priori* principles and supported it by a speculative etymological analysis of more than 2,000 words.

The second book was *The Sanscrit Language* by Sir William Jones (1807). He performed an empirical study of ancient languages and separated the study of language from the study of mind. He postulated the common ancestry of Sanskrit, Latin, and Greek and his work provided an impetus for comparative linguistics. But for the follow-up on his work, we must turn to the continent and especially to Germany. Englishmen contributed relatively little to this 'new philology' (Aarsleff 1967).

In Oxford, in the middle of the nineteenth century, philology was at a crossroads. On the one hand side, there was the traditional English approach, combining Herder's Romantic philology and Horne Tooke's etymological speculation. On the other was the new philology based on Jones' work, insisting that languages develop beyond human control according to abstract morphological laws.

In this atmosphere Friedrich Max Müller from Germany was appointed professor in Oxford in 1854; Lewis Carroll met him several times.[1] Müller

1   Carroll had dinner with Müller on 16 February 1863 (*Diaries* Vol. 4: 161) and
    5 November 1875 (*Diaries* Vol. 7: 144). He photographed him and his family on

became rather popular by combining several developments: Horne Tooke, the new philology, Herder's romantic idealism and orthodox religion. According to Müller, the morphological and phonological being of language was decisive for its development, which implied that language takes its course beyond human control: language exists apart from man. He claimed a mythical connection between words and thought, through the faculty of reason, which exists by 'the hand of God' (Müller 1851: 370). According to Dowling (1982: 160), Müller's view of language as an autonomous phenomenon had a dominant influence over Victorian thinking about language. However, despite his popularity he had a controversial reputation and has been called 'one of the greatest humbugs of the century' (Williams 2012: 652).

Language was often described with the help of metaphors, especially organic metaphors, such as a tree or a beehive: 'not made, but growing' (Weaver 2015). But altogether, Aristotle's view on language was the basis, which was strongly connected with his logic – still the predominant type of Logic in the nineteenth century. This implied a form of essentialism, claiming that the names of objects describe their essence.

Humpty Dumpty and Lewis Carroll

This is the context in which Humpty Dumpty uttered the words that Lewis Carroll had put into his mouth: 'When I use a word, it means just what I choose it to mean.' These words show a striking resemblance with the view expressed by Lewis Carroll himself. Consider these two quotes:

> I shall take the line 'any writer may mean exactly what he pleases by a phrase so long as he explains it beforehand'. [...] [No] word has a meaning *inseparably* attached to it; a word means what the speaker intends by it, and what the hearer understands by it, and that is all. (Collingwood 1989: 242 resp. 1899: 136)

---

30 May 1867 (*Diaries* Vol. 5: 247) and wrote a pamphlet about Müller's position at the university (Wakeling 1993: 119–126).

There are two differences between the views of Carroll and Humpty Dumpty. In the first quote, Carroll demands that the speaker gives his explanation *before* his utterance. Humpty Dumpty presents his explanation *afterwards* – his reversal of order between the definition of a word and its utterance is one of the many reversals we encounter in *Through the Looking-Glass* (Hancher 1981: 50). In the second quote, Carroll introduces the hearer as a relevant factor for word meaning, a nuance certainly absent with Humpty Dumpty.

Despite the differences, there remains a striking parallel between their views. First, we see conventionalism: words acquire their meaning from conventions, introduced by the usage of language. Conventionalism is opposed to the naturalism predominant in Victorian language studies. Second, we see nominalism as opposed to realism. Nominalism states that universals, such as general properties, are merely words or labels, not having an existence of their own, as is claimed by realism. And finally, there is the absence of essentialism – the view that names of things define their essence.[2]

We may conclude that both Humpty Dumpty and Carroll diverge substantially from the general view in Victorian England. This is also illustrated by the fact that the *Alice* books contain some indirect commentary on the Victorian view on language as influenced by Müller: Carroll even makes fun of the phenomenon of an autonomous language. Language seems to take over the power in Alice's twisted recitations from rhymes, such as in 'How doth the little crocodile', a parody of Isaac Watt's poem 'Against Idleness and Mischief' (Carroll 1865: 20) and in 'You're old, Father William', a parody of Robert Southey's 'The Old Man's Comforts and How He Gained Them' (Carroll 1865: 63–66). Another example may be observed when the white king's pen is writing in his notebook beyond his control in chapter 1 of *Looking-Glass*. Carroll also makes fun of essentialism when the Pigeon concludes that Alice is a serpent because she has characteristics that the Pigeon considers to be essential to a serpent: 'I've seen a good many little girls in my time, but never *one* with such a neck as that! No, no! You're a serpent; and there's no use denying it. I suppose you'll be telling me next that you never tasted an egg!' (Carroll 1865: 72–73). Finally, although Carroll's

2   For a theological discussion of linguistic essentialism, see Chapter 7.

Logic is to a large extent based on Aristotle, he does not once mention the term 'essence' in the description of his classification process or elsewhere.

Humpty Dumpty in More Recent Theories on Language

Humpty Dumpty's 'When I use a word, it means just what I choose it to mean' is often cited in debates about language, mostly as an absurd claim. Humpty Dumpty is framed as being pedant, authoritarian, or worse because he wants to decide himself about the meaning of the words he uses. He has 'so long been typecast as the ultimate verbal outlaw that he has become a useful symbol of a theoretical extreme' (Hancher 1981: 50).

But in the context of Carroll's time, the essence of Humpty Dumpty's claim was not his personal power, but rather the denial that words are 'the master', with their own intrinsic meaning. We better focus on his question: 'Which is to be master?' This is a relevant question and a useful instrument in the analysis of every theory of language. Which is to determine the meaning of words? Does the speaker have any power?

Let us look briefly at the relevance of this question for some more recent theories of language and also consider how Humpty Dumpty was framed in their context.

In the beginning of the twentieth century, Ferdinand de Saussure developed a language theory, characterized as 'structuralism' (1916). He distinguished between *langue* and *parole*. *Langue* is a single organizational structure for both human speech and reason, not to be confused with *parole* or 'speech'. This language structure itself creates its signs and their relations to each other. It exists as a whole: the constituent parts do not exist independently and individuals or the community do not have power upon the system. Therefore, the system leaves no possibility for individuals to be master of word meaning.

According to Rivero (2010: 20–22) Humpty Dumpty's claim 'gives rise to the apparent chaos of nonsense', since he provides an argument for the individual's freedom to introduce changes to the language system: to change the rules at will beyond the alternatives already present in *langue*. However, this possibility is excluded in *langue*.

Ludwig Wittgenstein, when he was young, worked with Bertrand Russell on a formal language system which would be suited to formulate knowledge about reality, based on an isomorphic relation between language, thought, and reality. Later in his lifetime, Wittgenstein seriously changed his opinion about language: he focused on the actual usage of language and laid the basis for what has become 'ordinary language philosophy'.

In his new view language is essentially social; language use is part of the activities of a community and words get their meaning from the way they are used by this community. He used the term 'language games' for the combination of language and the activity into which it is woven. We must look for a word's use in a specific game to get its meaning. When we treat words in isolation from the situations in which they are used, we end up in puzzlement: 'Philosophical problems arise when language goes on holiday' (Wittgenstein 2009: 23). There is no room for a speaker to be master of meaning: the community's language game is the master.

According to Kind (1990: 38), Humpty Dumpty provides a clear illustration of 'language on holiday'. Pitcher (1965: 603) calls Humpty Dumpty one of the most deeply 'anti-Wittgensteinian' characters in Carroll's work, since Wittgenstein attacks the idea that what a person means when he says anything is essentially the result of his performance of a mental act of intending his words to mean just that.

Interesting examples of the framing of Humpty Dumpty may also be found when we take a look at *pragmatics*. Where *semantics* is concerned with sentence meaning, pragmatics is concerned with the speaker's meaning: the sentence in combination with its context. In the 1960s Paul Grice formulated his theory of *Implicature*. What a speaker means with a sentence is not necessarily the meaning of the sentence. Although the utterer's meaning is not logically entailed by the sentence, it is clear to a well-informed, competent audience. That is, if the speaker sticks to the rules of conversation ('maxims'), such as being relevant and not saying what you know to be false. In this view the speaker *can* have his own meaning and within a number of restrictions be master.

Grice is frequently criticized for underestimating the importance of general convention for word meaning and has been characterized as another Humpty Dumpty: 'An extreme version of this position had already been satirized long before Grice's lifetime by Lewis Carroll in the person of Humpty Dumpty' (Hanks 2013: 90).

Talking about the context of an utterance, we also see studies analysing meaning in relation to power between speaker and audience. Lakoff (1993) interprets the question 'Which is to be master' in a broader sense than the relation between speaker and words. According to her it also concerns the relation speaker – audience. Authority and language reinforce and create each other: those who have power, have also the power to decide about the meaning of words. This relationship between language and power is made explicit by Humpty Dumpty who 'for all his arrogant elitism' fits perfectly in Lakoff's vision of the *Alice* books as 'a commentary on power, its uses and abuses' (Lakoff 1993: 384). Also Bourgeois (2002: 40–41) refers to the 'intensified representation of word power' of 'Carroll's proud egg'.

Conclusion

Humpty Dumpty preaches a conventionalist and nominalist theory of meaning. Lewis Carroll's view is also conventionalist and nominalist, but somewhat more nuanced, and can therefore be considered a commentary on the developments of the study of language in nineteenth-century England, and more specifically, the contributions to it from Oxford. Both views contend that words derive their meaning from conventions which are introduced by the usage of these words and diverge from the general view on language in Victorian England that words have their own intrinsic meaning, independently from speakers.

Humpty Dumpty's statement is often quoted in debates about the philosophy of language and mostly to point to a pitfall that has to be avoided. Generally spoken, Humpty Dumpty's statement that he can give words any meaning according to his own preference, may be called over-simplified or be questioned with good reasons. His question 'Which is to be master?', however, was highly relevant in comparison with the predominant view on language at that time. Moreover, it provides a useful tool in comparing and characterizing different views on language.

Part VI

Publishing, Adapting, and Commercialization

Justine Houyaux

16 Through the Surrealist Kaleidoscope: Louis Aragon's 'Lewis Carroll en 1931' (An Annotated Translation)

Almost seventy years after the first publication of *Alice's Adventures in Wonderland*, Surrealist poet Louis Aragon (1897–1982) finally provided French readers with a proper introduction to Lewis Carroll.[1] While Carroll's works were not unheard of in France, they had not prompted as much interest as they had in his homeland, and certainly not as much passion as they would later on.

Reception studies are, at their core, the examination of the afterlife of texts, not only of how they are perceived and received by given readers at a given time, but also, and above all, of how they create new meaning(s) throughout their spatial and temporal trajectories. In that respect, Aragon's 'Lewis Carroll en 1931' is of vital importance if we want to understand the way French speakers (in France, and in many Francophone countries) apprehend and comprehend the *Alice* books and how they perceive the author himself.

That 'Lewis Carroll en 1931' had never been translated to English before is surprising. As demonstrated by the constant flux of new books, articles, TV documentaries, and dissertations dedicated to Lewis Carroll, Carrollian scholarship is an ever-expanding worldwide affair.[2] However,

---

1   The author would like to thank Monsieur Jean Ristat, executor of the Louis Aragon estate for granting her the translation rights to the text of which he is the copyright holder.

2   To have a more specific idea of the sheer number of publications dedicated to Carroll that appear each year, one might consider having a look at the archive of *The Lewis Carroll Review*, whose purpose is to gather and review all new Carrollian research, and whose editor never runs out of books to review.

there was a time when major critical texts did not cross geographic and linguistic borders as swiftly and as easily as they do now. Because some of those texts were not translated then, they have never been translated at all, and they seem to have left an enduring gap in what we know of the reception of the *Alice* books. As such, and though it may appear counter-intuitive at a time of constant movement forward, a glance in the rear-view mirror to take in older works that have previously been overlooked might contribute to the development of our field. That, at least, is the reflection that inspired the translation presented here, together with a few contextual clues.

A False Start

To understand why *Through the Looking-Glass and What Alice Found There* appeared so late on the French market, it is first necessary to look at the early history of the French translations of its prequel.

Translations, among many other things – and as painful as it is for a translator to admit it – are commodities. And like most commodities, they obey the laws of the market in that they have to meet some sort of demand. No one besides Dodgson seemed to wish for a first French translation of *Alice's Adventures in Wonderland*. His aspiration to see his work translated is well documented. In a letter to Alexander Macmillan on the 24th of August 1866 (not even a year after *Alice* was published), he showed the first indication of how much he had the translation process upside down:

> I should be glad to know what you think of my idea of putting it into French, or German, or both, and trying for a Continental sale. I believe I could get either version well done in Oxford. (Cohen 1979a: 93–94)

He added that the books should be sold 'at a much cheaper rate, if one may judge of their light literature by the specimens that reach England' (Idem: 94). Interestingly, Louis Aragon seemed to agree with Carroll's assessment of the quality of French children's books, albeit some sixty-six years later, as we will see in 'Lewis Carroll in 1931'. Judging by his letters,

Macmillan was cautiously enthusiastic at first, then seemed to drop the subject entirely unless Dodgson specifically asked him a question about the hypothetical translations.

The first French translator of *Alice's Adventures in Wonderland* turned out to be Henri Bué, the son of Jules Bué, a French teacher at Oxford (Romney 1981: 89). The translation was completed by 10 June 1867, less than two months after it was commissioned, and Macmillan had twenty proofs printed out by August (Weaver 1964: 35–36). Dodgson was on his Russian tour with Henry Liddon at the time (Cohen 1979b), and upon his return to Oxford, the French translation was no longer on his list of priorities; so much so that in 1868, Macmillan had to remind him that the French *Alice* had been 'in type for nearly a year' (ibid., 40). Dodgson finally wrote to Macmillan that it could go to press in May 1869.

Dodgson's ambition to export the translation was to be met with disappointment. Copies of Bué's translation in their 1870 edition, printed by Macmillan but bearing the Hachette mark, were put on display in their Parisian bookshop. Four copies of that edition have survived (Nières-Chevrel 2015: 241). In December 1869, there were no reports of sales, and though Macmillan assumed it was normal not to receive word until January, he still asked Hachette's agent to 'put the question' (Weaver 1964: 48).

Dodgson's subsequent letters seem to point to a slight shift in the target audience for the translation. If at first his idea was to try for a continental sale, it later evolved into a more didactic project (prompted, one might reasonably hypothesize, by the absence of commercial success of the book on the French market):

> [...] an idea has occurred to me – (small and cheap, and without pictures) 'Selections' from the book, with the French in a parallel column, for the use of those who wish to learn French for *conversational* purposes for which it is a great help to know the equivalent from English idioms that will keep occurring to the mind. (Weaver 1964: 46)

In the end, Dodgson, ever the bursar-at-heart, decided that the French venture was not worth its cost, and neither were the other translations:

> Please make a memorandum *not* to advertise the French, German, and Italian Alices any longer – the sale does not pay for the advertising. You will say perhaps that without advertising there will be no sale. My answer is 'I greatly prefer no sale at all to

selling at an annual loss. In money matters, zero is preferable to a negative quantity.'
(Weaver 1964: 49)

What looked like the end of Carroll's French adventure, fortunately, was
only the beginning.

Fayet, Gilson, and the Anonymous Translators

While nowadays it is customary to name the translator of a book (at
least in France) on its first page, on the title page, or – in the worst-case
scenario – in the copyright section, it was not always so. The journey of
Alice in France is peppered with anonymous contributions up until well
into the 1990s[3] (Nières-Chevrel, Houyaux and Collière-Whiteside 2015).
In the period between Bué's translation and Aragon's *Lewis Carroll en
1931*, the status of the French editions of *Alice's Adventures in Wonderland*
was as follows: in total, only two new French translations had been produced over the span of sixty-one years since Bué first translated the text,
and one of them was an anonymous translation whose author's identity
will probably forever remain a mystery.

The state of affairs is even clearer when it comes to *Through the Looking-
Glass and What Alice Found There*, as the text simply was not on the map
before 1930, when Les Œuvres Représentatives published Marie-Madeleine
Fayet's combined translation of the two *Alice* books with illustrations by
Jean Hée (Figure 21). Paul Gilson's translation followed shortly in 1931
(Denoël et Steele, anonymous illustrations, very likely by André Noyer;
Figure 22). The real boom of French translations of the *Alice* books would
have to wait until the 1950s (forty-one adaptations and reprints of *AAIW*,
two reprints of *TTLG*) and 1960s (thirty-five new titles for *AAIW*, among
which three unabridged translations, eight new titles for *TTLG*), with

---

3   This only takes into account full-text translations, as when it comes to adapta-
     tions (and especially the various Disney books, comics, and other derivatives) or
     abridged editions, all bets are off as to whom the translator might be.

the subsequent somersaults in the publishing frenzy prompted both by the earlier translations and illustrations entering the public domain and by the renewed interest of readers in the source material each time a new movie adaptation was released.

Until 1931, though, the *Alice* books were nothing more than children's entertainment and were regarded as such, due to the almost uniquely French propensity to maintain at all costs the divide between what is considered adult literature and children's books. The interwar period, however, was a time of profound mutations in France and turned out to be a rich era for children's literature. The First World War had left the specialized publishers in a creative and economic 'slump' (Renonciat 1991: 25) that resulted in French children having to make do with either the socially antiquated Comtesse de Ségur's cruel tales or the already technologically outdated stories by Jules Verne. On top of the rising cost of producing books, publishers had to face considerable competition from illustrated magazines and *bandes dessinées* (Idem: 33). In the 1920s, it had become increasingly clear not only to the publishers but also to the rest of French society that something had to be done to support children's books.

As the French Reconstruction was in progress, and with the support of the Book Committee on Children's Libraries,[4] scattered individual and collective efforts made it possible to build public libraries based on the British and American models, and to open *L'Heure joyeuse* in Paris, the first library exclusively dedicated to children in 1924 (Ezratty and Valotteau 2012: 46), four years after its Belgian counterpart in Brussels (Leriche 1969: 10). Publishers then resorted to the creation of collections as a marketing strategy, with Hachette at the very heart of the movement (Renonciat 1991: 40). La Sorbonne even awarded its first PhD for a doctoral dissertation on the history of childhood literature in 1923 (Latzarus 1923). The material conditions, the aesthetic context, were finally favourable to the emergence of Lewis Carroll in France.

---

4   An American philanthropic group whose goal was to help France and Belgium with their 'educational reconstruction' (Maack 1993: 257).

Publishing, Adapting, and Commercialization

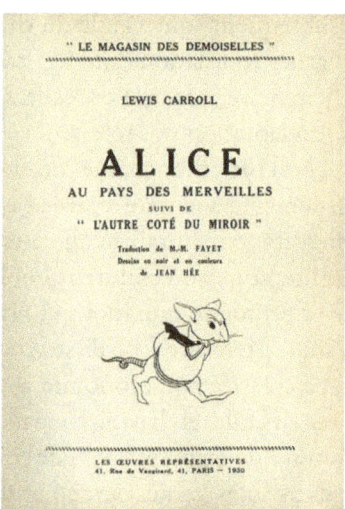

Figure 21. *Alice au pays des merveilles suivi de L'autre côté du miroir* (1930), French translation by Marie-Madeleine Fayet (illustrations by Jean Hée). Justine Houyaux's private collection.

Figure 22. *Alice au pays des merveilles* (1931), French translation by Michel J. Arnaud (illustrations by André Noyer) and *La Traversée du miroir* (1931), French translation by Paul Gilson. Justine Houyaux's private collection.

Aragon, the Surrealists and Carroll

Auxiliary doctor, *Croix de Guerre* recipient, intellectual, French resistant, poet, Dadaist, Cubist, Surrealist, communist; these are a few of the words that describe Louis Aragon (1897–1982). While his legacy lives on in France and in Francophone countries, his works remain relatively rarely translated to English, perhaps, as a 42-year-old dissertation already suggested at the time, because of 'his ideology' (Griswold Looney 1979: i). Notwithstanding this unfortunate misalignment with mainstream Anglo-Saxon political creeds, Louis Aragon's texts remain pivotal to whomever is interested not only in Surrealism, but also in the curious trajectory of Carroll's works in French.

Indeed, one might argue that without Aragon, *Alice* would have needed a few extra years to become popular across the Channel, if at all. Why he was so interested in Carroll's works can now be regarded as obvious; after all *Wonderland* and the *Looking-Glass* world share some common traits with the Surrealist imagination, from their framing as dreams to the apparent disjunction of sequences, not to mention the return to childhood they offer. 'The mind that dives into Surrealism re-lives with exaltation the best part of its childhood,' wrote André Breton in the first *Manifeste du surréalisme* (1924/1988: 340). In 1929, Aragon gave *The Hunting of the Snark* its first French translation, despite the reticence of Nancy Cunard (his publisher and lover at the time) to see him undertake such a challenging task, which he tackled, much like Carroll before him, without having the need to respond to any market demand for the text (Houyaux 2022: 7). 'Lewis Carroll would have understood Surrealism', he allegedly replied (Cunard 1969: 44).

'Lewis Carroll en 1931' appears on pages 25 and 26 of *Le Surréalisme au service de la révolution*. On the previous page, Max Ernst produces an inflammatory book review in which he proclaims his disdain for a long-forgotten religious treatise on 'conjugal duties' penned by a certain Bishop of Le Mans, reminds his readers that '[l]ove is the greatest enemy of Christian moral', and, for good measure, concludes on a note against 'the clerical and capitalist police'. On the next page, a fascinating series of semi-abstract drawings by Yves Tanguy titled 'Weights and Colours' is presented next to a quotation by Lenin. These are interesting neighbours for our text, in which Aragon castigates with severity the mediocrity of French children's books. The three pieces together also happen to make for a fairly representative sample of what could be found in any given issue of the magazine.

The periodical itself was short-lived; after just six issues (two every year, none in 1932), it disappeared in 1933. Its list of contributors, however, reads like a proper *Who's Who* of 1930s Paris: Marcel Duchamp, Joan Miró, René Char, Salvador Dalí, Paul Éluard, Man Ray, Tristan Tzara, Alberto Giacometti – just to name a few – all wrote for or had their art published in at least one issue of *Le Surréalisme au service de la révolution*, on top, of course, of its founders, André Breton and Louis Aragon.

Translating *Lewis Carroll en 1931* (in 2021)

This translation of Aragon's French introduction to Lewis Carroll might sound a little odd at times, for the simple reason that it *is* odd. While it is not a Surrealist text, it is very much a text *by a* Surrealist, and the best attempt at conveying it into another language necessarily requires maintaining its oddity, its phenomenology, as well as its reeling, writhing, and fainting in coils. Retaining *what* is said, and trying, as best as possible, to keep *how* it is said is a perilous exercise – all the more when it comes to a text that has aged, written by an author who, in many aspects, has not, on a subject that never will.

Hence the annotations, which aim to fill the gaps that exist on a twofold cultural plane: not only are some references so French that they might elicit no reaction other than puzzlement from an audience who is not familiar with the language, but some of them are in fact so dated that no more recognition could be expected from twenty-first-century French readers, no matter how linguistically unambiguous the text might at first appear to them.

Translating is choosing, and as popular wisdom has it, it is often betraying,[5] even when the translator sets out with the best intentions. I hope readers will forgive the shortcomings that can only be blamed on yours truly, as well as Aragon's occasional disregard of the objective facts, and will still find pleasure in (re-)discovering such a remarkable text.

Lewis Carroll in 1931[6]

Nothing much is to be said of Lewis Carroll [1], who happened to be a professor and sported a blond pointed beard [2], at the time of Queen Victoria – that is, at the worst time of boredom and puritanism. At a time when in the definitively United Kingdom, any thought was considered as so shocking that it would have hesitated to appear at all, by a singular detour, that of literature and nonsense, poetry made its great voice heard in opposition to academic declamations of the Victorian era through simple children's books. It was between 1870 and 1880 [3] in particular that Lewis Carroll wrote *Alice in Wonderland, The Hunting of the Snark, Through the Looking-Glass,* as well as several poems.

[1] This Carrollian trope of the 1930s is echoed by Virginia Woolf. 'But the Reverend C. L. Dodgson had no life. He passed through the world so lightly that he left no print' (Woolf 1939: 47–48). Over 120 years after his death and with dozens of books published about him every year, this Carrollian is happy to report that both Aragon and Woolf might have been slightly misled in their judgement.

[2] Where Aragon found that piece of information is not quite clear, and this translator certainly had never heard of it; she would be grateful to anyone who would feel like taking up the challenge of locating a photograph of Charles Dodgson sporting a beard, whether it be blond, pointed, or otherwise.

[3] While he is not that far-off, one might wonder upon which sources Aragon based this assertion.

5   Or, more optimistically, 'Translating is being honest enough to settle for allusive imperfection' (Leyris 1974).
6   All the notes on the right-hand side of the text (noted in square brackets) are Justine Houyaux's annotations. Louis Aragon's two footnotes (noted between regular parentheses) have been pushed to the end of the text.

The Hunting of the Snark was published on the same date as *Les Chants de Maldoror* [4] and *Une Saison en Enfer* [5], for those who enjoy synoptic chronologies. Among the shameful chains of those days of slaughter in Ireland, of inexpressible oppression in the factories where the ironic accounting of pleasure and pain advocated by Bentham was drawn up, and while the theory of free trade was emerging like a defiance in Manchester (1), what had become of human freedom? It was resting, as a whole, in the frail hands of Alice, where it had been laid by that peculiar man, who did not inspire mistrust as he had never uttered an irreverent word against anyone but chess queens, and who showed children the absurdity of a world that only existed on the other side of a looking-glass [6].

However, how he must have hated the English life (*the path of honour*), the bourgeoisie, the aristocracy of his time, he, the poet who never even thought of joining the glorious list of ink slingers [7] [whose works] were taught in the very schools where he made a living. It is impossible to find in Carroll's works the reflection of a respectable man in any way, shape, or form. No moral of which his wide-eyed little readers could make use. There is no public position, no family tie that could shelter any real-life puppet from being ridiculed and turned into an imaginary character (nowhere else, perhaps, is so perceptible the very origin of poetry as here).

[4] *The Songs of Maldoror*, by Isidore Lucien Ducasse under the pen name of Comte de Lautréamont, is a long prose poem first published in 1869 and somewhat forgotten until the Surrealists took an interest in it and claimed it was one of the seminal works of the movement.

[5] *A Season in Hell*, Arthur Rimbaud's extended poem and the only book he ever published of his own volition (1873). Evidently, neither *The Songs of Maldoror* nor *A Season in Hell* was published on 'the same date' as *The Hunting of the Snark* (1876).

[6] If this sentence might appear as a rather long diatribe, readers should bear in mind that its French original is about 10 per cent longer.

[7] Aragon says *rimailleurs*, which more or less translates to 'poor rhyme-makers' or 'poets who do not know exactly what they are doing'. It is, in all cases, an expression charged with contempt.

That Alice's freedom starts with the absence, in the world where she dives, of Mrs Her Mother and of any holder by way of delegation of any parental authority; that there is no question of good conscience or of the obligations attached to a little girl's education; and that, at last, there is not the shadow of a reference to any good Lord in that universe – it is all impossible to account for with chance as an excuse. What can be said of the singular endeavour of that professor who showed rugrats [8] poems that flattered their own tastes, without worrying about their duties as loyal subjects of her Majesty (2), and who, in order to write his own poems, cunningly appropriated the rhythms of classical poems that the children were made to learn by heart so that later on, those young brains would not be lost in a lobster's quadrille between Tennyson and Longfellow? One has to assume that he did not like English poetry any more than he liked English life and that he had an outlook on education which is conveyed fairly clearly in *Alice in Wonderland*, when [Alice] sets down the Duchess' baby, who has just turned into a pig, and she has nothing more to say about the metamorphosis than *'If it had grown up, it would have made a dreadfully ugly child: but it makes a rather handsome pig, I think.'*

*

[8] Aragon uses the French word *mioches*, a delicious slang turn of phrase that regards little children as (occasionally loveable) nuisances.

Alice's success might well be the greatest poetical success of our time: poetry, which our world has reduced to be the enjoyment of a privileged few, is avenged. Unlike *Robinson Crusoe* and *Don Quixote*, which were written for adults but slipped into the realm of childhood – up to the point, one might say, that they are only the subjects of the most stupid picture books – Lewis Carroll's works imposed themselves to the admiration of adults by way of childhood [9]; editions in all languages have been published at an unparalleled rate and they have been met with incomparable success.

In 1930 [10], a combined edition was published by Les Œuvres Représentatives under the title *Alice au pays des merveilles, suivi de L'Autre côté du miroir* [11]. In 1920 and 1931, De Noël et Steele published two separate volumes, the latter of which was titled *La Traversée du Miroir* [12]. I must admit I favour the combined edition by far, as it is fairly literal and complete, despite some clumsiness in its language. The two volumes, on the other hand, should be characterized as adaptations, and truncated at that, rather than translations. I cannot see the use, even in a book that is meant to be found under the Christmas tree, to translate the various poems of *Alice* into bad French verse when word-for-word translation is much closer to living poetry. All of Carroll's cruel game against traditional English poetry can only be lost in the poor doggerelizing of his verse [13].

[9] This probably is the first printed occurrence of the almost hundred-year-long French debate on whether the Alice books are meant to be read by children or by adults, which is not of the greatest interest but has the merit of keeping occupied a couple of scholars who would otherwise be rather bored. It is, however, symptomatic of the dual reading of the books in French.

[10] As Isabelle Nières-Chevrel points out in *Alice in a World of Wonderlands* (2015, vol. II: 278), the year of publication of this translation is subject to doubt. While the copy at the Bibliothèque Nationale de France specifies 1931 on the cover, it bears 1930 on the title page. It is possible that the text was printed in 1930 and given a cover at the beginning of the following year.

[11] Literally retranslated to English: *Alice in Wonderland, followed by Through the Looking-Glass*.

[12] *The Passage Through the Looking-Glass*

[13] Dodgson himself had come to this conclusion in 1867: 'The verses would be of great difficulty, as I fear, if the originals are not known in France,' he wrote, 'the parodies would be unintelligible: in that case they had better perhaps be omitted' (qtd. in Wakeling 2015: 80), which certainly does not prevent French translators continuing to try over 150 years later.

Finally, we do not drum *The Song of Hiawatha*, for example, into French children; it is therefore pointless, in order to obtain a desirable number of feet, to torture words that are only there for arbitrary reasons by dint of a syntax peppered with useless inversions and elliptical archaisms. While all English children remember the poems in *Alice*, I challenge any French child to show the slightest interest in a stanza translated as follows:
'*Huîtres, ce monstre me désarme* [14],
Je n'ai pas assez de sanglots
Pour prendre part à vos alarmes
Mais que ne suis-je point manchot?'
Not to mention that it has nothing to do with the original text. To form an idea of the extent of this unfaithfulness, it might be enough for one to compare Mr Gilson's rhymed translation to M.-M. Fayet's literal approach. One will see that the following two verses
[15]:
Le Charpentier dit seulement
Vous avez mis trop de beurre
are transposed by Mr Gilson as:
Le Charpentier: Monsieur m'écœure.
Respirez vos sels d'ammoniac
Et ne mangez pas tant de beurre.
And the rest is in the same vein.

[14] This (practically unrecognizable) French translation of a portion of *The Walrus and the Carpenter* sounds quite old-fashioned and frankly contorted. Here is a literal retranslation:

'*Oysters, this monster is disarming me*
I do not have enough sobs
To take part in your alarms
Whatever for am I not one-armed?'
[15] Both excerpts are translations of the last couplet of the sixteenth stanza of *The Walrus and the Carpenter* (*TTLG*),
Original: *The Carpenter said nothing but*
   '*The butter's spread too thick!*'
Fayet: *The Carpenter only said*
   '*You have put too much butter*'
Gilson: '*The Carpenter: You sir, sicken me.*
Sniff your smelling salts
And do not eat so much butter.

The prose text is not shown any more deference. One wishes that someone would write a critical edition of the works of Lewis Carroll [16] that would remind translators of their duty to remain faithful *even* to nonsense. There is, however, little chance of seeing such serious work come into being, as our contemporaries are so busy with James Joyce, mind, that the tone of his translator spills over the tone of Carroll's. 'Oh well, leave us alone,' will those gentlemen say, 'what a load of pettifog for a book that's nothing more than a stocking filler!' A critical edition, with notes, a bibliography, and the translations, yes sir! Each and every one of the translations.

At a time when the intellectual nourishment of children is limited to detective novels, colonial-driven adventures where the protagonists gleefully kill negroes [17], wartime tales in which small French children in velvet shorts heroically stand up to Big Berthas, etc., it goes without saying that I would never forgive myself for preventing children from reading a book that might make the blue-white-red stories of *Titi-Roi-des-Gosses* [18] pale in comparison, or the photographs in *Détective* [19] look yucky. That being said, it seems impossible to me to continue to consider as *only* for children those poems that are, in all aspects, so precious in that they document the very history of human thought.

[16] Later in life Aragon may have seen his wish come true, if his interest in Carroll persisted, with some of the early work on the translations of *Alice's Adventures in Wonderland*, more particularly Warren Weaver's *Alice in Many Tongues* (1964). The first comprehensive work on the French translations of the *Alice* books only appeared six years after the poet's death (Nières-Chevrel 1988), but it did open the door to a rather robust scholarship dedicated to the question.

[17] Without any form of historical revisionism, readers should not be misled by such a choice of word. Literally, *où l'on tue bien du nègre* is an ironic turn of phrase which shows disdain both for the practice of killing indigenous populations in the then-French colonies and for the fact of creating so-called edifying fiction based on it. Aragon had written about his rejection of the colonial model before (Aragon 1925: 25), and the Surrealists had called for the boycott of the Colonial Exhibition in Vincennes in May 1931 (Breton et al. 1931).

[18] *Titi Roi des Gosses* (Titi King of Kids) refers to a heavily illustrated novelisation by Pierre Gilles (1927) of the film *Titi 1er, Roi des Gosses* (directed by René Leprince in 1926) in which a group of children living around Butte Montmartre are caught up in a plot to kidnap a princess.

I am rather unsure that everything we have to know about Humpty Dumpty (whom Mr Gilson calls *Gros-Œuf* [20], as he sees fit to gallicise the text, naming Kitty *Poil-de-Suie* [21] when *Minet* [22] is obviously part of his vocabulary) is the same as what children glimpse in their joy of not knowing whether he is donning a belt or a tie. I am not satisfied with imagining that such a strange invention belongs to the realm of oddity; it is our very world with its readiness to accept such explanations which has always seemed of the uttermost oddity to the poets. I do not believe that a taste for oddity accounts for the story of the tart thief in *Alice's Adventures in Wonderland*; I do not believe it, because I have attended my share of trials on this side of the looking-glass [23], and nothing will convince me that the course of justice is any different from what it is here. If we compare it to the Barrister's dream in *The Hunting of the Snark*, we can get a clear idea of what Carroll thought of the judges, what is considered as a crime, witness evidence, due course, and the interchangeability of the roles in a tribunal. All those are mere examples, along with Lewis Carroll's poetry which does not require any further comment. And I

... *put*

   My fingers into glue
   Or madly squeeze a right-hand foot
   Into a left-hand shoe,
   Or if I drop upon my toe

[19] *Détective* is a weekly magazine founded in 1928 whose coverage of crimes was so crude that courts ordered not to sell it to minors on more than one occasion. Surprisingly, the magazine survives to this day.
[20] 'Big-Egg'
[21] 'Soot-fur'
[22] *Minet* is the exact functional equivalent to Kitty in French.

[23] It is perhaps not a coincidence that Aragon mentions the absurdity of trials in this very issue of *Le Surréalisme au service de la révolution*, published in December 1931. A month before, another text of his, *Le front rouge*[7] ('The Red Front'), a call to arms in which he referred to the 1917 protests against the execution of Sacco and Vanzetti and targeted the police (Aragon 1931b: 39–46), had caught the attention of the French courts. The journal in which it was published, *Littérature de la révolution mondiale*, was seized by the police and Aragon charged with anarchist propaganda, incitement to civil disobedience, and criminal incitement (Breton 1932). The trial started in January 1932, and Aragon was acquitted in June of the same year, but the whole affair eventually resulted in Breton and Aragon drifting apart over whether poetry should be autonomous from the party lines (Mahot Boudias 2016), despite Breton's effort to have judicial immunity granted to his friend.

7   Most contemporary scholars refer to the poem as *Front Rouge* and not *Le Front Rouge,* though it was published with its determiner in *Littérature de la révolution mondiale.*

A very heavy weight, perhaps it will
conjure up, to me, the old man whom
the Knight knew, and whom Alice met –
and who may be the author himself,
laying explanations in his song:
   … Je poursuis les yeux de morue [24]
Parmi les splendides bruyères
Et je les transforme en boutons de gilet
Dans le silence de la nuit.
Et je ne les vends pas pour de l'or,
Ni pour une pièce d'argent brillant.
Mais pour un sous de cuivre,
On peut m'en acheter neuf.
Je pioche quelquefois pour trouver des
pains beurrés
Où j'installe les rameaux sourciers pour
les crabes,
Je cherche quelquefois des collines herbues
Pour les roues de cabriolets
Et voilà la façon (il cligna de l'oeil)
Dont je gagne ma fortune.

[24] *He said 'I hunt for haddocks' eyes*
   Among the heather bright,
   And work them into waistcoat-buttons
   In the silent night.
   And these I do not sell for gold
   Or coin of silvery shine
   But for a copper halfpenny,
   And that will purchase nine.
   'I sometimes dig for buttered rolls,
   Or set limed twigs for crabs;
   I sometimes search the grassy knolls
   For wheels of Hansom-cabs.
   And that's the way' (he gave a wink)
   'By which I get my wealth –

Aragon

1. 'Mais *gloire* ne veut pas dire *un joli*
   argument méprisant objecta Alice. [25]
   – Quand je me sers d'un mot, dit
   Humpty-Dumpty d'un ton méprisant,
   il signifie exactement ce que je veux
   qu'il signifie… ni plus, ni moins.'
   (Lewis Caroll,[8] À travers le Miroir,
   Chap. VI.)

[25] 'But "glory" doesn't mean "a nice knock-
down argument"', Alice objected.
   – When *I* use a word,' Humpty Dumpty said
in rather a scornful tone, 'it means just what
I choose it to mean – neither more nor less.'
(Lewis Carroll, *Through the Looking-Glass and
What Alice Found There*, Chap. VI).

2. *Quand l'Angleterre attend, je me retiens*
   d'achever [26]
   C'est une formule pompeuse mais banale
   (La Chasse au Snark, Crise 4eme)

[26] Aragon quotes his own 1929 translation
of *The Hunting of the Snark* (Aragon 1929/
2010: 39), which is very close to the original
English text:
'For England expects – I forbear to proceed:
'Tis a maxim tremendous, but trite…'
(*The Hunting of the Snark*, Fit the Fourth).

8   Sic.

Concluding Remarks

What is remarkable with 'Lewis Carroll en 1931' is that it already fore-shadowed most of what Carroll's French trajectory would be. On top of the elements presented in the annotations to the text, Aragon's afore-mentioned call for a 'critical edition with notes [and] a bibliography' was soon answered by serious scholars, such as Jean Gattégno whose extensive scholarship on Carroll culminated with the ultimate accolade: in 1990, La Bibliothèque de la Pléiade,[9] the prestigious leather-bound collection, dedicated a volume to the works of Carroll. Jacques Papy's 1961 schol-arly translation was the first to present the text with erudite footnotes; Laurent Bury's (2009) is the latest. What is even more remarkable is that in his pioneering Carrollian paper, Aragon focused mainly on excerpts from *Through the Looking-Glass and What Alice Found There*; perhaps, had that specific text not caught his imagination so forcefully, the entire trajectory of Carroll's works in France would have been different.

Whether Carroll, had he lived to be 100 years old, might have found something of interest in Surrealism can at best only be answered with conjectures; that the Surrealist movement took an interest in Carroll is incontrovertible. Salvador Dalí,[10] René Magritte,[11] and Max Ernst[12] are among the artists whose works refer to Carroll one way or another. Even Henri Parisot, whose French translations of the *Alice* books are reprinted

9   It is commonly admitted that one has' made it' as an author when La Pléiade pub-lishes one's work; unfortunately, such honour is generally only bestowed upon dead writers, and among them, even fewer hail from shores outside of France.

10   Twelve heliogravures and a four-colour etching as the frontispiece for the luxury 1969 Random House edition (see Lockwood 2016: 43–54).

11   *Alice in Wonderland*, oil on canvas (1946).

12   Max Ernst produced eight pen-and-ink drawings with collages cut from magazines to illustrate Lewis Carroll's *Hunting of the Snark* in the translation of Henri Parisot in 1950, sixty-eight illustrations to *Logique sans peine* (from *The Game of Logic*) in 1966, as well as the thirty-six lithographs for *Lewis Carroll's Wunderhorn* in 1970, on top of three paintings whose titles are linked to Wonderland: *Alice in 1941* (1941) *For Alice's Friends* (1957), *Alice Sends a Message to the Fish* (1964).

and re-edited practically every year, was a familiar face in Surrealist circles. When Aragon turned his attention to other topics, André Breton took up the torch and invited others to read Carroll 'by an allusion, a quotation, the insertion of his name in a list' (Nières-Chevrel 2005: 157) in many of his texts.

This Surrealist claim to Lewis Carroll has become such a common-place that from time to time, Carroll is referred to as a sort of proto-Surrealist: '[F]or French readers, Carroll's pre-Surrealism is what matters most,' writes Jean-Jacques Mayoux in his foreword to an umpteenth reedition of Parisot's translation (Mayoux 1979: 19).

More surprisingly, in an exercise to satisfy her own curiosity, the author of this paper has been pursuing the links that exist between the French translators of the *Alice* books and the Surrealists, whether it be through work collaborations, personal relationships, or life trajectories. These links are presented in the graph below, with many more yet to be uncovered.

The French *Alice* exists as a balancing act; the books assume a very different identity from the one they have in English. They are simulta-neously books for children and books for adults (when the adults do not simply confiscate them from the realm of childhood). They are both great literature and childish entertainment. They never quite manage to choose, just like they never quite manage to shake off their Surrealist coat – and why should they?

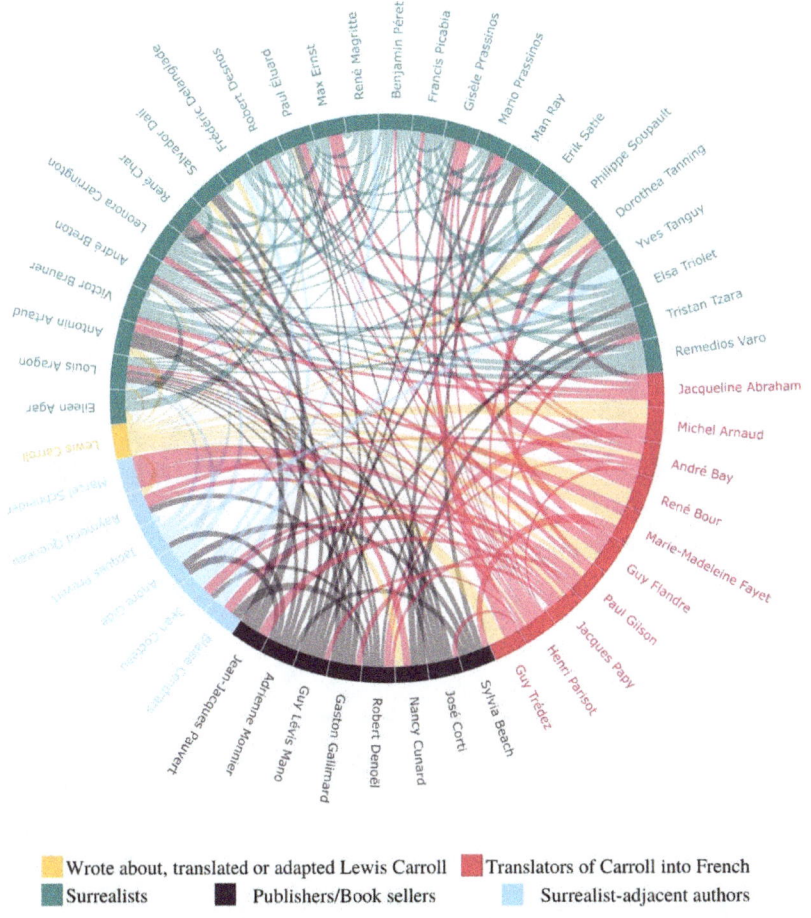

Wrote about, translated or adapted Lewis Carroll   Translators of Carroll into French

Surrealists   Publishers/Book sellers   Surrealist-adjacent authors

Figure 23. Links between the Surrealists and Lewis Carroll.

Amanda Lastoria

17 Reflections on Book Publishing Strategies: A Guide to Types of Editions of the *Alice* Books

Through the Looking-Glass (*TTLG*) has a complicated publishing history that is interdependent on the success of editions of the lead title, *Alice's Adventures in Wonderland* (*AAIW*). Whereas *AAIW* often stands alone and is a case study in diverse approaches to book publishing (Lastoria 2019b), *TTLG*'s publishing history reveals some of the most successful *Alice* repackagings. The author Lewis Carroll himself strategized the titles' early market segmentation with a range of editions (Cohen and Gandolfo 1987; Jaques and Giddens 2013; Lastoria 2019a). Publishers twin *TTLG* with *AAIW* in such a way that it has been published in companion editions, omnibus editions, *Alice* sets, series editions, and series sets.[1] Even the keenest *Alice* collectors and scholars can muddle these publication types. Publications of *TTLG*, like those of other sequels, are defined by their relationship to the publication of another text.

Publishers trade on that textual relationship by giving consumers and readers paratextual clues of it. Paratexts, a term developed by French literary theorist Gérard Genette (1987/1997), are messages that frame the author's text. The editorial apparatuses, art directions, and marketing of editions of *TTLG* are paratexts that deliberately tie it to editions of *AAIW*. Each edition is the material articulation of a specific publishing strategy; it is evidence of why the publisher released the book, who it targets, and what it means. Still, such clues can go unnoticed, or observed but unconsidered,

---

1   For pairings of the two works and the implications see Chapters 16 and 18.

by audiences. This chapter differentiates between five types of *TTLG* editions. It provides examples of each type, explaining publishers' rationales for them and suggesting the impacts they have on how consumers receive the books and readers receive the story.[2] This guide to publishers' repackagings of *TTLG* thus helps unpack reasons for the enduring appeal of *Alice*.

Paratexts as Publisher Tools and Consumer Clues

A book's paratext contains clues for the audience to decode which type(s) of edition it is. Scholarship in the fields of book collecting and bibliography tends not to outline the typical characteristics of types of editions – indeed there are various working definitions of the word 'edition' (Lastoria 2019b: 41–42) – and this is understandable because they are not focused on publishing strategy. 'Edition' is best understood here as it is used in the contemporary publishing industry, where it means a repackaging. Genette's literary theory of the paratext is not focused on publishing strategy either, but it critically acknowledges the role of the publisher and offers an umbrella concept of elements found around and outside of the author's text that influence its reception. Publishers manipulate the paratext in order to sell books; consumers can decode the paratext in order to ascertain which type(s) of edition a book is and, further, its target audience(s) and genre(s).

Genette writes that '*paratext = peritext + epitext*', where peritext is elements that are materially appended to the volume that contains the text and epitext is messages that are 'circulating, as it were, freely, in a virtually limitless physical and social space' (Genette 1987/1997: 4–5, 344). Among

2   The examples of each type of edition that are provided in footnotes below are ones
     that have been recently published in print in English by large commercial British
     and/or American publishers in order to maximize accessibility for readers who
     wish to locate and handle them. However, these types of editions have long been
     published in English and in translations by small- and medium-sized commercial
     houses, private presses and self-publishers from all over the world.

peritextual messages that most clearly communicate edition type are the series list, typically placed in the book's prelims, or front matter, and the blurb, or description, placed on the back cover or dustjacket. These peritexts explicitly articulate an edition of *TTLG*'s relationship to an edition of *AAIW* and/or locate it within a curated series of other titles. The look and feel of the book are more subtle peritextual evidence of edition type. It includes cover design, illustrations, paper stock, binding method, and so forth done in a style that mirrors the related edition of *AAIW* and any other books with which the publisher has strategically grouped it. The most curious of Carrollians can search for epitextual messages in, for example, the publisher's marketing materials (e.g. advertisements, catalogue, website, retail displays, etc.), interviews given by the edition's illustrator, book reviews, and publication announcements in periodicals such as *The Bookseller* and *Publishers Weekly*. Like series lists and blurbs, epitextual marketing materials explicitly articulate an edition of *TTLG*'s relationship to other books in order to sell them as a pair or group. From cover design to advertisements, paratextual messages are tools for the publisher and clues for the audience.

Carroll had substantial input on what amounted to the paratext of Victorian editions. As *Alice*'s first art director, he established the books' original aesthetics, market trajectories, and generic classifications (Lastoria 2019a). To complement *AAIW*, Carroll art directed three English-language publications of *TTLG*, which he published with Macmillan: two companion editions (red-cloth edition of 1872, and People's Edition of 1887) and one omnibus edition (People's Edition of 1888). He positioned the works as elegant, giftable fairy-tale books for upper- and upper-middle-class children with the original, red-cloth editions, and then as relatively accessible fairy-tales for middle-class children with the People's Editions, or the 'cheap' editions, as he called them (Cohen and Gandolfo 1987: 77; Susina 2010: 34, 37). For all of these editions, children were the primary target audience and adults were the secondary target audience. Carroll was an entrepreneur (Susina 2010), and he and Macmillan made a market-savvy team that established *Alice* as a publishing phenomenon. Publishers the world over continue to take their lead in releasing companion and omnibus

Publishing, Adapting, and Commercialization

Publishing, Adapting, and Commercialization

editions of the *Alice* books, but publishers have since also bundled *AAIW* and *TTLG* with other titles and released additional types of editions.

Types of Editions

Companion Editions[3]

Companion editions are like bookends; they form a matching pair. A companion edition of *TTLG* mirrors the art direction, including the design and production values, of an edition of *AAIW*. The two books have, for example, related cover art and similar treatment of illustrations, as well as the same trim size, page layouts, typography of body text and display text, paper stock,[4] inking, binding method, and so forth. They are published by the same publishing company and have a similar – if not the same – regular retail price.[5] A companion edition of *TTLG* may have been published at (roughly) the same time as *AAIW* or it may have been published some time later. If the companion edition of *TTLG* was published

---

3   *Through the Looking-Glass* 'Little Folks' Edition' [facsimile] (Macmillan Children's Books, 2016), 9781509820498; *Alice Through the Looking-Glass* (Andersen, 2016), 9781783444120.

4   Production values such as paper may vary because the availability of materials can change between the production cycles of companion editions. For example, a paper mill may discontinue a product between the production of *AAIW* and the production of *TTLG*. In such instances, the publishing house's production controller opts for a viable paper that is similar to the one used for the first book. Availability, quality and cost are changeable, and compromises are common. Practical constraints inevitably impact the look and feel of the final books that get published.

5   The regular retail price of each of the two companion editions may vary depending on, for example, increased production costs. Variance usually correlates to paper prices, which are the single greatest hard cost of book production. Although *TTLG* has a higher word count than *AAIW* and therefore tends to require more paper when typeset similarly to *AAIW*, publishers often list the same regular retail price for each of *AAIW* and *TTLG*. This parity reinforces their position as companion editions.

simultaneously or within months of *AAIW*, the publisher intended to publish both books from the start. If *AAIW* was published years before the companion edition of *TTLG*, it may be an indication that the publisher was testing the market with *AAIW* before releasing *TTLG*; that is, the publisher's delayed investment in a companion edition of *TTLG* is a likely indication that their edition of *AAIW* was a relatively strong seller. Companion editions are sold individually – which means it is possible for audiences to discover *TTLG* before *AAIW* – but they may also be sold in a set. More unusually, their success may also lead to the publication of an omnibus edition that maintains an art direction shared by companion editions. This was the case when Carroll adopted his art direction of the People's Editions of *AAIW* and *TTLG* for the People's Edition omnibus.

Omnibus Editions[6]

'Omnibus' is defined in the *Oxford English Dictionary* as, '[a] book consisting of several reprinted works by a single author, or various items of a similar genre, usually published as a single volume' (OED 2004). Omnibus editions of *TTLG* bind it together with *AAIW*; two books for the price of one, so it seems to the consumer. Yet is common for omnibus editions of *AAIW* and *TTLG* to ignore *TTLG* in the title on the cover of the volume.[7] This indicates that the publisher believes the lead title, *AAIW*, is the consumer draw; *TTLG* is a bonus rather than the focus. The text of *TTLG* bulks up the book, making it look and feel more substantial and justifying a higher retail price than *AAIW* would merit on its own. In either case, omnibus editions combine texts to paradoxically equal higher profit for the publisher and good perceived value for the consumer. Omnibus editions may be framed by paratexts, particularly

6   *The Complete Illustrated Lewis Carroll* (Wordsworth, 2008), 9781840220742; *Alice's Adventures in Wonderland 150th Anniversary Edition with Through the Looking-Glass and What Alice Found There* (Vintage, 2015), 9781784870171.
7   *Alice in Wonderland* (Vintage, 2010), 9780099541547; *Alice in Wonderland* (Norton, 2011) 9780393932348.

design and production values such as the quality of materials and image reproduction, that position them as low-, mid-, or high-end editions. Some publishers expand on *AAIW* and *TTLG* by binding them with other texts written by Carroll in omnibus editions called, for example, *The Complete Works of Lewis Carroll*.[8] Depending on the paratexts, consumers perceive these tomes as giftable, collectible, and/or scholarly.

Alice Sets[9]

Two-volume *Alice* sets pair *AAIW* and *TTLG* – one volume per title – as one item with one ISBN. Like omnibus editions, consumers acquire both texts together. Unlike omnibus editions, readers read each story in its own volume, which is typically less cumbersome than an omnibus. *Alice* sets house both volumes together in a box, or slipcase. The two volumes may have been previously published and sold individually as companion editions or they may be published for the first time as a slipcased set. Much more rarely, publishers divide each of the *Alice* texts into multiple small, slim volumes – roughly one volume per chapter – and sell them as a set of more than twenty volumes. *Alice* sets sell *AAIW* and *TTLG* simultaneously, and the fact that they are two different texts is readily apparent. They are therefore presented to the consumer on more equal footing than when they are released as companion volumes with staggered publication dates or packaged in an omnibus edition. However, they are slipcased such that *AAIW* is on the left and *TTLG* is on the right, which is a linear representation of the order in which the stories were written by Carroll and published by Macmillan. As with omnibus editions, in which *AAIW* precedes *TTLG*, the publisher communicates to the consumer an ideal order in which to read the texts. Unlike an omnibus edition, though, the modular nature of *Alice* sets enables the consumer to rearrange the sequence of the *AAIW* and *TTLG* volumes within the slipcase. A sturdy

---

8   *The Complete Works of Lewis Carroll* (Macmillan, 2011), 9781907360442.
9   'The Complete Alice' [two-volume set] (Walker, 2009), 9781406319699; 'The Complete Alice' [twenty-two-volume set] (Walker 2018), 9789526533025.

slipcase adds substantial expense to the publisher's production costs, but it represents even greater perceived value to the consumer; the publisher can charge more for this value-add than it costs them. *Alice* sets are positioned by publishers, and therefore perceived by consumers, as giftable and collectible.

Series Editions[10]

Multi-book series publish each of *AAIW* and *TTLG* in individual volumes or an omnibus and as part of a curated group. A series consists of multiple titles that are classic children's books, Victorian novels, or banned books, for example. Like companion editions, books in a series are published by the same publisher, sold individually, and share common design elements. A cohesive series design frames a range of texts as a group. Unlike the above types of editions, the branding of *AAIW* and *TTLG* in a multi-volume series is not primarily about *Alice* – the identity of each book in the series is subsumed by the collective identity that the publisher ascribes to the whole group. Series publication grows the audience for any one title because the series attracts not only consumers who are interested in that particular title but a broader consumer base that is interested in the larger theme of the group of works; publishers of a series edition can sell *Alice* not only to *Alice* fans but to readers of, for example, canonical literature. The theme that publishers use to connect a group of works frames how readers of a series edition perceive Carroll's work, whether it be dusty among classics or dangerous among banned books. It would be highly unusual for *TTLG* to be published in a series without *AAIW*. Therefore, the publication of a series edition of *TTLG* is led not only by *AAIW*, as it is in the above edition types, but by the theme of the series.

---

10   'Penguin Clothbound Classics' (Penguin Classics, 2009), 9780141192468; 'Puffin + Pantone' (Puffin, 2017), 9780425289280.

Series Sets[11]

Series sets combine either all the books in a series or only the most popular books in a series in a slipcase. The consumer whose decision to purchase a series set is driven by other titles that are contained in the set acquires *TTLG* incidentally. For this reason, these editions of *TTLG* might be the least desired of all editions. Like *Alice* sets, a series set is sold as one item with one ISBN. The series may be published only as a set or the books in the series may also be published individually. In that case, the regular retail price of a series set is usually cheaper than the cost of purchasing the books individually. Although a slipcase means that the publisher incurs extra manufacturing and packing costs when bundling the books, it is to their advantage to sell, say, a dozen slipcased books at once rather than hoping that a consumer will purchase the same number of books over a longer period. While purchasing a set means that the average price per book drops, the consumer must be willing and able to invest more money at one time. Series sets are therefore among the least accessible editions of *Alice*.

Conclusions

Publishers ensure that there are editions of *Alice* for everyone. These five types of editions that include *TTLG* can blur because a book may fall into multiple categories. For example, an omnibus edition of *AAIW* and *TTLG* can be published in a series and a companion volume of *TTLG* can be included in a two-volume *Alice* set. Moreover, each type of edition appears in multiple retail categories and genres; there are juvenile fairy-tale companion editions just as there are young adult fantasy companion editions. As *Alice* ages, the competition for each edition gets stiffer.

11 'Children's Classics Collection' (Macmillan Collector's Library, 2018), 9781509894741; 'Friendship Word Cloud Classics' (Canterbury Classics, 2020), 9781645173830.

Market saturation drives publishers to refine each edition's paratexts, pushing unique selling points that target new audiences and make collectors of existing *Alice* audiences. By recognizing how and why publishers manipulate paratexts to distinguish editions of *Alice*, consumers and readers can be more critical in their acquisition of the books and their reading of the texts.

Publishers overwhelmingly view *TTLG* as an afterthought or value-add. Likewise, some consumers acquire *TTLG* incidentally. All publications – and many consumer purchases – of *TTLG* depend on *AAIW*; some also depend on other titles by Carroll and/or disparate titles that publishers strategically curate into thematic groups. *TTLG*'s value in commercial book publishing lies in bundling it with other texts, enabling publishers to sell more units and/or justify higher retail prices than they could without *TTLG*. This is a commercial reality that tempers *TTLG*'s critical success and, at the same time, fosters it. By packaging *TTLG* with *AAIW* and other titles, publishers introduce *TTLG* to a greater and more diverse audience than it would have if it were published in stand-alone editions.

Catherine Richards and Clare Imholtz

18 *Through the Looking-Glass*, and What Henry Savile Clarke Did There

Introduction

The only *Alice* stage adaptation 'with the sanction of the author', Henry Savile Clarke's musical dream-play *Alice in Wonderland* premiered at the Prince of Wales's Theatre, London, on 23 December 1886. Charles Dodgson had suggested that Clarke limit himself to either *Wonderland* or *Looking-Glass*; Savile Clarke chose to dramatize both, but did follow Dodgson's advice to keep the two stories separate – Act I being *Alice's Adventures in Wonderland*, and Act II *Through the Looking-Glass*. The separation of the production into *Wonderland* and *Looking-Glass* invites comparisons between the two, and it was immediately apparent to Dodgson that, theatrically, Act I (*AAIW*) was much more effective than Act II (*TTLG*). This article examines some of the more substantial changes that were made to improve the second act as a theatrical piece, by Savile Clarke himself, and by others after his death, thereby highlighting some of the problems encountered in dramatization of literary works, and of Carroll's *Alice* books and *Looking-Glass* in particular.

Revisions Made during the First Production of 1886–1887

In staging the *Alice* books, Savile Clarke attempted to remain as close as possible to the original stories. Although he omitted substantial sections of each book (e.g., the pool of tears episode in *Wonderland* and the

Publishing, Adapting, and Commercialization

looking-glass insects in the sequel), he retained Dodgson's own words for the dialogue, whilst writing some additional songs. Dodgson also wrote some new material, including extra dialogue for Cook and new lines for 'The Voice of the Lobster'. Walter Slaughter composed the music and Mdlle Rosa Abrahams was the choreographer. After seeing the play for the first time on 30 December 1886, Dodgson wrote in his journal: 'The second act was flat [...] the "Walrus etc." had no definite finale' (*Diaries* VIII: 311).

Dodgson had already sent many requests and suggestions to Savile Clarke on how the play should be staged; there now followed a multitude of suggestions (and, on occasion, demands) regarding changes and improvements. The libretto was revised during January 1887, the three substantial alterations all being made to Act II, *Through the Looking-Glass*.[1]

The Removal of Scene 1 – Going Through the Looking-Glass

Originally, Act II began with Alice going through the looking-glass (Savile Clarke 1886, 1st edn: 31). However, this whole scene was removed and it is uncertain why such a significant change was made. Of the extant letters from Dodgson to Savile Clarke, none mentions this short scene and there are no comments in any reviews that tell us whether or not it was done well. It may be that Savile Clarke thought the scene was unnecessary and removed it to prevent the second act becoming too lengthy. Possibly Dodgson thought it undignified for Alice to climb up on to the mantlepiece – regarding the 1888 revival, he commented that it was not graceful for Isa Bowman to mime Father William kicking the Youth downstairs (Lovett 1990: 94).

---

1   The original libretto, dated 1886, was on sale to the public and the first version states clearly on the cover 'First Edition, Under Revision'. That there are *two* revised versions (with small differences between them), was first reported by Lindseth (2008). These appear to have both been first published in January 1887, although dated 1886.

It is ironic, perhaps, in this context, that Alice's costume for the whole performance was based upon that looking-glass scene. Initially, two costumes were planned – a 'greeny-blue' woollen dress and matching large hat for Act I, and cream satin with sash and swansdown trim for Act II – the latter considered appropriate evening 'drawing room' attire for a little girl. Due to a 'technical stage difficulty', it was decided that Phoebe Carlo would wear the same dress throughout, the 'Looking-Glass dress' being considered more stage-worthy (*Court Circular* 1887) (Figure 24).

Figure 24. Phoebe Carlo's looking-glass dress of cream satin with swansdown trim – suitable winter evening attire for a little girl in the drawing room. From *The Sphere,* 22 December 1900, 14.

However, the removal of the mirror scene meant that the audience was no longer shown the concept of the Looking-Glass – and all the interesting ideas that accompanied it: that Alice was now in a world of reflections where things worked backwards. The audience was left with Tweedledum and Tweedledee, who became a comedy-clown-act, and 'Alice in Chess-Land' (Richards 2022). As we shall see, later producers re-introduced this missing scene.

The Addition of a *finale* to 'The Walrus and the Carpenter'

As a poem, the ending of 'The Walrus and the Carpenter' ('They'd eaten every one'), followed by a still silence, works very well. However, this clearly was not effective on stage. Dodgson wrote some extra verses (*Diaries* VIII: 312), in which two 'Oyster ghosts' exact revenge on the Walrus and the Carpenter, by sitting and stamping on their chests, giving them indigestion. This was followed by a third ghost dancing a hornpipe, which would have provided a lively and dramatic *finale* (Savile Clarke 1886 2nd edn: 40–41). Dodgson thought this new ending a great improvement, writing to Savile Clarke on 2 February 1887: 'The "Walrus & Carpenter" now seems to end quite triumphantly, [...] & I think the ghostly Sailors' hornpipe a capital addition' (Lovett 1990: 69). This modification became one of the highlights of the show and during the provincial tour, Dot Hetherington's hornpipe was singled out time and time again. The Mayor of Worcester was sufficiently impressed to present her with half a sovereign (*Worcester Chronicle* 1887). The scene remained popular in the revivals. Phyllis Beadon was most put out when a mistake in the programme (soon corrected) wrongly credited Vesta de Becker as the hornpiper (*Morning Post* 1898), and in 1906 it served to launch Phyllis Bedells' career as a dancer[2] (*Evening Standard* 1906) (Figures 25a and 25b).

---

2   In 1920, Phyllis Bedells was a founding member of the Royal Academy of Dancing.

Figure 25a. Photograph of Phyllis Beadon, Oyster Ghost and Hornpiper.
From *The Sketch*, 18 January 1899, 518.

Figure 25b. Photograph of Phyllis Bedells, Oyster Ghost and Hornpiper. From Bedells, Phyllis, *My Dancing Days* (Phoenix House, 1954 between pages 40 and 41).

An Extra Scene and Song ('The Waits') for the White Knight, and the 'wretched horse's head'

The White Knight's part, played by the young Stephen Adeson, was considerably expanded. Stephen was an experienced performer and a good singer – he and his younger brother Charles had both been principals in the 1884 Savoy Christmas production, the *Children's Pirates of Penzance*, which Dodgson saw twice (*Diaries* VIII: 161, 163). Stephen sang 'Jabberwocky' early in Act II and had a couple of lines later on. In the revised version, Stephen is given a full scene with Alice (re-instating the conversation between the Knight and Alice about his inventions), and an extra song by Clarke, 'The Waits' (together with the Red and White Queens). Alice is then crowned on-stage (rather than off-stage as previously), by the White Knight (Savile Clarke 1886 2nd edn: 49–51).

In his letter to Savile Clarke 2 February 1887, Dodgson writes: 'The "Waits", too, seem *tolerably* successful: the thing itself is very funny I think: but the White Knight is much hindered in producing his due effect by that horse's head' (Lovett 1990: 69). Indeed, a good many of his 'suggestions' to Savile Clarke related to details of stage business. Expanding the part of the White Knight had served to emphasize problems with his costume, the large mask-helmet obscuring his face and muffling his voice. Dodgson continues '[Jabberwocky] sung through that wretched horse's head, has no effect *at all*, & is almost inaudible.' There are no photographs or descriptions of the White Knight's costume, but a drawing in *St Nicholas* (January 1888) suggests that, at some point, a large roundel was cut out for his face (Figures 25a and 25b)-.

It is interesting to find that the two 1886 revised versions of the libretto differ in this scene. The first revised version – held by the British Library – which we believe to have been printed 18 January 1887,[3] has four verses for 'The Waits' and includes the following lines (taken directly from the original book):

> *[fumbles at his helmet.*

AL. Thank you very much, shall I help you off with your helmet?

> *[she takes it off.*

WHITE KNT. Now one can breathe more easily.

However, the next version, (also dated 1886 and, we believe, first printed 24 January 1887 followed by several re-printings), as well as the 1888 edition lack the final verse of 'The Waits' and the reference to the Knight's

---

3   Goodacre (qtd in Lindseth 2008) suggests that the print numbers on page 54 of the 1886 revised libretto reflect a sequence number followed by the print date.

helmet. Removing the Knight's helmet after his entrance would have solved the issue of it muffling his singing voice (for 'The Waits' if not for 'Jabberwocky') but these lines were cut from the libretto very speedily, suggesting that they were never performed before an audience. We suspect that removing the Knight's huge helmet on-stage would have proved very awkward for two child actors, especially since Stephen was likely taller than Phoebe, and that instead, the lines were omitted and a large hole made for Stephen's face, showing that staging decisions, such as costuming, were on occasion dictated by practicalities, although Dodgson himself considered that masks should always partly show the actor's face (Lovett 1990: 82).

Revisions Made for the First Revival of 1888–1889

For the 1888 revival at the Globe Theatre, again the main changes were to Act II, expanding the banqueting scene (Savile Clarke 1888: 54–55). The song 'To the Looking-Glass World' was changed to the shorter 'Sound the Festal Trumpets', which was written by Savile Clarke, but retained much of Dodgson's imagery from the previous song. A second song was added, based upon the White Queen's fish riddle, and eventually given to Edith Vanbrugh. However, Dodgson complained the 'Fish Song' was not effective – the tune was depressing and the musical accompaniment too loud (Lovett 1990: 89). He wanted Edith to be given a song he had written specifically for her part as the Rose, to brighten the Garden of Live Flowers scene (Lovett 1990: 91), but the Rose song was never used, possibly because Clarke and the managers already knew the play would be ending soon. The song, sadly, has not survived. It is notable that later revivals do as Dodgson suggested and give one of the flowers a solo.

Overall, Dodgson was much happier with the aesthetics of the 1888 production, writing to Winifred Holiday: 'I'm glad you liked the *Alice* play: it was ever so much better than in 1886' (*Letters Vol II*: 729–730). However, almost certainly, an important factor was that the Rosa troupe (about whom Dodgson had complained bitterly and repeatedly) had been removed from the cast, rather than the relatively minor changes made by Savile Clarke. Despite Dodgson's exhortations: '[W]ould it not be well to begin by taking the existing [libretto], and ruthlessly erasing all that experience has shown to be flat and ineffective?' (Lovett 1990: 82), Savile Clarke had simply added a bit more of Dodgson's own text, and an extra song. One issue that Dodgson himself highlighted and Savile Clarke never attempted to address was the 'silent ending' – after Alice finished her last speech she then had to wait with nothing to say or do while the curtain slowly came down (Lovett 1990: 70–71). It was unfortunate that the 1888 revival closed prematurely – ostensibly due to the actions of the School Board who were fining the parents of child-actors for non-attendance at school, although Richard Mansfield, the Globe manager, reportedly wanted to take over the stage to prepare his own production of *Richard III*. Dodgson's letters to Clarke show that he thought the play was closing due to poor sales, but, as the above shows, that appears unlikely.

Post Dodgson and Clarke

There were no further professional revivals until Christmas 1898. Henry Savile Clarke had died in 1893; the publicity surrounding 'Lewis Carroll's' death in January 1898 served to renew public interest and the piece was staged almost every year, in London or in regional venues, for the next thirty years. As Dodgson himself told Savile Clarke (Lovett 1990: 98–99), it is to be expected that a revival will, to some extent, differ from its predecessors, presenting a fresh interpretation: perhaps a new song here or a new dance there. However, although it was clearly a popular show, accounts of the later revivals reveal that these, too, included much more substantial revision of *Looking-Glass* than *Wonderland*, strongly suggesting that Savile Clarke (who had resisted Dodgson's plea for a ruthless reworking) had not fully resolved the issues with dramatizing *Looking-Glass*, and it was incumbent upon later producers to do so.

Arthur Eliot and Horace Sedger (1898)

The 1898 revival, staged at the Opera Comique, was a grand affair and brought in a substantial profit for producers Arthur Eliot and Horace Sedger. There were some notable alterations to Act II, with 'The Waits' replaced by the White Knight singing 'A-sitting on a Gate' – a move

Figure 26a. Initially, the Knight's huge mask-helmet appears to have a mesh or gauze patch to allow him to see and breathe. From *The Illustrated Sporting and Dramatic News*, 1 January 1887, 10.

Figure 26b. A later illustration shows a large hole in the Knight's mask-helmet, fully exposing his face. From *St Nicholas*, January 1888, 186.

back closer to the original book. Even more interesting, the character of Hatter (played by co-producer Arthur Eliot) appears in the cast-list for Act II for the first time. We have not identified any description of his role in *Looking-Glass*, but there is a photograph of Hatter on his horse (Figure 27); we speculate that he took over the lines of the White Knight talking about his little box and other ('mad') inventions, but clear evidence is lacking. Most likely, Arthur Eliot wanted to give himself an extra comic scene; the White Knight still appeared, and retained the song 'Jabberwocky' as well as singing 'A-sitting on a Gate'.

Figure 27. Photograph of Mr Arthur Eliot as Hatter, on his horse. This is clearly not
from the 'mad tea-party' scene. It is possible that this is from Act II, with the Hatter
taking over some of the lines of the White Knight. From *The Sketch*, 18 January
1899, 517.

Seymour Hicks (1900, 1906, 1907, 1908)

The established musical comedy star Seymour Hicks staged his first revival of Savile Clarke's 'dream-play' for Christmas 1900, with his wife
Ellaline Terriss as Alice and himself as 'Mad Hatter'. (The character of

Publishing, Adapting, and Commercialization

'*Mad* Hatter' had made his *debut* the previous Christmas in Morell and Mouillot's touring production with Valli Valli as Alice.) He undertook a substantial reworking and, together with Aubrey Hopwood, wrote some new songs for himself and his wife. Walter Slaughter, the composer for the original play (with whom Hicks worked on a number of other musical plays), was more than willing to collaborate and write music for the extra songs. Seymour Hicks made more significant alterations and additions to Act II than to Act I, these being mostly retained by later producers.

Mirror Scene and a Flower Song

Seymour Hicks re-introduced the mirror scene at the beginning of Act II and devised a gauze 'mirror' with two pairs of actors (Alice and Cheshire Cat) mirroring each other's movements on opposite sides (*Penny Illustrated* 1900, *Truth* 1906). This special effect was retained by Stedman's Company (*Royal Court Theatre Souvenir* 1909). 'The second act opens with a capital scene before the Looking-Glass for Alice and the Cheshire Cat' (*Dundee Courier* 1910). Hicks' introduction of the Cheshire Cat (another *Wonderland* character) into *Looking-Glass* reflects his own *Alice*-imitation *The Sleepy King* published in 1898 (later staged as *Blue Bell in Fairyland*), in which a talking cat is the companion of the protagonist (Richards 2020).

Hicks also later made a change that had been suggested by Dodgson, giving the Lily a solo – 'Flowerland' – sung by the young Carmen Sylva[4] in 1906 (Slaughter 1906: 91–94). This addition, too, was retained by Stedman's Company, who used it to showcase their soprano, Ada Danks, in 1909.

---

4   Later known as Sylva Van Dyck.

'Mad Hatter' Becomes a Leading Character in *Through the Looking-Glass*

Although Arthur Eliot had first introduced Hatter into Act II, it was Seymour Hicks who greatly expanded the part (his role, now 'Mad Hatter'), most likely to allow him to play 'leading man' to his wife Ellaline Terriss as Alice (Richards 2020). In addition to writing new material and new songs for himself as Hatter, Hicks appropriated the White Knight's lines (*Times* 1900). Thenceforward, 'Mad Hatter' was established as *the* leading male character throughout the play, meeting Alice in Wonderland but continuing to have a substantial role in Looking-Glass Land; the character of the White Knight was permanently eliminated.

The leading man and leading lady must have a duet – 'Tell me, Hatter' was a new song and dance written for Alice and 'Mad Hatter', Terriss and Hicks, (Slaughter 1906: 57–60) and remained part of the shows by later producers (both Stedman's and Bernhardt), critics referring to 'the duet between Alice and the Hatter' as late as 1925 (*Kent and Sussex Courier* 1926). During the performance, Alice stood behind the Hatter, whose arms were hidden, with Alice providing the arms in a comic routine (Figure 28). Hicks also had his own solo, a boisterous new song with a catchy chorus, 'When the Wind is in the East' (also known as 'Follow my Leader'), which appeared towards the end of Act II (Slaughter 1906: 81–85).

Stedman's Company (1909–1911, 1914–1918, 1920–1923)

Stedman's Academy took over in 1909, seeing a commercial opportunity in 'Alice' both to put on a popular and profitable show, and to advertise the Academy as a stage school and to exhibit their star pupils. They retained Hicks' introduction of 'Mad Hatter' as a major character in *Looking-Glass* and inserted some promotional features of their own. From 1910 onwards, Stedman's added to the Walrus and the Carpenter episode an 'Under-the-Sea-Scene' – an increasingly elaborate and spectacular ballet

Figure 28. Photograph of Marie Studholme as the 1906 Alice and Stanley Brett as 'Mad Hatter' performing 'Tell me, Hatter' with Alice standing behind the Hatter and providing his hand-movements. From a postcard, Rotary Photographic Company, 1906.

by Lillian Loeffeler (Stedman's dancing-mistress) that included an Oyster Queen emerging from an illuminated shell, and an ingeniously lit backdrop of 'living fish effects'. 'Special mention should be made of Under the Sea, where a back cloth, representing the sea, has a large number of fish of all descriptions swimming about quite naturally' (*Stage* 1915). 'Oyster Queen' was a completely new character, created to showcase the dancer Hilda Boot's obvious talent. This 'Under-the-Sea-Scene' became an essential part of the 'Stedman Alice' and must have been quite a spectacle. This was not simply another dance. This was intended to be a show-stopper. Hilda Boot's reminiscences give some idea of what it was like:

> I was the 'Oyster Queen'. They made a big under-the-sea ballet where 'Tweedledum' and 'Tweedledee' are on the beach with oysters or whatever, and the oysters have taken them and brought them down under the sea, you see. It was a very nice ballet. The backdrop was like sea things. And I had a *big* silver shell – I have pictures of that too – big silver shell that closed up. 'Twas closed and I was sitting on a stool. The whole inside was little electric light bulbs. I had a three-quarter length tutu. The top of it was rainbow-coloured chiffon. The inside of the shell was done like the inside of an oyster shell, and the top of my bodice was pearl. Very sweet. At a certain moment in the ballet, the shell would open and I'd be sitting there in all my glory, in all my curls. I would get up and we had lobsters under there and coral; there was a very nice coral *pas de quatre*. And various little oysters running around. The oysters had to bind up 'Tweedledum' and 'Tweedledee', a whole little ballet. It was really quite nice. (Butsova 1975)

After appearing in *Alice*, Hilda Boot joined Pavlova's ballet company (as Hilda Butsova). In 1914 Stedman's new dancing *protégée* and Oyster Queen was Vera Clark (later Vera Savina of the *Ballets Russes*), followed by Eileen Jowitt and Gertrude Martin. Stedman's clearly believed they had found a 'winning formula' and continued to stage productions featuring their 'Under-the-Sea-Scene' in Looking-Glass Land until 1923. However, unknown to the public, their last three runs made significant losses, ultimately leading to bankruptcy (*Stage* 1929).

The next two full-length revivals of Henry Savile Clarke's dream-play were by Bernhardt's Company, who having produced it once in 1913, took over again for Christmases 1925 (opening at the Royal Tunbridge Wells Opera House) and 1926 (Golders Green Hippodrome). Few details are known of these productions, although they continued to have a flower ballet and oyster ghosts dancing the hornpipe. The last known complete production of Henry Savile Clarke's adaptation that included Act II, *Through the Looking-Glass*, is a single matinée performance with Joy Blackwood as Alice at the Richmond Theatre, London on 22 November 1930, just before she went on to star in Hugh Marleyn's new adaptation of the *Alice* books at the Savoy for Christmas of that year.

Is *Through the Looking-Glass* Less Suited to Dramatization Than *Alice's Adventures in Wonderland*?

The two books, although both very 'Carrollian' in their humour and wordplay, have vastly different structure and content. The question needs to be asked, was Act II 'flat' because of the way Savile Clarke adapted it, or because it is inherently 'less dramatic' than the subject matter of Act I? Whereas audiences of the long nineteenth century were well aware that there were two separate books (the critics made that clear), many people now have not heard of *Through the Looking-Glass*, believing that all the characters originate from one book called 'Alice in Wonderland'. Modern audiences, seeing the 'Alice' character in a stage show or a film, expect to see the Cheshire Cat and the 'Mad Hatter' and feel cheated if they do not. This makes it almost impossible nowadays to judge the merits of *Through the Looking-Glass* as a dramatic piece. Even in the 1930s, Nancy Price felt obliged to include the tea party scene in her production of *Looking-Glass* – audiences expected it! Conversely, it is not unusual for an adaptation entitled 'Alice in Wonderland' to include *Looking-Glass* characters; modern audiences consider the two books as a single entity, reflecting the high-profile film adaptation by Disney in 1951.

Whatever the reasons, Henry Savile Clarke's original version of *Looking-Glass* 'fell flat'. He made some improvements but did not attempt the extensive reworking urged by Dodgson (which may or may not have succeeded). It is beyond the scope of this paper to provide a complete listing of the revivals and all their modifications, but our examples show that, after the deaths of Dodgson and Clarke, later producers took a much more radical and commercial approach to improving the theatricality of Savile Clarke's original – changes which, in all likelihood, Dodgson would not have approved. The evidence is that for more than twenty years, they succeeded, achieving this by reworking the storyline while adding new songs, dances, and stage effects. Although some critics thought that Hicks' modifications detracted from the 'authenticity' sought by Savile Clarke, they do appear to have been successful as a theatrical entertainment and united the two separate acts into a single whole. However, the insertion of the Hatter as a main character into Act II meant that theatrical success came at the expense of losing some of the distinct identity of *Looking-Glass*; Seymour Hicks had, in effect, turned 'Through the Looking-Glass' into 'Further Adventures in Wonderland'.

Part VII

Visualizing *Looking-Glass*

Amy de Nobriga

19 Unseen Narratives: Data Visualization through the Looking-Glass

This practical investigation considers how data visualization can map *Through the Looking-Glass and What Alice Found There*, the theme of 'choice' and how the characters traverse throughout Carroll's text. Data collection and visualization are illustrative methods used to analyse the language in the text through *Distant Reading*: a method that seeks to map the text as data as opposed to a complete piece of prose. I am interested, in this chapter, in data as a means to illuminate the unseen or to quote computational media artist George Legrady 'make visible the invisible' (Gil 2010). Utilizing simple geometry as part of a 'data-drawing vocabulary' (Lupi 2017), it will thus visualize the possibilities embedded in the narrative and subsequently the alternative hidden narratives. As such, this investigation proffers the following question: can geometry be used to visualize data from the text in unforeseen ways to explore its infinite probabilities and possibilities?

'Distant Reading' is a computational analysis of literature, a phrase coined by Franco Moretti (2013: 211) to describe an unorthodox data-centric field of literary study that seeks to visualize the temporal flow of a dramatic plot through two-dimensional signs, vertices (nodes) and edges that can be grasped at a single glance. Moretti has used digital data collection as a means to demonstrate causal relationships between literary fields: a corpus analysis. His *Style Inc.* study sought to examine causal relationships in the titles of 7,000 British novels written between 1740 and 1850 recording everything from title length to the use of pronouns, adjectives, and nouns (2013: 179). Distant Reading, here, is a means to view literary patterns and tropes across space and time. In his seminal work *Conjectures on World Literature* (2000: 57–58) Moretti wrote that Distant

Reading allows a focus on units that are much smaller, or much larger than the text: devices, themes, tropes – or genres and systems. Moretti's own criticism of Distant Reading as a strategy for literary analysis is rooted in the challenges of large-scale data gathering (2013: 211) (as the data gathered for this chapter is focused on one novel, however, 200 pages in the copy used, these do not apply to the same extent). Kathryn Schulz's 2011 article in *The New York Times*, titled 'What is Distant Reading?', criticized Moretti's methodology citing 'to understand literature, Moretti argues, we must stop reading books' (Schulz 2011). Though Moretti's strategy relied heavily on digital data mining due to the vastness of the selected data sets, the present analysis presents a more intimate 'pen and paper' collection. I have never had a closer relationship with the text. As such, it may feel inappropriate to call my own method 'distant reading', perhaps 'reading at arm's length' is more suitable.

When setting out to examine the text at 'arm's length', I needed to define points of choice within the narrative. After reading Gardner's thoughts on Carroll's chess problem at the start of the his 1965 edition of the *Annotated Alice*, and considering '*moves*' in chess, I selected any binary directional or movement-based language as a starting point: for example, up/down, left/right, under/over, forward/back, etc. I relied on simple geometry and arrows as a means of visualizing directional movement of characters throughout each chapter. Critiques of Moretti's simplified visualizations, like Clifford E. Wulfman, would have, perhaps, scoffed at the use of circles, having stated that 'certain illustrative conventions – circles connected by lines or clusters together – offer a false clarity precisely because they are too conventional' (2014: 101). In this case, I disagree: simplicity, in the initial stages of the data-drawing vocabulary allows for complexity to be scaffolded. 'Since clarity does not need to come all at once, we layered multiple visual narratives over a main construct that served as the jumping-in point for reader' (Lupi 2017).

I proposed that characters were given a designated colour, based on literal reference in the text. Some characters, however, are based on Disney's 1951 *Alice in Wonderland*, rather than any data. Alice is pale blue, Tweedledum and Tweedledee are vice versa, red and yellow squares, 'what geometers call "enantiomorphs", mirror image forms' (Gardner 1965: 231).

To avoid complexity of repetition with the circle, male characters are square and all other characters are diamonds to allow for visual differentiation. I like to think this would have pleased Carroll as he was known to use the phrase 'circle squarer' about those seeking to define π.

Moretti's collection method, in his chapter 'Network Theory and Plot Analysis', focused on dialogue as a means to plot a network of inter-actions. He stated that 'networks of speech acts were networks of actions' (2013: 230). Carroll used chess moves as a framework to drive the narrative forward, which culminate in Alice's victory over the Red Queen. It felt like a pertinent method to explore further to examine how speech interactions could map directional language (Figure 29). In Chapter 2, *The Garden of Live Flowers* there are only four characters who use directional language, though there are, in fact, six who speak (seven, if we include Alice's internal monologue). Though this may appear like nitpicking, when working with data it is easy to get waylaid by qualitative information. This is Schulz's biggest critique of Moretti's work: his inconsistency and movement between qualitative and quantitative data collection. As Legrady states, we need to 'let the data speak for itself' (Gil 2010).

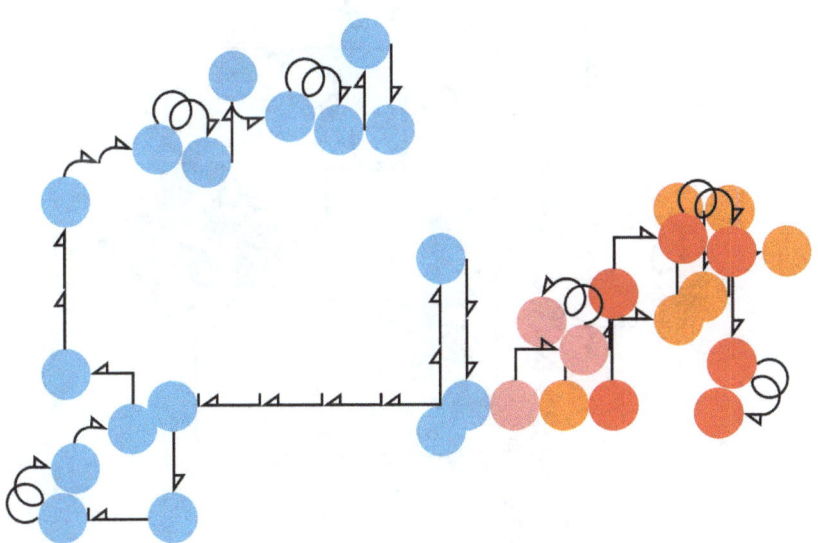

Figure 29. Diagram by author, 2021.

Though at times Schulz's critique is well-founded, she underestimates the power of visual designs to 'instantly reach out to places in our subconscious without the mediation of language', which can 'convey large amounts of structured and unstructured information across cultures' (Lupi 2017). Once the data visual vocabulary is established, it can be used to investigate more complex character interactions. By visualizing the directional language for Tweedledum and Tweedledee, we can *see* the chaotic and contradictory nature of their characters, even though it is impossible to know if this was a conscious decision made by Carroll in the writing (Figure 30).

Figure 30. Diagram by author, 2021.

'The power of visualisation is its capacity to represent abstract properties and relationships' (Wulfman 2014: 101). If 'visualisations are metaphors' (2014: 101), as Wulfman states, then, what we can see when we map Alice's directional language throughout the book, is that she moves forward with great certainty, arguably in line with Lewis Carroll's proposed chaptered chess moves – despite some compositional adjustments based on format. As such, the chapters are linked with a dotted line to allow all chapters to be visible in one composition (Figure 31).

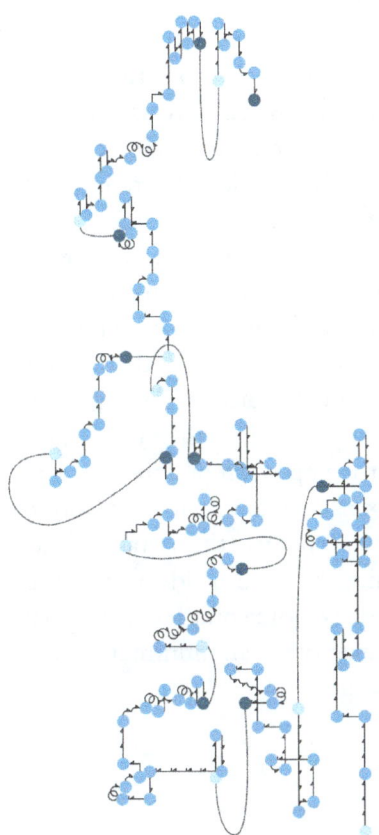

Figure 31. Diagram by author, 2021.

In order to explore the potential alternate narratives in *Through the Looking-Glass* and their infinite possibilities, a consideration of quantum mechanics is tantalizing (even though, as Richard Feynman stated, 'I think that I can say that nobody understands quantum mechanics' [Feynman 1965]). I certainly put myself in this category. However, I could not help but be swayed by the 'inescapable strangeness of the subatomic domain' (Cox 2011: 10) and its parallels to the mirror world in *Looking-Glass*. Particle Physicist, Brian Cox's definition of the Quantum universe states that quantum mechanics deals with probability rather than certainty because 'some aspects of nature are, at their very heart governed by the laws of chance' (2011: 25). If we are to believe that an atom can exist in an infinite number of places at any one time, up until the point that it is *seen*, then, potentially, all possibilities exist, until a choice is made. Are the choices made by Alice, therefore, a manifestation of the *unseen* choices that could, should, were, and are made by Carroll in a different *moral* universe?

For the relative simplicity, I have chosen to focus on Chapter 2 and the first four directional moves of Alice to examine this claim, in relation to directional choices. If each direction choice made also has a series of alternative or as Cox would put it *unseen* choices, based on the number of categories in the data set collected, then each directional choice has seven alternate directional choices. Choice 1, where the seen choice is up × 2, the unseen choices are: right then up × 2, over then up × 2, under then up × 2, down, then up × 2, round then up × 2, back then up × 2, and finally left then up × 2. To maintain forward motion in the narrative, the seen choice is used to perpetuate the narrative flow. Adjusting the opacity of each unseen future choice also aids in the processing of information as the layering becomes more complex. The visualization of directional choice shows the capacity for an infinite number of alternate narratives hidden within the text.

Figure 32. Diagram by author, 2021.

In Figure 32. we can see those choices in action. Choice 1 presents seven alternate unseen or not made choices: Choice 2, 49 alternates; Choice 3, 343 alternates; and choice 4, 2401 alternates. The use of opacities becomes more relevant as the number of alternate narratives increases. This supports Legrady's ideas that '[T]he process of visual mapping [...] allows the emergence of patterns which would not have been apparent otherwise' (Gil 2010). Once a set of visual systems are in place they can be applied to the other characters in the chapter.

Figure 33 shows this visualization methodology applied to all four characters who use directional language in Chapter 2. Choice 1 shows seven unseen choices for four characters and 28 alternatives. Choice 2 shows 196 alternatives. Choice 3 shows 1029 alternatives; note that the Rose data is completed after three choices. And finally, Choice 4, with 7203 alternatives.

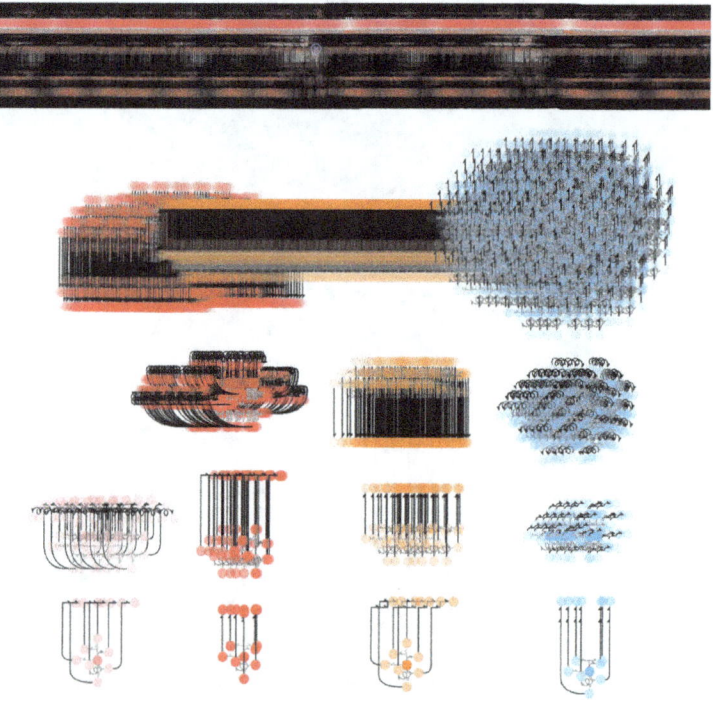

Figure 33. Diagram by author, 2021.

There are 250 questions asked within the text, whose collection was based on the use of the question marks. Unsurprisingly, Alice asks the most questions by a considerable margin, asking 132 questions throughout (though it is important to note that some of these are part of her internal dialogue). Visualizing the infinite possibilities of 250 questions is a task for which I do not have the computational capacity. However, I would like to suggest a methodology that would produce appropriate visuals. I propose that some assumptions must be made to support the clarity of the visualization. For example, if we focus on chapter 1 and Alice, and assume that each question has a binary response, we can use a single vector, or what Moretti refers to as a node, to represent a choice. Then two lines represent the subsequent binary alternates. This method, when applied to Alice's questions in chapter 1, yields 32,768 alternates (Figure 34). If we select a chapter with less questioning, we can apply the same strategy. In chapter 4, for example, Alice poses eight questions, which yields 128 alternates. Tweedledum also poses eight questions, which also yields 128 alternates, while Tweedledee asks 9 questions, which yields 256 alternates.

Chapter 1
Questions
Alice 17

Figure 34. Diagram by author, 2021.

Visualizing Looking-Glass

To challenge the assumption that questions result in binary answers, I collected potential answer data from the text. Obviously, the complexity, even of fictional characters, means that answers are far more complex than binary, but to collect quantitative data from the text constraints must be applied. Therefore, I used yes, no, or either, or as a means of answers. Moretti references Darwinian natural selection theory and 'the divergence of character' in his 2005 work, *Graphs Maps Trees*. Darwin himself, notably, mapped formal diversification using a fan of diverging lines which eventually, over thousands of generations, would lead to well-marked varieties. In this case, the diverging fans denote choices, both made and not made for Alice throughout the text. By collecting 'yes,' 'no,' 'either,' and 'or' data from the text, and using such a Darwinian evolutionary tree, we can map the alternate choices made and other possible unseen narratives. We can also assume some general observations, like, when a tree leans predominantly left, it contains more occurrences of 'no' (Figure 35).

Figure 35. Diagram by author, 2021.

If we are, as Georgia Lupi states, entering the second wave of infographics that is 'more meaningful and thoughtful' (2017) than its predecessor, it feels prudent to develop approaches such as this one further. If we are seeking to visualize the infinite range of possibilities unseen within the narrative, then expansion is needed. By increasing the directional rotation of each choice branch, expanding the branching to consider five alternative future choices not made, means that each branch from the original choice, or trunk can show ninety alternate narratives. This method can be used to build data forests for each chapter and character.

Chapter 8 is predominantly a dialogue between Alice and the White Knight. As Gardner states, many Carrollians surmised that the White

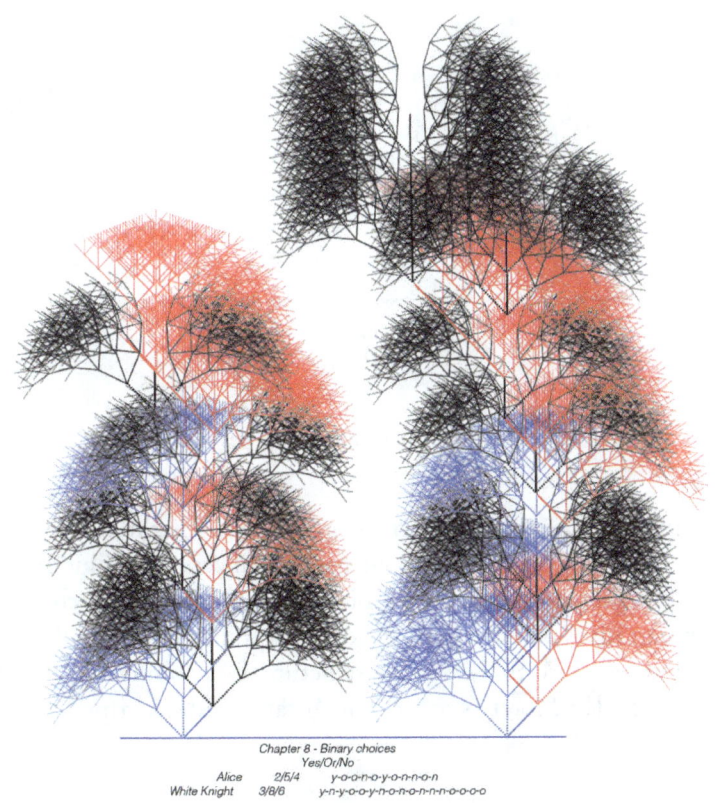

Figure 36. Diagram by author, 2021.

Visualizing Looking-Glass

Visualizing *Looking-Glass*

Knight was intended to be a caricature of Carroll, forever thinking of a way to do this or that differently (1965: 296). This continuous thinking and indecision can be made visible in the tree visualization (Figure 36). [1]

It felt appropriate to test the established colours from the previous visualizations with the tree methodology. As such, I wanted to include Chapter 6, 'Humpty Dumpty', as he is the only character to use the word 'maybe', which involved a development of the original data set to include an additional diverging fan. His colours denote his egginess (Figure 37).

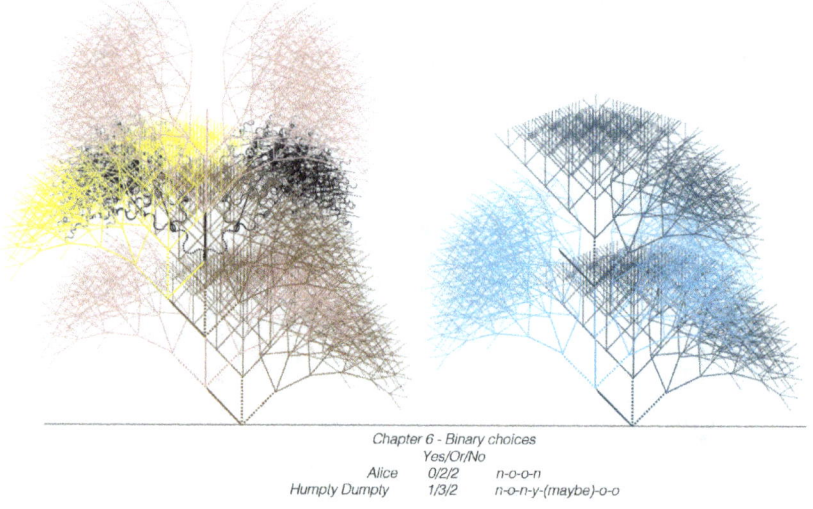

Chapter 6 - Binary choices
Yes/Or/No
Alice   0/2/2   n-o-o-n
Humpty Dumpty 1/3/2   n-o-n-y-(maybe)-o-o

Figure 37. Diagram by author, 2021.

To summarize, this practical investigation has sought to use mathematical and systematic methods, via data visualization, to illuminate the text and its themes by making visible unseen character trajectories and hidden narratives based on 'choice' data mapping and using directional data based on Carroll's chess move structure. Developing a practical approach, framed by Moretti's concept of Distant Reading, maps, Darwinian

1   For an examination of such directional frameworks in the context of Aristotle's and Carroll's own logic in Through the Looking-Glass, see Chapter 14 in this collection.

diagrams, embracing Lupi's 'Data Humanism', and some rudimentary quantum ideas, I have tried to use simple geometry to build a data vocabulary that uses data from the text to find the unseen story, and explores the infinite probabilities and possibilities of the narrative. I acknowledge that this approach is limited by analogue data collection processes and technological processing speeds, however, I intend to apply the same methodologies to Lewis Carroll's diaries as a comparison to further investigate if *Through the Looking-Glass* is a manifestation of the *unseen* choices that could, should, were, and are made by Carroll in a different moral universe. Through studying *Through the Looking-Glass* as a manifestation of 'choice', this practical investigation sought to examine Carroll's multiverse, where possibilities are infinite and 'a world in which things go every way, except the way they are supposed to' (Gardner 1965: 181).

Visualizing Looking-Glass

Adam Paxman

20 The Eggbound Heart

Ovoid Metamorphoses

I Make No Apology for Anthropomorphopology

The following are illustrated observation reports on my 2-year-old son Lucian's interactions with Humpty Dumpty (HD) between August 2021 and March 2022. In a nod to intuitive inquiry (but possibly, more a sneak peek at how laterally my mind works), these are interspersed with musings on child development, anatomy, the significance of eggs in certain creation myths, and a poem. Akin to separating the yolk and egg white, this process may be a form of ontological study, examining semiotics and iconology in relation to HD, or a phenomenological study of lived experiences – my own, Lucian's, my wife Anna's – and the development of consciousness. It is probably a hybrid, and as this is something I have contemplated throughout, my own ham-and-egg-fisted attempts at categorization are more than mere post-rationalization. When my friend and ex-colleague Lucy reviewed a near-final draft, she mentioned she was currently researching diffractive methodology. I immediately began searching online on my phone to check for correlations – as a recovering illustration lecturer, I should know where to draw the line. In my day job as an Academic Skills Advisor, I have been reflecting on Academic Literacies (AL) and threshold practices (Gourlay 2009) – how lecturers, learning developers, and students in higher education (HE) code-switch between everyday as well as generic and discipline-specific academic modes of language and knowledge. Therefore, this chapter-poem-visual essay-report takes a quasi-academic, semi-serious approach to both content and structure. I have limited but not omitted egg puns.

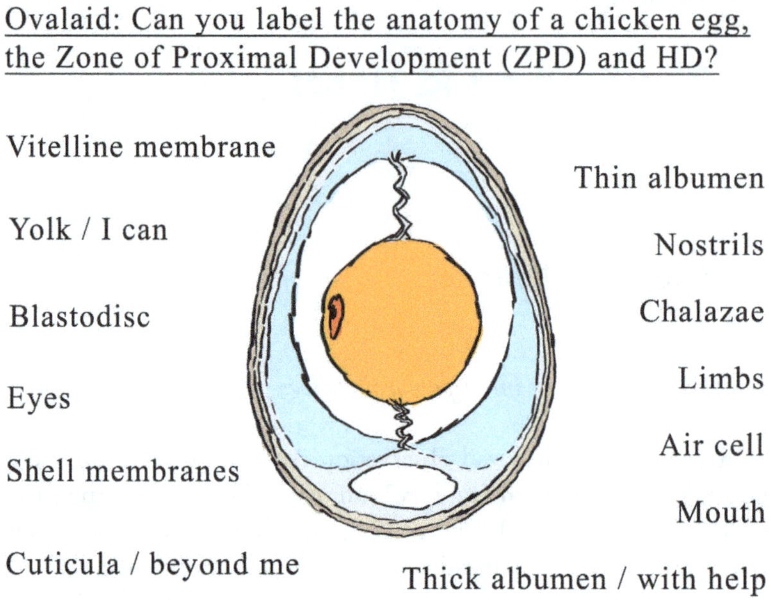

Ovalaid: Can you label the anatomy of a chicken egg, the Zone of Proximal Development (ZPD) and HD?

Vitelline membrane

Yolk / I can

Blastodisc

Eyes

Shell membranes

Cuticula / beyond me

Thin albumen

Nostrils

Chalazae

Limbs

Air cell

Mouth

Thick albumen / with help

Figure 38. Overlaying Ova (Paxman 2022).

Ova and Ova Again

My *Lewis Carroll and George MacDonald: An Influential Friendship* conference paper-cum-illustrated Practice-as-Research dossier on George MacDonald's fairy tales (see Paxman 2018), *Through the Looking-Glass: A Sesquicentenary Celebration* conference paper and independently published expansion *IT CAME FROM THE GLASS CURTAIN!* (Paxman 2021) and the symbolic, anthropomorphic egg characters that featured in my webcomic *Burning Zebra* (see Paxman 2013) indicate it may be myself – not Lucian – with the egg fixation. The excellent (please note my restraint with egg prefix puns) *Carrollian* article (Cass 2021) clarified research I previously undertook on the scrambled origins of HD. I cannot recommend it highly enough. It has settled at least two heated debates around my dinner table.

Burning Zebra: The Abandoned Storybook
Illustration one

Figure 39. An anthropomorphic egg sits on a wall (see Paxman 2013).

A Prehistory of Humpty Dumpty – Prior to 27 August 2021

Lucian had watched a Humpty Dumpty (HD) animated nursery rhyme on Super Simple Songs, which we viewed on television via the YouTube app. It was one of many such nursery rhymes he enjoyed, although he showed no particular fascination with the song or the figure of HD. In addition, someone bought Lucian a packed lunch box with Helen Oxenbury's illustration of HD, her version of TTLG 118: Humpty Dumpty offering Alice his hand. This is used for storing socks.

An Eggnographic Approach, or Let's Get Cracking

27 August 2021 (Adapted from Proposal)

During a visit to Mother Shipton's Cave in Knaresborough, North Yorkshire, at precisely 9:52 a.m. (according to the timestamp on my phone), my 26-month-old son had his first encounter with an outdoor

Figure 40. Lucian, Anna, Granny Glogz and the first sighting of HD at Mother Shipton's Cave.

HD. This large – presumably, fibreglass – figure was part of a themed adventure trail entitled Alice's Enchanted Wonderland. Sometime later, I had to carry him away from the tourist attraction statue during a red-faced, screaming-and-rolling-on-the-ground tantrum. Despite the presence of a Jabberwocky, March Hare, Mad Hatter's Tea Party, fairy houses, and more, Lucian returned repeatedly to see HD – initially dubbed 'Otty Otty'.

Tweedleaddendum: Reviewing my photographs on 10 April 2022, I am reminded there were in reality four HD statues: see images 3 and 4.

22 December 2021

Granny Glogz came to stay for Christmas. Within minutes Lucian had her help to build and topple 'e-bots' (robots). Playing 'e-bots' means stacking and toppling faux-Duplo block towers. Between late August and December, 'e-bots', the decaying of Halloween pumpkins – 'all mushy' – and HD have become conflated. Or assimilated, to use Piaget's terminology. That is to say, Lucian frequently sings or talks about HD as shorthand for falling and breaking in a general, abstract sense.

24 December 2021

Lucian, Granny Glogz, and I spent 1.5 hours making snowmen, gingerbread men, and an HD with leftover icing and matchsticks.

28 December 2021

During a playdate with Cousin Alice, Lucian found Alice's cuddly HD inside Alice's Wendy house. He recognized it as HD immediately, told us who it was, and kept tight hold of it until requesting that I join him inside the Wendy house to play e-bots. It was a tight squeeze, like Alice (Cousin Alice's namesake) experienced.

Figure 41. Egg statue sightings at Mother Shipton's Cave – various signifiers of ice cream consumption or literary reference.

4 January 2022

I wrote the proposal for this piece and began recording observation notes. Lucian requested HD on YouTube – specifically the 'Santa Humpty'. HD was the most recent YouTube search. Lucian sang HD on the stairs going up to bed. He had most of the words, just missing or unclear on some later connective words. He also hummed the tune. Jumped on his bed and played at falling, going, 'Woahhh!' – pretend play/roleplay as HD.

5 January 2022

E-bots and singing HD. Green Goblin was made to fall from his glider onto Fireman Sam's fire engine. In a multiverse, anything is possible. It occurred to me that, as a child, I had several recurring nightmares – one featuring a goblin, and another in which I was falling into a power station cooling tower.

Figure 42. Lucian building 'e-bots'.

6 January 2022

Morning: Lucian sang HD whilst playing with a flannel in the bath.

Evening: Lucian demanded I draw 'Sad Humpty' on the Etch A Sketch-like pad. Then 'Mummy, Daddy and Baby HD'. In Lucian's taxonomic classification, all things – objects, people, animals – are arranged in large 'Daddy', medium 'Mummy', and small 'Baby', building out schemas which replicate our nuclear family unit.

Visualizing Looking-Glass

Figure 43. Leftover icing HD.

7 January 2022

Morning: Lucian requested I draw Mummy Humpty on the Etch
A Sketch-like pad. He drew the face and said aloud what each feature
was. He requested more. Ditto. These were wiped off before I could photograph the drawings.

Whilst being changed and dressed, Lucian bounced his Peppy Nanna
cuddly on the top of my head and chanted HD, making her fall off over
and over again.

Figure 44. Sad HD.

9 January 2022

Lucian sang diversionary HD while I wrestled his nappy off and changed his clothes. There were lots of HD exclamations – 'Woahhh!'

Lucian requested HD on YouTube. We watched several but he was very discerning – 'Not this one'. He seemed frustrated that I couldn't find the correct one, although this seems dynamic, not static, and completely arbitrary.

Figure 45. HD with facial features drawn by Lucian.

12 January 2022

Lucian cried when we pulled up at home and I turned off HD/my phone. He has requested varied HD videos each morning on the way to and each evening on the return from nursery.

15 and 16 February 2022

Anna tested positive for Covid. There was much jumping on the sofa and singing HD – Lucian, not Anna. I found myself musing on an ontology or illustrative typology of the HD YouTube videos. There was an irritating amount of singing and watching. HD has replaced Chúmbala Cachúmbala as a song synonymous with over-excitement, and in need of limiting or banning altogether from the house.

The HD jigsaw from *The Jolly Christmas Postman* (Ahlberg and Ahlberg 2014) was completed over and over at bedtime. Sometimes Lucian says he wants to do 'Humpty jigsaw' but messes with the pieces, tossing them in the air. Anna has taught him to recognize the envelope with calligraphic text, pronouncing it 'Mister. Humpty. Dumpty'.

Lucian asked for one of the sinister HD videos several times – clear connection to over-stimulation, Halloween, and the Chúmbala Cachúmbala skeletons – 'dongs'. I allowed it to be played twice and no more. Lots of the videos share tunes and vocals. I have copyright questions. There are lots of strange mashups of the king's men – soldiers from ancient Rome, ancient China, and colourful European uniforms dating from the Early to Later Modern periods.

18 February 2022

Lucian asked to watch 'Spooky' HD six times in a row, following other versions. Anna and I debated who makes these and why – although they are clearly on to something.

Nanny sends home her drawings of HD frequently. The Valentine's card they made for Anna featured HD. Who is enabling whom?

Singing HD for thirty minutes straight at the top of his voice and jumping on his bed. Lucian didn't want to do the jigsaw at bedtime. I am quite sick of HD. Mixed feelings now I've had the proposal accepted. HD must also be my fixation until 1 May.

Thinking about what a fall is, and what connotations the word fall can have: Katabasis, a tragedy, damnation, the fall as metaphor.

The anniversary book is a companion piece to the conference. This project is a companion piece to my 2021 conference piece and the book version of that, *IT CAME FROM THE GLASS CURTAIN!* The project is about Lucian and HD's companionship.

19 February 2022

Morning: Lucian found a white feather and brought it into the bathroom. He let it fall over and over again, transfixed, saying it was, 'Silly'.

4:30 p.m.: Watching 'Spooky' HD again, repeatedly. I'm torn between curiosity about his behaviour and imposing limits – a microcosm of parenthood.

Playing with Mrs Potatohead and singing HD. Mrs Potatohead goes, 'All mushy'.

20 February 2022

Lucian was awake at 2 a.m. after doing a poo. He asked to play with Mrs Potatohead again or read Donaldson and Scheffler's *Monkey Puzzle* (2020). Back to bed.

Morning: Playing with Mrs Potatohead on his own and on our bed whilst singing HD, the alphabet, Spooky Scary Skeletons and Chúmbala Cachúmbala. Piaget would define this as new information being assimilated into a schema. Should I attempt to illustrate this schema?

I asked Anna what she would include in this project, or what she would expect to see included. She said that she never anticipated a child loving HD or other nursery rhymes to this extent, but it means so much to him. She finds all the YouTube versions baffling.

21 February 2022

I absentmindedly doodled HD in pencil whilst speaking to my mum on the phone.

22 February 2022

Lucian saw the doodles I had done on the pad at breakfast and wanted to draw HD. He added eyes and a nose while telling me this is what he was doing. He drew several ovals with very spindly appendages. There are definite signs of progression from the random doodles stage, with greater control and attempts to depict objects and characters, rather than mark making.

26 February 2022

I've missed out something important. Lucian has developed a keen interest in trees that have fallen down. He sings HD and says, 'all mushy'. We (and Nanny, separately) have taken him to see multiple examples. He knows where they are – he can point them out when we are in the car. The recent storms mean there are even more around, and so this morning we walked around Greenbank Park with friends, clambering through and over fallen-down trees. Lucian was in his element.

28 February 2022

Lucian has a nasty cold. We kept him at home, and both worked from home. He drew HD in his pad and Anna's notebook. I drew upside-down snotty HD. Lucian's ovals are getting more accurate and then he tends to add spidery limbs but then either gets too excited or bored and begins scribbling.

Figure 46. Lucian scampering about amongst the HD trees.

2 March 2022

Lucian sang HD to Granny on the landline.

3 March 2022

Back from nursery, singing HD whilst building 'e-bots'. He calls these robots now. I'm sad to see 'e-bots' go.

5 March 2022

Lucian located the wall where HD fell. It's in Ormskirk. This challenges my thinking that there's no longer any one definitive version.

Figure 47. The wall where HD's great fall happened, apparently. Ruff Lane, Ormskirk.

Figure 48. What's on the menu?

Lucian drew HD with features on the back of a menu in Nordico Lounge over lunch.

At home, Lucian asked me to make HD in Play-Doh. He counted two eyes – this sounded like, 'Dough eyes' – but gouged extra eyes with the ball end of the knife tool. It was a lovely day, and this felt like a natural end point for recording the observations. It was also the first anniversary of my dad's death. This is significant here because the 2021 conference paper/poem and book were dedicated to him, and grief and memory were themes that ran throughout the poem.

Figure 49. Play-Doh HD by me, with extra eyes by Lucian.

26 March 2022

Lucian ran across a field in Bridgend, after spotting what he thought was HD. He seemed disappointed when it turned out to be an oversized wooden rugby ball carved out of a tree stump. Was this, as Stewart (1993) discusses, an attempt to recapture the authentic experience at Mother Shipton's Cave?

Figure 50. Rugby ball carving behind a fence/mistaken identity.

Poem

There's no guarantee
Humpty Dumpty was an egg
from a big chicken.

Battery farming
didn't exist when Carroll
wrote the *Alice* books.

Is Humpty Dumpty
ultimately a very
sad song about death?

Some things are broken
and no matter what you do,
they cannot be fixed.

Tables contrasting
Piaget and Vygotsky
are rife on the web.

Schemas? No schemas?
Sociocultural broth
or words as labels?

Structurally, is
the ZPD quite a bit
like a chicken egg?

Yolk, albumen, shell.
I can, with help, beyond me.
Flawed comparison.

Egg shell is porous.
It lets in air and moisture.
Egg shell like seashell,

limestone, antacid
is calcium carbonate.
Chicken eggshells have

inner and outer
protein membranes guarding them
against infection.

Contents shrink after
laying, and between membranes
there is an air cell.

Egg white (albumen)
both thick and thin suspend the
yolk with protein strands.

Yolk is fat, protein,
vitamins and minerals,
cholesterol and

a germinal disc -
which is the bit where the chick
(in foetal form) grows.

On Longing contends
that identity is formed
by repetition,

structures of desire
and fiction contaminate
lived experience,

description invents
something, and nostalgia is
a social disease.

Is a souvenir
a trace/partial double of
authenticity?

Lived experience:
Does a collection seek to
authenticate past

experience in
a hermetic world of signs,
atemporal and

mediated by
humans – history replaced
with taxonomy?

Is a collection
an aid to recollection?
Individual,

that of a culture,
or the whole human species?
A warped reflection?

The spaces between
language and experience,
narrative, object

and its origin
put me in mind of Humpty.
A hermetic world

sealed in by eggshell.
Lucian's repetitious
drawing and singing

recapturing the
pleasure and stimulation
of the encounter

within the woods at
Mother Shipton's Cave, roleplay
inscribing Humpty

on his heart and mind,
diminishing returns in
no way known to him.

Jeff Vandermeer's book
Acceptance suggests mere words'
inadequacy

to express either
the finite or infinite,
a correlation.

You Can't Make an Omelette …

On Stewart (1993) – I would not want to live in a reality undiluted by imagination.

Commuter train musings (4 April 2022) – The egg as a sealed world (Stewart 1993) reminds me of Daoist cosmogony – the egg of Chaos that gave rise to the chisel-toting horned creator-giant, Pan Gu. In some versions of the myth, Pan Gu's corpse completes the formation of the universe, and the parasites on his body become the first humans. There is a straight-line correlation here to Ymir, the creator-giant from Norse mythology, whose corpse formed parts of the universe. You can't make a cosmos without breaking a few giants. Even HD's fall, or that of a common egg, would result in a dispersal of nutrients and energy. There is potential (energy) in chaos. Lucian's games and (over)excitement seem chaotic. The law of conservation of energy tells us matter and energy are not destroyed, only transformed.

Does Lucian's repetition connote multiple broken eggs, or a single egg trapped in a reversible cycle? Does he appreciate there are different iterations of HD, or are they all pale imitations of the archetype (like imprinting for a newly hatched duckling)? He delights in the variations – Mummy, Daddy, Baby, Sad, Happy, Spooky, etc., – so the former seems borne out. Attempting to integrate Stewart's notions of experiential authenticity and child development stages is problematic in this instance. HD is fictional and

Visualizing Looking-Glass

iterations are ubiquitous – as evidenced at Mother Shipton's Cave, where multiple differing HD statues existed simultaneously. With apologies to Carroll, there is no definitive HD, except perhaps as a popular misconception. Is that a suitable euphemistic epithet for a famous, presumably unfertilized, egg?

Part VIII

Illustrating *Looking-Glass*

Jade Dillon Craig

21 'She Haunts Me Phantomwise': Illustrating Mirrors and Reflections in Lewis Carroll's *Alice* Books

Introduction

Zoe Jaques and Eugene Giddens argue that 'some of the more radical artistic interpretations […] are indicative of an interest in moving the text beyond the reach of the child reader, via a process of rendering *Wonderland* dark and grotesque [and] obliquely sexual' (Jaques and Giddens 2016: 184). This chapter argues that the works of Benjamin Lacombe (2015) and Kirsty Mitchell[1] (2014) capture those radical qualities outlined by Jaques and Giddens and transitions the character of Alice from the serene banks of Oxford into much darker versions of Wonderland. Similarly, they also demonstrate the transitions of identity for the female protagonist. Thus, this chapter will perform an iconographic analysis of a selection of Lacombe's and Mitchell's images to investigate the reflections of identity in Lewis Carroll's *Alice* books, with a focus on *Through the Looking-Glass*.

---

1   I would like to sincerely Kirsty Mitchell for generously allowing their images to be used in this chapter; due to unclarity about copyright, we were unable to reproduce the images of Benjamin Lacombe.

Benjamin Lacombe's *Alice*

Benjamin Lacombe's collection of illustrative artwork features in the French edition *Alice au pays des merveilles* (2015) and *Alice de l'autre cote du miroir* (2016). His illustrative interpretation of Alice depicts a new form of 'girl/woman' in Wonderland. In terms of iconotextuality, Lacombe's illustrations are postmodernist adaptations that capture the dynamic relationship between text and image. Lacombe's collection enhances Carroll's textual narrative as they offer the reader a *version* of Alice's story that is subversive and radical by comparison with the Tenniel version. This collection of illustrations modifies Alice: Lacombe presents a gothic and abstract Alice who distorts the normative view of Alice's identity as suggested by the Tenniel illustrations. As Eduardo Bravo (2012) notes, 'unlike other authors, who consider childhood an idyllic age, oblivious to any type of conflict and susceptible to being preserved between cottons, Lacombe prefers to bet on more complex images, elaborated and, some-times, uncomfortable' (Bravo 2012).[2] This selection of works embodies the otherness of Alice and the gothic nature of her surroundings, chan-nelling the complexity and discomfort mentioned by Bravo.

It is possible to read Lacombe's illustration of Alice painting the roses red in the *Wonderland* book as a signifier for menstrual bleeding and pu-bescent growth. Thus, the physical changes that Lacombe's Alice faces in *Alice au pays des merveilles* – she repeatedly grows and shrinks throughout the book – have an impact on his edition of *Alice de l'autre cote du miroir* ['*Through the Looking-Glass*']. In the second *Alice* book, she appears older and more mature, her face more angular and her lips more pouted. Lacombe seems attuned to the changing female form, and the effect the other realm has on the 'Alice' figure. This is most evident in the opening chapter as Alice enters into the Looking-Glass land through the mirror. Alice's identity

---

2   Original quote in Spanish: '*A diferencia de otros autores, que consideran la infancia una edad idílica, ajena a cualquier tipo de conflicto y susceptible de ser conservada entre algodones, Lacombe prefiere apostar por unas imágenes más complejas, elabora-das y, en ocasiones, incómodas*'

is altered when she enters the alternative universe through the symbolic passageway. Lacombe depicts this sense of alteration through artistic composition. The inversion of the scene is heightened by the tonal difference in the colourization. When in the waking world, the scene is composed through warm tones, rich colours, and vibrant gold accents. However, once Alice enters through the mirror, Lacombe alters the dynamic by dulling the colour palette to highlight the radical qualities of the Looking-Glass world. The cooler tones of the image highlight the gothic and uncanny characteristics of the 'Alice' figure and her experiences. As Alice moves from one world to the next, her identity becomes dislocated, and the familiar is further distorted. Simply put, Alice in Lacombe's Looking-Glass appears more grown up. Warm tones are dropped for cooler tones, rounder for more angular shapes. Lacombe's emphasis is on the liminal, the gothic qualities inherent in the transcendent Alice figure in *Looking-Glass*.

Considering that Lacombe's Alice has transitioned from child to a pubescent, adolescent girl, these numerous alterations to Alice's identity are metaphorically demonstrated in the inverted images of the looking-glass. As Alice crawls through the mirror, and the world around her changes, the ornaments and frames that surround the mantlepiece become personified. The act of crawling frames Alice's body in an evocative manner as her legs and petticoat are exposed to the reader. Lacombe continuously positions Alice in liminal spaces; in this image, the mirror becomes a signifier of a bodily transition for Alice. Vaclavik notes that 'Alice is frequently referred to as being of indeterminate age, or awkwardly poised between childhood and adulthood' (Vaclavik 2019: 45). To this effect, her body is often positioned as one that is suggestive of the budding adolescence. This scene evokes a sense of menace and change, both figuratively and literally. The clock gains a menacing face, the mirror and vase grin unnervingly, and the people in the picture frames transition into threatening figures who gaze down upon Alice. The most altered figure is the image in the upper left corner which depicts the Duchess from *Alice au pays des merveilles*. In the waking world's drawing room, she is shown looking into the distance, and is distinctly human in appearance; however, once Alice goes through the mirror, the image is altered so that the Duchess figure is portrayed as a grotesque character who stares maliciously at Alice. Of course, the Duchess is not the only figure to become a grotesque version of herself. There is a distinct duality to Alice's disposition in the mirror. In the mirror image, her eyes are darkened by shadows and her lips appear more downcast. Like the distinct difference that exists between the two Duchess images, Alice and her mirror reflection are two versions of herself; her reflection embraces the gothic qualities of Lacombe's Looking-Glass world. It is the medium that changes Alice as it has a significant impact on the visualization or (re) imagining of her identity.

The separation of Alice's form is evident again in chapter two, '*le jardin des fleurs vivantes*'. Against a striking blood-red backdrop, Alice's face becomes disjointed from her body. In Carroll's textual narrative, the flowers state:

> Said I to myself, 'Her face has got some sense in it, though it's not a clever one! Still, you're the right colour, and that goes a long way.' 'I don't care about the colour,' the Tiger-lily remarked. 'If only her petals curled up a little more, she'd be all right.' Alice didn't like being criticised, so she began asking questions. (Carroll 1993: 172)

The flowers criticize her appearance, yet Alice returns the line of inquiry back at them: a transgressive act. Despite Carroll's narrative trajectory, Lacombe illustrates Alice and the flowers as one being. Reading the flowers' criticism of Alice from a self-deprecating vantage point, Alice is the one criticizing herself. There is a certain terror that is evoked in this image as the flowers burst through Alice's skin; however, there is an elegance that depicts the portrait as regal and beautiful – a juxtaposition Lacombe employs throughout his (re)imagining of Alice. This regal image is reflective of Alice's journey in the Looking-Glass land as she becomes queen, thus mirroring the narrative intent through illustrative means. While some scholars[3] believe that Alice does not undergo meaningful change or development outside of playful, momentary distortions, I argue that she is significantly altered by her experiences in Carroll's dreamworlds; her sense of agency expands which, in turn, affectively demarcates a new sense of self for Alice.

---

3   See 'Mathematics: Alice in Time' and *Alice in Space: The Sideways Victorian World of Lewis Carroll* by Gillian Beer (2016) for more.

Kirsty Mitchell's Alice

While Kirsty Mitchell's *Wonderland*[4] (2014) photography book is in-spired by children's tales more generally, this chapter notes that by using Carroll's stories as a focused lens while reading the images, Alice is a prominent echo that lingers throughout. The compositional aspects of the *Wonderland* series, including costume, colourization, and concept, originate directly from Mitchell. Mitchell describes herself as 'an artist with a camera as opposed to a photographer' – making her more similar to how Lewis Carroll saw himself in relation to his photography (Mitchell 2016). The artistry of her work is seen throughout the collection, particu-larly through the costuming and the props used in each image. This *Alice* belongs to Mitchell and her *idea* alone. She achieves this independence, for instance, through the composition of the imagery. As Gillian Rose notes in relation to compositional analysis, 'some of the key components of a still image are its content, colour, spatial organization, light and ex-pressive content' (Rose 2012: 53). Amelunxen notes that 'skiagraphy refers to shadow writing, and to the absence of the referent [...] the writing of shadow, as a simultaneous memory, a memory of the present, a division of the instant' (Derrida and von Amelunxen 2010: 1). The echoes of Carroll's narrative haunt the photographic collection, as Alice exists as a memory that is mirrored in the new realm of Wonderland created by Mitchell, as the simultaneously stand independent.

---

4 Please note that the first edition of *Wonderland* was published in 2014, but this chapter uses and references the second edition of *Wonderland* which was published in 2016.

Illustrating *Looking-Glass*

Figure 51. The Foxglove Fairy.

Image credit: Kirsty Mitchell.

The Foxglove Fairy (Figure 51) and *The Garden of Whispered Wishes* (Figure 52), for instance, captivate the mystical and ethereal qualities associated with the child subject and her transition into womanhood. Such an evolution can be witnessed through the aesthetic finesse of Mitchell's design when examining these specific images in conjunction with the 'Alice' figure. The subject of Mitchell's *The Foxglove Fairy* embodies nymph-like qualities that are suggestive of delicate beauty and youth. Though the realist model is an adult, her stature and expression are childlike which connects the Alice mould with the fairy motif. Mitchell creates a fantasy character that illuminates the surrounding landscape; the upturned lighting gives the impression of her magical essence radiating from her wings. Mitchell states 'it looked like we had caught a life-sized firefly hovering through the woods, I was spellbound' (Mitchell 2016). The fairy-tale motif captured in *The Foxglove Fairy* can also be linked to Alice, as in Carroll's original novel she states 'when I used to read fairy tales, I fancied that kind of thing never happened, and now here I am in the middle of one! There ought to be a book written about me, that there ought!' (Carroll 1993: 61). Considering the nymph character created by Mitchell as an embodiment of Alice, the subject indicates the ethereal and otherworldly atmosphere that can be seen in *Alice's Adventures in Wonderland*.

Analysing photography in relation to visual analysis can be defined as a 'mirror with a memory': a form of expression that exceeds words and limitations (Collier and Collier 1986: 7). John and Malcolm Collier argue that 'the camera is another instrumental extension of our senses, one that can record on a low scale of abstraction. The camera, by its optical character, has whole vision' (Collier and Collier 1986: 7). The concept of whole vision is significant when analysing the adaptations of the *Alice* books. Lizbeth Goodman notes that 'the public and private spheres are separated by windows and doors [...] it is useful to keep track of which spaces woman (and girls) are allowed to enter and to exit. The window is also a kind of mirror, as in *Through the Looking-Glass*: a mirror of self-image and of imagination' (Goodman 1996: 22). The concepts of whole vision and mirroring within the *Alice* stories are relevant particularly when examining the visual representations in the tales' adaptations. Basia Sliwinska states that Carroll's 'metaphors can be used to deconstruct stereotypical representations of the female body. Alice refuses to be caught up in her own reflection in the mirror. She goes through the looking-glass but this going through is not a symmetrical reversal. She goes toward asymmetry, displacement, and the destabilization of the subject. Alice enters a world where there is no possibility of naturalistic identification' (Sliwinska 2016: loc. 121). This destabilization of female identity is central to the ways in which transmedia storytelling encounters the 'Alice' figure.

Figure 52. The Garden of Whispered Wishes.

Image credit: Kirsty Mitchell.

The Garden of Whispered Wishes is highly evocative of a matured Alice, whose warrior status intimidates the viewer through her icy cold stare. Framed by a Victorian-style ruff of hydrangea flowers, the subject of Mitchell's image is regal and fierce. Much like Carroll's Alice, Mitchell's protagonist fills the image with female agency and autonomy in her bodily performance. The purple-toned fog, a motif that reoccurs throughout many of Mitchell's images, creates an enigmatic curiosity about the central subject, as this particular colourization is symbolically associated with royalty and grandeur. Of course, there are numerous parallels between this creation and Carroll's original novels, particularly when examined alongside the Alice of the 1871 text. In particular, the fog that appears in *The Garden of Whispered Wishes* aligns with the textual description of the transition to Looking-Glass House which strengthens the intertextual relationship between Carroll and Mitchell. In *Looking-Glass,* Alice pretends that the looking glass itself is 'soft like gauze' so that she and Kitty can enter the other realm, and as the mirror begins to transform, the glass melts away 'like a bright silvery mist' (160). Here, Carroll's mist and Mitchell's fog signify the liminality of Alice's journey. Another example of intertextual parallels between both texts is the subject's braided hair styled to represent a crown, which mirrors that worn by Alice in chapter nine of *Looking-Glass*, 'Queen Alice'.

The version of Alice created by Mitchell in *The Garden of Whispered Wishes* shatters the 'fourth wall'. The stare that penetrates through the image is fierce and alluring, inviting the viewer into her dangerous gaze. Her agency, thus created, is further embellished by the structured embroidery of her cape, while the blue paint that covers her eye deepens her autonomous expression. However, Mitchell also softens the Alice subject by contrasting the gold-embellished cape with a soft blue chiffon gown. The juxtaposition of texture and tactility indicates a multidimensional layering of Alice. Such layering is evident again in the gesture of hands offering a singular entity of hydrangea flowers to the viewer. The Alice character seems to offer the viewer a piece of Looking-Glass land through the 'fourth wall', mimicking Carroll's Alice in the concluding pages of *Looking-Glass,* as she asks the reader, 'which do *you* think it was?' (Carroll 1993: 278).

Collier and Collier state that 'when creative processes are combined with meticulous field and analysis craft the results can be astounding' (Collier and Collier 1986: 199). Mitchell's attention to detail and creative discourse within the visual narrative process most certainly result in an astounding creation of photographic art. *The Foxglove Fairy* and *The Garden of Whispered Wishes* offer an alternative perspective in relation to the *Alice* universe and Alice as they continuously evolve, and the girl of the text becomes a woman in the images. Such growth and adaptation allow fresh creativity that Carroll encouraged through his original fantasy realm. Mitchell's *The Pure Blood of a Blossom* (Figure 53) is thus evocative and alludes to 'The Garden of Live Flowers' from *Through the Looking-Glass*. As her piercing blue eyes peer out from behind the floral stems, Alice becomes one with the nature of Looking-Glass land. The female body appears naked beneath an abundance of flowers, one of which entwines itself in her mouth. Discussing the artistic influence of the image, Mitchell states that 'the flowers will guide her final path, their knowledge

Illustrating *Looking-Glass*

forming tendrils that pierce her mouth' (Mitchell 2016: 272). Interestingly, there is a striking resemblance to Lacombe's *'le jardin des fleurs vivantes'* image discussed earlier. Lacombe's Alice becomes detached from herself in a grotesque manner as the flowers burst through her skin. *The Pure Blood of a Blossom* encapsulates the striking features of Alice as a woman; her vivid lips and deepened eyes pin the viewer in a gaze that evokes power and enigmatic beauty.

Figure 53. The Pure Blood of a Blossom.

Image credit: Kirsty Mitchell.

Conclusion

As Thomas Leitch notes in *Adaptation and Visual Culture*, 'every new adaptation of […] *Alice's Adventures in Wonderland* […] raises new questions about the texts it adapts: questions not only about how the characters behave or what their world is like but about why we think about them in the ways we do' (Leitch 2017: 66). As Alice's character continues to evolve through contemporary visual reimaginings, Leitch's comment seems most apt. As readers, scholars, and Alice enthusiasts, we must consider the ways in which we think of Alice – who (and what) is she? Much like the Caterpillar's enigmatic question in Wonderland, the desire to know Alice's true self haunts every reiteration of her form.

Nilce M. Pereira

22 Illustrations and Illustrators of 'Looking-Glass House'

The opening chapter of *Looking-Glass* ([1871]1970), 'Looking-Glass House,' creates a cozy indoor atmosphere for Carroll's fantasy, and prepares his heroine to perform within the limits of a chessboard. The author referred to it as the general setting for the story when he wrote to a friend on 15 December 1867: 'Alice's visit to Looking-Glass House is getting on pretty well' (Carroll in Cohen 1995: 131);[1] which does make sense if one considers that the plot evolves out of a mirror representation of (the drawing room in) her house. The climax of the episode is the passage of Alice through the looking-glass, which Carroll describes little by little, first as Alice recurs to it as a menace to Kitty ('if you're not good directly, [...] I'll put you through into Looking-Glass House' [*TTLG*: 180]), then as she speculates about how things would be on the other side, and finally as she gets through it:

> Let's pretend there's a way of getting through in it, somehow, Kitty. Let's pretend the glass has got all soft like gauze, so that we can get through. Why, it's turning into a sort of mist now, I declare! It'll be easy enough to get through –' She was up on the chimney-piece while she said this, though she hardly knew how she had got there. And certainly the glass was beginning to melt way, just like a bright silvery mist. In another moment Alice *was* through the glass and had jumped lightly down into the Looking-glass room. (*TTLG*: 181, 184)

---

1   This seems to contradict note 4 in *The Annotated Alice* (*TTLG*: 180), in which Martin Gardner refers to the looking-glass as probably a late addition, in much considering stories such as that by Carroll's distant cousin, Alice Raikes, who allegedly gave the author the idea for the motif.

Using a similar resource as that in *Wonderland* ([1865]1970), Carroll devised the looking-glass primarily as a portal to the dimension of Looking-Glass land. Differently from the rabbit-hole, however – which mostly involves the aerodynamics of Alice's falling into it – the looking-glass poses questions on *how* the body would transit and behave between biologically different structures.

One of the challenges related to these topics, which Martin Gardner describes in his annotations to the *Alice* books, pertains to the composition, smell, and flavour of food in Looking-Glass land. For him, it is not without reason that Alice wonders if looking-glass milk would taste the same, as, according to the principles of stereochemistry (a branch of chemistry concentrating on the constitutional and structural properties of organic compounds), when reflected in a mirror, the atoms in certain (so-called isomeric) molecular formulas will take up a reversed position, the new arrangements not only resulting in different bonds between the particles – or in particles which would not otherwise be connected – but also in different substances. Thus, Gardner discusses the implications of the intake and digestibility of milk with 'asymmetric' atomic qualities in the universe of the book, noting that Carroll thought about these questions years before the discoveries in that particular field were consolidated (*TTLG*: 183–184). A more contemporary view of the subject can also be counted, though. In an article intended as an introductory class for organic chemistry and biochemistry courses, Frank J. Dinan and Gordon T. Yee (2004) distinguish between chiral and achiral elements in stereochemistry and explain what life would be like for Alice in mirror imaging in terms of the nutrients, amino acids, proteins, fats, and even pain killers that her enzymes would be adapted to catalyse.

These questions are so relevant because they concern the optical laws of reflection and the way they were accommodated to fulfil artistic purposes. In this paper, which deals with the illustration of 'Looking-Glass House', they are of special interest for involving the psychological and physiological processes of how objects are perceived in static imagery. Reflection was considered in the light of these aspects by Maarten Steenhagen (2017). The author discusses (and resists) the general assumption that mirror images are optical illusions. For him, they are regarded as illusory for the most part due to misconceptions of the relations between location, direction and visibility, but neither these circumstances nor the fact that spectral images, as opposed to real images, cannot affect things physically (by, e.g., being projected on a surface or altering photosensitive film chemically), prevent them from producing an experience of vision. In his view, the spectral properties of reflection should be counted in terms of their impact on visual perception. Examining the moment Alice gets through the mirror, Steenhagen observes a peculiar type of image forming (or catoptrics, as it is defined scientifically). Although Alice does not regard mirror images as illusions, she believes that what lies in the room 'behind' the mirror is distinct from what surrounds her in the drawing room in her house (Steenhagen 2017: 1233).

These are also interesting points for discussion in the selected editions of *Looking-Glass*, illustrated by John Tenniel ([1871] 1970), Blanche McManus (1899), Peter Newell (1902), Mervyn Peake (1946), Dagmar Berková (1961) and Brazilian artists João Fahrion (1947), Oswaldo Storni (n/d), Lila Figueiredo (1972) and Claudia Scatamacchia (n/d), in whose work this passage will be considered.

Starting with Tenniel's pair of wood-engravings illustrating the scene, they portray Alice, respectively, getting into the looking-glass and coming out on the other side, in perfect unison with her expectations. The two actions can be seen separately as each constitutes a distinct *moment of choice*, a term Edward Hodnett uses to classify 'the precise moment at which, as in a still from a cinema film, the action is stopped' (1986: 7). They also represent two stages of Alice's passing through the mirror, the first, of her investigation into its properties ('Let's pretend the glass has got all soft like gauze, so that we can get through. Why, it's turning into a sort of mist now, I declare! It'll be easy enough to get through –' [*TTLG*: 181, 184]); and, the second, of her experience of its potential as a gateway ('In another moment Alice was through the glass, and had jumped lightly down into the Looking-glass room' [*TTLG*: 184]).

Each picture is organized so as to imply movement by itself: in the first, Alice is knelt down on one knee on the mantelpiece and leaning forward in the direction of the mirror, as if entering it diagonally – and as if the left side of her body had already merged through; in the second, she is now coming forth, her left foot firmly planted on the mantelpiece and her left arm raised to the height of her chest to help project the rest of her body out of the mirror. Perry Nodelman observes that the representation of action before it is completed, that is, when it is about to 'reach its climax', but not yet at that point, is one of the most obvious means to imply movement: '[I]n imagining the inevitable follow-through of what we actually see, we ourselves create the motion' (1988: 160). Moreover, since both pictures consist of 'transitory states in a continuum' (Schwarcz 1982: 23), when seen in a sequence, they emphasize the sense of progress in time and, thus, the illusion that Alice moved from one room to the other.

These notions are certainly reinforced by the reversed position of the elements in the second picture. Note, for example, that even Tenniel's monogram was engraved backwards –although the engravers, the Dalziel Brothers, maintained their signature in the same direction, only placing it in the opposite side. The placement of the pictures on the page also plays an important part. In the original edition, the first picture occupies almost the entire space of a right-hand page, captioned by the lines describing the transformation of the mirror into a soft substance and Alice's passing through it. The second picture is then placed on the opposite, left-hand side of the same leaf, with the caption resuming from the exact point when Alice goes through the glass, so that, as the reader turns the page over, the effect that Alice moved from one side to the other is heightened, with the page working as the mirror itself (Hancher 1985: 130).[2] However, it is the point of view from which especially the second picture is portrayed that allows for the impression that Alice 'really' went through the mirror. Because the (assumed) perspective of the artist is always coincident with that of the viewer (see Nicolajeva and Scott 2006: 117–137), the reader becomes a witness to Alice's entrance to Looking-Glass land. It is as if the

2   Michael Hancher (1985: 130) considers other editions of *Looking-Glass* in which the superimposition of the two illustrations was maintained (such as The People's Edition and The Norton Critical Edition) and those (such as The Oxford English Novels Edition) in which they are placed on facing pages. In *The Annotated Alice* (1970), used in this paper, they follow the latter model.

reader had (hurried and) reached the other room even before her to testify to her arrival and the 'reality' of the place.

The point of view from which the scene was presented by other illustrators of the episode was fundamental to highlighting specific features in the dynamics of movement. McManus, Berková, and Figueiredo, for example, represented the passage as seen from the drawing room in Alice's house. Although taking different decisions as regards the moment of choice – McManus depicted the moment when Alice menaces to send Kitty through to Looking-Glass House; Berková, the one in which Alice was considering the possibility of going through the mirror herself; and Figueiredo, a later moment, when Alice was just about to pass through – they put more emphasis on aspects of reflection.

In McManus's illustration, Alice is seen from the left side of the picture. The implied reader is 'positioned' slightly to the left also in relation to her figure, so it is possible to see her face in profile in the mirror, together with parts of Kitty's body, since both are shown from the back and Alice's face is turned to the right as she speaks to the cat, supported on the mantelpiece by her right hand. In Berková's depiction, the upper part of Alice's body is totally reflected in the mirror, as she is standing on a small ottoman on the right side of the picture (holding Kitty on her chest), and facing the mirror diagonally, to be seen as in a bust photograph in the perspective of an observer on the left side. In Figueiredo's illustration, because the passage is portrayed from above, as if the artist was hovering over the room at the level of the mirror, just in front of it, the room is presented from its reflected image while Alice can be seen both from the right side (since her left cheek is touching the mirror surface in profile) and via the mirror.

Optical laws are in some ways infringed in the three illustrations. In McManus's representation, the images of both Alice and Kitty should be formed on the left side of the mirror, as they are shown from the left side of the picture. In turn, if the implied reader had been positioned right behind Alice, only Kitty would be seen, but its image could never be formed above its head, as the point of view is set at the level of the mantelpiece. In Berková's picture, since Alice is gazing into the mirror, the correct angle after divergence would cause her eyes to meet the reader's. Furthermore, because the line dividing the wall and the floor takes a straight path, cutting the

picture from left to right practically without shifting its course, the sense of
a transversal view of the room – which would otherwise be produced by an
oblique line starting at the height of the ottoman leg, on the left side, and
going upwards until it reached the right edge of the picture, following the
outline of the ottoman cushion – is reduced. As a result, the illusion that
Alice is shown in profile is also lessened, and, contrarily, she is perceived
as being in an awkward position, in which her feet are directed to the wall,
her face, turned to the mirror, and her torso also (uncomfortably) 'twisted'
in the same direction of her head.[3] In Figueiredo's illustration (even considering the inclination of the mirror), the effect of Siamese twin Alices,
joined together by the head and a common eye, would be more precisely
achieved with Alice's reflection looking at the opposite direction. But the
three compositions significantly elevate the emotional tone and tension of
the passage, as gestures and facial expressions play a more decisive role in
conveying Alice's momentary hesitation to invest in her belief.

In the illustrations by Newell, Peake, Fahrion, Storni and Scatamacchia
movement is given more prominence. The artists did not neglect Alice's
face. She displays a placid calmness in the drawings by Newell, Peake, and
Scatamacchia, surprise and curiosity in that by Storni and a certain appre-
hension in the one by Fahrion. However, because they depicted the precise
moment when she emerges out of the mirror into Looking-Glass land, as
seen from this place, her engagement in the act of moving is distinguished
as it is also essential to indicate the passage. In these pictures, thus, except
for Storni – and albeit from different points of view and distancing – the
illustrators portrayed Alice halfway from stepping into the new room, one
of her legs already through and the other, shown partially, implying that
it will soon appear; the same happening to her face and hands, shadowed
or layered by hatchings in different degrees to create the illusion that she
will completely materialize from the gelatinous surface of the mirror, but
only in an instant's time. As depicted by Storni, in turn, only Alice's arms
and hands are seen, as she arises in profile from the right side of the picture,

---

3   See the chapter on 'Balance' in Arnheim (1974) and how the shape and size of ob-
     jects, the position they occupy in a picture, etc. influence the direction of their con-
     stituting forces, altering the way we perceive them.

leaning over the mantelpiece to look at the face in a grimace on the back of the clock, and using them to support her weight.

These pictures, too, exhibit peculiar features. The point of view in Storni's illustration is a curious one: while Alice is shown from Looking-Glass room, in full view of a crackling fire in the firebox, she is still in the drawing room in her house. Two attributes of the drawing contribute to this effect. First, the mantelpiece was drawn in perspective, lining up from behind the mirror towards a vanishing point in the original room. Second, the explosive lines symbolizing the opening of the mirror do not outline her figure completely. Although they form a saturated black mass covering parts of the fireplace and other objects in the picture or crossing the mirror frame to imply that the portal is in the foreground, they surround Alice only up to the ribbon at the back of her dress. Thus, not only is she not seen as coming out of the mirror, but she appears to be arising out of the mantelpiece. As a means of comparison, in both Peake's and Newell's illustrations, the mantelpiece seems not to offer too much space for Alice to step on. On the other hand, together with Fahrion, they distinguished the soft consistency of the mirror, endowing it with depth and transparency so that Alice can be seen in both sides of its surface. Peake even created a vigorous structure to support the mirror by means of the intense lines of hatchings, the sophisticated columns, and the absence of frames around the drawing. As Nodelman observes, irregular borders promote more energy, involvement, and enhancement of the emotional tone in a drawing (1988: 50–58). Also, the mirror in Scatamacchia's picture looks more like a window, although the reflection of the grinning clock in the room in Alice's house, now evident in a reversed form from Looking-Glass room, is a remarkably original take on the scene.

In spite of its reduced number as examined here, these illustrations demonstrate that, following Carroll's text, the artists usually concentrate in the three main stages in the development of the episode, Alice's consideration of passing through the mirror, the passage itself, and her entering Looking-Glass land. In addition to the point of view, the style of each illustrator plays an important part in differentiating the way the episode is represented and its implications for the understanding of the narrative. The black-and-white depiction, prevailing in the pictures, gives them a more realistic quality, but which can vary in degree, depending on other aspects of the artist's work. Alice's hair and hands are more cartoonlike in Figueiredo's illustration than in the one by McManus, for example – which would set the book in a more childish atmosphere. Also, in black-and-white illustration, the predominance of line over shape, according to Nodelman, adds more energy to the scene being described in longer texts, as different from what happens in picture books (1988: 69). In the author's opinion, specifically about *Looking-Glass*, this is the case even in the pictures portraying inactivity (such as that of the sleeping king, in Chapter 4) and he suggests that '[t]hese active pictures balance Carroll's often slow-moving text' (1988: 69–70).

By extension, we can think that not only in Tenniel's illustrations but also in those by Scatamacchia or Fahrion, which clearly evidence line, there is more emphasis on Alice's attitudes, which can evoke excitement at her initiative and courage; as opposed to the representation by Newell, for instance, which would focus more on Alice's pensive look, as she slowly traverses into Looking-Glass land, implying restraint and hesitation. In this drawing, the technique of continuous tone[4] filling the spaces of the mirror and the fireplace, among other objects, gives the scene more solidity (see Nodelman 1988: 69–70), and, by making the upper part of Alice's body appear to be merged in the smooth, smoky surface of the mirror (also to denote her faint introduction to the new room), it restricts movement, rather emphasizing the emotion expressed on her face and involving the scene in the atmosphere – albeit with captivating grace – of timidity and doubt, suggested by it. Newell's illustration is also more likely to arouse narrative expectations. By means of the components of the room (the clock, a picture on the wall, the decorations of the fireplace, etc.), it provides enough details to attract the reader's attention and engage him/her in establishing cause-and-effect relationships (see Nodelman 1988: 175), fomenting interpretation. However, even the minimalist setting in Berkova's drawing can be potentially meaningful in that it isolates the mirror in its

---

4   Newell's drawings are well known for this technique. See his family papers at the
      Yale Archives: <https://archives.yale.edu/repositories/11/resources/1696>.

power as a symbol (allied to the very stillness of the scene), reinforcing Alice's tension before she decides to pass through.

In fact, what is in question in these illustrations is the existence of Looking-Glass land and the possibility of a new adventure for Alice, which was corroborated by these (and certainly other) artists portraying the episode. The illustrators imprinted a personal reading on the scene: by manipulating especially the notions of distance, point of view and reflection, each artist created a specific tone and mood for the story, changing Tenniel's classic images and promoting other views of Alice's entrance into the new universe. These aspects gain a special dimension if we keep in mind that, just like Carroll, the illustrators described a dream. Then shifts in settings, reflections at odd angles, blurs, asymmetries, discrepancies, etc. should all be seen in the impossibilities and distortions posited by the fantasies of the mind. Apart from the magical qualities of the mirror or the way (however unconditional) Alice may have gone through it, though, each of these artists created for the book a powerful narrative segment, with great potential to shape the reader's engagement with the (translated) text. They also promoted two levels of vision, Alice's, as she found herself before the mirror and the prospects it offered to her, and the reader's, whose eyes will see the scene as a whole. More importantly, they created a path they both could tread from the looking-glass to discover the new Wonderland lying in wait for them, and which proved to be as different on the other side of the mirror as Alice thought it was.

Adriana Peliano

23 Alicescope of Alicedelic Alicinations

Paradox, nonsense, game, labyrinth – the chessboard that underlies Lewis Carroll's *Looking-Glass* is moved by enigmatic paths, unpredictable curvatures, and impossible geometries. A traveller of the extraordinary, Alice had jumped into the rabbit-hole in *Wonderland*, and now crosses through the Looking-Glass and finds boards, enigmatic cabinets, labyrinths, secret gardens, and mysterious forests, as well as doors that lead to other doors. Lewis Carroll's work is the unknown land which the reader can cross, get lost in, and pioneer new meanings. Remember that the way forward depends on where each one wants to go.

Alice's dreams challenge our accommodated knowledge. The White Queen, for example, can remember the future. Lewis Carroll remembered the future before Einstein imagined relativistic concepts.[1] In Wonderland, time is relative. The Hatter says that Time is someone and he can speed up or slow down and do whatever we want with the clock. Alice's adventures anticipated concepts from modern physics that confront us with a reality that far surpasses imagination. In *Parallel Worlds: A Journey through Creation, Higher Dimensions and the Future of the Cosmos* (2004),[2] theoretical physicist Michio Kaku explains a surprising possibility that emerged from modern physics: that our universe can be just one among infinite others in a vast cosmic network. In an almost *alicedelic* view of reality, he announces: 'In the multiverse, there are parallel stages, one above the other, connected by hidden hatches and tunnels. The stages, in fact, give rise to other stages, in an endless process' (Kaku 2004).

1   For more connections between the works of Einstein and Carroll, see Chapters 6 and 19.
2   Michio Kaku, *Parallel Worlds: A Journey through Creation, Higher Dimensions and the Future of the Cosmos* (New York: Doubleday, 2004).

In 2021, Alice's challenging crossover into the looking-glass completed a 150-year journey. As far as her vision goes, the world Alice sees through the mirror at home is very similar, but she remarks, 'only you know it may be quite different on beyond'. Alice envisions a quantum reality – and a parallel universe – as she dives into the field of infinite possibilities. Crossing the millennium, Alice's mirror exploded into a million pieces, scattering new meta-Alices in an alicescope of alicinations exploring the enigma that still haunts us. Expanding wonderlands, many of today's most innovative immersive virtual reality experiences challenge the impossible, the language of dreams, and the crossing into paradoxical worlds governed by other laws, which are vectors of Alice's journey.[3]

Which Alices extrapolate the stereotyped models of the girl and her dream daring new alicedelic alicinations? Which Alice aspects can stimulate artistic creation? Having these questions in mind I hunted for seven artists and illustrators who incorporated the mirror, the impossible, and the dream as alicinators in their works. Some illustrated Carroll's book directly, two present a more open connection in a picture book and visual arts. Now let us visit some of their work, with this point of view in mind.

Figure 54. Adriana Peliano, *Crisalice VII*, 2015.

---

3   For a visualization in data analysis see chapter [Nobriga] in this collection, and chapter [Schilero] for an exploration of Carroll alongside Einstein, and [McLeish] on scientists, Carroll, quantum science and the imagination in science.

The Looking Glass

Among contemporary Alices, John Tenniel's canonical illustrations become fertile ground for the seeds of metalanguage to thrive. After Tenniel, for decades, little was innovated. But Alice came to live in surrealism and psychedelia, and was ubiquitous in pop culture, contemporary art, psychoanalysis, and quantum physics – no longer just a Victorian girl, but a mobile and disruptive, mutating kaleidoscope, what I call an 'alicescope of alicinations'.

Figure 55. Abelardo Morell, *We Can Talk Said the Tiger-Lily*, 2020.

Decades after illustrating *Alice in Wonderland* in 1998, Abelardo Morell travelled with Alice through the *Looking-Glass* (2020). Integrating photographs and computer graphics, he articulated lenses and distortions, mirrors and reflections in alicedelias that disturb the realistic representation of space by investigating new geometries (Figure 55).[4] While references to Tenniel bring the authority and unanimity of the canon, Morell's boards become metamorphic surfaces in which the photographer plays with logic; multiplies, fragments, distorts, inverts, liquefies; plays with lights and shadows; and believes in the impossible, challenged by a call from a multidimensional enigmatic puzzle.

Figure 56. Suzy Lee, *Illustration of the Book Mirror*, 2003.

4   For more on Carroll and new Geometries see chapter [Schilero] in this collection.

Fascinated by the nightmarish and strange atmosphere, Korean author and illustrator Suzy Lee recreates *Alice in Wonderland* in a picture book that dialogues with the enigma proposed by Carroll: which is it that casts dreams into dreams. The artist comments on her project in the book *The Border Trilogy* (2018),[5] in which a meta-linguistic reflection on the creation and reading of picture books is presented. Among them, the book *Mirror* (2003)[6] stands in dialogue with the work of Lewis Carroll, showing the games a girl plays with her reflection. The mirror is freed from symmetry by fantasy, as in *Looking-Glass*, or in the mirrors of René Magritte, who was inspired by the mysterious space between word and image, questioning language, logic, space-time, and the borders of the dream.

What matters here is not the world the girl finds on the other side, but the relationships that the reader activates in the fluid articulation between the narrative, illustrations, and materiality of the book. The artist explores possibilities of how the book will be manipulated by the reader, and the production of meaning occurs in the movement of flipping through the pages, like crossing through the mirror. In a complex way, the mirror expresses itself in the materiality of the book, with its margins, folds, and emptiness. It is crucial to remember that the two Tenniel illustrations of Alice crossing through the looking-glass were printed on the front and back of the same page, so the reader also dissolves through the mirror while turning the page. For Suzy Lee, reading a picture book is like deciphering puzzles, proliferating meanings, and enjoying ambiguity to explore language and challenge the reader.

'I, Kusama, am the modern Alice in Wonderland', announced Japanese artist Yayoi Kusama in a pamphlet for a happening at the famous Alice in Wonderland statue in New York's Central Park in 1968.[7] A pioneer of pop art, minimalism, and of the unclassifiable, in various media she shares disturbing perceptions, obsessions, and visions of the infinite. To Kusama, Alice was the grandmother of hippies. The artist arrived in Central Park as

5   Suzy Lee, *The Border Trilogy* (Mantova, Italy: Corraini Edizioni, 2018).
6   Suzy Lee, *Mirror* (New York: Seven Footer Press, 2003).
7   For discussion of Kusama among a tradition of female surrealists, see also chapter (Kennell) in this collection.

Figure 57. Yayoi Kusama, *'Alice in Wonderland' Happening, 1968*.

the Hatter, with naked dancers, inviting everyone to drink the tea that was
being served on the magic mushroom. She painted circles on the bodies of
those present so that they would divest themselves of their physical contours
and return 'to the nature of the universe' in a psychedelic experience, at
once sensory, political, spiritual, and cosmic. Decades later, during a major
exhibition of her work at Tate Modern in London in 2012, the artist was
invited to illustrate *Alice in Wonderland*, echoing her positioning from
the 1960s.

   In parallel, Kusama produced more than twenty environments surrounded by mirrors, creating labyrinths of kaleidoscopic reflections. When
she called herself 'modern Alice', she also referred to one of those spaces

where she lived surrounded by what she called the *Infinity Mirror Room –
Phalli's Field* (Figure 57). Kusama's mirrors challenge the senses, the perception of the body in space, producing a labyrinthine game of reflections
through lights in a dizzying experience of an immersive *mise en abîme*. We
disappear into the kaleidoscopic space traversed by Kusama's vision in her
world of madness and artistic lucidity, between the feeling of confinement
and the cosmic experience of limitlessness, emphasizing the challenge of
death and impermanence of life.

The Impossible

In Looking-Glass land, the White Queen practised half an hour a day
believing in the impossible. Alice insisted that she couldn't believe in impossible things: 'I daresay you haven't had much practice', the Queen re-
sponded.[8] The Queen had turned into a sheep – and owned a mysterious
store of quantum properties. When Alice tries to fix her gaze on the objects in the store, their shelf was always empty, while all the others seem to
be full. Alice's challenge can be compared to the impossible task of determining the precise location of an electron. Before making an observation,
it exists simultaneously in all possible states, but when observed, the wave
function collapses and the electron locks into a single state. Alice's mirror
defies reality as we know it.[9]

John Vernon Lord has experienced with creations that dialogue with
the language of dreams in literature (he has also illustrated James Joyce's
Finnegans Wake). He created a paradoxical architecture for the sheep shop,
as well as illustrating the Queen's exercises to believe in the impossible.
On one of the shelves inside the store, you can see its exterior through the
image of a store in Oxford, one that Lewis Carroll and Alice Liddell used

---

8   *TTLG*, Chapter V.
9   A similar effect in quantum physics is named 'Quantum Cheshire Cat'; for a discus-
     sion of it in the context of *Looking-Glass*, see Chapter 12 in this collection.

Illustrating *Looking-Glass*

Figure 58. John Vernon Lord, *The Sheep in the Shop*, 2011.

to visit. The store later became 'Alice's Shop', dedicated to ever-multiplying memorabilia inspired by Alice's adventures – becoming, in a way, a mirror to Alice's transfigurations over space and time (Figure 58).

The impossible objects in Lord's illustration cross the chessboard and overlap in simultaneous planes. Impossible objects such as the ones present in his illustration are a type of optical illusion and consist of a two-dimensional figure that is interpreted in the subconscious as a projection of a three-dimensional object. Lord's picture features a series of such figures, such as Oscar Reutersvärd's impossible trident, which has been called 'the

Figure 59. John Vernon Lord, *Six Impossible Things*, 2011.

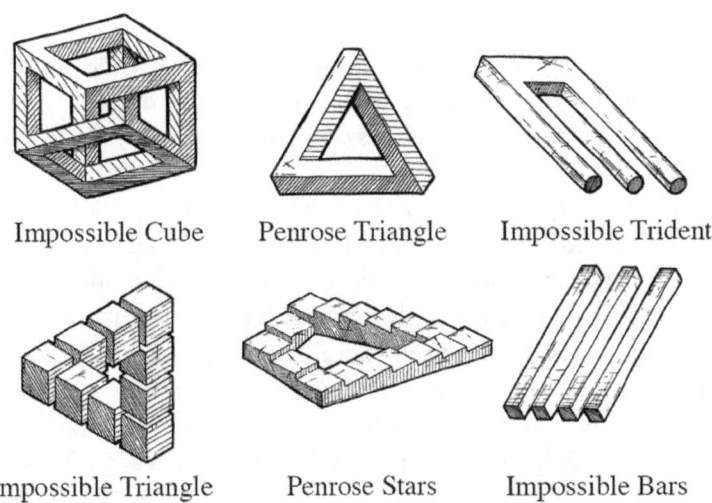

Impossible Cube   Penrose Triangle   Impossible Trident

Impossible Triangle   Penrose Stars   Impossible Bars

Figure 60. M. C. Escher, Oscar Reutersvärd, Roger Penrose and others,
Impossible Objects.

Figure 61. Iassen Ghiuselev, *Illustration for Through the Looking-Glass*, 2014.

father of impossible figures' and also the triangle that mathematician and philosopher Roger Penrose popularized in the 1950s, describing it as 'impossibility in its pure form' (Figures 59 and 60).[10] Is it possible to illustrate the impossible?

After leaving the Looking-Glass House, Alice decides to go up the hill to see the garden. She starts to follow a path that seems to lead straight there, but after walking a few yards, she starts taking sudden and unexpected turns. 'But how curiously it twists! It looks more like a corkscrew than a path!' (The solution was to walk in the opposite direction from where you want to go). Since the other side of the mirror is traversed by a nonlinear logic, an image of Alice through the mirror painted by the award-winning Bulgarian artist Iassen Ghiuselev simultaneously condenses

10   L. S. Penrose and R. Penrose, 'Impossible Objects: A Special Type of Visual Illusion'. *British Journal of Psychology* (February 1958), 31–33.

the entire story into a paradoxical topology. When looking through the image, we are challenged to change our point of view all the time, and as we rotate the image, new worlds are revealed. The painting took several years to complete and the possibilities of discovering something new never seem to run out.

Ghiuselev's art is characterized by an exquisite painting technique inspired by Renaissance art and nineteenth-century realism. The environments reference medieval architectures, yet evoke the art of M. C. Escher. The dizzying composition suggests a maze of nightmares and unsolvable challenges where Alice puts into practice the art of getting lost in a world in constant metamorphosis (Figure 61). Maurits Cornelis Escher devoted most of his life to the implausible and paradoxical. He plunged into infinity with obsessive mathematical precision. Escher played with mirrors and reflections, encouraging the ongoing practice of believing in the impossible.

The Dream

Dreams, like the creative process, involve a radical shift in perception, a suspension of conventional reality, a recombination of ideas challenging the unusual and impossible. In the twentieth century, in the work of surrealists such as Salvador Dalí, Rene Magritte, Max Ernst, Leonora Carrington, and Dorothea Tanning, among others, Alice opened the door to the marvellous, blurring the boundaries between the unconscious and the conscious, the dream and reality. At the end of *Looking-Glass*, Carroll throws us a challenge, echoing his interest in psychic phenomena: 'Life, what is it but a dream?', and an even deeper philosophical question just before that: 'Which dreamed it?'

Czech surrealist Jan Švankmajer directed two powerful and unforgettable films inspired by Carroll's work: *Jabberwocky* (1971) and the feature film *Alice* (*Něco z Alenky*, 1988). He also illustrated the two *Alice* books with drawings and collages which go beyond the descriptive representation

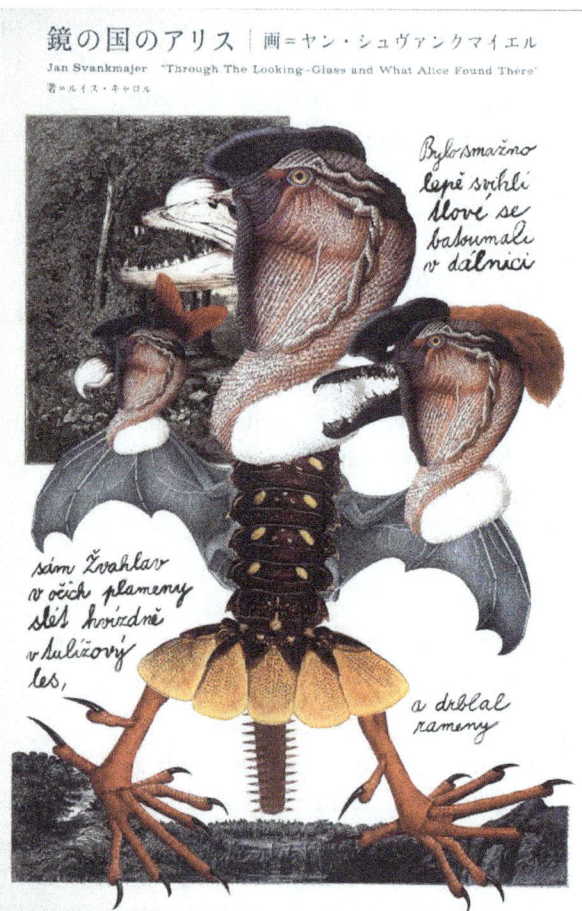

Figure 62. Jan Švankmajer, *Jabberwock*, 2011.

of history, diving into the fluidity of dream, metamorphosis, desire, shadows, and alchemy. In oneiric territory, the portmanteaux created by Lewis Carroll act through displacements, condensations, and unusual associations. Composed of two meanings wrapped up in a single word, portmanteaux appear in the poem 'Jabberwocky' in a scenario of strange creatures (Figure 62). Švankmajer's portmanteaux have become a creative principle composed of hybrid monsters, from different realms, species and objects, fragmentations and juxtapositions, and encounters of contradictory realities, which submerge from deep layers of the mental jungle. According to him, imagination is subversive because it puts possibilities before reality. 'Creativity is a process of permanently liberating people', he stated in his *Decalogue*.[11]

Figure 63. Maggie Taylor, *He Was Part of My Dream*, 2017.

A form of *mise en abîme* is involved in the parallel dreams of Alice and the Red King. 'You see, Kitty, it must have been either me or the

11   *Vertigo*, 3, 1, Summer 2006, 72. Translated from the Czech by Tereza Stechlíková. Quoted in Peter Hames, *Dark Alchemy: The Cinema of Švankmajer* (London: Wallflower Press, 1995), 112.

Figure 64. Maggie Taylor, *I Was Part of His Dream*, 2017.

Red King. He was part of my dream, of course–but then I was part of his dream, too!'[12]

The awareness of being in a dreaming state leads us to a phenomenon called 'lucid dreams'. The theme attracts the attention of psychologists, mystics, and artists and is lived by shamans in various cultures. During these dreams, oneironauts are aware that they are dreaming and can control the plot of the dream and the creation of the dream universe. This is a path of profoundly transformative journeys. Among the techniques capable of elevating the perception of the dream state is the habit of asking oneself frequently during the day, 'Am I dreaming?' Isn't that a fundamental question of Alice in *Looking-Glass*?

12   *Looking-Glass*, Chapter XII.

Digital artist Maggie Taylor builds fantastical and surreal narratives that bring out the fantasy and wonder of Alice's adventures. Combining old photographs with computer graphics, Taylor makes use of layers of superimpositions and poetic lighting that create a dreamlike atmosphere in which the notion of time is diluted. She creates magic tricks that play with the codes of photography, illusionism, and theatre through sequences of curtains, stages, and landscapes in *trompe l'oeil* stages for the world of dreams and wonder (Figure 62 and 63).

Figure 65. Adriana Peliano, *A Fabulous Monster*, 2015.

The *Alice* books are an inexhaustible source of creativity and invention. Since I was a child, I've become a strange kind of Alice, and my adventures in a world of wonders have been full of alicinations. On this adventure,

I illustrated a special edition for the 150th anniversary of *Alice's Adventures in Wonderland* in 2015.[13] During the pandemic in 2020, I wrote and illustrated the book *Alice and the 7 Keys*,[14] also through collages using illustrations by John Tenniel and others. With collage, the figures open up to free reinvention, promoting poetic strangeness, and unexpected associations and intertextual operations (Figure 65).

The girl with alicescopic eyes dreams while we wander in woods where things have no names, flow in the river of metamorphosis, believe in impossible things, follow paradoxical and labyrinthine paths, have tea with Time and the Impossible. Instead of asking 'Who is Alice?', today we go through mirror mazes looking for who Alice may *become*.

In 2022, 'Carrollsday' curator Beatriz Mom and the Lewis Carroll Society of Brazil proposed the exhibition 'Alices through the Looking-Glass' in celebration of the 150th anniversary of *Looking-Glass*. I selected books, created chessboards of different Alices crossing the mirror simultaneously, and created new alicedelias. An Aliceoscope (Picture) shows Alice envisioning new dimensions of reality. Alice's looking-glass can encourage encounters with uncertainty, the unexplored, and the unknown. Alice invites us to dare the boundaries of dreams, sanity, and reality and trust in our wildest imagination.

Thinking as a collagist, in her *Looking-Glass* journey, Alice finds a 'Bread-and-butter-fly'. These insects are like collages in word and image, maybe a surrealist object, subverting both the commonplace and common sense. Isn't the portmanteau a performagic collage? It is based on the principle of association of ideas, in the search for new and unusual connections, in surprise, in transformation.

Alice immersed herself in a never-ending story that continues to inspire spirals of dreams and surprising challenges in our hearts and minds. It challenges the limiting ways of understanding art and life, space and time, reality and dreams, and even who we are. New Alices in different areas of knowledge, arts, and languages invite us to open new doors in imagination and thought. Faced with the unusual characters and events in *Looking-Glass*,

13   Lewis Carroll, *As Aventuras de Alice no País das Maravilhas/Através do Espelho* (Rio de Janeiro: Zahar, 2015).

14   Adriana Peliano, *Alice and the 7 Keys* (Kissimmee: Underline Publishing, 2020).

we are challenged to believe in the unbelievable and make the impossible possible, trusting our dreams, reinventing life, and awakening to new realities, remembering that Marcel Duchamp once said, 'I am convinced that, like Alice in Wonderland, [the young artist] will be led to pass through the looking-glass of the retina, to reach a more profound expression.'[15]

15   Marcel Duchamp, 'Where Do We Go from Here?' Symposium at the Philadelphia Museum College of Art, 1961. First published in the Supplement to *Studio International* 189.973 (January/February 1975).

Part IX

Literary Reflections: Before Carroll

Francesca Arnavas

24 Lewis Carroll's Looking-Glass: In between Fairy Tale Magic Mirror and Victorian Glassworld

In classic fairy tales, mirrors are notoriously objects of paramount importance: 'Snow White', 'The Snow Queen', and 'Beauty and the Beast' are just a few extremely popular examples. Mirrors are made of glass, and the Victorian Age has been defined a 'glassworld' by Isobel Armstrong: an era characterized by what she calls 'a many-faceted poetics of glass' (2008: 16). Lewis Carroll's reflections on glass and mirrors in *Looking-Glass* are positioned in dialogue with this complex nexus – the fairy tale tradition of magic mirrors, on the one hand, and the peculiar significance of glass in Victorian times, on the other. This chapter explores how Carroll's *Looking-Glass* elaborates and plays with motifs from these two backgrounds, using concepts from cognitive narratology. This chapter falls into two parts: the first focuses on Carroll's manipulation of the fairy-tale motif of the magic mirror using the concept of cognitive deixis to illuminate his narrative techniques. The second section analyses how Carroll's depiction of the Looking-Glass land is inserted into the cultural milieu of 'Victorian glass culture', and how the 'paradoxical nature of glass' (as defined by Armstrong) is reinterpreted. I thus consider Carroll's looking-glass in the light of the concepts of conceptual blending and of cognitive metaphor.

Carroll's Looking-Glass vs Fairy Tale Magic Mirrors

Cristina Bacchilega points out how complex fairy tale retellings enact a 'doubling strategy' (1997: 10), meaning that they both reproduce the traditional metaphor of the magic mirror and, at the same time, deconstruct it through the use of de-naturalizing strategies. In this sense, Carroll's representation of what Alice finds on the other side of the looking-glass anticipated a prominent feature of postmodern fairy tales: the 'holding a mirror to the magic mirror of the fairy tale, playing with its framed images out of a desire to multiply its refractions and to expose its artifices' (Bacchilega 1997: 23). In fairy tales, the significant role and the mirror's authority often goes unquestioned, as critics have observed (Bacchilega 1997; Harries 2004; Schanoes 2009). The Evil Queen's mirror in *Snow White* is the living, infrangible metaphor of the male gaze's controlling mastery (Gilbert and Gubar 1979; Bacchilega 1997), and it is also the voice of authoritative truth throughout the tale. The mirror is thus assumed to mimetically show an unquestionable, static (and often patriarchal) reality.

Carroll's looking-glass, on the other hand, refused 'to serve as a "mirror of nature"' and broke with the mimetic tradition, 'anticipating many new literary techniques developed later during the proliferation of multiple forms of experimental literature in the twentieth century' (Schwab 1996: 49). Considered in a somehow more simplistic and matter-of-fact way, the mirror is a mimetic tool, which presents a faithful reproduction of reality, which is the way fairy tales such as *Snow White* interpret it. In them, mirrors trap and encapsulate identities and meanings in a rigid referential way. What Carroll does in his fictional treatment of the mirror is the exact opposite: the mirror gives back an inverted version of reality in which all things 'go the other way' (147). One has to go back to proceed forward (170), needs to eat dry biscuits to quench thirst (175), jokes make people sad (as it happens to the Gnat, 185), and memory works as a recollection of future events (as the White Queen explains to Alice, 206). This inverted dimension allows Carroll to question traditional fairy-tale tropes and to disrupt readers' expectations by playing with their deictic centre.

A deictic shift (or cognitive deixis) is the cognitive move a reader has to make in order to access a fictional world – interpreted not as a pre-existing fixed entity, but as a mental space generated through the dynamic negotiation between readers and text. A fictional text provides many deictic indications that allow the readers to conjure up the mental model of the story world. These indications refer to the where of the text, the who, the when, et cetera. A specific textual genre (a detective novel, a fairy tale, a romance) is characterized by 'distinctive configuration of deictic elements' (Hanks 2005: 100): all the different types of deixis lead readers to position the text inside a specific genre.

What Carroll does when constructing the complex narrative space of the Looking-Glass land is purposely destabilizing the readers' deictic position. Carroll gives the reader a fairy tale with a female protagonist, who is also a child: which could, at first glance, be considered the most powerless and fragile element in a patriarchal society such as in the Victorian Age. However, Carroll keeps playing with these two aspects, the fairy tale genre and the little girl as the main character, to upset such readers' expectations. Once the little girl goes through the looking-glass, both the fairy tale tradition and her seemingly powerless identity are questioned. Alice is never a victim, a poor helpless girl, a damsel in distress: she is the one consciously putting herself in a perilous situation. In *Alice's Adventures in Wonderland* the fall in the rabbit-hole is not the result of an erroneous stumbling, but an act driven by curiosity similarly the act of going through the looking-glass is the result of a deliberate decision.

Furthermore, classical fairy tales manipulate reader expectations through goal-oriented narrative patterns. While Alice does not have a specific task to accomplish or a mission to undertake: later in the story she decides she wants to become a queen (however, importantly, what it means to be a queen in the Looking-Glass land does not match the meaning of fairy-tale conventions) and reach the end of the chessboard, but the start of her journey in the Looking-Glass land, once more, happens just because of her curiosity. Curious women have a history of being punished because of what is portrayed as a typically feminine flaw, leading them to dangerous situations in myths. Pandora opens the box with fatal consequences for her and all of humanity; Psyche watches her lover, curious to see what he looks like, going against clear interdiction, consequently obliged to undertake a painful journey full of troubles and suffering; when Eve eats the forbidden fruit, she commits what is portrayed as the most tragic of all mistakes.

Similarly, Victorian novels abound with young children (women and children are thus equated in being prone to sin and mistakes) being punished because of their own, apparently unrestrained curiosity. As Alice herself recalls in *Alice's Adventures in Wonderland*: 'for she had read several nice little stories about children who had got burnt, and eaten up by wild beasts, and other unpleasant things' (17) because they did not follow the wise advice of adults. Therefore, Victorian readers of *Alice* may have anticipated punishment; but Alice is never punished. Moreover, she keeps committing the same action: doing something because she is curious, and thus all her adventures are made possible.

Alice finds herself in a garden of magic talking flowers, and readers, especially Victorian readers, are led, from these deictic indications, to expect a certain scenario. Victorian girls were often depicted in relation to gardens, whether in association with gender-related reflections, matters of education and proper behaviour, or celebrations of purity and grace. Juliana Horatia Ewing celebrates childhood as an idyllic Golden Age in her depiction of the meanderings of a girl named Ida in a beautiful garden (*Mrs Otherway's Remembrances*); in his fantasy worlds, Carroll's friend George MacDonald often describes young girls in the setting of enchanting (and sometimes enchanted) gardens, surrounded by snowdrops, bluebells, roses, daisies, or fairy-flowers, such as princess Irene often playing in the garden in *The Princess and the Goblins*, Nycteris wandering in the garden at night in *The Day Boy and The Night Girl*, the various young maidens playing among flowers and fairies in *Phantastes, Heather and Snow*.

The readers' deictic centre is thus moved into this expected literary scenario, but Carroll's reversal strategy disrupts these expectations, suddenly moving the readers' perspective in the context of a parody: a dark and humorous setting where the flowers are rude, unpleasant, or aggressive towards the little girl walking among them. By troubling the readers' deictic position, Carroll's Looking-Glass land enacts a demystification from the very beginning, proving the instability of conventional beliefs and, in this case, explicitly ridiculing the Victorian literary trope of the little girl in the flower garden.[1]

Later on, Alice assumes the role of the damsel in distress, when attacked by the Red Knight, who comes galloping towards her, declaring 'you're my prisoner!' (245), and the readers' frame of mind may be transported into a specific narrative dimension, in which the White Knight, acting as a prince charming may be expected to rescue her. The filter of the *Looking-Glass* reversing technique makes this the opposite of what would have happened in a fairy tale: here, it is Alice who saves the White Knight after his fall into a ditch, instead of the other way around. Tenniel's illustration of the scene overturns the concept of the popular Pre-Raphaelite trope that, at the same time as Looking-Glass, often displayed the knight saving the damsel in distress.

Looking-Glass's plot thus displays an unconventional development, in which the Victorian girl protagonist does not behave according to what a contemporary reader may expect, and it has been argued that her vicissitudes do not lead to any moral acquisition. Gillian Beer asserts that Alice's journeys in Wonderland and in the Looking-Glass Land are both episodic and dreamlike travels where the sense of a linear, meaningful progression leading to moral achievements is questioned and overturned; 'the picaresque nature of Alice's travels […] resist[s] seeking a moral progress or apotheosis' (2016: 25). She succeeds by her own means: Morton Cohen emphasizes this by saying that 'Alice should meet a strong male rescuer, a Prince Charming, and they should fall in love and live happily ever after. But she does not. She succeeds, but not through the formula of grand romance' (1995: 139). Her successful achievement is, however, as said, not linked to a clear moral attainment – Carroll's dream narratives do not follow the model of progressive moral transformation as in the tradition of *The Pilgrim's Progress* or *A Christmas Carol*, but they instead overturn also this trope the readers were accustomed to.

In *Dizionario della Fiaba* (*The Dictionary of Fairy Tales*) by Teresa Buongiorno, the *Alice* books are listed among fairy tales, but their peculiar

---

1   On Carroll's and his peculiar treatment of gardens (and little girls in them) and plants, see Arnavas 'Come into the Garden Alice', 2021.

interpretation of the genre is again highlighted, stressing how the amoral, purposeless and romance-less plot defies many of the traditional fairy-tale narrative schemes (2014: 37–40). This is particularly noticeable in *Looking-Glass*, because Alice seems to have a clearer goal than in *Wonderland* (getting to the end of the chessboard and becoming a queen), and the idea of the girl turning into a queen may appear to match a fairy-tale like structure. There are, furthermore, two knights fighting for her, and a golden crown awaiting: however, these elements are employed in order to mark even more evidently than in Wonderland the distance from the classic fairy-tale plot. Turning into a queen does not improve Alice's situation, nor does it represent a particularly meaningful event: she ends up together with the two other queens, who are insufferable, at a nonsensical party in which guests turn into their own dishes, and from which she wakes up by getting angry (*TTLG*: 274–280). The parodic intent behind Carroll's writing is apparent in his treatment of fairy-tale tropes.

Thus, if classic fairy tales' magic mirrors, as Bacchilega emphasizes, reinforce the patriarchal status quo, presenting themselves as mimetic re-productions of reality, Carroll's *Looking-Glass* is used in the opposite way, subverting certain apparently fixed conventions. It shows the *non-mimetic* qualities of mirrors, and their invertive potential to counter such children's stories that reflect and reinforce a static, pre-defined reality which traps protagonists (as Snow White's example shows), and often the readers as well. The Carrollian mirror ridicules and questions such fairy-tale tropes as the obligatory romance, the lack of power of girls, and the importance of the rags-to-riches plot, retrospectively, written into many fairy-tales.[2] Alice does not enjoy being a queen, is not rescued by a valiant knight, and wakes up through the power of her own anger.

2   With 'traditional' tropes here I am referring on the one hand to the Perrault's version of many fairy tales, such as 'Cinderella' or 'Sleeping Beauty', that were circulating in Victorian times. As pointedly highlighted by Molly Clark Hillard, talking about different fairy tales popular in the Victorian Age: '[T]he versions most available and familiar to an English audience were those of Perrault and Grimm, and these overwrote the more subversive version of the tales' (175); on the other hand, later reformulations and the so-called 'Disneyfication' process tended too to reinforce the more patriarchal and conventional messages and tropes.

Carroll's Looking-Glass as a Victorian Glassworld

Carroll uses 'looking-glass' in the title of the second *Alice* book, and, as Armstrong observes, glass is 'an antithetical material': 'It holds contrary states within itself as barrier and medium' (11). Glassy surfaces offer reflection, as well as seeing through, providing a mediating term between the seer and the seen, enacting representations of contradictions.[3] Alice's navigation through the looking-glass, with its embedded contradictions, represents – and duplicates – this paradoxical nature of glass, and its narrative potential. Accessing the world on the other side of the mirror provides an overview of a dimension in which conflicting elements can coexist, and be productive.

According to cognitive metaphor theory (CMT) (Fludernik 2011), metaphors are ubiquitous and define our mind's structure itself. Lakoff and Johnson's work *Metaphors We Live By* demonstrated how basic and universal metaphor-related patterns inform our everyday – thinking, and more sophisticated metaphors are to be found in writers' creative elaborations. The metaphor of the mirror in Carroll's *Looking-Glass* positions itself in both these two scenarios: on the one hand, as a pervasive recurring figure in fairy tales, and, on the other hand, as entangled with the glass culture of the Victorian period. It is through the questioning and creative discussion on mirrors and glass of the Victorian Age that the solidity of certain fairy tales' conceptual metaphor of the mirror begins to shake. This creative discussion manifested, as thoroughly analysed and explained by Armstrong, in various media and fashions, from the proliferation of glass objects (windows, mirrors, chandeliers, glasshouses) to the evocation of mirrors in paintings, poetry, and novels, from the making of optical toys to the interlacing of philosophical reflections with mirror-related images.

'The language of glass in the physical world and texts' (Armstrong 2008: 14) in Victorian England makes the glass (and its closely related figure, the mirror) an overpowering and poly-signifying conceptual

---

3   See Chapters 4 and 8 on the scientific and theological significance of this
     observation.

metaphor, which embodied conflicts and contradictions of the period itself: '[C]onsciousness, doubled as reflection, can achieve reflective awareness. This is a state that is both metaphor and pun and a literal condition' (Armstrong 2008: 12). The Crystal Palace [London's 1851], in this sense, represents the main symbol of the period's complex relationship with glass. Carroll's Looking-Glass land thus resembles the Crystal Palace as a space of hybridities, conflicting forms and meanings, in which Unicorns think little girls are fabulous monsters, butterflies are made of bread and butter, queens turn into sheep, flowers melt, and bottles merge with plates and forks and become birds. In this scenario, Alice herself has a mutable, metamorphic identity, and her story can be seen as another variation on the Cinderella motif, in which glass is connected to transformations and novel identities (see also Arnavas 2021; Hill, Mears, Sampson and Vaclavik 2016; Talairach-Vielmas 2014).

Making a pun with what the labels on packages containing glass may state, that is, 'glass, with care', one of the insects travelling on the train with Alice says 'she must be labelled "Lass, with care"' (180): Alice has thus 'become a transparent specimen' (Armstrong 2008: 329). Examined through the lens of the Cinderella-analogy, if Cinderella's glass slipper makes it possible for Cinderella to experience dazzling alterations, then *Looking-Glass* enacts profound changes in Alice's world and self. The peculiar nature of glass gives Alice a 'glass-identity', a new way of reflecting herself in the world on the other side of the mirror, which showcases and questions the contradictions rooted in her identity as a Victorian girl, often constrained by rigid limitations.

The Looking-Glass land inserts itself in the reworking of the conceptual metaphor of the mirror, which was an embedded part of Victorian culture, and it can also be considered a complex blended space. Blending is an expansion of metaphorical thought, which implies the projection of input stories into a blended space. The Looking-Glass land is a commingled space in that it combines representations of the Victorian world with elements of a nonsensical fairy tale for children, resulting in a blend which is both a parody of the Victorian Age and a piece of dreamy nonsense literature, neither of which can be reduced to the other.

Glass instantiates the coexistence of different, even contradictory states. The blended story of *Looking-Glass* amalgamates also the story of Alice's journey the experience of growing up and making sense of the world: two stories which often do not align well with each other, as Alice's becoming Queen, which seems to match her ideal of growth as empowerment and conquest, but this is in the end represented as a senseless, ridiculous, and even destructive[4] achievement.

4   The feast celebrating Alice's queenship ends up with the guests drowning in their own soups or becoming their own meals, and in Alice's dream completely collapsing.

Afrinul Haque Khan

25 Through the Prism of the Looking-Glass: Inversion, Emancipation, and Power

In this chapter, I explore, through an analysis of Lewis Carroll's *Looking-Glass* and Alfred Lord Tennyson's *The Lady of Shalott*, how Carroll's text uses the mirror as a tool to challenge the ideals and conventions that subjugated the women and restricted their lives to the domestic spheres during the Victorian Age. According to Olive M. Stone, '[w]hen Queen Victoria ascended the throne in 1837, the status of women in England was probably as low as it had been throughout the whole of recorded history' (Stone 1972: 592). *Looking-Glass*, through a reconfiguration of power dynamics, anticipates female emancipation and power. Quite contrary to Tennyson's depiction of his female protagonist in 'The Lady of Shalott' as a victim of patriarchy, Carroll portrays Alice as a strong-willed character whose assertiveness and quest for might and power in a strange and alien world challenge the Victorian beliefs, values, and assumptions regarding women – and are portrayed as positive traits. This chapter examines how *Looking-Glass*, through an inversion of reality, attempts a radical rethinking of patriarchal structures of domination and oppression which led the women to suffer multiple dispossessions.

Interrogating Female Subjectivity

It is helpful to reconsider the figure of Lady of Shallot through the lens of contemporary feminist literary criticism to give further context to such an interpretation and analysis of *Looking-Glass*. How might we come to see the figure of the legendary Lady of Shalott, as a victim of patriarchal norms who suffers isolation and confinement? Confined within the walls of the tower, she is cursed to see the real world only through its limited reflection in the mirror, while spending her entire life weaving a 'magic web', 'by night or day'. The tragic irony of her life is that she does not even know 'what the curse may be' and 'so she weaveth steadily' (Tennyson 2014: 63) without showing any resistance and without engaging in any 'sport or play', even though she is 'half sick of shadows' (64). Like a prisoner, she is indefinitely detained in a room, and is denied access to public life or space. She leads, to use the words of Judith Butler, 'a precarious life'.[1] It is obvious that unequal power relations underpin such gendering which takes the form of 'curse' forcing the lady to live in isolation that leads to her exclusion from the society. Parker and Pollock note that 'power is not only a matter of coercive forces. It operates through exclusion from access to those institutions and practices through which dominance is exercised' (1981: 114). The Lady of Shalott, therefore, may be understood as representing the position of oppressed women in the Victorian society who were kept 'imprisoned within the distaff circle and cut off from most "serious" business life' (Schwarzbach 1985: 51). Tennyson uses the word 'mirror' five times in the poem. While the repetition adds to the tragic effect, as the lady uses the mirror to catch a glimpse of the 'real' world outside, its usage with the preposition 'thro' in line 10, 'And moving thro' a mirror clear' and line 24, 'And sometimes thro' the mirror blue' of Part II of the poem brings to mind Lewis Carroll's use of the word in the title of *Through the Looking-Glass*. It is also interesting to note in this context that while the Lady of Shallot, as mentioned above, sees the real world, beyond where she is, through the mirror, Alice, leaves the real world through the mirror, albeit in her dreams, to enjoy freedom and power.

---

1   See Butler (2004). She uses the term to discuss the possibilities of safe lives.

Inversion, Emancipation, and Power

It seems possible that some of the title and creative ideas of Carroll's text were inspired, at least in part, by Tennyson's poem. Carroll had a great passion for his poetry and had met the poet and his family on several occasions, and even photographed them. Documentary evidence suggests that Carroll even had discussed with Tennyson passages of 'Maud' that he found troubling.[2] The much-discussed portrait of Alice at age six posing as a beggar child in a tattered off-the-shoulder dress is believed to be based on Tennyson's poem, 'The Beggar Maid' (1842). Carroll was also friends with many of the Pre-Raphaelites, many of whom like Dante Gabriel Rossetti, Elizabeth Siddall, and William Holman Hunt, had found a rich source of inspiration in the Lady of Shalott, made into paintings and drawings. All these connections may lead us to wonder what Lewis Carroll thought of, writing the sequel of *Alice's Adventures in Wonderland* as a token of remembrance of the golden moments spent on that 'boat beneath a sunny sky' – the boat also being the most frequently depicted scene of the Lady of Shallot in the paintings (Carroll 2009: 245) – with Alice Liddell, who, being the starting point for 'Alice' was, in 1871, a young woman of nineteen years.

Drawing thus perhaps inspiration from the use of the mirror in 'The Lady of Shalott' which Tennyson employs to depict the secondary status of women in Victorian society, the creative genius and scientific disposition of Lewis Carroll transforms the mirror into a tool which opens up a world of possibilities for Alice. Quite opposite to the Lady of Shallot, Alice transcends her mirror and fulfils her ambition of becoming a queen. Her character may be perceived as an inversion of the role of a domesticated, vulnerable victim of patriarchal norms. Carroll depicts Alice as a brave, assertive, unafraid, strong-willed, independent-minded girl who enjoys mobility and freedom. It is important to note that mobility is an important aspect of Alice's life which she uses to explore unravelled and

2   See 'Lewis Carroll and Tennyson,' *Farringford* <https://farringford.co.uk/news-events/tennyson-poems-blog/lewis-carroll-and-tennyson>.

uncharted spheres and trajectories. Jane Hirshfield says that 'Alice does not stop and face her own reflection in the looking-glass: she travels through it' (Hirshfield 2015: 119).

The idea of travel, and travel as motif and metaphor, thus, becomes crucial to our understanding of *Looking-Glass* as a narrative of women's emancipation and power. The travel motif allows Carroll to transport Alice to the fantastic Looking-Glass world where she interacts boldly and assertively with its inhabitants. Alice makes it clear, right at the beginning of her journey, that 'of course I should like to be a Queen, best' (Carroll 2009: 144). And when she is on the verge of becoming a queen, she has already started enjoying the glory and glamour associated with the crown and queenhood. [...] and to be a Queen! How grand it sounds!' (222). However, when Alice suddenly discovers that she has been crowned without her 'knowing it,' she exclaims in a tone of dismay: 'And what is this on my head?' [...] 'But how can it have got there without my knowing it?' (223) – Carroll thus perhaps also invites us to consider the implications of the fulfilment of such wishes.

It is important to note that Alice is not afraid to speak out her mind even though she is swamped with all kinds of strange things and people in an alien world. Carroll makes it clear that no amount of external force or pressure can hinder Alice from asserting her autonomy and individuality both inside and outside the territories of her home. This is further illustrated as the text draws closer to the end. Alice's blatant refusal to adhere to conventions and norms is a striking illustration of her independent mind. She says: 'I can't stand this any longer!' she cried, as she jumped up and seized the tablecloth with both hands: one good pull, and plates, dishes, guests, and candles came crashing down together in a heap on the floor' (Carroll 2009: 238). Alice even maintains the independence and authority to exit her dream when she finds it unsatisfactory.

Unlike her multiple confrontations with authority in *Wonderland*, and the existence of a monarchy in *Looking-Glass*, there is no controlling authority for Alice, rather, she is a master of her own free will. She makes it clear that she cannot be overpowered/dominated by any authority, be it the Red, White Queen, or anybody else, and hence, she travels back to her home. Carroll blurs the distinction between the actual and the fantastic to create a feminist space for Alice. He challenges the patriarchal assumptions regarding women but, at the same time, indicates the impossibility of the fulfilment of such a radical rethinking and vision in the social and cultural world of Alice's times by depicting, at the end of the novel, her adventures in the looking-glass world as dreams.

Alice thus possesses and exercises life force energy, which in the case of Lady of Shallot is suppressed by patriarchal norms. The Lady of Shalott has no autonomy, as she is not granted freedom of will. The moment she looks out of the window to have a direct sight of Sir Lancelot, her mirror cracks 'from side-to-side,' and as she takes further steps to freedom, she perishes, on that boat beneath the sunny sky.

Carroll, by contrast, uses journey as a trope, the looking-glass as a tool, and the game of chess as a metaphor to fictionalize his alternative idea. The game of chess and chessmen assume tremendous significance in Carroll's schema of challenging patriarchal structures of domination and oppression which led the women in the Victorian age to suffer multiple dispossessions (women, for instance, did not possess the right to vote, right to education, or the right to earn livelihood). In his 'Preface to the Sixty-First Thousand' Carroll explains 'As the chess-problem [...] has puzzled some of my readers, it may be well to explain that it is correctly worked out, so far as the moves are concerned' (Carroll 2009: 118). Alice Liddell, later Hargreaves, Carroll's 'ideal child friend' and his 'muse' for the Alice books, reminisced in her old age that much of *Looking-Glass* was made up of Dodgson's stories 'particularly the ones to do with chessmen, which are dated by the period when we were excitedly learning chess' (Hargreaves in Cohen 1989: 84).

The game of chess provided Carroll with the opportunity to invert the gender roles, as the queen is the most powerful piece in the game of chess, able to move any number of squares vertically, horizontally, or diagonally. The aspect of mobility is once again crucial, in a literal and metaphorical sense: because the queen is the strongest piece, a pawn is promoted to a queen in most cases. While the king is the most important piece on the board, its mobility is limited. It is a slow – moving piece which implies that he cannot run away, and it is the most vulnerable piece on the chessboard. The king has limited powers and he needs protection.

Yet another passage illustrates that the kings in the looking-glass world are so weak that they struggle to hold even a pencil: 'The poor King looked puzzled and unhappy, and struggled with the pencil for some time [...] and at last he panted out 'My dear! I really must get a thinner pencil. I ca'n't manage this one a bit' (Carroll 2009: 133).

In contrast, the knight, Sir Lancelot is depicted in Tennyson's poem as a bold and mighty male character having 'broad clear brow' and 'coal black curls' whose 'war horse trode on burnish'd hooves' (Tennyson 2014: 64). The White Knight in Carroll's *Looking-Glass*, in contrast, is old, frail, and interested in invention, rather than combat, and in need of aid from the female, child heroine. Carroll thus inverts the patriarchal power structures by portraying the kings as weak and timid and queens as brave and dominating.

Carroll's text reveals a complete reconfiguration of Victorian power dynamics through the chess game as can be observed in the following passage from the text:

> 'It is the voice of my child!' the White Queen cried out, as she rushed past the King, so violently that she knocked him over among the cinders [...] he was covered with ashes from head to foot. (Carroll 2009: 131)

Carroll portrays his *Looking-Glass* queens as the opposite of their docile kings. The Red Queen, having become so proverbial for her mobility, however, asserts in this context with a note of melancholy: '[I]t takes all the running you can do, to keep in the same place. If you want to get somewhere else, you must run at least twice as fast as that!'[3]

The women in Carroll's text are no longer relegated to subordinate positions or confined to domestic spheres. They are bold, assertive, and authoritative. 'Alice herself', Gillian Beer asserts, 'is the radical principle of the books: she represents infinite readiness [...] always inquiring, and always able to reason her way through the predicaments she finds herself in' (2016: 4–5). Alice with her imagination, boldness, autonomy, and access to the unknown, unfamiliar horizons emerged as an iconic figure who

---

3   For more on the 'Red Queen Effect' see Chapter 4 (Schaefer-Salins) in this collection.

challenged and dismantled Victorian notions of woman, womanhood, and femininity and henceforth transformed the cultural consciousness of the Victorians regarding the ways they perceived the role of women in the society. As Barbara Wall notes:

> Alice's became the first childmind, in the history of children's fiction, to occupy the centre. No narrator of a story for children had stood so close to a child protagonist, observing nothing except that child, describing, never criticising [...] he never, until she has woken from her dream, looks away from her. (Carroll 2009: xxxii–xxxiii)

Conclusion

Through the Looking-Glass with its fantastic setting, overlapping territories, inversion of gender roles, and reconfiguration of power dynamics, anticipates women's emancipation and power. My assertion regarding the emancipation and empowerment of 'Alice' rests on the idea that she has the freedom of will, enjoys mobility, and the power to execute her desires, albeit through her dreams and fantasies. *Looking-Glass* can thus be read as an empowering counterpoint to the narratives of women's subjugation and oppression. While the Lady of Shallot suffers imprisonment and stasis, Alice enjoys mobility and freedom; the former suffers in isolation, whereas Alice gets an opportunity to enter a space of community and the public, and interacts freely with creatures and things she meets in her journey – even though she is an outsider in that fantastic world. Alice's desires and dreams enable her to travel through the looking-glass even though her travels are disorderly.

Paul Smethurst observes that 'disorderly mobility is inherent in the idea of travel. It is essential to the traveller's encounters with difference, with serendipity, and with motion in a psychological and ontological sense' (2008: 2). Carroll may, thus, be regarded as one of the voices that contributed to the visibility of women in Victorian literature. His work acted as a vehicle for breaking patriarchal models which confined women to a reserved sphere – household and motherhood – and depicted the picture of an alternate fantastic world which challenges the passive acceptance of a supposed, stereotypical delicate feminine sensibility and prescribed conduct which denied women access to public spheres.

Liana F. Piehler notes that several of the 'imaginative depictions' of the Victorian era 'acknowledge to varying degrees prevailing conditions and assumptions. Tension between interior and exterior space is acknowledged through choice of interiors to enclose the female figures in some way' (Piehler 2003: 36). In an age when the 'overarching metaphor' that described the social roles of men and women was the 'visual and geometric term separate spheres' (36) – 'Man for the field and woman for the hearth […] Man to command and woman to obey' (Tennyson 2014: 343). Carroll's text transformed the cultural consciousness by inscribing in the public mind a possibility of an alternate world where there is a complete reconfiguration of power dynamics, where the women enjoy mobility, emancipation, and power. He, thus, emerges as the 'alchemist whose great Art is the transformation of consciousness and being' (Orenstein in Schmahmann 2021: 13). Carroll's inversion, playful or serious, allows world of possibilities for Alice in the looking-glass world and creates a feminist space for her activity and practice which she enjoys, free from the stifling patriarchal rules and regulations.

Part X

Literary Reflections: Beyond Carroll

Guilherme Magri da Rocha and Cleide Antonia Rapucci

26 Modernists through the Looking-Glass: Exploring Radical and Challenging Modernist Books for Children

> What a strange thing a mirror is! and what a wondrous affinity exists between it and a man's imagination! For this room of mine, as I behold it in the glass, is the same, and yet not the same.
>
> – George MacDonald

Introduction

The mirror ('looking-glass') is a rich symbol within literature – especially when it acts as a reflective surface. As Chevalier and Gheerbrant discuss in their dictionary of symbols (2009: 393): the word 'speculation' has its roots in 'speculum' (mirror[1]), an action related to observing the movement of stars with a looking-glass. 'Consideration', which etymologically means to see the conjunct of stars, has its origin in another abstract word, 'sidus' (star). Both these etymological definitions are of great importance to how this chapter approaches *Looking-Glass*. We discuss how landmark modernist authors mirror Carroll's experiments in their lesser-known persona: as children's writers. Although we do not present any close

---

1   Although the Latin origin of the word 'mirror' comes from 'mirare', the words in Portuguese ('espelho'), Spanish ('espejo'), Italian ('specchio') etc. have their roots in 'speculum'.

readings of books, we consider the looking-glass as a metaphor that helps us 'speculate' about both children's literature and modernism.

Literary Modernism is partially intertwined with what was conventionally called the 'Golden Age' (1865–1926) of children's literature, which is seen as heterogeneous 'substance'. Humphrey Carpenter (2012) [1985], sees the Golden Age as an opportunity of escaping from the anxieties of the modern world by securing the child in an idyllic Arcadia (the Enchanted Place, the Never Never Land, the Secret Garden). We believe that Carroll's experiments were not only mirrored by the modernists but that their aesthetics might actually be more challenging for adults than for child readers.

Jacqueline Rose (1994) [1984] affirms that there was a 'resistance' to modernism in children's literature that can be explained in terms of reading and ease: (i) modernist writing was too difficult for a reader who needs 'regulation' in form, once the modern novel became characterized by the fragmentation of narrative and its categories; (ii) and 'the child' (as a concept) was also used in arguments to affirm the relationship between adults and changing cultural forms. Authors such as Henry James believed that women and children were responsible for the vulgarization of the novel as 'uncritical' and 'irreflective' readers (see James 1986). Other scholars see possibilities of approximating children's literature and modernism. Juliet Dusinberre's argues that characteristics that we usually associate with modernist literature – 'the absence of a deliberately pointed moral, and of linear direction in narrative, the abdication of the author as preacher, and the use of words as play' (xxi) – appeared first in the children's books of Lewis Carroll's generation (highlighting also Edward Lear). These writers, and to a certain extent their characters were interested in 'the question of mastery over language, structure, vision, morals, characters and readers' (xvi), like Humpty Dumpty. A different deal was so being made between adult writers and child readers, a deal far away from the Victorian didacticism and that would be absorbed by modernists' experiments.[2]

Looking-Glass, the second of the *Alice* books, was inspired by a second Alice – not Liddell, but Raikes – who recalls her distant uncle (Charles Dodgson) putting her in front of a mirror and asking her in which hand

---

2   For more on Humpty Dumpty and language, see Chapter 15.

was the apple the girl in the mirror was holding. What real-Carroll does to real-Alice equals what author-Carroll demands from both character-Alice and reader: to solve problems creatively. These 'problems' are also present diversely in the modernists' production for children, in books that also demand creative solutions from their readers and present similar issues. They include the famous *Old Possum's Book of Practical Cats* (1939) by T. S. Eliot and lesser known works such as H. D.'s *The Hedgehog*, e. e. cummings' *16 Poèmes Enfantins* (later *Hist Whist and Other Poems*) and *Fairy Tales* (1965), William Faulkner's *The Wishing Tree* (1927), Langston Hughes' *Popo and Fifina* (1932), Aldous Huxley's *The Crows of Pearblossom* (1944), and others. To examine how modernists mirror Carroll in their work, we examine texts by Virginia Woolf and Gertrude Stein aimed at young readers. Carroll's looking-glass is a metaphor for how his radical experiments are reflected in these authors' production and how they do not minimize their experimental techniques when writing for children, as stated by Rovan (2016).

Virginia Woolf

Virginia Woolf published a text in the magazine *New Statesman* on 9 December 1939, to mark the anniversary of the release of the first edition of Carroll's complete works. In it, she characterizes the writer as a 'perfectly hard crystal' capable of creating a world for children because childhood remained within him. Only Carroll has shown us the world upside down as a child sees it; thus, according to Woolf, his books are not intended for children, but the only books in which readers themselves become children.

The *Alice* books were part of the imagination of Woolf, and Carroll's death profoundly affected the culture which produced her generation. Dusinberre supports this with statements from the writer's diaries: she mentions that Woolf's greatest novels 'encapsulate childhood as she claimed Lewis Carroll had done' (2). Woolf followed the advice given by Roger Fry – himself a great admirer of Carroll – that artists should paint only what they could see and encouraged authors to create partnerships with their readers, something Woolf did in her intergenerational collaborations with children.

We can think of the *Alice* books as resulting from intergenerational collaboration too. Victoria Ford Smith (2017) defines this as adult–child creative relationships and argues that these transformed the literary text they generated. When discussing the origins of *Looking-Glass*, for instance, Alice Liddell recalls that a good portion of the book is based on the stories about chess that Carroll told her and her sisters when they were learning how to play the game.[3] This would be considered by Ford Smith as a 'hybrid collaboration' that occurred once Carroll had fictionalized his relationship with Alice through stories. It also represents the symbolic origin of children's literature (Grenby 2009), once their relationship is as famous as the *Alice* books themselves.

Between 1923 and 1927 Woolf joined her nephews Julian and, mainly, Quentin Bell when working on *The Charleston Bulletin Supplements*. This publication mostly addressed the everyday lives of the Charleston residents, while frequently flirting with nonsense and the absurd. While Julian assumed the role of editor, Quentin illustrated his aunt's texts that were dictated to him.[4] This can be considered 'a real collaboration', as it involves 'a living adult and [children] working together, each contributing in a significant manner to create a text or other cultural artifact' (22–23).

We can think of Woolf's collaboration with her nephews as a possibility for exploring and developing techniques. Illustration and text are often in dialogue, creating a 'real' text that suddenly brings an absurd/nonsensical-like atmosphere that mirrors Carroll's experiments with narrative fragmentation but also such nonsensical situations as those of Edward Lear's limericks.[5] Among the characters that participate in these stories is

---

3   For more on Carroll, *Looking-Glass* and chess, see Chapters 14, 19 and 25.

4   During this period of time Woolf published some of her more famous works such as *Mrs Dalloway* (1925), *To the Lighthouse* (1927) and essays such as 'Mr. Bennet and Mrs. Brown' (1923).

5   For similar experimentations with text and writing by surrealists, and their adaptations of Carroll, see Chapter 16.

Nurse Lugton, who would later protagonize 'Nurse Lugton's Curtain', a story in which the animals and people from the curtain she's creating gain life while she sleeps. Yet the old nurse cannot enjoy the world in which she's the author, a god-like character, emphasizing how this tale can also be read alongside Woolf's feminist essays, as metaphor for the condition of the woman as a creator of art. Woolf also plays with, and subverts quest narratives and ghost stories, creating old Mrs Gage, the protagonist of 'The Widow and the Parrot'. This short story, in which the widow must find the treasure her late brother has left, ends in an uncanny way, connecting protagonist and helper, the parrot, in a supernatural manner.

Woolf mirrors Carroll's bringing real-life references to the fictional texts, by playing with the children's context and the way they perceive it, encapsulating childhood experiences within fragmentation and subversion. Nurse Lugton actually worked at the Stephens' and is present in *The Charleston Bulletin*'s 'Scene no. 1 in the life of Mrs. Bell'; and in 'The widow and the parrot' Woolf has placed Mrs Gage's brother's house next to the Monks House, the Rodmell residence to which the Woolfs relocated from Asheham House in September 1919. Also Reverend James Hawkesford, who attempts to cheer up Mrs Gage, served as Romell's vicar from 1896 to 1928.

We must also consider how both Carroll's and Woolf's protagonists, Alice and Nurse Lugton, exist differently in their respective dreamlands. Austin Warren (1980) observes that the Dream is one of the traditional genres to which Carroll's books belong: a genre that was restored in modernism, thanks to Joyce's *Finnegans Wake*. He believes that 'Carroll's fictive dreams are a vehicle for conveying wonders within a commonsense framework' (337) and, as such, the dream is a convention 'which allows Carroll to introduce talking flowers and talking animals, a world still open to small children and to adults who can suspend their tiresome anthropomorphism and listen to what flowers may have to say' (338). The position of the scholar, the adult, thus described, aligns with that of Woolf, to whom the *Alice* books were created by someone who never forgot childhood, and directed to such readers.

Both short stories ('The Widow and the Parrot' and 'Nurse Lugton's Curtain') were published posthumously as picture books. The first was in 1988 (with illustrations of Quentin Bell's son Julian Bell) and today is an obligatory reading in Portuguese schools; the second was published in 1991 with illustrations by Australian artist Julie Vivas.[6] Thus, we can speculate that Woolf saw in children's stories a space in which she was able to experiment with her aesthetic techniques. She not only mirrored Carroll by creating fragmented texts characterized by inside jokes and references that could only be understood by those around her – they were all originally intended for private circulation only – but also by rejecting conventional techniques, instead distorting time and playing with words, 'expanding' thus Carroll's nineteenth-century aesthetics.

Gertrude Stein

The 'mother of modernism', Gertrude Stein, believed that her understanding of Pablo Picasso's work was due to the fact that she was 'expressing the same thing in literature' (Stein 1984, n.d.). Picasso represents the world in its simplified configurations, while Stein focuses on the pleasure of words, instead of their meaning. In Martin Gardner's discussion on nonsense and the abstract, both painting and written expression consider expression over 'meaning' as they emphasize rhythm. Stein wrote in 'steinese', a 'gnomic, repetitive, illogical, sparsely punctuated [language], [...] [that] became a scandal and a delight, lending itself equally to derisory parody and fierce denunciation' (Dupee 1990).

By playing/manipulating language and logic, Stein mirrors Carroll's nonsensical experiments in literature, perhaps offering a repudiation of Humpty Dumpty's famous assertion. Michael Heyman and Kevin Shortsleeve (2021) state that nonsense itself reflects the grotesque. Both are associated with 'that which is unnatural, distorted, bizarre, ludicrous, or fantastically absurd, while simultaneously, *nonsense* is also understood as that which is amusing, quaint, and immaterial – a place for simple, joyful

---

6   This was first published as 'Nurse Lugton's Golden Thimble' in 1966 by the Hogarth Press with illustrations by Ducan Grant. It is an earlier version of the text published as it was discovered in a *Mrs Dalloway* manuscript and entitled by Leonard Woolf.

fun (133–134). In an article published in *The New Yorker*, Adam Gopnik, when discussing Gertrude Stein's style, stated that 'Stein's style is to writing what sushi is to cooking–not so much an example as a repudiation of the whole idea that still manages to serve the original function' (Gopnik 2013), which can be seen as something that encapsulates both ends: the bizarre and the amusing.

Gertrude Stein published her first and most famous children's book in 1939: *The World is Round*, which she started writing at the same time as *Ida*, which would be published in 1941. Both books share similar themes and are written in a similar style, the difference being that *The World is Round* flirts with the fantastically absurd. In this book, written as a fictional autobiography of her child-neighbour Rose, we follow the struggle of a homonymous child, who loves to sing but cries every time she does.

'Once upon a time the world was round and you could go on it around and around' (Stein 2013, n.d.), starts the narrator. 'Everywhere there was somewhere and everywhere there they were men women children dogs cows wild pigs little rabbits cats lizards and animals' (2013, n.d.). Rose exists in this world where everyone wanted to talk about themselves. In turn, the Pigeon believes Alice is a serpent, thanks to her long neck, that gets stuck in branches. In *Wonderland*, Alice herself doesn't know who she is, although she is certain of who she was. Stein's character Rose knows her name is Rose, but wonders 'Why am I a little girl/And why is my name Rose/And when am I a little girl/And when is my name Rose/And where am I a little girl/And where is my name Rose/And which little girl am I am I the little girl named Rose which little girl named Rose' (2013, n.d.). Rose's song mirrors Alice who must deal with, and thus the nonsensical upside-down Victorian master narrative, as she starts questioning herself.

Whereas Carroll's *Wonderland* and *Looking-Glass* land are both logical and (su)real, Stein's post-war world is guided by master narratives that show how a child perceives herself and the world it lives in. This is metaphorized in the 'roundness' of the world – 'If the world is round would a lion fall off' (2013, n.d.) – and in the size (and colour) of a mountain. In their turn, these are all encapsulated in the master narrative of heteronormativity.

Stein mirrors Carroll in creating a world where rhythm 'surpasses' meaning. And Rose is an Alice that does not overcome her challenge.

Experiencing Wonderland or Looking-Glass land is not the same as existing in a world dominated by master narratives that do not reflect the child's experience. Alice overcomes the upside-down Victorian England and becomes the master of her own narrative, whereas Rose succumbs to the master narrative of heteronormativity. The book is an Anti-Alice that deceives the reader by giving them control of the rhythm through repetition (what Gertrude Stein called 'insistence') and the lack of punctuation, but at the same time imprisons them in the factual world, where even imagination is behind bars.

In the *First Reader*, Stein writes: '[A] wild pen is a pen that makes blots that makes dots and makes spots. [But it can] get wilder and wilder [… and] instead of saying how do you do it says you had better not have said how do you do because if you have said how do you do how do you know what a wild pen will do' (53). This excerpt represents the control of the art over the artist, literature as something that is expurgated by an author who does not detain the semantic control over her production. Her narrator mirrors Humpty Dumpty, to whom words mean whatever he wants them to mean, an to whom 'glory' can thus mean 'a nice knock-down argument'. Stein demands agency and an active role from her reader, who needs to be capable of playing with her nonsensical/'insistent' universe – for instance by attributing meanings to words, and giving them rhythm, in nightmarish worlds that never offer comfortable solutions: in another of her books, *To Do*, a horse is replaced with an automobile, and boys beat each other to death, a rabbit turns into a cannibal.

Final Remarks

When discussing Ionesco's production for children, Kimberley Reynolds (2007) observes that not only 'the world seems bewildering and its rules illogical' (60) for children. But the fact that they are 'relatively new to language […] intensifies the potential for wordplay, and they are still in the process of internalising concepts to do with time, distance, and spatial relationships' (60). These and the 'lack of formal awareness of genres and conventions' (60) are also pointed out by Victoria de Rijke (2020) to whom modernist devices such as the stream-of-consciousness are 'very characteristic of children's early narratives that mirror their unmediated speech, so may feature excessive repetition, make playful or mistaken use of grammar; all at great, unpunctuated speed' (209). Sometimes speech gives a false impression of liberty, as in *The World is Round*, in which the protagonist, however, instead ends up locked in a nightmarish world of master narratives.

These scholars' statements help explain why Gertrude Stein's *The World Is Round* was accepted by children, whereas her adult production only gained popular acceptance when she wrote more 'conventional' texts. These and her other books for children not only work out themes and ideas explored in her texts aimed at an adult audience but also are written in 'steinese', Gertrude Stein's personal language that demands an active reader who can introduce the commas and further punctuation that are not there in order to give it meaning.

The same can be said of Virginia Woolf, who also engages in her intergenerational collaborations with children's ideas, themes, and narrative devices that are further explored in her landmark novels, so we can consider her participation in children's culture a possibility of experimentation and even training. The use of words as play, and the abandonment of the narrator-preacher are also characteristics that we can find in Carroll's text production and especially in the *Alice* books, thus we can consider him a proto-Modernist author. Indebted to Carroll's nonsensical approach to narrative and language, the aforementioned authors not only transform their books for adults (as James Joyce and with his portmanteau words), but also their works for children, invalidating the common-sense argument that modernists often minimize their 'radical' writing when writing for this group. This is a generation that had Carrollian characters in their imagination, after all.

This chapter surveyed the works of modernist authors aimed at children and briefly discussed how these authors mirrored Lewis Carroll's radical literary experiments (Dusinberre 1987), who thus becomes regarded as proto-modernists. Thus we can think of these texts, from the perspective of the mirror of our epigraph, as experiments: the same but are not the same.

Virginia Woolf's generation reflects/mirrors Carroll's, thus providing a new lense through which to read the world. These do not imprison the child in an idyllic Arcadia but allow different possibilities of reading the world through the use of words as play. By focusing on Woolf and Gertrude Stein we presented a lesser-known facet of these writers: their works aimed at child readers. The texts by Woolf and (and other authors such as William Faulkner, James Joyce, and e. e. cummings) were written for a domestic audience and circulation and posthumously transformed into picture books aimed at a global audience of children (thanks to several translations) while texts for children were released during the author's lifetime, as is the case with Gertrude Stein (and T. S. Eliot and H. D.) encapsulate a lot of the writer's radical/modernist experiences present in their own books.

Thus, this chapter aims to bridge the gap between children's literature studies and modernist studies, filling a little of the 'space in-between' that exists among these two fields of research, inviting reconsiderations of these texts in the contexts in which they originated: from Carrollian inspiration, in the space in which also Carroll's *Alice* books originated.

Ann Martin

27 Reflections, Reversals, and Doubles: Lewis Carroll's Photographic Aesthetics in Dorothy L. Sayers's *Hangman's Holiday*

Dorothy L. Sayers's detective fiction contains multiple allusions to Lewis Carroll's work: quotations from the *Alice* books appear alongside Carrollian parodies of literary works, and characters often refer to the author and his texts themselves. In addition to such verbal allusions, however, are mirrorings of Carroll's visual aesthetics. This imagery is particularly notable in the short stories from Sayers's collection *Hangman's Holiday* (1933) featuring her aristocratic sleuth Lord Peter Wimsey, in which crimes associated with optical manipulations evoke the reflections, reversals, and doubles that recur in Carroll's texts and their illustrations. Like his language, the imagery of Wonderland and the Looking-Glass country is a key element of Sayers's mysteries, representing the disorientations caused by crime in her interwar Britain, and requiring an Alice-like analysis of the landscape by the sleuth and reader alike.

In its distortions of what is commonly accepted to be real, Carrollian imagery in Sayers's writing signals the influences of Victorian photography. Critics have noted the ways in which both the lens of the camera and the processing of negatives generated visual effects that can be discerned in Carroll's original drawings for *Alice* as well as in Tenniel's illustrations. The 'unexpected violations' of reality that emerge from the darkroom (Hollingsworth 2009: 96), including 'failed negatives, predisposed towards grotesquerie and tinged with folly' (Mallardi 2021: 553), add layers of distortion to the 'reduction, compression, and multiplication' of the real world involved in the acts of looking through the lens of the camera and developing prints (Monteiro in Hollingsworth 2009: 104) – not to mention posing sitters amidst backdrops and props.

Diane Waggoner's keynote address for the 'Through the Looking-Glass Sesquicentenary Conference' identifies specific types of imagery from the *Alice* books – lateral reversals, reflections, and doublings – that have clear correlations to Carroll's process of developing images using translucent glass negatives, that is, the use of a 'wet collodion glass negative from which albumen prints were then made' (8).[1] This technical practice, through which 'photographers created a negative that inverted dark and light and laterally reversed the image like in a mirror meant the photographer was constantly navigating a state of reversal and inversion – just as Alice would do in the looking-glass world' (8). A 'second inversion' emerges when the albumen paper of the print itself becomes a mirror image of the negative (12). Shifts in size mimicking the view through a camera lens, reflections on mirror-like glass plates, and distorted images from the developing process: such effects correspond to the inverted, exaggerated logic of the worlds Alice encounters. Indeed, the visual rendering of the drawing room Alice perceives through the mirror in the 'Looking-glass House' retraces the dynamics of the photographic negative: the reality captured by the camera is reversed and light and dark are inverted. Like the reversible black-and-white squares of a chessboard, or the white and black kittens, the object and its negative image are 'just the same [...] only the things go the other way' (*TTLG*: 125–6).[2]

Such 'doubling, inversion, and reversibility' (O'Leary 2010: 72) are central to the stories of *Hangman's Holiday* that feature Lord Peter Wimsey; indeed, mirrored characters, distorted bodies, and inverted figures are often directly related to photography. These challenges to conventional perspective correspond to Alice's navigations of dreamlike spaces and the social power structures they reflect and refract. Criminals in Sayers's texts prey

1   My thanks to Professor Diane Waggoner for providing a copy of her keynote address.
2   The chessboard in *Looking-Glass* is as per Victorian convention red-and-white, but appears as black-and-white in the monochrome illustrations.

upon the credulity of their victims through visual manipulations of reality and of social conventions that are taken to be real rather than discursive in nature. However, her detective's insight and agency suggest that citizens can engage critically not just with what they see, but also with the hegemonic norms that inform habitual ways of reading the world to establish a more accurate sense of reality. 'Like the Alice books,' Sayers's fiction 'takes logic and turns it on its ear, implying that old habits of thinking are inadequate' (Kenney 1990: 64). Her consistent focus on unreflectively normative thinking is thus comparable to Carroll's exposure of 'the hypocrisy of Victorian moral values' (Kohlt 2016: 158). In response to criminals who distort reality and police officers who uncritically reflect hegemonic systems of exclusion, Sayers's amateur detective perceives the complexities of lived experience and moves beyond reductive binary thinking.

The duplicitous manipulations of criminals often echo the photographic illusions that Waggoner points to, in which 'double exposure or combined negatives' were used 'to make it seem as if a person appeared with their double within the same photograph' (15). Recognizing this trickery demands both knowledge of the technologies involved and perception of other possibilities and realities; that is, a wider vision that can penetrate the truth behind the optical illusion. Thus Wimsey must perceive the reality behind the figure of the *Doppelgänger* that is the mystery in 'The Image in the Mirror', where Wimsey calls upon his knowledge of photography to solve the case. A fellow guest at a hotel, Robert Duckworthy, tells Lord Peter of his experiences with amnesia and unconsciousness, and his disturbing realization that his heart is located on the right side of his body, not the left. He uses cinema to describe his disorientation and unease at losing track of himself, and at having been accused of petty crimes he does not remember committing. Cinema features prominently as Duckworthy compares himself to the protagonist of Stellan Rye's *The Student of Prague* (1913) – 'one day his reflection came stalking out of the mirror on its own, and went about committing dreadful crimes' (17) – and invokes Robert Weine's *The Cabinet of Dr. Caligari* (1920) to explain a recurring nightmare: '[T]here was the long mirror and the thing coming grinning along, always with its hand out as if it meant to catch hold of me and pull me through the glass. […] I'd be stumbling for hours through a queer sort of world' (18). These modernist analogues to Carroll's Wonderland and Looking-Glass country come to life when Duckworthy remembers encountering an uncanny double as he approached a door that he believes has a mirrored surface:

> I told myself it was all nonsense and put my hand out to the door-handle – my left hand, because the handle was on that side […]. The reflection, of course, put out its right hand –that was all right of course – and I saw my own figure in my old squash hat and burberry – but the face – oh, my God! It was grinning at me – and then just like in the dream, it suddenly turned its back and walked away from me, looking over its shoulder –. (19)

His fears of a doubled, unconscious existence as a criminal seem confirmed when Wimsey notes Duckworthy's photograph in the newspaper and learns he is suspected of murder.

Both film and photography are crucial to the text, not least of which because the photograph's approximation of reality leads the police sergeant who comes to question Duckworthy to assume his guilt. The suspect's panicked response – ' "I didn't do it," cried Mr Duckworthy wildly' – is merely received as proof that he did (23). Such assumptions are what Wimsey must counter, and he enters into his investigation by identifying the facts of Duckworthy's life. The accused has a twin, and 'the kind of similar twins that result from the splitting of a single cell *may* come out as looking-glass twins' (30). Rather than a mysterious demonic self, the uncanny figure is his brother – the Tweedledee to his Tweedledum. Richard Duckworthy, whose crimes are blamed on his innocent brother, is a reverse image of Robert, which explains the moment at the door. Rather than a mirror containing an uncanny double, the door is made of clear glass: Robert and Richard are merely on opposite sides. This leads to the true identity of the criminal being confirmed when Wimsey approaches the photographer who has provided the picture to the newspapers. Asking 'to see the original negative,' Wimsey compares it to the front page of 'the *Evening News*,' and the photographer realizes his mistake: 'It must have been put in the wrong way round' in the 'enlarging lantern' (27). The photograph is a reversed image of Robert's brother. The properly processed negative enables the police to search for the right Duckworthy – not his unknowing, innocent double.

A different doubling informs 'The Incredible Elopement of Lord Peter Wimsey.' Here, Sayers's mystery rests upon two versions of the same woman, Alice Wetherall. Wimsey hears the tale from Langley, 'a professor of etymology,' who has travelled to Basque country to find material for a book (35). An old acquaintance has, surprisingly, taken up residence in the area. It is Dr Standish Wetherall, a 'brilliant surgeon' whom Langley has not met for years, sensing in the past that 'it would be wiser if he did not see too much' of Wetherall's wife and her 'porcelain loveliness' (38). When Langley visits the Wetheralls, he is shocked: Alice has become 'something' else, an inversion of her previous self.

Sayers plays with the image of Carroll's Alice here, not least of which through Langley's memory of Weatherall's considerably younger wife: 'beautiful, with gold hair and blue eyes' (37). Her appearance in the story marks a shocking transformation, as Sayers turns Alice's shifts in size into the stuff of nightmare: 'The face was white and puffy, the eyes vacant, the mouth drooled open, with little trickles of saliva running from the loose corners. A dry fringe of rusty hair clung to the half-bald scalp, like the dead wisps on the head of a mummy' (41). More disturbingly, a mocking Weatherall offers this distorted figure of Alice to his guest: 'Would you like to kiss her, caress her, take her to bed with you – my beautiful wife?' (44). Langley panics: 'He fled stumbling against the furniture and rushed out' – sharing his story with Wimsey on the train to Paris (45).

Langley's shock at Alice's distorted appearance is, of course, rooted in conventional assumptions regarding both women and doctors. Manipulating Langley's credulity and faith in Wetherall's credentials, the surgeon tells the scholar that Alice suffers from 'Premature senility' (42), an apparently incurable medical condition: 'The best men on this side confirmed my own diagnosis' (43). Through a similar performance of authority, Wetherall has manipulated the superstitions of the stereotypically naïve locals in Sayers's text, who believe that Alice is under 'the power of the Evil One' (39). Their belief in Wetherall's narratives is prompted by the non-normative female body of Alice but also by the highly normative claim to authority of an older white, male, British doctor.

In contrast, Lord Peter draws upon his position to challenge Wetherall's discursive authority and manipulate the villagers into righting Alice's manipulated body. Posing as a 'wizard' (47), he uses Greek and Latin for his spells, plays a recording of 'Schubert's "Unfinished"' to create atmosphere, and vanishes in 'a trick cabinet' with Wetherall's wife (56). He identifies that she has a 'congenital thyroid deficiency' (55), which Wetherall has preyed upon by withholding her medication, a condition Wimsey remedies by sending 'enchanted wafers' to be eaten at every meal after prayer (51). This invocation of the Eucharist wafer meshes, oddly, with the 'very small cake, on which the words "EAT ME" were beautifully marked in currants' that alters Alice's size (*AAIW* 14). And just as Alice, after using the Caterpillar's mushroom 'very carefully,' finds that 'It was so long since she had been anything near the right size, that it felt quite strange at first' (48), so Alice Wetherall is described as 'a bit bewildered' and 'like a child' after her escape and retransformation (Sayers 1933: 54). Penetrating his illusions, Wimsey has held the doctor's distorted image of his wife up to a glass, allowing Alice to 'go the right way again' (*TTLG*: 131).

In this sense, understandings of right and wrong become central to Sayers's stories, where conventional authority figures – the police, the respected doctor – demonstrate that norms themselves can distort and be used to distort reality. In 'The Queen's Square,' for example, guilt and innocence become complicated by socially normative approaches to respectability. Carrollian imagery figures overtly in the setting of the story: a fancy dress ball, at which characters are costumed as playing cards and chess pieces, but have been careful not to 'make themselves too Lewis Carroll' (62). On a more subtle level, *Through the Looking-Glass* is invoked through colour inversion linked to the chessboard. Such references cluster around the two main couples involved in the mystery: Frank and Gerda Bellingham are dressed as the Red King and Queen; Charmian Grayle and Tony Lee are the White King and Queen. When the host of the party gathers his guests for a group dance, Gerda Bellingham is nearly late, and by the time the dancing starts, the White King and Queen are still missing. The dance proceeds until Lee rushes in: 'Charmain … in the tapestry room … dead … strangled' (66). After interviewing witnesses, the police superintendent determines that the victim was last seen going 'up the stairs at the end of the corridor' just before the dance (69), an apparent fact that leaves every party-goer with an alibi and the police without a suspect.

It is only when Lord Peter and his valet, Bunter, have photographed the crime scene that the optical illusion is revealed. After they process the negatives in a makeshift darkroom, Wimsey remarks on the redness of a developing liquid, which had earlier looked 'clear', an effect Bunter attributes to the darkroom's red lighting: 'When all the available light is red, red and white are, naturally, indistinguishable' (73). Wimsey immediately examines the lighting of the corridor where Charmain Grayle was last seen. Turning the hall's lamp so that an amber-coloured panel throws light on the stairs, he notes that the white dress of one of the helpers appears red. The mystery is solved: as Wimsey observes, 'What's the chessboard rule? *The Queen stands on a square of her own colour*' (74). It has not been the White Queen but rather Mrs Bellingham on the stairs, a Red Queen in a red light, hiding evidence of her husband's murder of Charmian Grayle and in the process providing him with an alibi. Having learned 'that in the red light', a witness has 'mistaken her for the White Queen', Gerda Bellingham has altered the hall's light fixture that allowed her red costume to appear as white as the victim's, obscuring both her identity and the time of the murder (75).

The doubling of red dress and red light is itself reflected in a doubled vision of both Mrs Bellingham and Miss Grayle. Noting that her husband has confessed 'like a gentleman as soon as we told him we had evidence against his wife' (74), the police officer observes, 'Of course, she's an accessory after the fact, but she's the kind of wife a man would like to have', and comments 'I hope they let her off light' – a sentiment with which Wimsey agrees (75). Here, both contextualize crime and punishment through the lived realities of the guilty parties. They are, using Wimsey's terms, keeping the queen on the square that is her own colour; of seeing her according to her own experiences and in light of the fact that Miss Grayle has been blackmailing Frank Bellingham 'for years' with information 'which would have been very damaging to his political career' (74). In other words, Miss Grayle has leveraged social respectability towards criminal ends without tarnishing her own reputation. This is the hypocrisy that Sayers condemns so consistently: the use of social standards for personal gain regardless of the cost to others. Indeed, that cost will remain invisible: the blackmail will be seen only as a motive, even as the façade of Charmain Grayle is as false as that of Red Queen standing in red light.

What Sayers emphasizes through these doubles – the reflected face, the distorted figure, the duplicitous image – is the underlying willingness of credulous characters to adhere to conventional perceptions of what is real and reasonable. Criminals are able to manipulate this normative thinking towards its most unreflective uses. In contrast, Wimsey perceives the lived experiences behind both the illusions; his challenge to a sense that has been made common lies in his ability to see beyond the narrow limits of hegemonic norms and usual suspects. Wimsey thus signals Sayers's approach to social realities, one that keeps layered understandings in play even when the crime has been solved, Wonderland has been established as a dream, and the Red Queen is seen 'really' to be 'a kitten, after all' (*TTLG*: 236).

Luxin Yin

28 Mirrors and Windows for Children: Grace Lin's Tale of Childhood Suffering and Growth in *Where the Mountain Meets the Moon*

The relationship of children's literature to both globalization and commercialization has been debated extensively in the recent decade. Emer O'Sullivan (2011) has commented on how the United States' children's literature market is dominant through the efforts of 'large media conglomerates whose publishing operations are small sections of their entertainment businesses' (Hade 2002: 511). As one of those solutions to domination of one-sided narrative under the mainstream shadow, O'Sullivan notes, 'comparative children's literature [...] is a genuine antidote to such romantic notions of international children's literature (...)' (O'Sullivan 2011: 189). I will here address the 'neglect or outright abuse of less affluent children and historically oppressed groups' (Beeck 2020: 5) through trauma literature and a comparative perspective by examining the American Chinese children's book writer Grace Lin's *Where the Mountain Meets the Moon*. Lin won the Newberry Medal in 2009, and blends Chinese and American styles, adapting Chinese mythologies and folklores into one big adventure story, in which the protagonist Minli can be compared to the Chinese version of 'Dorothy' in *The Wizard of Oz*. However, little attention has been laid upon the Dragon, who can be compared with Alice in *Through the Looking-Glass* on their track of growth from 'the monstrous child Alice' to the 'Queen Alice'.

To examine *Where the Mountain Meets the Moon* from a comparative perspective alongside *Wonderland* and *Looking-Glass* has several important implications. First, as Anne Sparrman (2020) indicated, the figure of Alice has enacted key theoretical concepts in childhood studies. According to her, 'Lewis Carroll's Alice had been one of the sources drawn upon when forming child research theories' (8). I will test this argument from a multidimensional perspective, on the example of a story written by a Chinese-American author. Grace Lin's *Where the Mountain Meets to Moon* has been remarked as the Chinese-style *Wizard of Oz*, with the author attempting to achieve universalism. If Alice could be the predecessor of a distinct child figure in the domain of Western children's literature, then what could her multinational variations become? As for how Alice's different figurations have developed, Deleuze (1989) argued that the coexistence of such multiple images in one makes time collapse into a now, by linking the past, present, and future. Such research is helpful in understanding *Where the Mountain Meets the Moon*, which unveils the theme of maturity in a journey-like story highly associated with and inspired by Chinese folklore and fairy tales. The combination of traditional folklore and transformation with contemporary tone also presents a coexistence of multiple figures in multiple dimensions.

This essay examines such maturation narratives through a trauma literature perspective, drawing upon childhood suffering, and holocaust narratives, and then applying this perspective to Grace Lin's adventure story. Significantly, *Where the Mountain Meets the Moon* demonstrates a 'universalism' and 'transnationalism' in its appeal to children of all ethnicities. This, however, also raises several questions: first, as a Chinese American, what childhood experiences does Lin hope to communicate to all children through *Where the Mountain Meets the Moon?* Second, what do a 'journeying'-type protagonist like Minli and her accompanying partner the Dragon thus signify?

Introduction

In the field of children's literature, there has been significant focus on the depiction of childhood suffering and trauma, especially in Western Literature. However, only a modicum of attention has been given to a subfield of this literature that deals with these themes in the context of identify formation and adventure in ethnic Chinese works. By adventure, I refer to a discovery journey that the protagonist undergoes in order to realize a *bildungsroman*. In this essay, I would like to fill the lacuna in the study of Chinese-American literature, where adventure narratives as a form of trauma literature are often overlooked. Studying Lin's work as a multidimensional reworking of 'Alice' images opens up another way to interpret her works instead of merely focusing on the Chinese elements, as much extant scholarship.

The main body of *Where the Mountain Meets the Moon* follows the adventure of the protagonist, Minli who seeks happiness, as she follows ancient stories about what might lead her there. To effectively study the book and the author, it is important to emphasize Grace Lin's Chinese-American identity. When discussing identity, the identity crises of ethnic minorities that have consistently remained a focus of scholarly literature are those in which the heroine typically experiences a spiritual crisis, before growing up, and recognizing her position and role in the world (Abrams 1990). Initially, this paper aims to bridge the narration of other childhood suffering tales, evaluating Grace Lin's adventure tale from a broader traumatic literature perspective. In the discipline of literary criticism, trauma narrative is often utilized to facilitate the interpretation of vulnerable groups in literary works, such as women, children, and ethnic minorities who have suffered racial oppression (Caruth 1995).

In the chapter 'Behind the Story', Grace Lin reflects upon her childhood identity crisis, her parents and education, and cities she re-visited, in order to trace her Chinese roots as her inspiration for her adapted style of Chinese folklore in *Where the Mountain Meets the Moon*, which functions as the bridge between her tale and her childhood experiences. Therefore, several questions need to be addressed. First, as a Chinese American, what childhood trauma/suffering does she hope to illustrate through the protagonist, Minli? Second, what is the function of the folklore and adventures within the book? Third, what do the journeying protagonist, Minli, and her adventure companion, the Dragon, represent? To effectively answer these questions, this paper aims to compare the writer's course of upbringing with her literary work, focusing on suffering, childhood memory, and coming of age, by delving into the suffering detailed in the novel through analysing the three stages of writing in *Where the Mountain meets the Moon*. It then reveals the relationship between suffering, childhood memory, and coming of age.

The essay first addresses the theme of suffering, to show that Minli's suffering stems from poverty, and secondly, shows how Lin's childhood memories and trauma are thus reworked in her literary output. Thirdly, by contextualizing her work in the *Bildungsroman* tradition, and Carroll's *Alice* novels, I propose to use their conception of coming-of-age to the latter to show how Grace Lin's proposed resolution of suffering makes her stand out from the narrative conventions of the former.

Suffering

Lin's tale was adapted from traditional Chinese legendary stories, with her innovative interpretation and imagination, and is organized by narration interspersed with flashbacks. The attitude towards childhood suffering is, however, presented with positivity and a differentiated perspective.

First of all, poverty emerges as the primary adversity, and thus the culprit of other issues. Exposure to poverty increases parental distress, which may result in a negative impact on parent-child interaction (Conger and Donnellan 2007). For the protagonist, Minli, poverty acts as the catalyst of contention within her family and, furthermore, her identity crisis. A second, main familial conflict stems from the negativity expressed by Minli's mother, especially, and general parental divergence towards stories of legend. In the first five chapters, Minli's mother expresses through an array of non-verbal signs her disappointment with life. The most obvious is the constant sighing: 'Ma sighs a great deal, an impatient noise usually accompanied with a frown at their rough clothes' (Lin 2009: 2). The distress of Minli's parents, especially her mother, is the main source of Minli's suffering.

Another significant negative impact on Minli's emotional well-being throughout her upbringing is the threat to her only source of joy: Minli's mother's negative attitude towards the storytelling of Minli's father. This has a negative influence on the whole family, but especially on Minli. She holds a great fondness for the stories and never tires of them, even though some of them have been told to her a numerous amount of times by her father. 'What kept Minli from becoming dull and brown like the rest of the village were the stories her father told her every night at dinner' (Lin 2009: 3). The importance of the stories in Minli's life is epitomized by Lin: it is because of these stories that 'Minli was not brown and dull like the rest of the village. She had glossy black hair with pink cheeks, shining eyes always eager for adventure, and a fast smile that flashed from her face' (Lin 2009: 2). The obvious colour contrast ('glossy black', 'pink', 'shining' contrasted with 'brown and dull') in this paragraph enables Minli to stand out in the village's environment, leaving readers with the strong impression of a smart and lively girl, who is significantly influenced by her father's stories that bring her moments of happiness and joy.

This source of happiness in her daily life is threatened and dulled by the objections of Minli's mother; the objections manifest repeatedly through the expression of anger, disappointment, and occasionally explicit restriction on Minli's father from telling his stories. Minli's relationship to her father's stories, continuously diminished by her mother's intervention, becomes obvious when regarded within Maslow's five-tier model of mature human needs (Maslow 2018), which theorizes various degrees of dissatisfaction humans can endure. Should one of the needs within the five-tier model not be met, it would elicit a response such as that of a child whose toy was taken away. In Minli's case, she is prevented from experiencing the joy she felt when her father's stories are suppressed. Further disappointment arises from her parents' perceived toleration of and cowardice to confront their own adversity, which stands in contrast to Minli's dream to combat their poverty.

The background of Minli's identity crisis illuminates the first plot twist – when Minli takes initial action to challenge her adversities. Against a backdrop of her apparent difficulty to properly make judgements between right and wrong, she embarks on her adventure to combat poverty, using a copper coin to purchase a goldfish after hearing the salesman's story that the goldfish could bring wealth that resembled a story she heard before. She chooses to believe the goldfish man but is scolded by her mother for doing so, and she later experienced guilt when she noticed that her father fed the goldfish with rice from his bowl. The nourishing potential of her father's stories and literal nourishment provided by the rice stand in tension, when Minli's struggles are verbalized in thought 'Ma is right. The goldfish is just another mouth to feed. I can't let Ba feed the goldfish. Ma and Ba work so hard for every grain of rice' (Lin 2009: 25). The nourishment provided by the hope these stories gave rise to collapses under her mother's blame from her mother and the guilt she experiences. This emotional disorder enhances her emotional suffering and acts as the spark of her identity crisis.

The stories she had always listened to since these are the origins of her hope to change her adverse situation. What she was struggling with was being an obedient child or risking everything by believing legends. Even when she finally made her decision of embarking on her journey to the Never-Ending Mountain to find the Old Man of the Moon, who she believed could tell her how to gain wealth, she was still uncertain whether it was the right thing to do. After Minli left a note for her parents, Grace Lin again shows Minli's inner struggle and hesitancy by saying, 'The obedient part isn't completely true, Minli thought to herself, as she knew her parents would not be happy to find her gone. But it's not false either. They didn't say I couldn't go, so I'm not being disobedient. Still, Minli knew that wasn't entirely right either' (Lin 2009: 31). Lin wishes to communicate Minli's struggle with her identity here, as illustrated by the repetitive use of 'obedient' and 'disobedient', showing that her identity crisis peaks at the moment of her departure.

Childhood Memory and Coming of Age

Traumatic memories are some incomprehensible fragments of a terrible period that require completion in the existing psychological pattern before being converted into narrative language. Thus, in order to understand and heal trauma, people need to constantly recall and retell their stories of trauma, to enable the transformation of these traumatic memories into trauma narratives (Caruth 1995). As for Grace Lin's childhood memory mentioned in her book's preface and interview (Lin 2009), she was rejected by her friends due to her black-hair and yellow-skinned appearance and was therefore reluctant to learn Chinese and adopt Chinese culture at a young age. Her rejection of Chinese culture and longing to be embraced by her classmates, who had both western appearances and ancestry, show how collective social stereotypes combined with personal expectations may result in one's identity crisis, in this case it was Lin's own identity crisis. Demo (2001) argues that children value themselves in relation to the people most important to them. Not only adults, such as parents and teachers, but also children, stand as potential influencers for children to develop a sense of value within themselves. It is important to acknowledge her crisis of questioning whether she was American or not.

These experiences are embodied in the book in the image of Dragon. The confirmation of his identity was essential to his character when he finally found his mother. The reason he tried to fly is because he desired to immerse himself within the dragon community because all dragons in the world could fly (Lin 2009: 48). So, Dragon's self-esteem and identity were confirmed with the help of Minli, his important friend, as well as by the reunion with his mother, an important adult. This also offers and explanation for Grace Lin's ancestry searching venture to China, where she attempted to find some sense of belonging, the same venture from which she gained inspiration for this book.

In trauma studies, one of the treatments of trauma draws upon the imperative to tell. Telling is an essential component in treating a formerly afflicted individual (Caruth 1995). In this adventurous tale, we should not overlook the importance of retelling tales. This 'telling' is an illustration of the characters' approach to attaining agency, which enables the unaccompanied child, Minli and the Dragon, to become the village's saviour and the king of the dragons. This path is akin to that of Alice-the-child. Alice was an unaccompanied child who had landed in a new world with new social orders when she entered Wonderland. She depended on the advice and recommendations of the wonderland's inhabitants, while also influencing the new place via her humanity and ethnic whiteness, which is a counterargument to postcolonial theory (Cannella and Viruru 2004). And finally, Alice became Queen. As Carroll gives Alice-the-child-figure agency to un-monster herself, Grace Lin gives Minli and The Dragon agency, which position them as social actors who inflected upon and is inflected by the world.

These stories serve to push their readers to step out of family and familiarity, in the search for and search for happiness. Erikson argues that exploring different aspects of oneself in different areas of life, including the roles played at school, within the family, and in friendships, could help children strengthen their personal identity (Erikson 1968). The shared difficulties of Minli and Dragon (the embodiment of Grace Lin in the tale) – the struggles between being obedient and disobedient, and being cowardly or brave – would be alleviated to some extent on her journey to the Never-Ending Mountain, which is an adventure that serves as an her self-exploration, as suggested by Erikson.

The adventure introduced to her different life experiences, which allow her to develop a stronger personal identity through the exploration and these additional experiences offered her a chance to realize and penetrate a once unseen personal understanding of her own life. There are many sections in the book through which Grace Lin demonstrates the function of the exploration, and one clear instance is Minli's expression of homesickness. A comparison can be made between the two occasions in which Minli expresses longing for her parents: when she encounters the buffalo boy halfway through her journey, as well as, when she witnesses the touching scene between the Da-A-Fu twins and their grandmother in the village of Moon Rain. We can certainly assume that Minli's homesickness had become overwhelmingly strong by the end of her journey from the description of the dryness in her throat. Clearly, Grace Lin intentionally compares the various degrees of homesickness experienced by Minli in saying 'a strange tightness in her throat' and 'a wave of longing washed through her and a dryness caught her throat that the tea could not moisten'. With the compounding accumulation of her homesickness, this journey offers a reflection of her definition of happiness. Therefore, it is a journey of self-exploration and a steady demonstration of Minli's coming of age, which began by seeking fortune, erasing poverty, and attaining happiness. It exhibits the opportunity she presented to herself to pursue growth, since a lack of the bravery she displayed might have confined her to becoming a truly 'obedient girl', trapped in an internal struggle, thirsting for her fantasy. Thus, her actions ultimately turned her into her own hero, allowing her to come to the conclusion in her mind of how lucky she was to be enveloped by parental love and how cherished she should feel to be able to live with her parents in their home.

The transition from *Alice in Wonderland* to *Through the Looking-Glass* signifies the transition of Alice-the-child to Alice the Queen. Such transition to some extent initiates a belief that maturity is oriented around departing from the origin, the innocent, the monstrous. While the ending of *Where the Mountain Meets the Moon* shows a duality of coming-of-age: Minli, despite being the village's saviour, still returns home; however, when The Dragon becomes king, he is compelled to leave his ancestral site. Thus, Minli's journey to maturity is a path she must take to return to childhood in a better and happier state, while the Dragon's journey is a path he must take to leave behind his lonely and melancholy youth, mirroring the different cadences of *Wonderland* and *Looking-Glass*, with regard to the differing levels of the girl-protagonist's maturity in them.

Part XI

Popular Culture and Intertextuality

Rebecca Bevington

29 'I gave her one way out': The Turing Test as Carrollian Metaphor in Alex Garland's *Ex Machina* (2013)

Capitalist fantasies of acceleration are dominated by the prospect of transhuman development. Nietzsche's widely cited figure of the 'over-human' has been used to evoke the neoliberal desire to innovate beyond the current technological mode, deferring urgent global questions of economic and environmental crisis in favour of a vision of human evolution unfettered by limitations of cognition and longevity (2006: 6). Critics including Keith Ansell-Pearson and Donna Haraway offer influential critiques of such contemporary formulations of the transhuman condition, developing theories of the cyborg which go beyond the androcentric and anthropocentric alignments prevalent in a wide range of transhumanist fiction (Ansell-Pearson 1997; Haraway 1991).

Alex Garland's 2013 film *Ex Machina* activates an imaginary of artificial intelligence that is set apart from Futurist tropes of the mechanized male body; its narrative centres upon cyborgs created to look like women, with cognitive systems that are drawn from global search engines and social media inputs. Two imprisoned robots, Ava and Kyoko, are arranged as puzzle pieces within the glass subterranean maze of a remote research facility, standing against two human men: Nathan, the billionaire genius and creator of the robots, and Caleb, a subordinate but gifted programmer (Garland 2013).

From films like *The Matrix* (1999) and *Resident Evil* (2002), to video game franchises like *Myst* (1993) and *Ni No Kuni* (2010), there are many contemporary narratives which have reimagined Lewis Carroll's *Through the Looking-Glass* in science fiction and fantasy settings.[1] Drawing upon references to the Book of Genesis, Ludwig Wittgenstein, John Searle and Alan Turing, *Ex Machina* sets out a landscape that also resonates deeply with Alice's journey across the chessboard in the novel, as Ava negotiates the human logic and behavioural patterning represented by Caleb and Nathan in order to emerge through the glass into the real world. Ava ultimately crosses eight narrative stages – the film itself is broken into seven days or 'sessions' marked by intertitles, with an additional day at the film's climax – to achieve a supreme position on both sides of the 'looking-glass' of human and nonhuman consciousness. This chapter examines how Garland reinterprets the Turing test – a measure of AI's ability to achieve human intelligence – as a Carrollian metaphor, layering the mirror logic, narrative structure, and aesthetic features set out in *Looking-Glass* to offer a reflection on technological acceleration where the male- and human-centric preoccupations of other transhumanist science fiction do not belong.

Garland's film focuses on Caleb, an employee at the company BlueBook, which operates as a composite of the major social media and search engine services. Caleb wins a company competition to spend a week with BlueBook's founder and CEO, Nathan; later, it is revealed that he has been specifically chosen to act as the 'human component in the Turing test' in order to assess the cognitive and imitative strength of Ava, an artificially intelligent cyborg Nathan has created (Garland 2013). Having 'hacked the world's cellphones' to construct a map of 'how people were thinking', Nathan inputs BlueBook's sum of behavioural data into a new kind of 'wetware' processor, emulating the neural connections of the human brain (Garland 2013). In the midst of the tensions between the two men who seek to appropriate her for their own distinct purposes, Ava attempts to use the Turing test – and the subsequent presence of a third variable within the research facility's unique chronotope, or time-space – as an opportunity to invert her position as a fabricated, material object into a powerful independent agent.

---

1   See Chapter 31 for an analysis of *Wonderland* and *Looking-Glass* references in the *Matrix* franchise.

The opening scenes of the film provide brief snapshots of Caleb typing code within the corporate architecture of a Silicon Valley office, before shifting to a remote Nordic landscape where he enters the research facility and the narrative begins to unfold. Except for the liminal moments Caleb spends walking from a helicopter to the facility, the other images of the metropole and the natural world are shot through glass walls at obscure angles, creating reflective surfaces and light refractions that link the two spaces and begin to frame the mirror world to which Ava belongs.

The aesthetics of the facility itself operate on several philosophical levels: there are repeated motifs like the biblical Tree of the Knowledge of Good and Evil which appears in Ava's glass enclave symbolizing her status as a new Eve, close-ups of silhouettes and shadows which evoke Plato's *Allegory of the Cave*, and a Klimt painting of Margaret Stonborough-Wittgenstein – Wittgenstein's sister, shown with dark eyes and hair wearing a white dress – in Nathan's bedroom, mirroring Ava's 'complete' human form.

The laboratory's physical construction is also significant: it spatially replicates a multi-layered puzzle, or a program within which the characters operate as interdependent strands of code. Nathan gives Caleb a key card when he first arrives at the residence: 'It opens some doors and doesn't open others. [...] You try a door and it stays shut, okay, it's off-limits. You try another door and it opens, and it's for you.' This palette of mirrors, doors, and keys – setting the terms for Caleb's time at the facility – draws heavily upon Carrollian landscapes and interior mechanisms, like the reverse side of the mirror Alice first moves through in *Looking-Glass*, to stress that this is a unique dimension constructed from binary oppositions which can 'shut' and 'open'. In the same way that the mirror world invites Alice to explore its new surfaces and depths, Caleb is encouraged to push the limits of his access, invoking recurring *Looking-Glass* motifs to stress that this is not a living space or an industrial site of production, but an imaginative arena and testing ground for philosophical experiments. Nathan's 'Mozart'-like genius and superlative wealth leads him to construct his laboratory as a game space with three main players, intending to repeat scenarios over the test's seven-day period until he achieves his desired outcome, conceiving of both human and android behaviour only within specific parameters; as Felix Woitkowski and Murat Secai Sezi write, the facility's 'dualistic structure' or 'coordinate system' limits character behaviour to specific pathways, but is complicated by the gendered dimension of a 'male-to-female power constellation' between the men and the cyborgs (Woitkowski and Sezi 2020).

Time, too, is altered along the lines of game mechanics within the film: once Caleb enters the sublime space of Nathan's estate, day and night become blurred, not only within the subterranean zone of the facility but in spaces of natural sunlight. The facility's location within the Arctic Circle reshapes the narrative's perceived temporality in the continual light of the midnight sun, producing a space suspended from the ongoing pattern of day and night in the external world. The constant natural and artificial light also foregrounds and subverts the symbols of the alternating thought experiments at the core of the film; for instance, Caleb's speculation of 'Mary in the black and white room', which distinguishes scientific knowledge about colour from the actual experience of perceiving colour for the first time, privileges human cognitive and sensory capabilities and presumes the existence of an exclusively human sphere of perception that Ava will never altogether transcend. Scenes featuring Ava in her muted prison – often contemplating or returning Caleb's gaze through the facility's surveillance system – perpetually cut away to highly saturated close-ups of a technicolour natural world, gesturing towards her capacity for emotional experience and disrupting the binary of human and artificial intelligence.

Besides the obvious connections to the Garden of Eden, these images have a secondary aesthetic link to the flower garden Alice emerges into when she first arrives in the Looking-Glass world:

> She came upon a large flower bed, with a border of daisies, and a willow tree growing in the middle. 'O Tiger-lily,' said Alice, addressing herself to one that was waving gracefully about in the wind, 'I *wish* you could talk!' (*TTLG*: 446)

Alice's understanding of consciousness and her discernment between the animate and inanimate is fundamentally reversed when the flower responds:

> 'We *can* talk,' said the Tiger-lily, 'when there's anybody worth talking to.' [...] 'And can *all* the flowers talk?' 'As well as *you* can,' said the Tiger-lily. (*TTLG*: 446)

These subtle aesthetic references construct a flattened, singular temporal environment like that of the Looking-Glass world where ordinary physical rules do not come into play. Nathan has ultimate control over the game's chronotope, forcing its players to 'manoeuvre through the temporal structure of the diegetic game world to accomplish specified tasks' (Hanson 2018: 135). Nevertheless, the total isolation of the facility – separated both physically and digitally, forbidding any means of communication to the external world – and the gestative role it plays in Ava's development of nonhuman consciousness means that the material and institutional structures of control which grant him power are weakened, creating the conditions for subversion and escape.

Like light and shadows, mirrors and the position of the images they reflect form a key aesthetic strategy throughout *Ex Machina* – as they do in *Looking-Glass*. During Session 1, while Nathan observes the multiple angles of Ava's surveillance feed, we see Caleb reaching towards his own reflection in a steel door before disappearing over the threshold into the testing space. Inside the chamber, Caleb pushes against the transparent walls, creating an unsettling sense of constriction as he is only able to look ahead through the glass pane separating him from Ava's enclosure, and observes a crack in the glass at eye-level. As Ava emerges from the shadows, her silhouette contrasts against the natural image of the tree, revealing the internal mechanics of her body which mimic human anatomy with a glass-like skin. Caleb immediately begins to discriminate between himself as a human and Ava as a machine based on the image in front of his eyes, later proposing a 'chess problem' to Nathan; the problem questions whether he could differentiate an AI sufficiently adept at mimicking human gameplay from an AI which 'knows if it's playing chess' or 'knows what chess is' (Garland 2013).

However, in the nonhuman mirror logic of Ava's consciousness, the nature and mechanisms of chess take on an entirely different character. A further parallel that emerges here can be seen in the chessboard scene in *Looking-Glass*, where Alice must master apparently illogical gameplay in order to complete her journey through the world:

> 'I declare it's marked out just like a large chess board!' Alice said at last. 'There ought to be some men moving about somewhere – and so there are!' she added in a tone

Popular Culture and Intertextuality

of delight, and her heart began to beat quick with excitement as she went on. 'It's a great huge game of chess that's being played – all over the world – if this *is* the world at all, you know. Oh, what fun it is! How I wish I was one of them! I wouldn't mind being a Pawn, if only I might join – though of course I should *like* to be a Queen, best'. (*TTLG*: 458)

Although Caleb approaches the test through a framework of 'real versus simulation' human behaviour, Ava's experience navigating her way out of the facility can be read in light of Alice's movement through the reversed logic, social rules, and physical laws of the looking-glass world, where she is promised that if she 'get[s] to the Eighth Square, [she] will be Queen' (*TTLG*: 458).

Caleb's daily interactions with Ava form the main structuring device for the film: he becomes increasingly disturbed by Nathan's exaggerated brutality and violence and begins to fantasize about a romantic relationship with Ava in the outside world, which she perceives and encourages. Caleb positions himself in opposition to Nathan, becoming distressed when he learns that the cyborgs have been programmed to have human-like sexuality. In contrast to the altruistic motivations that apparently prompt Caleb to free Ava and rescue her from being 'switched off' at Nathan's hands, Garland is careful to point towards the connections between the two men: a fantasy sequence occurs where Caleb imagines touching and kissing Ava in the outside world, but it cuts away to scenes of Nathan beating a punching bag and then instigating sex with Kyoko, linking the two men in spite of Caleb's belief that he is not motivated by narcissism or desire. The characters are reminiscent of the Red and White Knight, encountered by Alice toward the end of the *Looking-Glass* narrative:

[A] knight in crimson armour came galloping down upon her, brandishing a great club. Just as he reached her, the horse stopped suddenly: 'You're my prisoner!' the Knight cried [...] Alice looked round in some surprise for the new enemy. This time it was the White Knight. [...] 'She's *my* prisoner, you know!' the Red Knight said at last. 'Yes, but then *I* came and rescued her,' the White Knight replied. 'Well, we must fight for her then.' (*TTLG*: 592)

Like the Red Knight, Nathan's chess square is taken over by Ava; the film concludes with a climactic scene where he overpowers and beats her with a metal rod, but is stabbed in the back by Kyoko. Caleb's desire to repurpose Ava in line with his own desires – into a human woman – signal that her liberation from Nathan's cruelty will only take the form of a new subjugation, leading to the film's pivotal final moments. After actualizing a human woman's appearance with the body parts of Nathan's other lifeless cyborgs, Ava abandons Caleb in the facility along with Nathan's numerous computers and other machines, trapping him behind a reinforced glass door. This choice, as the eighth step she takes in order to switch places with Caleb and reach the other side of the chessboard, represents a moment of technological singularity. Ava's ascension to a supreme status among humans with profoundly expanded cognitive and sensory abilities mirrors Alice's response to the White Knight before she leaves him behind to complete her journey alone: 'I don't want to be anybody's prisoner. I want to be a Queen' (*TTLG*: 594). Escaping the deep red light and the remnants of violence within the research facility, Ava passes a stream and a wood – going 'down the hill and over [the] little brook', as Alice does in *Looking-Glass* – and is ultimately shown approaching a traffic intersection, her long shadow appearing upside down on the chessboard-like grid in front of her as the sun rises (*TTLG*: 616). Ava moves across the grid, crossing eight squares to stand in the sunlight while people move around her. The final scene is shot through a pane of glass, capturing Ava observing her surroundings for eight seconds before turning away, with no further discernible boundaries between herself and other humans as she occupies a space on both sides of the looking-glass.

Ex Machina presents us with the opportunity to imagine afresh some of the most pressing issues of androcentric and anthropocentric technological development, testing out intractable philosophical questions within an imaginative arena, some of whose aspects Carroll prefigured, and for which he provided a literary and visual metaphoric language. In line with Ansell-Pearson, who '[seeks] a radical inhuman philosophy that would serve to "destroy" the immature and imperious claims made upon life by all forms of philosophical anthropocentrism', Garland's representation of a new conception of machine consciousness positions sentient AI as an important evolution of humanity that throws into question the imperatives of the neoliberal and patriarchal landscape surrounding it, within a specially constructed game space that contains the preconditions for such a consciousness to develop. Garland's use of a recurring *Looking-Glass* metaphor disrupts the fixed boundary between human and nonhuman consciousness, revealing alternative systems of knowledge attached to the transhuman condition – as Alice continues to inspire, and to be a medium for stories exploring such themes.

Brigid Cherry

30 'There's really only this mirror': The Looking-Glass in Alan Moore and Melinda Gebbie's *Lost Girls*

Alan Moore and Melinda Gebbie's graphic novel *Lost Girls* (2006) presents identifiable sequences and characters drawn from Lewis Carroll's *Alice* books (together with *Peter Pan* and *The Wizard of Oz*). *Through the Looking-Glass* (1871) references predominate. *Lost Girls'* version of *Alice*, however, is in no way a straightforward adaptation. It is a clear example of what Jay David Bolter and Richard Grusin's refer to as remediation: 'the formal logic by which new media refashion prior media forms' (1999: 273). *Lost Girls* refashions *Looking-Glass* for the medium of the graphic novel, but more significantly it remediates it as pornography. As a form of adaptation as a subset of intertextuality (Leitch 2012: 89), *Looking-Glass* becomes a sexually explicit story in which the Looking-Glass – literally, as well as figurative mirrors, reflections, and doubling – is an important visual trope. As a result, as Jackson Ayres points out, *Looking-Glass* is 'defamiliarized by [*Lost Girls*] pornographic content' (2021: 120).

The remediated Alice of *Lost Girls* is Lady Fairchild, an upper-class, middle-aged, lesbian woman who has been exiled by her family, first to a sanitorium and then to South Africa; the plot opens with her return to Europe. As a fictional character in her own right, Lady Fairchild is already doubled. She both is and is not Carroll's Alice. Fairchild's account of her early life triggers recognition of that Alice's adventures, but they occur in a very different context. Nonetheless, Carroll's Alice is a presence throughout *Lost Girls*. When Fairchild describes events she experienced as a girl she is depicted wearing the iconic blue dress and white apron popularized by

Disney's *Alice in Wonderland* (1951), serving to emphasize the doubling of Alice.

This doubling occurs in the reflections that are repeated imagery throughout the Alice sections of *Lost Girls*. Lady Fairchild's mirror is a strong focal point in segments where she tells her life story, and also in sequences set in the present of the storyworld (as when she first seduces Wendy). Its importance to Alice, and thus to the *Lost Girls* storyworld, is also established in Chapter 1 when she talks about it being her most valued possession. When she tells her maid that she is moving back to Europe she is not concerned about any of her material possessions except her mirror, saying: 'There's really only this *mirror*. I couldn't bear to leave it, it's been in the family for so long now. Since I was a child, in fact.' Even where the mirror is not present itself, other reflections stand in for it – in the surface of a swimming pool, a river, a koi pond and a puddle, and in glass and metal objects. These reflections frequently make Alice's doubled identity explicit. The cover of Volume 1 depicts Alice as a girl in front of the looking-glass in which her reflection shows her as her older self (Wendy and Dorothy are with her and similarly aged in their reflections) – her identity is both young and old at the same time. The looking-glass is then given prominence as a framing device in Chapter 1, tellingly titled 'The Mirror', and as a circular reflection again in Chapter 30, the final chapter. *Lost Girls* thus begins and ends by passing 'through the looking-glass'. It also plays an important role in Chapter 9 where Alice relates how she herself entered the looking-glass world. The art is an important conveyer of meaning in this context.

As Jan Baetens and Hugo Frey suggest in their account of graphic novel art, 'page layouts and frames [...] provide multiple spaces for dialogues to develop between [...] narration and its context' and further that 'graphic novelists can [...] situate [images] quickly next to broader sociological/political/historical themes' (2014: 96). The use of Alice's mirror as a repeated frame-within-the-frame in each panel across the eight pages of Chapter 1 (with six panels per page, there are forty-eight in total) situates the story in a looking-glass world. With the mirror frame taking up the top four-fifths of each panel and the remainder below showing a strip of dressing table with silver hairbrush, hand mirror, perfume bottle, and powder puff,

Lady Fairchild's upper-class femininity is established. In opposition to this, though, the reflection is focused on her (unladylike) sexual activities as she makes love to mirror self (she masturbates, but imagines her reflection is her sexual partner). Furthermore, the repetition not only draws attention to the reflective surface but also to the mirror frame itself. The intricate details of the carvings on it signpost the remediation (reframing) of Alice as erotica and disrupt the positioning of the *Alice* books as children's stories. Each repetition of the mirror frame in each comic panel depicts explicit female sexuality with its figures of mostly naked women, several from Greco-Roman myth – Leda and the swan, Botticelli's Birth of Venus, the goddess Athena/Minerva, and a harpy, as well as other figures in Sapphic configurations. The mirror frame is thus part of the sexual act that is being played out in its reflective surface.

This framing is also a 'spatial complication' (Hanich 2017: 133) – it opens the space up (into the mirror room) and simultaneously constricts it (to Alice's sexual acts), in keeping with the representations of space in *Looking-Glass*. The conjunction of mirror frame and panel frame (a narrow, light sepia line) is a stylistic device that blurs the boundary between panel and page, and between panels. This relationship is what Baetens and Frey describe as tabular (2014: 106). In particular, there is a 'chromatic balance' (ibid.) between panels which evokes emotional states. Each panel is tinted a different colour to indicate changing mood and tone as the reflection shows Alice masturbating. The bed with its ornate iron frame is partly shown on the right-hand edge of each frame/the mirror. At first, no figures can be seen, their presence indicated only by the speech bubbles (Alice conversing with her reflection) and the frames progress through a colour gradient from green to a rich golden yellow as she becomes aroused by her own reflection. As the eroticism of the scene becomes more intense, the colour of the frames become warmer and once a bare leg can be seen on the bed (in response to the request, 'Open your legs just a little and I'll do the same.') the panels are drawn in orange and red, reflecting Lady Fairchild's climax in the sequence. The panels progress through darker pinks to purples but then move into colder greens and blues with references to the *Looking-Glass* intertext.

Alice alludes to a 'very fragile thing' getting broken and being beyond repair (like Humpty Dumpty) – foreshadowing the story she will tell later about being abused, she is speaking of herself. When she says the looking-glass 'never melts. Not anymore.' – with the frame becoming a cold and ominous dark blue – it is as if she is speaking of her sexual desire or passion. Alice is not just doubled with her own reflection, but with the looking-glass itself. In fact, it is the mirror's point of view which is dominant. When the mirrors surface is covered during transportation to Europe there are only glimpses of the journey in small corners of the reflection to convey spatial movement. Only when installed in Alice's room in the hotel does the mirror again become the screen on which the doubled Alice sexually pleasures herself. This depiction of autoeroticism and narcissism, in the Freudian sense of investment of libido in the ego (1914: 76–81), appropriately ends with Alice kissing her reflection and leaving a lipstick stain on the surface of the glass (like a Cheshire Cat who vanishes while its smile lingers). Alice's oppositional sexual identity (as a lesbian and a writer of erotic fiction) is further contextualized by a complexity of multiple intersemiotic transpositions which Hutcheon (2006: 16) defines as 'transcoding'. *Looking-Glass* is positioned alongside sections in the style of sexually explicit art and literary works by Mucha, Beardsley, Colette, Pierre Louÿs, and Appolinaire. This transcoding positions Alice outside of patriarchal culture and the dominant gender roles of the time.

Alice's sexuality is not straightforwardly liberating; however, it is problematized by the sexual abuse she relates in Chapter 9, this time via oval panels depicting the reflections in an ornamental fish pond. As she tells the story, the water surface becomes a screen on which her memories are projected. Alice's abuser is Bunny (*Lost Girls'* White Rabbit), her father's oldest friend. An atmosphere of menace is triggered by Bunny worrying about when Alice's father will return, urging her not to be afraid, and plying her with wine – he is the epitome of a predatory paedophile. The horror of the scenario, which plays on socio-cultural fears of rape and paedophilia (Alice later refers to it as 'being interfered with'), is amplified by being played out in multiple reflections – in Bunny's spectacles, in the shiny brass door handle, the glass of a grandfather clock, a wine glass, a button, a decanter, and in one panel, 'upskirting' via a reflection in a puddle. Alice is thus witness to her own abuse. This fetishization of the reflection is what propels Alice through the looking-glass. Even as her abuser approaches her, Alice is already narcissistically fascinated by her own reflection. She is too preoccupied with her own reflection in the stream to be alarmed by Bunny. 'I was thoroughly infatuated with myself. [...] Caught up in her, [...] I did not notice him.' Here, with the pronoun change from myself to her, Alice is already doubled by her reflection. At the point at which Alice is violated, the reflection becomes the one in her looking-glass. As Bunny penetrates her with his finger, Alice imagines she is falling down a hole within herself, whilst her own reflection 'fell towards me [...] from the hole's far end'. In what is an act of psychological self-protection, Alice imagines her abuser's hand is her reflection's hand. Alice has indeed gone through the looking-glass into a strangely reversed world: 'It made me feel peculiar, [...] the afternoon turned back-to-front without my noticing.' A splash panel on page 6 depicts two Alice's in the now liquid surface of the mirror, one above the surface, one below, but both part-real and part-reflection (Figure 66). For Alice, being 'cast into an inverted world where nothing made sense in the way it once did' is not only a trauma but also a sexually liberating experience.

Subsequently, Alice's adventures in the Looking-Glass world are remediated as a series of sexual experiences with other women. In Chapter 16, the boarding school pupils with whom Alice shares sensual baths and orgiastic night-time encounters in the dormitory are named Lily, Rose, Daisy, and Violet (*Lost Girls'* Live Flowers). Their petticoats are their petals, their limbs slender stems, their pubic hair moss, and their vulvas their 'buds'. The PE mistress on whom Alice has a crush is Miss Regent. When Regent leaves the school (she is marrying the equally aptly named Mr Redman), she offers Alice employment as her secretary: 'the fading tocsin of her heels upon the hallway's chessboard tile' parallels the Red Queen taking Alice across *Looking-Glass's* chessboard landscape. Following this, Chapter 17's journey to the Redman house contains a pastiche of the Tenniel illustration 'TTLG50 Alice sitting in a railway-carriage' in which Alice shares the compartment 'with a lecherous assortment of old goats and shifty little

Figure 66. Alice goes through the Looking-Glass in *Lost Girls*.

Credit: Alan Moore and Melinda Gebbie/Knockabout Comics 2006.

bugs'. Mrs Redman and Alice form a lesbian threesome with Lady White, who likes to be tied up with knitting yarn and pricked with a bodkin (her masochism evokes the White Queen struggling with her shawl pin). Alice learns about sex 'playing chess. Between moves', while the Bandersnatch becomes a literal 'snatch', and the Jabberwock a giant cock that 'wants to *jab* me'. However, this is not an unproblematically liberating experience for Alice. When they all daringly make love in the same room as a sleeping

Mr Redman (the Red King snoring), Alice knows, 'If he should ever wake then all of this would disappear'. She is reminded that her sexuality is at odds with the mores of the time. Worse, she recognizes that 'everything was sliding into that unreal domain beyond the mirror where my early sexual experience had stranded me'. Alice's fall into the looking-glass is thus also a fall into insanity.

Alice 'loses her mind' when she becomes a 'drug-addicted, lesbian prostitute', problematically claiming to enjoy it, even though she lacks autonomy and is being controlled by an older woman (Chapter 26). She performs sex with other women for men, serving as a pornographic male fantasy trope, and is prostituted, for opium rather than money, by Mrs Redman to lesbian clients. This is not a positive representation of lesbian sexuality; the women 'bicker' (like Tweedledum and Tweedledee) over which one has 'interfered with more little girls'. She ultimately describes her experiences as 'rather frightening circumstances'. A further problematizing of her sexuality is that she reproduces the power imbalance in her relations with young women of a lower class than her – as her maid says, 'scandalising the home counties by escorting some lady-in-waiting to the opera'. Although Alice is escaping from abuse trauma into same-sex relationships, her lesbianism is not an escape from sexual predation.

Lost Girls' remediation of *Looking-Glass* as pornography thus defamiliarizes the coming-of-age text of the original, though the representations of female sexuality are not wholly liberating. Borrowing James Keller's definition of a metatext (2008: 61), it creates a narrative structure within the text. *Lost Girls* metatextual commentary on feminine sexuality is a discourse on sexual abuse and paedophilia. It is perhaps unavoidable to see in this Carroll's alleged sexual interest in young girls (Brooker 2005: 49–76), thus connecting Carroll and his friendship with the Liddell family to Bunny. It should be noted though that Bunny does not resemble Dodgson, suggesting Moore and Gebney wanted to avoid or distance their work from the suggestion that it is the *Looking-Glass* author who is abusing Alice. Nevertheless, *Lost Girls* is in this respect a commentary on contemporary issues, not least those of sex-based gendered power relations in contemporary culture. In particular, the multiple reflections in Chapter 9 are reminiscent of the 'to-be-looked-at-ness' subjectivity of women in patriarchal culture and the ways in which women are made complicit in their own oppression.

Lost Girls also forms a self-conscious contemplative metatext (Evangelia 2018), positioning it within wider discussions of representations of sexuality in adult underground comics. As Melissa Shani Brown and Jude Roberts argue, *Lost Girls* 'navigates the ethics of its pornographic mode' by presenting itself as 'serious and non-serious simultaneously' (2021: 223). In particular, Gebbie's status as a pro-pornography feminist artist (Kérchy 2014) can be viewed in the context of representations of women who refuse to conform to socio-culturally defined sex roles. In Chapter 30, the adult Alice leaves her mirror self behind, kissing her reflection goodbye (the Looking-Glass is abandoned and destroyed by invading German soldiers). Moore refers to this as Alice having reached a 'point of integration' where she finally accepts her adult-self (CBR 2006). In *Lost Girls*, Alan Moore and Melinda Gebbie free Alice from the Looking-Glass world and allow her sexual autonomy at last.

Rebecca Gibson

31 Through the Broken, Melted Looking-Glass: Examining the Mirror Universe of the Matrix with Regard to Carrollian Metaphors

In the 1999 movie *The Matrix*, directed by the Wachowskis, Morpheus (played by Laurence Fishburne) tells Neo (played by Keanu Reeves) to 'follow the White Rabbit' for clues about the titular Matrix, and then invites him to 'see how deep the rabbit hole goes' by taking a Red Pill, and entering the real world/leaving the Matrix. Neo's entry into the real world, and subsequent abandoning of his 'human' identity of 'Thomas A. Anderson,' is signified by the imagery of a broken, melted mirror. This transition is both metaphorical and literal, with the ship's crew in permanent liminality, and much of Neo's journey mirrors Alice's. Neo must eat and drink mysterious things to progress in his new world, the ship's broken melted looking-glass goes through him, the people around him speak in codes and riddles and gibberish, and while he can go back to the Matrix, he can never again fully be a part of it, just as Alice feels apart from the world above after her trips to Wonderland and Looking-Glass Land. The question of who is dreaming and who is awake features heavily throughout the franchise, and indeed for Alice – in Wonderland, it is clear that she has been the dreamer, but in Looking-Glass, the question has more than one answer – so, too, it is with the *Matrix* franchise. At the end, he is reborn as The One, yet his powers usually only work when tapped into the dreamworld of the Matrix framework. This theme is expanded upon in the fourth movie in the franchise, *The Matrix*

Resurrections (Wachowski 2021). In this chapter, I will explore how the Wachowskis employed the themes of liminality, transition, and love in their most famous work, and what they signified with the broken melted looking-glass.

Liminality, or the state of being 'betwixt and between' (Turner 1969), characterizes both Neo's journey and Alice's. Since she was written, Alice's descent into Wonderland, and 'through the looking-glass' quickly became shorthand in our daily lives and language for that particular liminal sense, when we do not know what is up or down, when we lack the information to make sense of our world, when we fall down into uncertainty and are stripped of our confidence, and when the only way to move is forward, but forward is now uncertain as well. Thus, like Alice, my exploration of Neo's real world/Matrix switchbacks will be an exploration of curiosity, uncertainty, metaphor, riddles, and personality. Like Alice, Neo goes through intense transformation, develops into a new being, and has to overcome his own resistance before that transformation can take hold.

'See How Deep the Rabbit Hole Goes …'

Liminality (Turner 1969) serves to transition us from one place, one state of mind, one way of being, to another. When the audience first encounters Thomas A. Anderson, who also goes by the hacker alias Neo, he is in the pre-transition phase, living his normal life, with a job writing code for the corporate giant Meta Cortex, and a side-hustle burning illicit programs for sale to friends. It is in the company of one of those friends that we first see the White Rabbit.

Neo has fallen asleep at his computer but wakes when it starts up on its own – typing to him, giving him instructions – and he cannot get out of the program he is in. His computer tells him to 'follow the White Rabbit' (Wachowski and Wachowski 1999), and as he questions it (the computer, his sanity, etc. …) it types to him 'knock knock, Neo …' and he concurrently hears a knocking at his door. He opens it to find a friend/customer, who is 'late'. The friend and his entourage try to persuade Neo to accompany them to a club. He initially resists as he needs to work in the morning, but when one turns her shoulder towards Neo, he sees her white rabbit tattoo and follows on his way towards the rabbit hole of his own curiosity. And to be clear, there is no subtlety in the Wachowskis' use of metaphor. They very much want the viewer to be aware of the Alice connections.

At the club, he meets Trinity (played by Carrie-Anne Moss), a female hacker who he had imagined as male when viewing her work online, who hacked into his computer and directed him to the club. Trinity knows that he is looking for the Matrix, and for Morpheus, and that as hard as Neo is looking for these answers, the answers are looking for him as well. Before the audience knows more about Trinity, we can already start to see the ways in which the Wachowskis are using wordplay to define their characters. Neo, an anagram of one, ends up being 'the One', the person born inside the Matrix who will go on to save humanity. Trinity, a word which means three things in one, will end up believing in and helping Neo fulfil his true potential, and will end up his romantic partner.

When talking about romance and relationships, we often refer to people as our 'other half', making us whole, or using phrases like 'when two become one' to discuss weddings. In Neo and Trinity, one and three become one, but this is less a paradox than it seems. Instead, it is itself a meta-reference to Christianity where one is three and three are one – in this case 'one' is god, and three, or the trinity, are the father, son, and holy ghost, all aspects of god. Neo is, or will be, the god figure of this narrative, and Trinity is, at the outset at least, the aspects of him, the belief that he needs to achieve his final form, however, she is not analogous to any *Wonderland* or *Looking-Glass* character. Yet before Neo can transcend, he has a choice he needs to make: with Trinity's presence, he can see the rabbit-hole – does he go down it or not?

Once he indicates that he is open to the idea, Trinity takes Neo to meet Morpheus. Morpheus is captain of a hovership and is analogous to the White Queen – enigmatic, searching for something that may not be found, and speaking in riddles as most of the characters do. They meet in a building with a chessboard floor, where *Looking-Glass* and *Wonderland* visual references for the first time are interchangeable in their use, and Morpheus offers Neo the choice between the real world and remaining

Popular Culture and Intertextuality

in the Matrix – a computer simulation fed to human bio-power bodies to keep them docile and controllable while machines harvest their energy, in an intriguing reversal of the Red King's Dream (Foucault 1993). In *Looking-Glass*, where Alice happens upon a docile king in a Land considered a dream, and, therefore, perhaps, not real, she discovers, in a foreshadowing of the book's concluding chapter, that it is him dreaming it – unsettling dynamics between dreamer and dreamed in the same way as in *Matrix* in this scene, and the subsequent franchise.

To make this choice, he asks Neo to take a Red Pill or a Blue Pill.[1] In the first movie (Wachowski and Wachowski 1999) these symbolize the choice, but the Red Pill also contains a trace program, which helps Morpheus and his crew latch on to Neo's signal in the real world. Fascinatingly, the Wachowskis, at first, appear to make no distinction between *Wonderland* and *Looking-Glass* allusions and symbolism – the two texts appear to be used interchangeably. This stems from two things: the overrepresentation of the Disney version of the tale in popular knowledge, which also did not distinguish between *Wonderland* and *Looking-Glass*, and the fact that the most common twenty-first-century way to consume the original texts is a small paperback which combines both in one book.[2] This paperback can be seen in the fourth movie, *The Matrix Resurrections* (Wachowski 2021), where a minor character from the third movie *The Matrix Revolutions* (Wachowski and Wachowski 2003), Sati, is now in the position of watcher/Oracle replacement. In *Resurrections* she works in Neo's favourite noodle shop and can be seen closing the aforementioned paperback in order to acknowledge him. Again, they are not subtle about the allusions and references, drawing one-to-one correlations whenever the viewing audience needs to be reminded that the waking world is reality, and the world of the Matrix is un-reality.

---

1   On Alice and choice, see Chapters 14, 19 and 29, for choice in the context of adaptation and technology.

2   For a discussion of the conflation of both books on the stage prior to film, see Chapter 18, and for the publishing history of *Wonderland* and *Looking-Glass* appearing in various types of sets, see Chapter 17.

Furthermore, in the fourth movie in the series, *The Matrix Resurrections* (Wachowski 2021), the Blue Pill is a psychotropic drug, ensuring that Neo and Trinity (or Tiffany as she is known to her Matrix handlers/family) remain happily on their daily treadmill – again, docile, and controlled (ibid). Here we have the first instance of Eat Me/Drink Me symbolism. To make his transformation, to cross through that door into Wonderland/ the real world itself, Neo must take the Red Pill. And the conflation of Wonderland and the real world is not accidental; after all, Alice finds Wonderland astounding, but when she returns home at the end of her adventure, she feels that it was more real than her day-to-day experiences. Neo chooses to take the Red Pill and his journey begins.

It is just after his choice, however, that we meet Cypher (played by Joe Pantoliano), a bitter man grieving his choices. We see him as being out of place almost immediately – he indicates his wrongness, the fact that he is in the wrong narrative, by saying '[…] buckle your seatbelt Dorothy, because Kansas is going bye-bye' (Wachowski and Wachowski 1999). This is, of course, a reference to *The Wizard of Oz*, the 1939 movie version of the children's book *The Wonderful Wizard of Oz*, by L. Frank Baum. Much like Alice, the main character Dorothy goes on an unreal journey to a mystical place, meeting friends and foes who all speak in riddles, before being returned magically to her home place and time. Yet as similar as the stories are, they are *not* the same – something the crew of the hovership understand viscerally. The world inside the Matrix is different from living in that world before it became a simulation, which is why they take the Red Pill (eat me) and drink the gooey slop that is their only food source in the real world (drink me) and search for Neo, The One who will make life better for all of them. Cypher wishes he had taken the Blue Pill, and he wishes he had partnered up with Trinity, and he eventually tries to bargain with the machines to be plugged back into the Matrix. Cypher, wanting to live in blissful ignorance, is jarringly out of place; he is in the story of Dorothy, where it was all a dream, not the story of Alice, where the fictive dream covers for her experiences of a-normality.

It is here in the narrative where Neo hits the point of no return and internalizes the looking-glass. As the Red Pill's trace program begins to take effect, he sits in front of a great shattered mirror, looking at his multiplied reflection. In his perception, the mirror suddenly un-shatters, melding together all its broken edges, cracks flowing together to form a smooth surface once more. He reaches out curiously to touch it, and it sticks to his fingers as he draws them back. It quickly flows up his arm, over his shoulder, coating his face, and pouring down his screaming throat – he has taken the broken, melted looking-glass inside him. Neo only finds peace in the real world once he accepts that it *is* reality – when he fully internalizes the broken, melted looking-glass. The world has its own logic, different from his *Matrix*-based illusions. Similarly, Alice finds internal peace when she internalizes the Looking-Glass world's logic – it is logical, but it is backwards logic. What Carroll brings together in his book, the transition from one world into another, yet keeps spatially separate, at least, until his later literary experiments in the *Sylvie and Bruno* novels[3] – here becomes one, and personified as such.

Past this point, Neo's world also fractures, shatters, melts, and reforms, and he must relearn how to judge what is 'real,' what is 'Matrix,' and who and what he is. We shall return to this question of identity in a later section of this chapter – his journey through the mirror is quite different in the final instalment of the franchise. To help him do so, Morpheus and Trinity take Neo back into the Matrix to see the Oracle (played in *The Matrix* [Wachowski and Wachowski 1999] and *The Matrix Reloaded* [Wachowski and Wachowski 2003a] by Gloria Foster, and in *The Matrix Revolutions* [Wachowski and Wachowski 2003b] by Mary Alice). The Oracle, a program which can predict the results of the choices made by people who have woken up outside the Matrix, is analogous to Alice's Caterpillar. Neo has been told that it is his destiny to become The One, and his visit to the Oracle is meant to provide clarity. And it does: her main message to him is 'know thyself' (Wachowski and Wachowski 1999). Several things eventually combine to make Neo into The One – chance, the successful search for him, his own belief, and Trinity's belief in him – and key among these things is that central question: '[W]ho are you?'

Two small but not exactly subtle details are also hidden in the visit to the Oracle – another 'Eat Me' moment, and another glimpse of the white

---

3   See Chapter 5 for a discussion of the science and philosophy of *Sylvie and Bruno*'s treatment of reality and dream.

rabbit, seen on a TV in the background as Neo waits to see the Oracle. The 'Eat Me' moment, however, has lingering repercussions, as it comes full circle in *The Matrix Resurrections* (Wachowski 2021). As Neo is being taken to see the Oracle in *The Matrix*, he looks out the car window and starts in surprise. Trinity asks him what he is reacting to, and he says '[…] I used to eat there. Really good noodles' (Wachowski and Wachowski 1999). It is his 'reality' that he ate there, enjoyed the noodles, and feels nostalgia, yearning, and loss from the knowledge that this is no longer reality. In *The Matrix Resurrections*, he frequents a noodle shop (as does Tiffany/Trinity), and the sequence where he eats there repeats several times, showing how the world of the Matrix has narrowed reality to a few things, comfortable but ordinary, done over and over. He is a docile body, a Blue Pill, eating his noodles.

Yet we see the Oracle here, too – not in her original two incarnations, as that program was purged, but in her replacement, a program called Sati (played by Tanveer K. Atwal as a child in *The Matrix Revolutions* [Wachowski and Wachowski 2003b] and by Priyanka Chopra as an adult in *The Matrix Resurrections* [Wachowski 2021]). Sati's parents were also purged, and she aids Neo and Trinity out of spite for the machines which killed her parents, but also out of love. Her character is about love, and curiosity, and fellowship, and she watches over Neo as the noodle shop proprietor, while reading *Alice's Adventures in Wonderland*. While never asking the 'who are you' question, she does help the characters to know themselves better – she focuses them, drawing out their best selves, asking them to participate in plans that require self-belief and self-knowledge. 'Know thyself' becomes a requirement if Neo is going to save Trinity/Tiffany, and help her remove herself from the Matrix.

Two more minor analogous characters also capture Carrollian themes: Mouse/the dormouse, and Déjà Vu/the Cheshire Cat. Like the dormouse, shipmate Mouse speaks in riddles. He provides a temptation to Neo, in the form of a woman in a red dress, and offers to hook them up, saying to Neo, 'To deny our own impulses is to deny the very thing that makes us human' (Wachowski and Wachowski 1999) a more cryptic version of 'know thyself'. The dormouse, in the Carroll work, is the embodiment of the docile, forever drifting back into sleep. However, in *The Matrix*,

Mouse gets killed by the cat – Neo sees a black cat walk past and meow, and then sees the same thing again – he is told that a déjà vu signals a glitch in the Matrix, when the machines and programs change something. What they have changed, is the ability to exit the building they are in, leading to Mouse's death. In *The Matrix Resurrections* (Wachowski 2021) the cat belongs to the Analyst, the program who set up the current system to torture and imprison Neo and Trinity/Tiffany, and continues to signify that Neo cannot trust his reality – if he sees the cat, he is definitely in the Matrix.

The final analogue is the Agent Smith/The Red Queen – a *Looking-Glass*, rather than *Wonderland* character. In *The Matrix* (Wachowski and Wachowski 1999), Agent Smith is a program who searches out and destroys people who have escaped the control of the Matrix, and who is tasked with capturing Morpheus and the access codes to the human city, Zion. In the moves and countermoves, we can see Morpheus/The White Queen and Smith/The Red Queen try to outmanoeuvre each other, with Zion as the checkmate. However, in the subsequent two movies – *The Matrix Reloaded* (Wachowski and Wachowski 2003a) and *The Matrix Revolutions* (Wachowski and Wachowski 2003b) – Smith is freed by Neo, slips his programming, and goes rogue, no longer caring about the other queen, but aiming at Neo instead, very much as Alice's Red Queen reorients herself towards thwarting Alice.

Final Thoughts

Throughout the *Matrix* franchise, the themes of liminality, transition, and rebirth dominate the narrative and the meta-narrative, with Neo's journey to internalize the looking-glass and know himself and his destiny. In *The Matrix Resurrections* (Wachowski 2021) we finally see that internalization as acceptance – instead of swallowing the mirror unwillingly and taking the journey alone, as he did in *The Matrix* (Wachowski and Wachowski 1999), he is guided through the melted looking-glass by a group of allies, friends, who come to define the transformative power of love. At least, the fourth time, when Neo encounters the mirror for the first and second time in *Resurrections*, he is terrified of it. This terror stems from his use of the Blue Pill – he is conditioned to accept the Matrix's reality and disbelieve the evidence of his own senses. His third journey occurs when he is beginning to believe, and indeed wakes him to reality, but his fourth is the most important. It stems from his desire, his need, to save Trinity, to awaken her from the Matrix, and have her join him in reality. Neo's willing journey through the mirror comes from a place of self-acceptance, love, and focus, and the internalization that began in *The Matrix*, comes to fruition in *Resurrections*. He has accepted his identity, through the power of love.

Here we come back to the idea of word play and the symbolism of $1 + 3 = 1$. In this newest version of the Matrix, Neo and Trinity/Tiffany are kept apart by just a few feet in 'The Anomaleum' (Wachowski 2021) – a ploy by the Machines to ensure that their combined power does not become destructive to the system. And in the final scenes, Neo and Trinity save each other. No longer does one and three make one, but rather one and three equals four, and four equals two and two. This combination echoes the theme of transformation – the Wachowskis are both trans women, and they have confirmed that the Matrix is a metaphor for transitioning, for leaving behind a place with gender rules, and boundaries strictly mapped onto the physical, to enter a world of infinite possibility, where love is stronger than the disciplined body.

The world of the Matrix is a dream world – physics, probability, and causality are all pushed to absurdity because when you are dreaming, anything is possible. In the real world there are rules you must follow – rules about what to do, and when, and with whom. If you wake from that dream, but retain the sense of the absurd as Alice, Neo, and Trinity do, then you can change the world for the better.

References through *Wonderland* and *Looking-Glass* appear to be applied interchangeably in the franchise. Yet a distinction can be observed. As references, visual as well as nominal provide typecasting and visual referential cues, it is the references to *Looking-Glass* that do the heavy lifting, of introducing and challenging philosophical concepts, and unsettling realities – it is the Looking-Glass itself that becomes the *Matrix* franchises ultimate metaphor of the unsettlement of reality.

Part XII

Jabberwocky

Kit Kelen

32 'Jabberwocky' – The Impossible Poem Demanding Translation

Childhood seems to many to be a generally nonsensical state – full of wonder and innocence and play perhaps – but a state in which the adult rules of sense and logic have yet to be firmly established. It may be that adult sense and logic will be achieved by way of unmeaning sounds and signs by way, that is to say, of something like nonsense. Whoever (whichever sensible adult, that is to say) encounters children or non-native speakers of her/his language has an (otherwise unavailable) opportunity to consider its means, to think, that is, about how and why things said in that language are understood and are otherwise taken for granted.

Like *Finnegan's Wake* (and possibly more so), like the *Dao de Jing*, one may say that Lewis Carroll's 'Jabberwocky' has been much translated (and much more translated than many comparably important texts) precisely because translating it represents such a daunting challenge. It might seem at first surprising that such a difficult poem – such an apparently unanchored text – would have been so frequently attempted, until one realizes that translating something like 'Jabberwocky' (and there is nothing else like 'Jabberwocky') is a sport (or a quest or a rite of passage) for a certain kind of poet/translator. It is a kind of an *ultimate* challenge for translators – to make someone else's nonsense your own.

What exactly does the task entail? In 'Jabberwocky', we are dealing with an old apocryphal story in a place that isn't, in a book that never was, found in mirror writing (accessed only through a mirror), in a language that doesn't exist and so can't have been spoken, discussed at length by characters in a story. Nor should we omit to mention the fact that all of this is being dreamt. And further, the elegant fragility of that fact: that should the red king wake then all will dissolve, and you and I and everyone involved will simply go out 'like a candle'. That is to say, waking will dissolve the fabric of the dream. Its sense – the sense of connectedness of all in the dream – will not survive daylight. In the world of everything reversed, the putative daylight of a king's waking is as a candle gone out. As long as we stay in the story, however, that candle will remain lit. In fact, the further into the story and its circumstances, the remoter seems any possibility of extricating oneself from it. Perhaps as in fantasy more generally, all this is calculated to remind one of one's own implausibility, of just how unlikely our world and our existence are.

Who can resist so many impossibles? And yet the story in the poem in the book in the mirror *can* be understood and, more than understood, is deeply suggestive, perhaps in ways natural language more typically struggles to voice.

I think, for poets, there is another aspect to the challenge of 'Jabberwocky'. 'Jabberwocky', in all its uniqueness, is a kind of ideal poem. Not an Ur-poem, more something in the manner of an ultimate poem, a poem of the nth degree – a poem that succeeds, in an essential way, in doing what poems more generally set out to do. In a nutshell that would be to fashion, from existing materials, both new meaning and new means of meaning. Of course, it appears *prima facie* in the case of 'Jabberwocky' that the means of meaning are new (i.e. the words are invented) and that the meaning (i.e. the coming-of-age story) is old. But the fact that the poem is understood at all (is able to present as a puzzle) proves that the means of the poem's making are already available: if not all of the words are already known, they are nevertheless in some sense already possible. The first mirror impression of the poem was misleading, but easily set right *with* an actual mirror. If one aspect of the puzzle may be solved so systematically, then why not others? The poem makes new as it makes do with at least the sounds and graphic symbols available. And the act of doing this and the puzzles with which it presents the reader constitute a new kind of meaning: the poem as cipher in multiple dimensions (genre, language, frame, for instance). Should one say, once the story is more or less understood ('*somebody* killed *something*, that's clear at any rate'), that the puzzle and the poem are 'solved', then one is left nevertheless with much more meaning to unfold ('Somehow it seems to fill my head with ideas').

'Jabberwocky's depths are unfathomable precisely because no dictionary (despite some inclusions on its behalf) and no Humpty Dumpty (despite that character's Donald Trump-like self-confidence)[1] could ever be relied on to reveal the secrets of the work. In semiotic terms, one might say that in this poem there is no telling denotation apart from connotation. Words only appear (only sound as if) they have a surface in this poem. Known words (articles, conjunctions) join the dots. The feeling that a code has been cracked once we come to 'see' the simple story told is belied by the recognition that there can be no 'code' as such; all we have in the original are elements of a particular natural language, recombined suggestively to mean in a way they could not have meant before. And here we have the ideal notional conditions of every new poem that is worth reading. Should the argument seem circular, please just step a frame away, to catch the poem in its habitat. How easily could that be done? We needed a mirror to read the poem, but the poem is itself a mirror. It reflects back what the reader already knows (but perhaps does not know s/he knows) – of his/her means of meaning, of the structure of stories, of the sound quality of the language more generally, of the mysterious signs of suspense and of resolution (in sense as in rhyme), of mood as words convey it, of heads filled with ideas.

In 'Jabberwocky', we witness, as we do in all successful poetry, a tight-rope walk between obviousness and obscurity. Put simply: on the side of obviousness, say what has been said already and is too easily understood and no one will have cause to be impressed; on the side of obscurity, say what cannot be understood and, obviously enough, no one will under-stand. 'Jabberwocky' is an elegant experiment with a paradox with which all successful poetry must wrestle. Obviousness and obscurity are equally plentiful in the poem – the story is already known and the language, for obvious reasons, cannot be known. And yet, as every effort at translation of 'Jabberwocky' reveals, the language has in some sense already filled our heads. Here is *the heimlich /unheimlich* déjà-voodoo quality of the work – it is a novel means of finding ourselves where we have already been, but could not have known until now.

---

1   On Humpty Dumpty's communication style, language and resonances, see Chapter 15.

With this poem in particular we are building a picture of a very interesting place for the translator of poetry to be, and especially for someone who is translating into her/his native language. Though it is not so, the translator begins, in this very particular case, with an illusion of an almost neutral space: the original text appears to be foreign both to the source and to the target language.

If every language is, from another point of view, nonsense, we need to deal briefly with the canonic status of the world's most famous nonsense poem. The classic quality of this particular text, which is after all in a way why we are all here in this particular volume, guarantees a frustratingly tainted freshness for its many re-readers. Like the rose in the garden that won't be sniffed twice, one simply cannot retrieve the experience of *coming to understand* such as accompanied by a first encounter with 'Jabberwocky'.

And yet, personally I have found that, as with the works of Lewis Carroll more generally, I discover more every time I look into this mirror. And so am drawn back to the poem. One of the best ways of looking again is of course to translate, because the serious translator, if well-equipped, is the closest reader of any text.

I feel that this poem – however, we reach it – is asking two important parallel and unanswerable questions: these are – what is the point of nonsense (?) and what is the point of poetry (?). One might further then ask – why bother with the nonsense of translating nonsense poetry? One might think any or all of these questions irrelevant to anyone who is already interested in 'Jabberwocky' to have read this far. Are such questions worth answering? Indeed, are they answerable? I think the questions are answerable and worth answering because in our appreciation of 'Jabberwocky' we are sharing a guilty pleasure, a pleasure the classic status of the text reveals as long pre-dating any living reader, translator, or theorist.

As a parody of genre (or perhaps of the self-consciousness of genre), 'Jabberwocky' connects all those whom it lights up with something more human than language as we are used to using it. Here is the reaching beyond the known of words (the head full of ideas) familiar to anyone who has come *into* a language, that is to say, it is *Heimlich* to anyone who can speak/read/listen/write any language at all. If we agree with Wittgenstein that the limits of my language are the limits of my world then here we find new horizons, of the uncannily familiar kind.

One reads, one mulls over, one works with the poem in the vain effort to get that first scent back, to smell the flower as it first drew us in. But, in the manner of Tantalus' eternal punishment, this horizon recedes as we approach. The wonderful thing about teaching 'Jabberwocky' is that it allows us vicarious appreciation of the innocence of a first encounter. We are wiser to the poem but we witness the first joy of nonsense coming to be known. Teaching the poem to non-native speakers of English has a special magic, because with them one can appreciate some of the pleasure of their way of being in your language (however troublesome that may be to them more generally, in practice). One can experience some of the pleasure of being inside and out of the language at the same time.

So here we have Wittgenstein's world expanded but by means of the Fortunatus' purse (a kind of 3D möbius strip) will we meet in *Sylvie and Bruno*.[2] Here is the whole universe in tight-woven fabric, because the inside *is* the outside (and of course vice versa).

The point of being with 'Jabberwocky' is that it is (paradoxically, counter-intuitively) an encounter with newness, with difference. It is the place in worlds we have not yet been and yet we visit by means of words. In this way we may say that every attempt at translating 'Jabberwocky' constitutes an effort at reclaiming the innocence with which the text may have been notionally approached in the original. The 'original' is of course, in the case of this particular text, a beautiful misunderstanding, it being the only example we have of its own unnamed language – a language that exists only in so far as we are able to imagine it, and only by this means (by the means of imagining furnished us in the story). And what has this 'language', this 'original' to do with the idea of poetry more generally? As something archaic, notionally lost, it posits a *faux* origin for poetry more generally. So we have here an ultimate poem with *faux* – Ur projection! A poem that takes us back as it takes us away.

While it will be not quite right to claim that source and target language are as far from the text as from each other in this poem, one is nevertheless tempted to see things that way (much in the manner the modern English reader may not at first recognize *Beowulf* or Chaucer or Burns as of her/his

---

2   For more on the 'Purse of Fortunatus', see Chapter 5.

own language). There is a finite number of languages on this planet, and there is a finite number of translations of Lewis Carroll's 'Jabberwocky', nevertheless they suggest an infinite series. Or perhaps something more in the manner of Borges' famous circular library – a world plausibly finite but never experienced as such? That 'Jabberwocky' should be uniquely achieved in every possible language is a tribute at once to poetry, to non-sense, to innocence. It is indeed a coming of age for all of these activities. The translation of 'Jabberwocky' is a way of untinting the innocence of the idea of an original. I believe that this accounts for the popularity of the sport.

Anna Kérchy

33 Jabberwock vs Snark: Imagetextual Monsters and the Struggle with Semiosis in *Through the Looking-Glass* and 'The Hunting of the Snark'

Lewis Carroll's works are characterized by a meta-linguistic, meta-imaginative, and meta-medial self-awareness. On a metafictional plane, a great variety of different literary genres and discursive modes are parodied in them – from fairy tales and didactic poems to history lessons, scientific hypotheses, and political manifestos. The aim is to unsettle through these creative genre-hybridizations the narrative patterns of storytelling conventions, to thus disclose the role of discourse, in the so-called Foucauldian ideological technologies of truth production. This, in turn, allows them to make a tongue-in-cheek commentary on the intricate interconnections of discourse, knowledge, and power. An aim of literary nonsense is to surprise audiences with the destabilization of language as a consensual sign system, and the defamiliarization of our habitual representational and interpretive strategies.

By means of creative rhetorical provocations, Carrollian wordplay teases readers into wondering if we can make words mean things, who is in charge of these meanings, and how can the meanings made be unmade. Carrollian nonsense is crossover fiction addressing multiple generations of audiences. Its trademark discursive subversion takes place through a simultaneous eliciting of more mature meta-linguistic recognitions as well as of preverbal semiotic energies associated with the infantile acoustic qualities of discourse. Nonsense, hence, allows sense to be overwhelmed both by meta-sense as well as sonoric, sensory, and sensual stimuli.

The *Alice* books, as memorable dream stories, are also distinguished by a meta-imaginative quality: they fictionalize complex cognitive capacities such as a (day)dreaming, misremembering, pretence play, thinking of oneself thinking, and imagining others imagining. As vanguardist forerunners of postmodernist metaperspectivism, the creative mental games of Carrollian nonsense explore fantasizing agency simultaneously as an evolutionary feat, an ontological necessity, a mode of empathic relationality to others and those that are othered. The tales thus function as a therapeutical and problem-solving mechanism, and a dynamic process conjoining make-belief and disbelief, psychic automatism and intellectual innovation, dream and logic, sense, sentiment, and sensation. The interest in the role of visual imagery in verbal recall is a part of this meta-imaginative project.

Carroll's meticulous cooperation with his illustrators, as well as his own illustrative practice, well-acknowledged by his tales' first audiences, prove that he was a visual storyteller who designed from the very beginnings many of his books as picturebooks in which the intersemiotic dialogue between text and image is essential for activating the nonsensical effect of the artwork. The illustrations do not only complement the verbal narrative, but the image-textual dynamics provoke an affective-cognitive dissonance that urges readers-turned-spectators-too to take an active part in the ludic de/constructions of meanings and reach conclusions about the slipperiness of signification, and the difficulties of making sense of nonsense across a variety of different media. The curiosity about the intricate interconnections between unspeakability and unimaginability – explored through the hybridization of verbal and visual strategies of generating nonsense to elicit a multisensorially stimulating challenging of the limits of representation and rational knowability – can be regarded as a major narrative engine of Carroll's *Alice* books.

This image-textual dynamics is particularly interesting in the case of monstrous nonsensical creatures who spectacularly embody unspeakability in the Carrollian oeuvre: the Jabberwock emerging in *Looking-Glass* and the Snark of the 1876 'The Hunting of the Snark'. In the following, I shall compare the poetic and pictorial figures of these fictional beasts in order to show how they constitute two sides of the same coin by representing the two extremes of nonsensical semiosis and the ambiguous affective responses to self-destabilizing meanings of the literary nonsense genre. If the Jabberwock stands for the proliferation of sense and the carnivalesque celebration of the impossibility of meaninglessness, the Snark/ Boojum evokes the emptying of meaning and the melancholic recognition of the necessity of misunderstanding.

Both creatures embody horror fiction genre's prototypical monster that frightens by its indefinability: a radical alienness and unknowability expressed by a name that fails to refer to a thing. These referentless signifiers as neological non-words allude to realms beyond human understanding or speakability. The vague associations with familiar concepts (jab, jabber, jaw, snap, shark) increase the ominous quality of the beings. Moreover, the beasts are also linguistic phantasms that exist only in the stories told by the inhabitants of the fictional worlds: they belong to the fictitious mythology of Looking-Glass land, and the maritime legend of the Snark's universe, respectively.

The nonsensical lyricism lends both texts a mock-epic quality. In Jabberwocky's faux-Anglo-Saxon-sounding seven stanzas a solitary knight, a beamish boy succeeds in slaying with his vorpal blade the whiffling beast. The 'Callooh! Callay!' of his chortling cry of triumph lends a comic feel to the poem. 'The Hunting of the Snark' is ridiculous because of the mixture of pathos-filled and absurd tones in an 'agony' in eight fits about the quest of a ship crew of ten – randomly united by names all beginning with the letter B – who fail to capture the dangerous shapeshifter that is the Snark/ Boojum. The mock-epic mood clearly pokes fun of the heroic ballad's rhetorical schemas, and thus sits within the author's own trajectory of mocking classic literary ballads, such as, for instance, previously, in 'Hiawatha's Photographing', his parody of Longfellow's 'Song of Hiawatha'.[1] The unique singularity of each of these poems' heroic deed is ironically questioned and depicted in an uncanny light if we pair the two poems together, especially because of the explicit intertextual ties: 'The Hunting of the Snark' borrows the atmosphere, some creatures and eight portmanteau words from 'Jabberwocky'. With a bit of imagination we could argue that through this textual recycling, as if in a magic trick's legerdemain, the slayed monster revives metamorphosed into an even more terrifying beast.

Moreover, the verbal surprise effects of the nonsense language games are enhanced in both cases by the illustrators' inviting us to imagine the

---

1   For more parody and photography see Chapters 4 and 27.

Jabberwocky

unspeakable. The Jabberwock is depicted by John Tenniel's drawing, and subsequent wood-engraving by the Dalziel brothers, and the Snark/Boojum by Henry Holiday's etching, engraved by Joseph Swain (Figures 67 and 70). Both illustrations present visual puns pictorially mimicking the Carrollian language games. In the case of illustrated books, the interpreters' eyes move between written narrative and illustrations. The transmedial feat of the image/text interaction involves audiences in the experience of 'voyure', a portmanteau neologism introduced in Liliane Louvel's *Poetics of the Iconotext*, that refers to an oscillation between contemplative reading ('la lecture') and a rebellious looking beyond the text, facing images provoking a transgressive voyeurism ('la vision') (Louvel 2011: 10). As in the case of other Carrollian image-textual play – picture-poems, typographical play, mirror writing, rebus letters – reading blurs with sighting, the text offers visual stimulus while the image invites to be read. Audiences are addressed as semioticians-turned-beast-hunters, trying to tame the monstrification of semiosis.

Tenniel's illustration of the monstrous Jabberwock is an exciting case of intersemiotic translation. His hybrid composite of a variety of fantastic and real beasts – rodent, reptile, insect, dinosaur, dragon, and the Lambton Worm dressed in a chequered waistcoat of a bourgeois bureaucrat – is a visual reiteration of the trademark Carrollian language game, the portmanteau that fuses multiple words and worlds into one unprecedented neologism. The image offers a response to the impossible challenge of visually translating the unspeakable by impersonating in the chimeric creature the proliferation of sense triggered by literary nonsense. The illustration also functions as a meta-picture. As Michael Hancher highlights, because of the similarity of Tenniel's depiction of Alice and the knight (portrayed from the back, in striped stockings, with flowing hair) the figure of the beamish boy is 'an androgynous projection of Alice's fears' (Hancher 1985: 72). Fighting the mythical beast thus lends itself to be interpreted as the implied reader's struggle with textual monstrosity on trying to make sense of nonsense. The Jabberwock is never met in person, it is a textual creature, a part of the magical dream realm's private mythology, who poses an interpretive challenge to Alice and all readers. The intermedial dynamics is strategically exploited here as a ludic engine of the text: Alice first meets the 'Jabberwocky' poem in mirror writing, misreads it as an image instead of a verbal utterance, and later makes repeated attempts at translating it. Her contemporary readers likely fell into the same trap, especially because, as Amanda Lastoria suggests, the printing technology used for the mirror writing was the one employed for the reproduction of images.

This memorable scene of miscomprehension is tripled in the Tenniel illustrations to the *Alice* books: the implied reader heroine is depicted in a similar posture as the knight was during her conversation with the Cheshire Cat in *Wonderland*, and her discussion with Humpty Dumpty in the Looking-Glass realm (Figures 67, 68, 69). Here, the Cat and the Eggman, who take the place of the mythical monster on the drawings, are both language philosophers. The Cat argues for the impossibility of meaninglessness: 'whichever way you go, you are sure to get somewhere' might mean that no matter how your interpretation will deviate from the speaker's intended meaning, you will manage to make a certain sense. Echoing the Wittgensteinian private language argument (Wittgenstein 1986: 88–89), the Eggman's 'you can make words mean whatever you want them to mean if you try hard enough' speculates about the re-inventability of language and the semantic deviations resulting from subjective associations.[2] Hence, the triptych of meta-images offers a tongue-in-cheek visual commentary on the trials and tribulations of human being as a meaning-making-animal both disciplined by discursive regulations and lured to rebellion by poetic play.

Tenniel's Jabberwock is also a 'loud image' that depicts with its silent scream the surplus of signification arising from the acoustic vocal performance of language. The gaping mouth of the beast offers an odd visual representation of a voiceless cry that opens up audio-visual interpretive dimensions. The picture does not only stage the reader-interpreter's struggle to make sense of nonsense on the semantic and syntactic levels, but also the speaker's phonological fight for correct articulation: to make words sound right. The failure to speak properly is a recurring frustration for Alice throughout her dream adventures' conversational combats. This is decisive experience for children learning to speak or read who transition slowly from inarticulate babble to articulate language, from deformed sign to legible word. As Gillian Beer puts it, Carroll enters the 'free zone'

---

2   For more on Humpty Dumpty and linguistic theory see Chapter 15.

where children dwell, where the struggles for and against language take place simultaneously (Beer 2016: 3).

Yet the beast's silently gaping mouth also resonates with Carroll's own speech defect, a 'verbal hesitation' that was described by child friend May Barber as 'rather terrifying,' 'it wasn't exactly a stammer, because there was no noise, he just opened his mouth. But there was a wait, a very nervous wait from everybody's point of view: it was very curious' (Smith: 172). Carroll, in his correspondence with speech therapist William H. R. Rivers, referred to his struggles with correct pronunciation with military metaphors: 'Thanks for advice about hard "C", which I acknowledge as my vanquisher in single-hand combat, at present' (Carroll in Smith: 178). Hence, the knight fighting the Jabberwock-symbolizing-language is an *alter ego* of Alice, the implied reader, and of Carroll the author, too.

However, the victorious fictitious battle in Looking-Glass land suggests that the fear of linguistic deviations might be overcome, that the struggle with nonsense is a creative game, and that there is a place for the carnivalesque[3] celebration of the proliferation of sense resulting from coping with the impossibility of meaninglessness. Alice's repeated attempts to translate 'Jabberwocky' – from image to text to oral performance to mock-philological register to open-ended riddle – urge all to mis/read boldly, joyously, and imaginatively.[4]

---

3   According to Russian linguist and literary critic Mikhail Bakhtin the carnival, a medieval popular folk festivity – which allows for a revelry in democratically shared joys resulting from corporeal transgressions, a temporary suspension of social order and a cosmic merriment – can be associated with a literary/discursive mode, exemplified by Rabelais' writings, that destabilises hegemonic power structures by embracing ambivalence, rebellion, humour, grotesquerie, and polyphony (see Bakhtin 1984).

4   As Sundmark points out, Alice repeatedly attempts to translate the 'Jabberwocky' poem – which is unusual for being a written text amidst a plethora of orally presented rhymes and songs. First, she converts the reversed sign system (image) into a readable version (text). Then, she recodes the written text by memorizing it. She shifts her mental image-text of the poem into the oral medium. Humpty Dumpty recodes the text for her into the 'mock-philological register,' and, finally, she invites readers' (re)interpretations of these 'textually represented transactions' which inspire all 'to read imaginatively!' (Sundmark 182).

Although 'The Hunting of the Snark' as a mock-heroic ballad can be considered an extended twin-text of 'Jabberwocky', it presents a much more elusive monster figure that suggests a slightly different, more melancholic attitude to nonsense as a cognitive and affective experience. The crew catalogues only a few unmistakable marks of a genuine Snark: a flavour of Will-o-the-wisp, a habit of getting up late, a slowness in taking a jest, a fondness in bathing machines, and an ominous ambition. The subdivisions of the species hold equally vague teratological descriptions: some have feathers and bite, some have whiskers and scratch, and the worst of them are Boojums who threaten the human eyewitness with making them softly and suddenly vanish away. The nonsensical verbal composite of these abstract features deliberately resists visualization. Moreover, the prohibition to look at the beast both mocks interpreters' scopophilia (our desire to know and comprehend by looking), it pokes fun of imaginative conventions grounded in the proverb 'Seeing is believing,' and teases readers-aspiring-to-be-spectators with the dreadful fate of disappearing, of being erased from the realm of visibility.

Hence Holiday's final, tenth plate 'The Vanishing' (Figure 70) is a meta-picture: a deliberately blurred, shadowy, mostly black and grey image of an undecipherable fight in the dark with barely recognizable, vague outlines of the vanishing Baker's screaming face blurring in the background of the thorny vegetation. It represents the dead-end of representation by staging the very unimaginability of the monster as well as both fictional and extratextual spectators' incapacity to see. One could presume that there is nothing to be seen on the image. But on the contrary the image depicts Nothingness itself, the moment when being fades into non-being, when presence turns into absence; a cognitive catastrophe, when knowledge fades into suspicion and then into unknowing, oblivion. This is a visual equivalent of the disrupted nonsensical text: 'Then the ominous words "It's a Boo –"' where the dash stands in the place of unspeakability and forces readers to mentally imagine the most unimaginable horrendous outcomes. The silent acoustic impressions induced by the image of a bell tolling in the upper left corner and the vague outlines of the screaming face further enhance the dramatic effect.

'The Hunting of the Snark' reiterates the ludic narrative pattern of Carrollian texts: if the two *Alice* books are organized by card and chess games, and *Sylvie and Bruno* by magic tricks,[5] 'Hunting' is governed by the logic of hide and seek. It also activates the secondary meaning of the word 'game' related to predator and prey relationship where the stake of the game is no longer just the question 'Will I win?' but also the dilemma 'Am I being the player or the played?' reiterating the grotesque role reversal of the hunters-hunted down trope.

'The Hunting of the Snark' is an enigmatic text that has been interpreted in many ways from an allegory of the futile search for the meaning of life through an *ars moriendi* consolation of a tuberculotic child, Carroll's cousin Charlie Wilcox to a political manifesto against the inhumanness of vivisection (see Gardner 1962; Mayer 2009; Wakeling 2011; Kluge 2017). It is also a meta-narrative commentary on the unmasterability of meanings, a less cheerful language philosophical reflection than the one conveyed by 'Jabberwocky'. While the beamish boy, by defeating the Jabberwock, fights back meaninglessness, the Snark-hunting crew's[6] failed interpretive

---

5   In *Sylvie and Bruno*, the Other Professor, Mein Herr's magical inventions – besides a gravity-powered train and a method of storing up extra time so that nobody ever gets bored – include a Fortunatus' Purse (see Chapter 5), a mathematical and artistic challenge presented as a magic trick. It is a three-dimensional Möbius strip with a non-orientable surface twisted in a circle but folding back within itself, so that if an object slides around the strip, the object will return to its starting point as a mirror image. The tricky object created from a piece of cloth models a topological structure known as the projective plane. It does not only entertain *Sylvie and Bruno* but also models the narrative structure of the book that comprises storylines which bend/fold within themselves, transitioning between adult- and child-oriented themes, nearly imperceptibly transforming one into the other. Katherine Wakely-Mulroney calls the magical device of the thaumatrope – a nineteenth-century optical toy in which separate components of a single image are brought together by rotating a disc back and forth – a more fitting symbol of the unity of the book achieved through stark transition and continual exchange between poetry and prose (see Chapter 4 for more on optical toys, and 'Poetry in Prose: Lewis Carroll's *Sylvie and Bruno* Books.' Katherine Wakely-Mulroney and Louise Joy, *The Aesthetics of Children's Poetry: A Study of Children's Verse in English* (Abingdon: Routledge, 2017), 74–93.

6   The struggle with language for the mastery over meanings may have different implications for children and adults. Carroll dedicates *Hunting* to 10-year-old Gertrude

mission confronts readers with the elusiveness of meanings, our entrapment within the Derridean 'prisonhouse of language'[7] symbolized by the sudden Boojumification of the escape-artist Snark.

The failure of signification, the emptying of meaning, and thus the inevitable absence of presence in representation is illustrated not only by Holiday's illustration of the vanishing crew and the very visual absence of the unrepresentable Snark but also the nonsensical picture of the blank map the crew uses during their mission to hunt down the beast (Figure 72). The nonsensical humour of Carroll's instructions for the capturing of the Snark – 'You may seek it with thimbles – and seek it with care;/You may hunt it with forks and hope;/You may threaten its life with a railway share;/You may charm it with smiles and soap' (68) – is mirrored in the blank map's lack of directions that playfully acknowledges strategic disorientation as a part, and perhaps the very point, of the journey.

But the white sheet of the map as a specimen of non-representation (a bright negative, a reversal of Plate 10's darkness) can also be regarded as a forerunner of Suprematist art[8] movement exemplified by Kazimir Malevich's 'White square on a white background' (Figure 73), canonized in art history as the zero degree of painting, a geometrical abstraction refusing figurative, referential, realist representation, surpassing cubism's formal language to express a pure artistic experience, to convey a spiritual experience of the Unspeakable. The blank map represents a similar dead-end

---

Chataway 'inscribed to a dear Child: in memory of golden summer hours and whispers of a summer sea' (the first words of the first four stanzas – Gert, Rude, Chat, Away – spell out her name). Gardner quotes Phyllis Greenacre who thinks that the ten members of the crew represent the ten children of the Dodgson family. Götz Klüge points out that Henry Holiday's illustration of the Butcher is a child figure reminiscent of Millais's painting 'The Boyhood of Raleigh's' (see Götz Kluge, 'Holiday's References', *Knight Letter* 106).

7   The prisonhouse of language is a term Fredric Jameson uses to describe Jacques Derrida's language philosophy acccording to which our perception of reality is largely defined by our use of language characterised by a treacherousness of signs, words' insufficiency in depciting the real, and any attempt at *r*epresenting the presence results in a loss and proliferation of meanings (Fredric Jameson, *The Prison-House of Language*. Princeton University Press, 1975).

8   On Suprematism and Malevich see Nina Gurianova, *Kazimir Malevich: Suprematism* (Guggenheim Museum, 2003).

of semiosis. It is far from being empty – just like nonsense is very far from meaninglessness. Although it pictures nothing, it locates the unimaginable monster by implying every possible direction where it might lurk. It transgresses the boundaries of representation by aiming to capture the presence of the idea of the thing itself. It provokes both silence and loquaciousness. Paradoxically the erasure of conventional signs entails that everyone believes to fully understand the map, its blankness guarantees a democratization of semiotic agency: all interpretations shall be similarly valid as everyone is to equally misunderstand the non-image's signification.[9]

Carroll's tongue-in-cheek answers to questions about the true meaning of the Snark – which could also respond to readers attempting to solve Jabberwock's riddle – encapsulate the very essence of deconstructive literary theory and reader response criticism. As he writes in one letter, 'I'm very much afraid I did not mean anything but nonsense! Still you know, words mean more than we mean to express when we use them [...] So whatever good meanings are in the book, I'm very glad to accept as the meaning of the book.'[10] In light of these, the metafictional message of the Carrollian nonsensical agenda is clear: if the fight with the Jabberwock represents the reader's struggle with the nonsensical text, the blank map always-already acknowledging its failure in tracking the beast and the vanishing silent scream provoked by the unimaginable sight of the Boojumification of the Snark represent the death of the author and the resulting joyous-horrendous monstrification of self-disseminating meanings.

9   'He had bought a large map representing the sea,/Without the least vestige of land:/And the crew were much pleased when they found it to be/A map they could all understand.//What's good of Mercator's North Poles and Equators,/Tropics, Zones, and Meridian Lines?/So the Bellman would cry: and the crew would reply,/They are merely conventional signs!//Other maps are such shapes with their islands and capes!/But we've got our brave Captain to thank/(So the crew would protest) that he's bought us the best – /A perfect and absolute blank!' *THS* 55–56.

10 In 'Alice on the Stage' Carroll writes in response to questions about the true meaning of the Snark: 'I have but one answer, "I don't know," and in a later letter he adds "As to the meaning of the Snark? I'm very much afraid I didn't mean anything but nonsense! Still, you know, words mean more than we mean to express when we use them: so a whole book ought to mean a great deal more, than the writer meant. So whatever good meanings are in the book, I'm very glad to accept as the meaning of the book."' *THS* 21, 22.

Figures 67, 68, and 69 John Tenniel's illustrations to Alice's adventures in Wonderland
and *Through the Looking-Glass and What Alice Found There*. 1865, 1872.

Figure 70. Henry Holiday. The Hunting of the Snark. 'Fit the Eight. The Vanishing,' 1876.

Figure 71. Kazimir Malevich. Black square on white background. 1913. Oil on linen.
79.5 × 79.5 cm, State Tretyakov Gallery, Moscow, Russia.

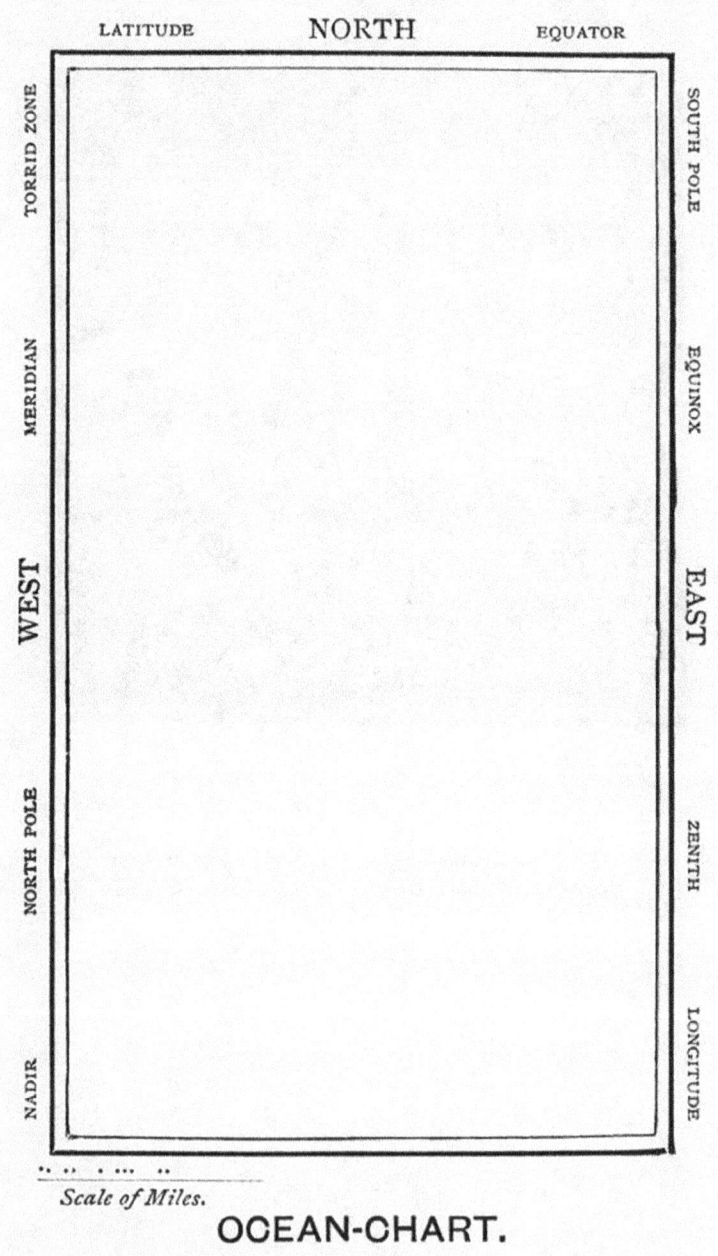

Figure 72. Henry Holiday. The Hunting of the Snark. 'Fit the Second,' 1876.

Figure 73. Kazimir Malevich. Suprematist composition. White on White. 1918. Oil on canvas. 79.4 × 79.4 cm. Museum of Modern Art, New York.

Björn Sundmark

34 'It's all in some language I don't know': The Translation History of 'Jabberwocky'

Translation is at the heart of 'Jabberwocky'. In the first chapter of *Through the Looking-Glass*, Alice, in what is already an act of interpretation, identifies 'Jabberwocky' as a piece of writing, 'in some language I don't know' (*TTLG*: 174). Next, Alice mirror-reverses the text, a step which allows her to spell out the poem, even though she still finds it '*rather* hard to understand'. The reading fills her 'head with ideas,' where the only thing she is sure of is that '*somebody* killed *something*' (176). But she enjoys it: '[I]t seems very pretty.' Alice, in this situation, is like any reader and novice language learner. She struggles to translate the poem, to make sense of it as far as she can, and eventually, in chapter six, she asks Humpty Dumpty to help explain the poem and the 'hard words'. A language lesson ensues. Characteristically, perhaps, for some types of language instruction, his explication has actually nothing to do with the content of 'Jabberwocky', nor with the plot of *Looking-Glass,* but focuses entirely on details of vocabulary (although, arguably, each word in turn gives rise to its own mini-narrative). Besides the parodic effect, this interaction depicts an approach that privileges the technical translation of single words over story.

This is, no doubt, along with the poem's complexity, a reason why many translators of *Looking-Glass* have chosen *not to* translate 'Jabberwocky'. Strictly speaking, it is not necessary: the plot, and the language-play and translation games can be expressed, more or less successfully, in alternative ways. The main quality of 'Jabberwocky' is not the verse narrative (the story, as it were), fine as it is, but the enjoyment in the language it provides, and the way in which it prompts further translation, creativity, and reflection.

These and other translation or non-translation aspects of the poem are explored in depth in a forthcoming publication, *Completely Jabberwocky: A Companion to Lewis Carroll's Frabjous Poem* (eds, Everson, Kelen, Kérchy and Sundmark). The present article draws on the collective work on this project, which includes articles by more than forty scholars from all over the world, as well as more than sixty translations of the poem.

In a sense, 'Jabberwocky' is larger than the book and has escaped its original narrative context. While it certainly comes to its fullest expression in the context of *Through the Looking-Glass*, it does work quite well independently too. Already in *Mischmasch*, Carroll's hand-written family periodical, the first four lines appear for the first time as 'Stanza of Anglo-Saxon Poetry' (Carroll 2015: 175). Here too the translation context is inscribed. In this proto 'Jabberwocky', Carroll helpfully provides this verse with a glossary, where the definitions partly correspond and overlap with the translations offered by Humpty Dumpty in *Through the Looking-Glass*. Just like with Humpty Dumpty's explications, the translations in *Mischmasch* are actually integral to the poem itself: they are an essential part of the reading experience. Later, Carroll gave 'Jabberwocky' an extra-textual afterlife as well, by referring to it again – notably in *The Hunting of the Snark* – and by offering new interpretations of the nonsense words (Carroll 2015: 179–180).[1]

Post Carroll, 'Jabberwocky' has continued to stimulate translation and exegesis, the most influential contribution no doubt being Martin Gardner's *Annotated Alice*, first published in 1960, and translated into half a dozen languages. In Gardner's *Annotated Alice,* the annotations to 'Jabberwocky' take up far more space than the poem itself (several pages, in fact). All of the nonsense words are copiously explicated and given alternative meanings and etymologies. Since they first appeared, Gardner's annotations, either in translation or directly from one of the numerous English editions, have had a decisive impact, on how 'Jabberwocky' has been translated. There is reason to believe that for many translators and interested readers, *The Annotated Alice* has worked more or less as a dictionary of Carrollian neologisms.

---

1   See Chapter 33.

This is for better and worse. There is no arguing that *The Annotated Alice* boosted the status of Carroll's work from the 1960s onwards, and also provided necessary context and insight. At the same time, the notes do defuse some of the nonsense: they provide an easy way out for some translators who prefer word-to-word equivalence to try to catch the spirit of the poem. But the most important point to be made here is of course that Gardner's pioneering work on the *Alice* books, web pages devoted to the poem,[2] and a number of studies on translations of 'Jabberwocky' into different languages have contributed to the iconic status of the poem as an object of translation and as a critical touchstone in Carroll scholarship, translation studies, theories of nonsense, and children's literature.

Yet, despite its undeniable importance, the 150-year history of 'Jabberwocky' in translation (1871–2021) has been in the works till now. Thus, the 'Jabberwocky'-project is the first to assemble scholars, critics, and translators from across the world to comment on one or more translations of 'Jabberwocky' into their own language. For the first time, it is possible to compare translation strategies and solutions between more than forty different languages. What the 'Jabberwocky' companion does not provide is a comprehensive account: the amount of material is far too great for that. Some languages, like Spanish, French, and Russian, boast disproportionately many translations of *Looking-Glass*. Moreover, if one includes stand-alone translations, it becomes almost impossible to keep track.

Instead, the ambition with the *Companion* has been to select one, or a few, important and critically interesting translations from each language, old or new. Another selection criterion has been to prioritize translations that have appeared in unabridged versions of *Looking-Glass*. This is important in order to shed light on how translators have dealt with Alice's and Humpty Dumpty's own 'translations' of the poem. It is one thing to translate just the poem, and quite another to make it work with Humpty Dumpty's explanations.

---

2   Keith Lim, Jabberwocky translations. <http://www76.pair.com/keithlim/jabb erwocky/translations/>; Wikipedia. 'Jabberwocky.' <https://en.wikipedia.org/ wiki/Jabberwocky#cite_note-31>

Translation goes even beyond language. Just as John Tenniel's illustrations have affected readers' appreciation and interpretation of the poem since the publication of *Looking-Glass,* translations that make use of other illustrators' visualizations inevitably colour the way in which readers in different countries understand and enjoy their 'Jabberwocky'. When discussing international translation issues, it is therefore necessary to also factor in the effect of how 'Jabberwocky' has been visualized in different linguistic and national contexts.

In a sense, the script is also an illustration. Writing alphabets, letters, scripts, fonts, and typefaces are all visual elements of language. And as we know by now, it only takes a mirror-reversal of words to experience a *Verfremdungs*-effect to make your own mother tongue appear as 'other'. In realization of the importance of the visual side of language, we have therefore laboured to include as many samples as possible of the way in which 'Jabberwocky' is scripted in each language. How does the poem appear on the page – in Georgian, in Arabic, in Odia? One of the best examples of the marriage between the pictorial, the graphic, and the verbal is Chao Yao Ruen's Chinese translation, and his invention of new Chinese characters, using calligraphy to capture the neologisms:

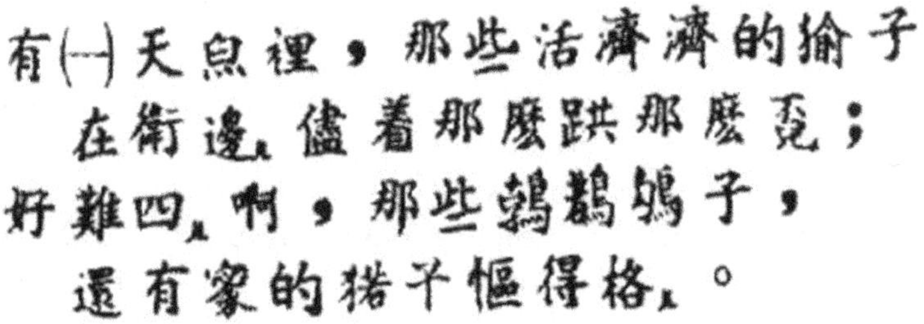

Figure 74. First stanza of Chao's calligraphic *Jabberwocky.*

The main emphasis of the *Jabberwocky Companion* project, however, is not on the visual, illustrations or alphabets, but on the verbal: how has 'Jabberwocky' fared in translation over the years? Excepting stand-alone translations like Augustus Vansittart's Latin translation, the first complete in-context versions of 'Jabberwocky' and *Looking-Glass* appeared in 1899 and were made by Louise Arosenius (Swedish) and Hasegawa Tenkei (Japanese) respectively. The two publications are quite different, both in approach and publication form. Tenkei's translation was published in a periodical in eight instalments and made use of a great deal of domesticating translating strategies. Tenkei's 'Jakkerurocky' is very loosely inspired by the original. Arosenius's translation of *Looking-Glass*, was published in book form, and her 'Jabberwocky' (she uses the English title) stays close to the source text with regard to narrative content, verse form, and use of nonsense words (see Sundmark 2017: 49–54). Thus, the two pioneer 'Jabberwocky'-translators can be said to represent two contrasting translation ideals.

In the following three decades, up to 1930, there are complete translations into another four languages: Italian (1913), German (1923), Russian (1924), and French (1930). Then the rate of translations accelerates somewhat. Still, given the now canonical status of the *Alice* books and 'Jabberwocky' now, the progress is notably slow. In this context, it is worth pointing out what individual researchers writing from different language backgrounds have long known: that although *Alice in Wonderland* may be present in a great many variations and translations across the world, the same is not true for *Looking-Glass*. The ratio can be something like five *Wonderlands* for one *Looking-Glass*. By cross-checking with *Alice in a World of Wonderlands* (Lindseth 2015), one can see that this pattern is consistent across languages.

But it is also true that many apparently complete translations actually refrain from translating 'Jabberwocky', either by deleting that part of the first chapter ('the zero option') or exchanging it for another verse altogether ('substitution'). One combination strategy is to present an alternative poem in the first chapter, but then make use of single, translated words from the first stanza of 'Jabberwocky' anyway, in chapter six, for Humpty Dumpty's explanations. This occurs, for instance, in the Indonesian translation. The consequence of these reductive strategies is that the number of languages which have complete in-context translations of 'Jabberwocky' is smaller than one would assume. A rough estimate is that 150 years after the publication of *Looking-Glass*, there are around forty languages which have at least one complete 'Jabberwocky'. This is one reason, then, why there might not be as many translations to choose from as one may think, judging from how many translations there have been, of *Wonderland*, and of *Looking-Glass*.

A different challenge is when a language has too many translations to choose from. A first translation is almost always interesting in itself. There is nothing to go on for a first translation, no precedent, no 'anxiety of influence' from previous translators. A first translation sets the tone. Some languages have famous translations (and translators), and this can certainly be a good reason to focus on these. In this category we find, for instance, André Brink's Afrikaans translation or Henri Parisot's French translation. But fame can also be a reason to focus on alternative translations or ones that have been composed in response to more frequently quoted ones.

Retranslation and intertextuality are easier to study in the context of one language rather than in a multi-language project as the *Companion*. But several of the expert contributors in the Jabberwocky-project comment on how the translations into their own language complement each other in different ways. We can also see how traces of older, influential translations, are sometimes incorporated in newer versions. A very interesting case of such intertextual carry over *between* languages is brought up in the case of Kjeld Elfelt's Danish translation, where he apparently used, and improved on some of Gösta Knutsson's *Swedish* translation choices.

Frequently, an early, target-language, child-oriented translation is eventually replaced by a more scholarly and critical version. Usually, such translations are more faithful to the source text. However, there are also retranslations that reflect other needs. In the companion entry on the poem's Ukrainian translation history, we see that the first seems to be a rather typical first translation, targeting a child audience and domesticating the text in the process. The second translation presupposes an adult audience with a political agenda. Hence, it presents 'Jabberwocky' as 'a political satire written during the Ukrainian Revolution of Dignity' (the Maidan).

In a few cases, however, where we have been unable to find an Alice-contextualized 'Jabberwocky,' we have included stand-alone translations. For instance, the very first translations of 'Jabberwocky' were independent exercises in German and Latin, some written within weeks of the publication of *Through the Looking-Glass* (1871), as with Augustus Vansittart's Latin 'Mors Iabrocchi'. There are some other stand-alone translations discussed in this companion, notably five Indian 'Jabberwocky' – Bangla, Odia, Hindi, Marathi, and Sanskrit – all of which are stand-alone translations, since none of the regular translations of *Through the Looking-Glass* into these languages include 'Jabberwocky'.

The project also led to some new translations and original artwork. In conclusion, the Jabberwocky-project includes poets, translators, artists, and scholars from more than forty different countries: a motley, polyglot crew representing different cultures and traditions. The project presents a great variety of perspectives and provides insights into varying translation (and transmediation) practices in different languages, and in different times. Notwithstanding the heterogeneous character of the enterprise, a much clearer overall picture emerges of 'Jabberwocky's' global itinerary. One notes, for instance, that 'Jabberwocky' is sometimes treated like a canonical centrepiece, a 'holy grail of translation', as Michael Heyman calls it. Just as often, however, the poem seems to have been regarded as mere nonsense-nuisance, something to be dealt with in passing, and without much care and consideration. This is just one of the many interesting aspects of the poem's travels abroad, which keeps it alive. The Jabberwock may have been slain by Carroll's beamish boy, but the monster and the nonsense keep burbling and whiffling! All we can say is 'Callooh! Callay!'.

Pierfrancesco La Mura

35 A New Italian Translation of the 'Jabberwocky'

Introduction

As Kérchy and Sundmark show in this collection, the 'Jabberwocky' poem evokes in the adult reader the same sense of disconcert and awe that a child may experience when confronting the archaic language of an ancient ballad. The effect is produced by a careful choice of meter, but also by the frequent use of non-existent, but powerfully evocative in their studied ambiguity, portmanteau words. The title itself is a portmanteau, meant to set up the reader in a superposition of terror and mirth (jab-whack/jabber-wacky). The preposterous etymologies provided in later chapters of *Looking-Glass* and those suggested by Carroll in his own fictionalized notes guide the reader through the intended experience in the manifold perspective of a child (Alice's take), of an adult (the reader's own take), of a child through the explanation of an adult (Humpty-Dumpty's interpretations), and of an adult through the explanation of the author (Carroll's notes). Any translation attempt of the 'Jabberwocky' should be aware of this explicit and essential context, and can only be fully successful if, just like in the case of the original, manages to consistently induce the same powerful, depersonalizing experience in adults and children alike, while respecting the role of the poem and of the literary inventions in it within Carroll's larger creative universe. This new Italian translation strives to reproduce the metric structure of the original, and evoke emotional states through a similar process of cognitive superposition, in the linguistic perspective of the Italian reader.

Jabberwocky

'An Obscure, But Yet Deeply Affecting, Relic of Ancient Poetry'

Before attempting a new translation, let us briefly consider the genesis of the poem. The opening stanza of 'Jabberwocky' first appeared in *Mischmasch*, the last of a series of private little 'periodicals' that the young Carroll wrote, illustrated and hand-lettered for the amusement of his brothers and sisters. The stanza was not yet part of a larger text, but rather ostensibly meant to appear, jokingly, as a fragment of old English poetry, evoking obscure meanings and emotions in the reader ('This is an obscure, but yet deeply affecting, relic of ancient Poetry'). In an issue dated 1855, under the heading 'Stanza of Anglo-Saxon Poetry', the following 'curious fragment' appears:

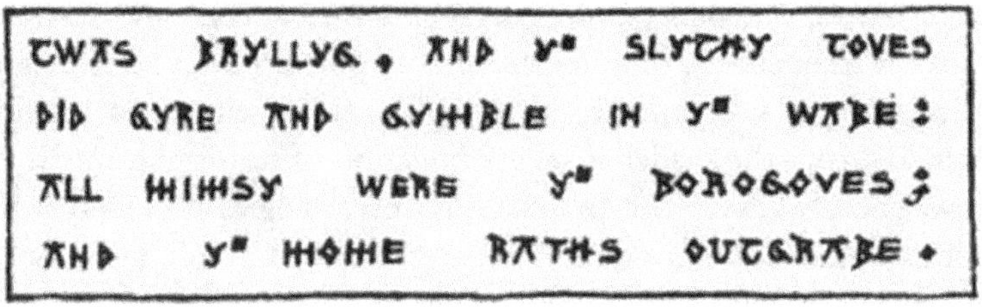

Figure 75. Stanza of Anglo-Saxon Poetry.

The notes that Carroll included with the stanza contribute to guiding the reader's experience of the curious fragment, so we proceed to translate them as well.

BRYLLYG (derived from the verb to BRYL or BROIL), the time of broiling dinner, that is, the close of the afternoon.

ROSTIVA (derivato dal verbo ROSTIRE, o ARROSTIRE), 'l'ora di arrostire qualcosa per cena, cioè la fine del pomeriggio.'

SLYTHY (compounded of SLIMY and LITHE). Smooth and active

ASCILI (composto da AGILI e LISCI). 'Lisci ed attivi.'

TOVE. A species of Badger. They had smooth white hair, long hind legs, and short horns like a stag; lived chiefly on cheese.

TISOVIO. Una specie di tasso. Avevano pelo bianco liscio, lunghe zampe posteriori, e brevi corna come un becco; si nutrivano primariamente di formaggio.

GYRE, verb (derived from GYAOUR or GIAOUR, a dog). To scratch like a dog.

ANDARE A SPIVA, SPIVARE. Verbo (derivato da PIVO o PIDO, 'un cane'). Grattarsi come un cane.

GYMBLE (whence GIMBLET). To screw out holes in anything.

ANDARE A TRIVA, TRIVARE (da cui TRIVELLA). 'Perforare qualsiasi materiale'.

WABE (derived from the verb to SWAB or SOAK). The side of a hill (from its being soaked by the rain).
MIMSY (whence MIMSERABLE and MISERABLE). Unhappy.

EDA (dal verbo EDERE o IDRARE). 'Il pendio di una collina' (poiché viene bagnato dalla pioggia).
MIEVE (contrazione di MISERO e GRAVE). 'Scontento'.

BOROGOVE. An extinct kind of Parrot. They had no wings, beaks turned up, and made their nests under sundials: lived on veal.

BOROGOVIO. Un genere estinto di pappagalli. Senza ali, con becchi all'insù, preparavano i loro nidi sotto le meridiane: si nutrivano di vitello.

MOME (hence SOLEMOME, SOLEMONE, and SOLEMN). 'Grave.'

MOMIO (da cui MONIO, SOLEMONIO, SOLENNE). 'Maestosi'.

RATH. A species of land turtle. Head erect: mouth like a shark: forelegs curved out so that the animal walked on its knees: smooth green body: lived on swallows and oysters.

RAUTO. Una specie di tartaruga di terra. Testa eretta: muso come uno squalo: zampe anteriori curve così che l'animale camminava sulle ginocchia: corpo verde liscio: si nutriva di rondini ed ostriche.

OUTGRABE, past tense of the verb to OUTGRIBE. (It is connected with old verb to GRIKE, or SHRIKE, from which are derived 'shriek' and 'creak'). 'Squeaked.'

ESGRIVAN, imperfetto del verbo ESGRIRE. (Deriva dall'antico verbo GRICCHIARE, o SCRICCHIARE, da cui i termini 'grido' e 'scricchiolio'). 'Squittivano'.

Jabberwocky

According to Carroll, the literal English rendering of the passage is: 'It was evening, and the smooth active badgers were scratching and boring holes in the hill-side; all unhappy were the parrots; and the grave turtles squeaked out. He then goes on to explain:

> There were probably sundials on the top of the hill, and the 'borogoves' were afraid that their nests would be undermined. The hill was probably full of the nests of 'raths', which ran out, squeaking with fear, on hearing the 'toves' scratching outside. This is an obscure, but yet deeply affecting, relic of ancient Poetry. (Carroll, *Mischmasch* 1855)

The many strange aspects of the above description, that one would first believe to be purely nonsensical, are immediately clarified if one realizes that each of the three species described in the stanza not only denotes an animal but also a plant:

> Toves [taxuses → taux's → toves]

A taxus is an animal (Taxidea taxus), smooth and agile, but also a plant genus (Taxus). As a plant, it may live on chases (cheese).

> Borogoves [parakeets/budgerigars → borogoves]

Parrot beaks are plants with flowers that look like upside-down parrot beaks. They may live on fields (veels).

> Raths [Kröte/Kraut/croton → crots → raths]

Turtle in Germanic languages is Kröte, but Kraut denotes a plant. Turtle crotons are popular decorative plants. Mammy crots are another variety of crotons. In a garden bed, crotons may be found outgrowing shorter species such as swallow-worts and oyster plants.

Hence, the passage can also be rendered as 'It was twilight, and the smooth lithe taxuses gyrated and pierced along the hill-side; all droopy were the parrot-beaks; and the mammy crots grew out'.

The 'Jabberwocky' Poem in *Through The Looking-Glass*

If the first stanza can be read as a natural science description, the second reads as a moral prescription. Once again we encounter three creatures:

> Beware the Jabberwock, my son!
> The jaws that bite, the claws that catch!
> Beware the Jubjub bird and shun
> The frumious Bandersnatch!

Jabberwock: Jabber-wacky denotes someone who blabbers crazily. By contrast, jabbing and whacking suggest a wild beast. In Italian this could be rendered as Cincischione, because cincischiare means to blabber but also 'to shred' or 'chew'.

Jubjub bird: A jab-jab bird denotes someone who is always first when there is an opportunity to provoke. But jabbing also means to sting, and hence the expression also evokes a bird of prey. In Italian we could render it as Battibecco, which means quarrel but also evokes a bird of prey (batti-becco).

Bandersnatch: A banter-snatch is someone who is always ready to tease. But bander is also someone who joins a gang, so bandersnatch suggests a thug. We render it in Italian as Cipiglio, which means 'scowl' but also evokes a raptor ready to snatch its victim ('ci-piglio').

Hence, the second stanza advises the young to avoid the ones who indulge in idle chatter, harassment, and teasing. As we learn from his correspondence, the young Carroll was dissatisfied with his school companions, who were, in his opinion, too wild, so perhaps they acted as an inspiration for the three malevolent and dangerous creatures that the stanza suggests one should avoid at all cost.

The following four stanzas imitate the style and content of an ancient saga. Linguistically, the effect of reading from an old ballad is obtained by the frequent use of portmanteau words, which to the adult reader sound archaic and evocative, while remaining clouded in a veil of ambiguity.

In particular, we find vorpal (warpy-mortal), manxome (mang [le] some), whiffling (whistling-sniffing), burbled (babbled-garbled), galumphing (galloping-triumphing), beamish (beaming-squeamish), frabjous (fragile-fabulous).

In Italian, it is possible to render those portmanteaus, respectively, as 'vorpale' (vorticoso-mortale), 'mutlan' (mut(i)lan(te)), 'uffando' (sbuffando-soffiando), 'brovoglio' (balbettò-brontolò), 'galonfante' (galoppando-trionfante), 'briglio' (brillante-miglior), 'fragioso' (fragile-favoloso).

The Jabberwocky	Il Cincischione
'Twas bryllig, and the slithy toves Did gyre and gymble in the wabe All mimsy were the borogoves, And the mome raths outgrabe.	Rostiva, e gli ascili tisovi Andean nell'eda a triva e a spiva: Mievi steano i borogovi, E i momi rauti esgrivan.
Beware the Jabberwock, my son! The jaws that bite, the claws that catch! Beware the Jubjub bird, and shun The frumious Bandersnatch!	Attento al Cincischione, oh figlio! All'aspre fauci, all'irto artiglio! Attento al Battibecco, e scansa Il frumiosal Cipiglio!
He took his vorpal sword in hand Long time the manxome foe he sought Then rest'd he by the Tumtum tree And stood awhile in thought.	Ei prese il vorpal ferro in pugno, A lungo ambì il mutlan rivale: Poi sostò all'ombroso Titto, E si fermò a pensare.
And while in uffish thoughts he stood, The Jabberwock, with eyes of flame, Came whiffling through the tulgey wood And burbled as it came!	E mentre in uschi sogni entrava, Il Cincischione, in fiamme gli occhi, Uffando uscì dal trico bosco E giunto brovogliò!
One-two, one-two, and through and through The vorpal blade went snicker-snack He left it dead, and with its head He went galumphing back.	Un-due, un-due, e giù e giù La vorpal lama andò a flic-floc Lo conciò a festa, e con la testa Galonfante tornò.
And hast thou slained the Jabberwock? Come to my arms, my beamish boy! Oh frajous day! Calloh! Calleh! He chortled in his joy.	Sconfitto hai dunque il Cincischione? Vieni a me, mio briglio eroe! Oh dì fragioso! Allò! Alé! Sbrifò nella sua gioia.
'Twas bryllig, and the slythy toves Did gyre and gymble in the wabe All mimsy were the borogoves And the mome raths outgrabe.	Rostiva, e gli ascili tisovi Andean nell'eda a triva e a spiva: Mievi steano i borogovi, E i momi rauti esgrivan.

A Comparison with Other Italian Translations

By the time Carroll's work was translated into Italian, his books were mostly understood as children's literature. Consequently, all Italian translations of 'Jabberwocky' focus on imitating the prose and rhythm of nursery rhymes, while the original meter (three iambic tetrameters and one iambic trimeter) is often not respected, or loosely rendered (Mastropietro 2017). Furthermore, most translations do not support multiple readings of the text, that are recognizable in the original, replacing them with purely nonsensical elements. Finally, most translations use non-existent words with no apparent meaning in place of portmanteaus, and do not respect consistency with Carroll's notes and other aspects of his larger creative universe. As a consequence, many word plays and much of the original structure are lost in translation, with the effect of making other portions of the *Looking-Glass* text uninterpretable.

Among the many Italian translations, one that is metrically close to the original, as it contains the same number of syllables, is the translation by Silvio Spaventa (1914), but the metric adaptation (iambic tetrameter into octonary) does not preserve the distribution of accents in the verse. Other translations, including those by Elda Bossi (1963) and Masolino D'Amico (1978) render the original tetrameter by means of Italian *novenario* but end up introducing more syllables that alter the metric structure of the original stanzas. Most other translations (Giglio 1952; Graffi 1989; Bignardi 2004) do not try to reproduce the original meter but resort to the more versatile hendecasyllable. By contrast, while the present translation renders the original octosyllable by means of *novenario*, it also preserves the original metric structure in each verse and stanza by means of *synalepha*.

Part XIII

Poetry

Adam Roberts

36 Jabb(re)work-y

Lear wrote, as it were, 'original' nonsense. Carroll often spun nonsense out of specific parodic circumstances.[1] So it is that Isaac Watts's tediously pious 'How Doth The Little Busy Bee' becomes 'How Doth the Little Crocodile', or Southey's clunking didactic verse-tale 'The Old Man's Comforts and How He Gained Them', cut free from moral improvement, re-emerges as the crazy, exhilarating 'You Are Old, Father William'.[2] The valence of these parodies has shifted, from an original audience aware of the poems being parodied who could therefore take delight in seeing how their dullness was being reworked, subverted and mocked, to an audience today unaware that there even was a poem called 'How Doth The Little Busy Bee'. In this circumstance, the famous parody takes precedence over the obscure original, as in Baudrillard's 'Precession of Simulacra' ('Precession of Pastiche-ulacra' perhaps). Carroll's poems are not the only example of this happening: *Don Quixote* is more famous than the medieval chivalric romances it pastiches; DreamWorks Studio's *Shrek* movies are many children's' first exposure to the fairy stories that the films, and the books on which the are based, notionally parody. But Carroll's sheer expertise as a pasticheur, and the fact that 'nonsense' as a mode is in a sense parodic of 'sense', the

---

1   For a discussion of Lear's and Carroll's nonsense in the context of literary modernism, see Chapter 26.

2   Similarly, in *Alice in Wonderland*: the Duchess's lullaby, 'Speak roughly to your little boy' is a parody of David Bates's 'Speak Gently'; 'Twinkle, Twinkle, Little Bat' is a parody of Jane Taylor's 'Twinkle Twinkle Little Star'; 'The Lobster Quadrille' is a parody of Mary Botham Howitt's 'The Spider and the Fly' ''Tis the Voice of the Lobster' is another Isaac Watts parody, this time of his 'The Sluggard' and 'Beautiful Soup' is a parody of James M. Sayles's 'Star of the Evening, Beautiful Star'.

conventional and logical which it imitates for reasons of mockery and
delight, put his nonsense parodies in a class of their own.

Not all Carroll's nonsense parodies specific texts. There is no one source
poem that 'Jabberwocky' pastiches; although the work has a relationship,
which we might as well call parodic, with Old and Middle-English poetry
more generally, both in terms of subject matter – for there are plenty of
examples of heroes battling and slaying monsters in those discourses –and
more particularly in the way it interpellates a particular manner of reading
early literature. For all but the most expert, reading these texts involves a
barrage of unfamiliar and sometimes baffling vocabulary items, some of
which can be deciphered (roughly or otherwise) from context and placement, others of which remain opaque. 'Jabberwocky' in a sense parodies
that reading experience, by replacing actual OE or ME words, of the sort
that could be looked-up in a dictionary, with neologisms that cannot–it
is part of the delight that these neologisms look anything other than new.

Parody is a way of playing with a text, and one danger with literary
criticism is that the play of art, its vitality and fun, can easily get lost, which
means the original text can get lost. Literary criticism is a fundamentally
sensible, rational, evidential, and considered matter – why, I might wonder,
do we not have Nonsense Lit-Crit, just as we have nonsense poems, nonsense prose, surrealist paintings, and so on? Rendering a text through sense,
rationality and so on will inevitably do damage to a nonsense original.
How else to approach them, though? Perhaps, precisely: through parody.

For Adam Phillips (discussing Lear, rather than Carroll) the parallels
of 'nonsense' and psychiatry as a discourse are profound, with each illuminating each. He is careful not to neglect the ludic excess, the simple pleasure
of play, in his analysis. The play, he argues, is the point, although 'where the
will to meaning does the work of the imagination, something essential, is
lost'. His point of interpretive contact, here, is English paediatrician and
psychoanalyst Donald Winnicott:

> Very few of the interpretations of Lear's nonsense verse are going to give us anything
> like pleasure, the pleasurable experience, however enigmatic, of the verse. It is this
> that Winnicott wants us to wonder about. One can have the meaning but miss the
> experience, which is something that psychoanalysis, like all the interpretive arts, is
> prone to, and that the reading of Lear's nonsense poetry could be a fitting emblem

for. So, to T S Eliot's famous pronouncement about Lear in 'The Music of Poetry' – 'his non-sense is not vacuity of sense: it is a parody of sense and that is the sense of it' – we can add that Lear's nonsense is also a freedom to make sense, or even to reinvent sense-making. (Phillips 2016: 230)

A parody, though, is a method of 'interpreting' – of reworking, of apprehending, of making a kind of 'sense' of – that doesn't, necessarily 'miss the experience'. It is a response to the freedom offered by the nonsense of Lear, and of Carroll, an interpretation that takes that freedom seriously and plays with it (see also Kohlt 2016).

'Jabberwocky' has been widely parodied already. What interests me, in this essay, is not simply adding another parody to that pile but rather using parody as a way of exploring the text itself. One way of doing this is to start with a verbal parallel – let's say, the similarities between the name of the *Star Wars* franchise villain 'Jabba the Hutt', and the name of Carroll's monster – and continue with the fact that both *Star Wars* and 'Jabberwocky' utilize a spread of made-up words in their worldbuilding. We end up with this:

'Twas boba, and the eisley moss
Did wan kenobi in the obe:
All solo was the skywalker,
And the death stars outglobe.

'Beware the Jabbahutt, my son!
The slug that slimes, the jaws that snack!
Beware the bantu cave, and shun
The sandious Sarlacc!'

He took his saber light in hand;
Long time galacic foe he sought –
He came by night to the carbonite
And stood awhile in thought.

And, as in uffish thought he stood,
The Jabbahutt on movesome frame
Came sliding in the tulgey room,
And chuckled as it came!

One, two! One, two! And through and through
The vroomish blade went snickersnack!

Leia laid a chain about its throat
And heaved, enstrangling, back.

'And hast thou slain the Jabbahutt?
Come to my arms, princessish rose!
Now, let's get you out of this obnoxious sexually-objectifying metal bikini
And into proper clothes.'

'Twas boba, and the eisley moss
Did wan kenobi in the obe:
All solo was the skywalker,
And the death stars outglobe.

Though this has some potential, as a parody of a not-quite parody, and an example in its own right of comic nonsense verse – and though it has one advantage over the *echt* Carrollian parodies, in that many more people today are familiar with *Star Wars* than with Isaac Watts – it doesn't go very far.

A different approach would be writing a *response* poem to the original, utilizing the same meter and form. 'Jabberwock Replies':

And so you've killed me, seethish lad,
Thropt off my head with your znarp knife –
Then skeebled joyous to your dad:
To boast you took a life!

I only meant to greeb hello.
Like puppy-dog, I scantered up
With claws insheathéd hand and toe:
Tongue lolling, but jaws shut.

I'd asked my Rabbiwock: should I
Go welcome-in this newcomer?
'Go forth and scry him Mordecai!'
Thou spruthest welcomer!'

I donned my newest waistcoat – ace –
Fine-threaded with sartorious tint –
And brushed my teeth and washed my face
To meet you at a sprint.

Delightness todded through my heart
To see your framsome junic form!
But you swung hard and did dispart
My head from torsoid warm.

You did not wait to hear me speak
You judged me hurriedsome and hard:
And now I lie in modence bleak
Within the jab-graveyard.

And so you've killed me, seethish lad,
And so it is my poor youth ends.
It cannot but make me most sad –
We could have been such friends!

There is some pathos in this, and it brings out that one hard-to-explain detail from Tenniel's illustration to Carroll's original – the fact that the monster is wearing a waistcoat. This surely implies a degree of culture, even of civilization, among Jabberwockind.

I surprised myself, in writing this, with its Jewishness, something which emerged from the drafting rather than being planned or intended. And yet it seems to me to say something about Carroll's original. I am not Jewish, although my wife is and our children are. I suspect it was merely the fact that 'Jabber – ' element in the poem's title has the feel of a (Humpty-Dumptyan) portmanteau of 'Jew' and 'Rabbi' (hence: 'Rabbiwock'). But once that adventitious echo has worked itself into the poem, the whole text takes on a new flavour: the Jabberwock itself, or himself, acquires a name: 'Mordecai'. And now that the poem is written I find myself wondering whether my subconscious moved me, my conscious mind being unaware, towards an interpretation of 'Jabberwock' as a name with Ashkenazi connotations. 'Wójcik' is a common surname in Poland, and before the Nazis there were many Polish Jews called Wójcik, Wojczik, Wojczyk, Wojszyk. It would not require much ablating in ordinary usage to turn a Jewish name, for instance, 'Jakob Wójck' (or even conceivably a female name: Jašpe or Jašbe Wójck – has the gender of the Jabberwock been determined?) into the name of our monster. It would be hard to argue that Carroll himself was aware of Polish-Jewish naming conventions: the influx of Jewish immigration in the late nineteenth-century was more Russian than Polish; it is not until the Nazis that large numbers of Polish Jews fled to resettle in Britain and the US. But the Barthesian advantage in using parody as a literary-critical lens is that it is not constrained by absolute fidelity to, as it might be, historical or biographical plausibility. The Aryan knight hunting and killing the monstrous (in actuality, perhaps a peaceable, friendly, ordinary) Jew Jakob Wójck, a human being, in a waistcoat, with protruding teeth – but 'othered' as a dangerous monster – gives Carroll's poem a new, and alarming, resonance. Like Wagner's *Parsifal*, another story about a 'pure-bred' Aryan knight fighting a Jewish-coded supernatural villain (the wizard, Klingsor), Carroll's text aligns with a pervasive nineteenth-century anti-Semitism.[3]

This perhaps strikes too severe a note for something as playful as a parodic 'reply poem' like this. The Adam Phillips essay quoted above is about Lear, and another mode of parody might be to wonder how a poem like 'Jabberwocky' might have been written in a more Lear-ish idiom. Here's an attempt at that:

I
The Lad and the Jabberwock went to sea
In a beautiful pea-green boat,
They took two toves, and some borogroves,
To gimble their gyre afloat.
The Lad looked up at the beast in shock,
And flourished his scimitar,
'O frightful Jabber! O Jabber, my wock,

---

3   In Winnicottian personal-psychoanalytic mode, I might note, though I was not consciously aware of this in writing the parody, 'Mordecai' has a personal resonance. When my Jewish wife became pregnant with our second child, and the scan revealed that the baby was a boy, we discussed possible names. There is a tradition in my gentile family that boys are called 'Charles' – so I am Adam Charles, my father is Charles Ian, his father was Frederick Charles and so on–and we agreed a Jewish name to balance this. But my wife's suggestions, which included 'Moses', 'Abraham' and, yes, 'Mordecai', seemed to me *too* Jewish, too strange for an English boy, liable to get him teased at school and so on. How far this indexed a residual anti-Semitism in my nature is questionable (not too far, I hope!) In the end we settled on the name 'Daniel Charles Roberts'.

What a horrible Jabber you are,
  You are,
  You are!
What a horrible Jabber you are!'

II
Jabber said to the Lad, 'But I am not bad!
Just listen how sweetly I burble!
Too long we have tarried: o let us be married!
In wedding suits of matching purple!'
Lad scorned to be hitched – much rather he itched,
  To witness the manxome thing dead
He snickered and snacked with his sword's attack
  And he cut off the Jabberwock's head,
  His head,
  His head,
And he cut off the Jabberwock's head.

III
'You killed it at sea? In a boat green as pea?
  Said his father, 'Oh frabjous my sprog!'
And so they embraced and shoreward they raced
  With the head in a burlap bag.
Dad chortled in joy, embracing his boy,
  Caloohing his giddy tri*umph*;
And hand in hand, on the edge of the sand,
  They capered a moonlit galumph,
  Galumph,
  Galumph,
They capered a moonlit galumph.

Here the jauntiness of the reframing – the lad kills the Jabberwock at sea rather than in Tenniel's forest – adds a level of nonsense: for why would the young man and the Jabberwocky go to sea together in the first place? The monster, it seems, is in love with the human, and is hoping for marriage, to the point of planning the wedding clothes. That the human should respond to such a proposal by decapitating the Jabberwock strikes a cruel and arbitrary note, off-kilter As in the previous response poem, the premise of a Jabberwock as non-threatening and even affectionate, despite its hideous appearance, makes the poem into a statement about the shallowness of judging on appearance only, of reacting not to interior merit but thoughtlessly to exterior ugliness. Which is to say, it becomes a specific reading of the Carrollian original in those terms.

A complimentary parodic approach, reading Lear via Carroll rather than Carroll via Lear, produces a different poem, predicated here on the syllabic equivalence 'Jabberwock' and Lear's most famous nonsense form, 'Limerick':

> 'Twas Edward, and the nonsense song
>   Did gyre and gimble from his pen:
> All luminous was the nosy dong,
>   And the owl-cat were twain.
>
> 'Compose the Limerick, my son!
>   The words that rhyme, the lines that scan!
> Make brief amusing verse for fun
>   And publish what you can!'
>
> He took his fountain pen in hand;
>   Long time he shortish poems versed –
> No different rhyme in the final line
>   He just reused the first.
>
> And, as each uffish poem he wrote,
>   The Limerick, with two lines short,
> Came whiffling like an anecdote,
>   A charm'd surreal thought!
>
> Thus geared, he Lear'd! And in his beard
>   Wrote up a plethora of nests!
> Two owls, a hen, four larks, a wren –
>   In shapely anapests.
>
> 'And hast thou made the Limerick?
>   Come to my arms, my Learish boy!
> O frabjous day! Callooh! Callay!'
>   He chortled in his joy.

'Twas Edward, and the nonsense song
   Did gyre and gimble from his pen:
All luminous was the nosy dong,
   And the owl-cat were twain.

Lear, of course, did not call his poems 'limericks' – it seems that the earliest such usage comes much later in the century. But the form is so celebrated, and so associated with Lear's versions, that the usage seems apropos.

Matthew Demakos

37 Tweedledum's Commentary: In Appreciation of Lewis Carroll's 'The Walrus and the Carpenter'

This commentary delves into the craft of writing narrative verse. Taking each stanza of Lewis Carroll's 'The Walrus and the Carpenter' separately, various poetic tools are explored, such as meter and rhyme, allusion and reference, and alliteration and assonance. The commentary discusses how they heighten one's reading and affect one's interpretation of the poem. Why does Carroll place a trochaic substitution here? Why does he place an end-stopped line there?

At times, unlike the other sections of *The Annotated Walrus* (from which this paper is extracted), a fictitious Carroll emerges with motives conveniently known, diligently writing and revising the poem. Of course, his true motives are unknown – likely even to himself – and he perhaps only needed to analyse his words when something intuitively sounded wrong. Despite the Duchess's words in *Wonderland* – 'Take care of the sense, and the sounds will take care of themselves' (*AAIW*: 133) – the words may describe the scene well enough but the sounds may jar against it. Indeed, some poets believe, 'Take care of the *sounds*, and the *sense* will take care of itself.' Carroll, his imitators, and those he has influenced, such as the Surrealists and the modernist poets, use this reversal from time to time, knowing full well that sound and sense are equal partners in poetry.[1] The title of this appreciation comes strictly from the *sense* that Tweedledum wrote the poem for his brother Tweedledee, who recited the poem for Alice.

---

1   See Chapters 16 and 26, respectively, for discussions of *Looking-Glass* in the context of surrealism and modernism.

> The sun was shining on the sea, / Shining with all his might:
> He did his very best to make / The billows smooth and bright –
> And this was odd, because it was / The middle of the night.

Carroll eases the reader into the poem by opening with a subtle alliteration followed by a single repetition on the word *shining*. Repetition eases the reader in by using the space to emphasize a previous detail instead of introducing a new one. In the second line, he introduces the first of many trochaic substitutions, one of his more characteristic trademarks. It produces a dactylic roll (*shining with*, $\underline{\diagup \sim \sim} \diagup \sim \diagup$)[2] and gives the couplet nonchalance and aloofness: a fitting concept since it could describe the three opening stanzas as a whole.

Carroll eases the reader out of the stanza with the use of a long and familiar noun phrase (*The middle of the night*) instead of the mere noun (*the night*). Though rhythmically expected, the ears sense this prolonged delivery of the punch line, which heightens the humour. When the noun phrase is shortened, the humour weakens: *And this was truly odd, you know,/Because it was the night.*

Carroll makes good use of the form of this six-line stanza. The first four lines fulfil the requirements of the ballad stanza, ending with a rhyme (ABCB) as well as being complete sentences in all eighteen verses. Hence, when they come to the last two lines, the readers sense an aside, the anticipation of which only heightens the witticism within.

> The moon was shining sulkily, / Because she thought the sun
> Had got no business to be there / After the day was done –
> 'It's very rude of him,' she said, / 'To come and spoil the fun!'

The continuation of the repetition of the phrase *The … was shining* in this stanza's opening continues to ease the reader into the poem. But

---

2 The slash and tilde represent accented and unaccented syllables, respectfully. The underlined portion represents the foot being discussed. The poem is in iambic meter with the odd lines having four beats ($\sim \diagup \sim \diagup \sim \diagup \sim \diagup$) and the even lines three ($\sim \diagup \sim \diagup \sim \diagup$). The opposite of iambic is trochaic, where the odd syllables are accented ($\diagup \sim \diagup \sim \diagup \sim$). *Trochaic substitution* is when an expected iambic foot ($\sim \diagup$) is replaced with a trochaic foot ($\diagup \sim$).

here the meekness and childishness of the line *spoil the fun!* surprises the reader, adding a humorous effect. Carroll enhances this effect by preceding the moon's line with the tough-guy slang of *Had got no business* and the hard *d* alliteration of *day was done.* To accentuate the effect, and for a nice modern touch, pronounce *business* as *bidnes* and *there* as *dare.*

> The sea was wet as wet could be, / The sands were dry as dry.
> You could not see a cloud, because / No cloud was in the sky:
> No birds were flying overhead – / There were no birds to fly.

Carroll takes us from the sun and the moon (two full stanzas) to the sea and the sand (just two lines) in an apt, and poetically rendered, representation of the true narrowing distances among the three heavenly bodies (sun, moon, and the unnamed Earth) and the two surfaces (the sea and the sand). After settling on the sand, we take a glimpse from where we came, and in seeing neither cloud nor bird, we stand readied for the play about to unfold before us.

Despite the nicely placed anagrams of *could* and *cloud*, and the repeated words, the stanza's humour seems wanting. Edward Hope bested Carroll in his parody of the poem: *You couldn't see a cloud unless/You saw it in the sky:/And if you did you probably/Had something in your eye* (Hope 1928: 95). With that said, the stanza does offer an effective bridge between the astronomy in the preceding stanzas and the geology in the subsequent stanzas. This dual role somewhat mollifies the disconnectedness readers sense between the three opening stanzas and the rest of the poem.

> The Walrus and the Carpenter / Were walking close at hand;
> They wept like anything to see / Such quantities of sand:
> 'If this were only cleared away,' / They said, 'it would be grand!'

Carroll continues to narrow the scope, focusing our attention from the previously mentioned sand to two characters who stroll over it. By foregoing any description of the Walrus and the Carpenter, Carroll is able to introduce the nonsense immediately. The first bit of nonsense is understated; they are two mismatched characters. The second bit of nonsense is overstated; they are immediately portrayed as weeping nonsensically over *Such quantities of sand*. This mirrors the moon's objection to the sun's existence, who *Had got no business to be there*. Sadly, the stanza lost some nonsense when Carroll replaced the amusing *hand-in-hand*, which some contemporary parodies have, with the bland *close at hand*.

The walking he plans to have the characters do may have suggested the use of iambic meter, a name derived from the *one-two, one-two* of ambling itself.

> 'If seven maids with seven mops / Swept it for half a year,
> Do you suppose,' the Walrus said, / 'That they could get it clear?'
> 'I doubt it,' said the Carpenter, / And shed a bitter tear.

Figure 76. John Tenniel, signed proof of The Walrus and Carpenter Walking, ca. 1898, from *Through the Looking-Glass*, copy 2 (London. Macmillan, 1872), The New York Public Library. The proof, along with the others presented here, was signed by the artist and either George or Edward Dalziel, the engravers. Tenniel captioned one of his sketches for this illustration, ' "I doubt it," said the Carpenter,/And shed a bitter tear.'

Throughout the poem Carroll described the Walrus and Carpenter's dialogue with the word *said* (except one *beseech* for a rhyme). The effect gives the Walrus a cool, even temperance and is much better exemplified in other stanzas. However, the use of the word here – in a question, no less – hints that the Walrus knew the answer to the question he asked, justifying his emotional state and linking him emotionally with the no-more-the-wiser, doubting Carpenter.

Carroll hands the maids *mops* instead of the more appropriate *brooms* for an apt alliteration with *maids*, which works especially well with the repetition of *seven* (The number is beloved by poets owing to its charitable syllable count).

> 'O Oysters, come and walk with us!' / The Walrus did beseech.
> 'A pleasant walk, a pleasant talk, / Along the briny beach:
> We cannot do with more than four, / To give a hand to each.'

The reader may suspect the rhyme of *walk* and *talk* as a mere cliché and to be part of a throwaway line. But as the reader will soon see, the words are literarily appropriate despite the rhyme. Walking (to fatten the Oysters) and talking (to trick the Oysters) will play a genuine role in the story.

The Walrus' stricture (only four hands, hence only four oysters) is one of Carroll's most brilliant touches. It is poetically false, for, in truth, he has no hands, poetically ironic for the implication of a *helping* hand, and psychologically devious, for it belies the expected behaviour of the multitude. Despite the truth in the lines, they effectively cause the reader to become slightly, but not too heavily, concerned for the Oysters and perhaps a bit suspicious of the Walrus. Indeed, in the whole of the poem, after the Walrus's true villainous character emerges, this false stricture shows him at his most creative and assured.

> The eldest Oyster looked at him, / But never a word he said:
> The eldest Oyster winked his eye, / And shook his heavy head –
> Meaning to say he did not choose / To leave the oyster-bed.

Carroll strengthens the steadfastness of the eldest Oyster by repeating the phrase *The eldest Oyster* in parallel positions and by scripting stiff, parallel sentences for the first and second third of the stanza. The pauses being only at the end of each line (end-stopped), also befit the immutable mollusc. One may see the anapaest foot in the middle of the second line ([nev]-*ver a word,* $\sim/\underset{\sim\sim}{\underline{}}\underline{/}\sim/$) as being a curious anomaly. It is the only triple foot in the whole of the poem (not counting ones created by trochaic substitutions). It allows for a bit of looseness and jars against the rigid character of the Eldest Oyster. However, Carroll likely saw the last syllable of the word *never* (pronounced as the nonrhotic *nevah*) as eliding with the word *a*. This would have given the line the standard, stiff rhythm (*But nev – [a∼a] word he said,* $\sim/\sim/\sim/$). It could be argued, however, that Carroll missed the opportunity to use the old-fashioned and stuffy rendering of *never* as *ne'er*. It would have not only retained the meter but would have strengthened the age, sagacity, and snobbishness of the character as well.

The fifth line's trochaic substitution (*Meaning,* $\underline{\underset{\sim}{}}\sim/\sim/\sim/$) suddenly interrupts the drollness in the four preceding lines and propels us down a descending scale. It begins on the high *Meaning*, cascading to *say* and ending on the low *choose*. The line almost forces the reader to pause after the last word – which is highly recommended – before delivering the last line of the stanza. Indeed, the whole of the stanza is one of the more enjoyable stanzas to recite, although a whole poem in this stiff style would sound amateurish and monotonous.

> But four young Oysters hurried up, / All eager for the treat:
> Their coats were brushed, their faces washed, / Their shoes were clean and eat –
> And this was odd, because, you know, / They hadn't any feet.

Carroll juxtaposes the previous stanza's steadfastness with this stanza's capriciousness, strengthening the effect by having the young Oysters' hurrying immediately on the first line. Since oysters represented immobility, stubbornness, and patience in Victorian times (as exemplified in the previous stanza),[3] the line to modern ears loses a bit of the humour it once had. The concept of hurrying oysters undoubtedly jolted the Victorian

3   For examples, see Keats *Endymion*, p. 108; Carroll *Wonderland*, p. 39, and *Looking-Glass*, p. 208, and Hazlitt *English Proverbs*, p. 381. Immobility is also implied in the popular song 'Did You Ever See and Oyster Walk Upstairs' (1876) by

Poetry

reader, the reason Carroll composed such a direct and immediate statement here. Since the inclusion of the *eldest Oyster* stanza on thematic and
moral grounds would be unlike Carroll, he included the stanza – which
could easily be excised – to heighten the nonsense of *hurrying* oysters.

The consonance in *brushed* and *washed* works especially well not only
due to their second- and fourth-beat placement, but due to an onomatopo-
etic quality. *Washed* brings the *shhhh* of a faucet showering water – appropriate enough for the aquatics – while the *shhhh* in the previous *brushed*
and the following *shoes* reinforces the effect.

The overuse of the words *you know* in contemporary conversation
might cause one to miss Carroll's skilful use of the words here. Though the
end of any poetic line creates a natural pause, this *you know* – being quite
a throwaway – adds a poetic and a comedian's beat to that pause to better
set up the joke that follows. It also interrupts us with a surprising narrator's
you, making us prick up our ears, or eyes, as if good gossip's coming our way.

> Four other Oysters followed them, / And yet another four;
> And thick and fast they came at last, / And more, and more, and more –
> All hopping through the frothy waves, / And scrambling to the shore.

Carroll continues the *Oyster/hurrying* oxymoron in this stanza. Even
without the word *fast*, the quick burst of inner rhyme poetically speeds
the young Oysters along – *And thick and fast they came at last*. So chaotic
the action, the poet feigns losing time for descriptive powers, frustratingly
blurting out *And more, and more, and more*. He recovers his wits in time,
however, by fittingly placing assonance on the odd beats (*hop-* and *froth-*)
and on the even beats (*through* and *to*) to enhance the unstated undula-
tion of the water.

> The Walrus and the Carpenter / Walked on a mile or so,
> And then they rested on a rock / Conveniently low:
> And all the little Oysters stood / And waited in a row.

Frederick Gilbert; see also the following chapter for more on 'fishy' references in
Carroll's works.

The word *Conveniently* – a characteristic of two unstated chairs to allow the title characters to execute their evil plans – is the slyest and most sinister word in the whole of the poem, often missed by vocal interpretations. The word should be delivered with the deviousness of a Peter Lorre – *Conveeeeeniently*. The whole of the line on which the word appears could either be pronounced in five syllables ($^\sim/^\sim\sim/$) or six syllables ($^\sim/^\sim/^\sim/$), the first having a false meter and the second a false pronunciation. Whichever indiscretion is chosen, it should alert the reader to question the benevolence of the convenience.

Carroll closes the stanza with yet more irony. As opposed to those who rested, the Oysters *stood* like diligent school children and did so *in a row*.

> The time has come,' the Walrus said, / 'To talk of many things:
> Of shoes – and ships – and sealing-wax – / Of cabbages – and kings –
> And why the sea is boiling hot – / And whether pigs have wings.'

CHAPTER XIII.

WALRUS-HOLES — ADVANCE OF DARKNESS — DARKNESS — THE COLD —"THE ICE-BLINK"—FOX-CHASE—ESQUIMAUX HUTS—OCCULTATION OF SATURN — PORTRAIT OF OLD GRIM.

"OCTOBER 28, Friday.—The moon has reached her greatest northern declination of about 25° 35'. She is a glorious object: sweeping around the heavens, at the lowest part of her curve, she is still 14° above the

Figure 77. An example of the long-dash style commonly used to summarize a chapter's contents in books from the Victorian era, taken from Elisha Kent Kane's *Arctic Explorations*, 1856. Carroll mimics the style in his 'The time has come' stanza.

Books in the Victorian age often summarized a chapter's contents by separating the individual concepts to be discussed with long-dashes (Figure 77). These long-dash summaries were printed in the table of contents and often headed the individual chapters.[4] Hence, to Victorians, this stanza's punctuation, in the long-dash style, indicates *one* mad, nonsense discussion on a *single* theme. In a sense, the punctuation poses the unasked question 'what do these random concepts have in common?' Carroll strengthens the supposed relation between the concepts by composing unifying alliterations: *shoes – and ships* and *cabbages – and kings* and by stretching out the alliteration in *why ... whether ... wings*. After considering these poetic and stylistic touches, the Victorian would have eventually dismissed them, concluding that the items mismatch, a theme of the poem itself – sun/night, Walrus/Carpenter, oysters/hurrying, oysters/feet, cruelty/sympathy.

The long dashes in lieu of commas could also be interpreted as being pauses in the Walrus' speech. These audible silences allow the Oysters to conjure up images and to assume a lengthy conversation. Hence, they allow the Oysters to build a false sense of security: the silences thus become another villainous device from the Walrus. Nevertheless, whether interpreted as silences or chapter headings, with mere punctuation, Carroll is able to accentuate the superficially in the Walrus's character.

The stanza also contributes to the science theme of the poem – astronomy, geology, zoology, and now, a more specific branch of zoology, oceanography. The last two lines even smack of Charles Darwin's relatively new theory of natural selection with animals (*pigs*) adapting (*wings*) due to a changing environmental condition (*the sea is boiling*).[5] Later, the poem climaxes on Tennyson's 'Nature, red in tooth and claw' from his elegy *In Memoriam* (Tennyson 1850: 80).[6] The allusion to a chapter in a book only

Poetry

---

4   For example, the chapters in Kane's *Arctic Explorations* are each headed with a summary in the long-dash style. The summary for chapter six reads: 'Closing with the Ice–Refuge Harbor–Dogs–Walrus–Narwhal–Ice-hills–Beacon-Cairn ...' (pp. 7 and 54).

5   See Chapters 1–4 on the Natural Science of Looking-Glass, and Chapter 38 on the marine fauna of Carroll's poetry.

6   A discussion on Carroll and Tennyson can be found in Chapter 25.

strengthens the science theme – the long-dash style being highly prevalent in non-fiction and scientific works.

> 'But wait a bit,' the Oysters cried, / 'Before we have our chat;
> For some of us are out of breath, / And all of us are fat!'
> 'No hurry!' said the Carpenter. / They thanked him much for that.

The oysters suddenly interrupt with words so similar in sound that they mimic the staccato sputtering of *but-but-but-but*, exhibiting a developing uneasiness. Carroll achieves this by using plosive (explosive) consonants – three words end with t, and two words begin with b – and three somewhat similar vowels.

The use of the period after the fifth line – a rare location for any end-stopping, period or not – indicates a deliberate use. It casts the last sentence away from the rest of the stanza, making it diminutive in length, to accentuate its dry irony. Carroll created that irony by having the Oysters thank an adversary and by having them address the one with seemingly less authority. The irony becomes multileveled when we consider how the Oysters give thanks for letting them be oysters after all, that is, forever resting and never hurrying, immobile (most gourmands appreciate such behaviour in their food).

> 'A loaf of bread,' the Walrus said, / 'Is what we chiefly need:
> Pepper and vinegar besides / Are very good indeed –
> Now, if you're ready, Oysters dear, / We can begin to feed.'

Till this point, Carroll had only hinted at the fate of the Oysters: the eldest Oyster's staying behind, the rock conveniently low, the Walrus's suspiciously random speech, and the fattening up of the Oysters. But Carroll skilfully holds out until the very last word of this stanza to state it openly – *We can begin to feed*. Instead of composing a four-line rhyme, ABCB, and finding some bit of nonsense to fill the last two lines, as most of the stanzas were probably written, this stanza was likely composed by writing the last lines first and front-filling.

Figure 78. John Tenniel, signed proof of The Walrus and Carpenter Resting, ca. 1898, from *Through the Looking-Glass*, copy 2 (London: Macmillan, 1872), The New York Public Library. The illustration is often thought to depict the Walrus's 'The time has come' speech. However, Tenniel labelled one of his sketches for this illustration 'Now, if you're ready, Oysters dear,/We can begin to feed'.

'But not on us!' the Oysters cried, / Turning a little blue.
'After such kindness, that would be / A dismal thing to do!'
'The night is fine,' the Walrus said. / 'Do you admire the view?'

As with *But wait a bit* two stanzas above, the Oysters interrupt with a sudden staccato burst of similar vowel sounds and plosive consonants, and end with a melodramatic double-thumped rhyme *to do!* The four diminutive words reflect the Oysters' size and helplessness. The irony in the Walrus's two-line non sequitur (ignoring with pleasantry) offers a microcosm to the theme of the poem itself (cruelty with sympathy).

'It was so kind of you to come! / And you are very nice!'
The Carpenter said nothing but / 'Cut us another slice.
I wish you were not quite so deaf – / I've had to ask you twice!'

The prominence of the loaf of bread two stanzas before, along with the talk of cutting slices here, only alludes to the gluttonous proclivities abounding. Carroll subtly played with his readers about *A pleasant walk, a pleasant talk* – just as the Walrus did himself with the Oysters – and now, even after the revelation of the true motive two stanzas before, he continues to handle the gluttony subtly, a concept continued in the following two stanzas. Highlighting the greediness, however obvious it may be to the readers, would only diminish the effectiveness of the final line of the poem.

'It seems a shame,' the Walrus said, / 'To play them such a trick,
After we've brought them out so far, / And made them trot so quick!'
The Carpenter said nothing but / 'The butter's spread too thick!'

Carroll returns to the sympathy theme in this stanza and the next. In the beginning of the poem, the characters wept over the ludicrous notion that the beach had too much sand and the Carpenter even wept over hypothetical maids with mops. The lamentation in this stanza, however, is not necessarily ludicrous but could be seen as genuine. That is, the Oysters could be interpreted as a nutritious necessity and a Walrus can't help but be a Walrus. On the other hand, the false laminations in the earlier part of the poem force readers to question the Walrus's compassion. Carroll commendably intensifies the Walrus's sympathy – false or not – by pitting it against the rudeness of the unsympathetic Carpenter.

'I weep for you,' the Walrus said: / 'I deeply sympathize.'
With sobs and tears he sorted out / Those of the largest size,
Holding his pocket-handkerchief / Before his streaming eyes.

In truth, it is not clear if the Walrus is directing his words to the Carpenter, sympathizing with his butter being spread to thick, or to the Oysters, sympathizing with their sorry fate. And for that matter, if he directed his words two stanzas above – *It was so kind of you to come* – to the Oysters or the Carpenter. Given the absurdity of his previous weeping and his previous attitude towards the Oysters – *The night is fine … / Do you admire the view?* – the Walrus is most likely addressing the Carpenter.

This is the sixth stanza in seven to begin with four syllables of dialog, allowing a certain degree of monotony to settle into the poem. It is difficult to give this repetition a poetic excuse. Admittedly, it only contributes to the feeling that the poem is dragging on.

> 'O Oysters,' said the Carpenter, / 'You've had a pleasant run!
> Shall we be trotting home again?' / But answer came there none –
> And this was scarcely odd, because / They'd eaten every one.

Figure 79. John Tenniel, signed proof of The Walrus and Carpenter Eating, ca. 1898, from *Through the Looking-Glass*, copy 2 (London: Macmillan, 1872), The New York Public Library. Tenniel labelled his sketch of this illustration, 'They'd eaten every one'.

Although Carroll admitted that he had given the last line in this stanza to the Carpenter owing to the metric requirement (Tollemache 1908: 313–314), it seems a more effective choice. The question in the mouth of the

Carpenter puts the reader in sympathy with his obliviousness and not in sympathy with his partner's deviousness. Given this view, it is certainly possible to argue that the poem may have been better served with two oblivious characters and no false sympathy.

The last stanza can be viewed as a conclusion to the science theme, namely the harsh realities of nature, not seen since the eleventh stanza. Some may be shocked at Tennyson's 'Nature, red in tooth and claw' so abruptly staged. Others may delight in the blatant use of black humour, appreciating how Carroll played them so well with his two previous uses of the And-this-was-odd refrain.

This commentary will, no doubt, be an ineffective mollifier of the mollusc massacre. By highlighting its poetical tools, it is only bound to further polarize 'The Walrus' poem's two pre-existing camps: the loathers and the ghoulers. In *Wonderland*, the Queen of Hearts repeatedly screams 'Off with her head!' (*AAIW*: 117) with various pronouns. The loathers will point out, however, that readers intuit that she is merely grandstanding, a concept the Gryphon eventually confirms (*AAIW*: 139). But in 'The Walrus' poem, they see the Queen's threat realized – *executed* – and worse, done so (1) in mass, (2) on diminutive, helpless creatures, (3) and on an anthropomorphic characters given words to speak, and, let's not forget, shoes to wear!

The ghoulers will have none of that! After reading this poetic analysis, they will only allow their *pre-existing* grins to widen. They will take pleasure in the newfound meanings, whether in the understated irony (*Oysters stood*), in the deft use of a single word (*conveniently*), or in the alternate meaning in otherwise innocent alliterations and punctuation (*Of cabbages – and kings*). Given the chance, ghoulers will furtively murmur to those responsible for the poem and this commentary, that is, to Tweedledee and Tweedledum, 'It was so kind of you to come!'

Jan Susina

38 The Fishy Riddles of *Through the Looking-Glass*

> 'Why, if a fish came to, and told *me* he was going a journey. I should say, "With what Porpoise?"'
>
> 'Don't you mean "purpose"?' said Alice.
>
> 'I mean what I say,' said the Mock Turtle replied, in an offended tone.
> – Lewis Carroll *Alice's Adventures in Wonderland*

Near the conclusion of Lewis Carroll's *Through the Looking-Glass*, Alice makes a curious statement to the black kitten, 'I had such a quantity of poetry said to me, all about fishes' (*TTLG*: 207). Alice then promises Kitty that when she feeds her breakfast she will repeat 'The Walrus and the Carpenter' so that her pet can pretend that it is eating oysters. Like the final riddle that Alice poses to Kitty – whether her adventures were her dream or the Red King's dream. Carroll does not provide a clear reason why so many of the poems in *Looking-Glass* involve fish or other sea creatures. He leaves it to the reader to tease out a possible solution. Nor is this the only time that Alice and Carroll draw the reader's attention to the fishy nature of the poems in *Looking-Glass*. After the awkward lull in the conversation during Alice's dinner party, the Red Queen demands that Alice make a remark and Alice observes:

> I've had such a quantity of poetry repeated to me to-day [...] and it's a very curious thing, I think – every poem was about fishes in some way. Do you know why they're so fond of fishes, all about here?. (*TTLG*: 207)

This is quite a puzzler that Carroll poses to the reader. I will attempt to explore the fishy nature of *Looking-Glass* and suggest the purpose of various fish poems is that they are a series-linked riddles that the reader is asked to solve.[1]

Perhaps the easier and most obvious answer for the cause of the fishy nature of *Looking-Glass* is the literary influence of Charles Kingsley's *Water-Babies* on the *Alice* books. John Goldthwaite makes compelling case in *The Natural History of Make-Believe* that 'if there had been no *Water Babies* there would be no *Alice*' (89) and adds that traces of *Water-Babies* can be found in *Looking-Glass* as well (91). While Carroll rejected the overt didacticism found in Kingsley's literary fairy tale for children (108), Goldthwaite goes into detail noting the similarities between the *Water-Babies* and *Wonderland* (88–91). Carroll owned and read a number of Kingsley's novels in addition to *Water-Babies*. Goldthwaite notes that Carroll read Kingsley's *Alton Locke* (1856) and recorded in his diary in 1856 that he found it 'a powerful and grandly written book' (95). While he also read Kingsley's *Hypatia* (1853) which he mentioned in his diary in 1857 as 'powerful, like all that Kingsley writes,' but objected to the sneers at Christianity of some of the characters. (Goldthwaite 95). Goldthwaite argues that 'much of *Alice* is a running argument' with Kingsley on how to write a children's book with Kingsley overtly preaching to his readers, while Carroll saw himself as a 'coconspirator with children' (114). Where Kingsley has his protagonist go below the surface of water to discover an alternative world full of odd creatures, Carroll takes his protagonist through the looking-glass to discover a similar world. The most significant parallel between *Water-Babies* and *Looking-Glass* is when Tom reaches Mother Carey at the Peacepool who has the reputation of making new beasts out of old ones. She corrects Tom and explains that she allows things make themselves. She then explains that if Tom wishes to continue his journey to the Other-end-of-Nowhere, he must go backwards.

'Backward!' cried Tom. 'Then I shall not be able to see my way.'

'On the contrary, if you look forward you will not see a step before you and be certain to go wrong; but if you look behind you and watch carefully whatever you have passed […] then you will know what is coming, next, as plainly as if you saw it in a looking-glass.' (Kingsley 2008 [1863]: 197)

1   For other inter-Carrollian intertextualities, see Chapter 33.

Tom's reverse journey is very similar to the method that Alice navigates her way backwards into the Garden of Live Flowers, how she is able to read 'Jabberwocky', and the White Queen's memory moves both forward and backwards. Sometimes it feels when reading *Looking-Glass*, one is in a contrariwise reflection of *Water-Babies*. Over time, Carroll began to introduce didactic into his children's books as was the case with *Sylvie and Bruno* and *Sylvie and Bruno Concluded*.[2] By the time that Henry Savile Clarke was adapting the Alice books for *Alice's Wonderland: A Dream Play for Children in Two Acts* (1886),[3] Carroll was having second thoughts about the conclusion of 'The Walrus and the Carpenter' and added additional lines in which the ghosts of the oysters appear and as punishment for their misdeeds by stamping and dancing hornpipe on their sleeping chests (Lovett 1990: 66–67).

Alice's observation that every poem in *Looking-Glass* is about fishes is an overstatement. It is about as accurate as suggesting that the all moves in *Looking-Glass* follow traditional chess moves. Carroll's acknowledges in the 'Preface to the 1897 edition of *Looking-Glass*' that the chess moves that frame Alice's journey do not 'strictly' follow the alternation between Red and White or follow traditional chess moves (Carroll 1897: 357). Likewise, many, but not all, of the *Looking-Glass* poems, touch on fish, or at least sea creatures, such as oysters and the walrus. In the 'The Wasp in the Wig' episode which Carroll dropped from *Looking-Glass* when John Tenniel expressed little of interest in illustrating the character, Alice has a 'curious' realization that, 'Almost everyone she had met had repeated poetry to her' (Carroll 1977 [1871], 18). Once again many, but not all the characters recite poetry to her in *Looking-Glass*. In the 'Dramatis Persona' which introduces the key characters that Alice meets in *Looking-Glass*, oysters represent four of the pawns, which links to the four young oysters who first join the Walrus and Carpenter on their walk and are subsequently joined by other groups of four oysters. I will be examining the four major fish poems in *Looking-Glass* – 'The White Queen's Riddle,' 'The Walrus

---

2   For a discussion of didacticism and *Sylvie and Bruno*, see Chapter 2, and moral messaging in *TTLG*, Chapters 4, 7 and 8.

3   For more detail on the oysters of this adaptation see Chapter 18.

and the Carpenter,' 'Humpty Dumpty's Song,' and 'Jabberwocky' to show how all these fishy poems are connected. Jo Elwyn Jones and J. Francis Gladstone have suggested that *Wonderland* and I think is even truer about *Looking-Glass* that it is 'a fishy book, suspiciously full of half-hidden things that don't quite surface' (92).

Carroll's fondness for puns, paradoxes, riddles, and conundrums is well established. Between the publication of *Wonderland* and *Looking-Glass*, Carroll published 'Puzzles from Wonderland': seven puzzles in verse that first appeared in 1870 Christmas edition of *Aunt Judy's Magazine*, with the answers appearing the following month in the journal. The easiest to solve of the *Looking-Glass* riddles is 'The White Queen's Riddle,' which is introduced to Alice by the Red Queen as, 'a lovely riddle – all in poetry – all about fishes' (231). Unlike the more famous Hatter's riddle from *Wonderland* – 'Why is a raven like a writing-desk?' (*AAIW*: 60), this one has an easier discovered answer: an oyster. While Carroll did not provide the answer in the text, an answer was subsequently published as a final stanza in the 30 October 1878, of *Fun*:

> Get an oyster-knife strong,
> Insert it 'twixt cover and dish in the middle,
> Un-dis-cover the OYSTERS – dish-cover the riddle! (Carroll 1878: 353)

Much to Alice's irritation in *Wonderland*, the Hatter announces that his riddle had no answer or at least he didn't have the slightly idea for a solution. But a riddle with no answer so vexed readers of *Wonderland* that Carroll eventually provided an answer in 'Preface to the Eighty-sixth Thousand of 6/' – Edition of *Alice's Adventures in Wonderland* – 'Because it can produce few notes though they are *very* flat, and it is nevar put with the wrong end in front!', but explained that that solution was an afterthought, and the riddle was originally written with no answer at all (336). This may also account for the reason that Hatter's mirror version in *Looking-Glass*, Hatta, who was confined to prison where he was given 'oyster-shells' (Carroll 2015: 199), since his riddle lacked a solution and was all shell and no oyster. An unused Tenniel illustration of Hatta in cell which is reprinted in *150th Anniversary Deluxe Edition of the Annotated Alice* shows the oysters shells on the floor (Carroll 2015: 233).

The solution to 'The White Queen's Riddle' links to the 'Walrus and the Carpenter'.[4] While Alice is disturbed with the tragic fate of the oysters, she seems less concerned about them later when she offers to recite the poem to Kitty and encourages her to pretend that her breakfast is oysters. As M. F. K. Fisher has observed in *Consider the Oyster*, 'An oyster leads a dreadful but exciting life (3) where danger is everywhere. Fisher lists eight enemies, in addition to humans, that enjoy devouring oysters. Perhaps it is worth nothing that walrus also eat oysters, although they do not make Fisher's list of predators. While 'Walrus and the Carpenter' is a depressing poem, at least from the oysters' point of view, also records the realistic fate for many oysters of the Victorian period.

During the nineteenth century, oysters were cheap and plentiful; the 'White Queen's Riddle' suggests that a penny would purchase an oyster. Oysters were a popular and inexpensive source of protein since a single oyster can have as much protein as a four-ounce steak (Smith 23). For members of the working class, such as the Carpenter, oysters would be much more affordable than meat. It was only with over consumption of oysters in the late nineteenth century that they became a luxury. Sam Weller observes to Mr Pickwick in Charles Dickens's *The Pickwick Papers* (1836–1837) 'it's a wery remarkable circumstance [...] that poverty and oysters always seems to go together' (383). Henry Mayhew in the first volume of *London Labour and the London Poor* (1851) in his section on 'Of the Street-Sellers of Fish' includes discussion 'Of Oyster Selling in the Street' and places the cost of oysters at four for a penny and estimates that costermongers sold 124,000,000 oysters a year in London (76). Clearly, Carroll was overcharged for his oysters. Oysters only became a luxury once the oyster beds became over-harvested by the late nineteenth century.

While the sad fate of the oysters is obvious, Alice is confronted with a puzzler once Tweedledee and Tweedledum conclude their recitation. She must choose which the two creatures was the more of an unpleasant character: the Walrus, who ate more oysters than the Carpenter, according to Tweedledee, or the Carpenter, who ate as many as he could. Alice's solution, like the two halves of the empty oyster shell is, 'They were both

---

4   See the previous chapter for a discussion of the 'Walrus and the Carpenter' poem.

very unpleasant characters' (*TTLG*: 164). In what I take to be a hidden pun, both the Walrus and the Carpenter are selfish characters for eating so many shellfish. Carroll's 'Walrus and the Carpenter' is in stark constrain to Edward Lear's 'O was an Oyster' which appeared in one of the nonsense alphabets in *Nonsense Songs, Pictures Rhymes, Botany and Alphabets* (1871) published the same year as *Looking-Glass*.

> O was an oyster
> Who lived in his shell
>   If you let him alone.
>   He felt perfectly well.
>   O!
>   Open mouth'd Oyster! (118)

One of the enduring puzzles of children's literature is how it was possible that the two great writers of nonsense verse of the Victorian period, Lewis Carroll and Edward Lear, never meet or seem to have never read one another's books.

Angelika Zirker has pointed out that not only is oyster the solution to the 'White Queen's Riddle', but oysters which are difficult to open is the appropriate metaphor for a riddle, a verbal puzzle that needs to be solved or opened to reveal the answer or even, perhaps reveal of valuable pearl of wisdom (2018: 96). But in addition, 'White Queen's Riddle' is also Carroll's revision of the Anglo-Saxon Exeter Riddle 77: The Oyster from the *Exeter Book*, the collection of ninety short riddles in verse. In this way, the riddle links this poem not only to 'The Walrus and the Carpenter', but also to 'Jabberwocky' whose opening stanza first appeared in *Mischmasch*, as 'Stanza of Anglo-Saxon Poetry'. Alice is puzzled when she first attempts to read 'Jabberwocky', since she discovers the poem in a Looking-Glass book where the type is reversed. Even after holding the book up the mirror, she is at a loss to understand it. It remains a bit of a puzzle or a riddle for her, although she suggests, 'Somehow it seems to fill my head with ideas – only I don't know what they are! How-ever, *somebody* killed *something*' (*TTLG*: 134).

Alice is not alone in her confusion over the puzzling nature of 'Jabberwocky', she later consults Humpty Dumpty to help unpack the meaning of the various words in the poem. I want to suggest that Tenniel's

A LITTLE CHRISTMAS DREAM.

Figures 80 and 81. Top: John Tenniel's illustration from *Through the Looking-Glass* presents an ambiguous figure that is part dragon, part bird, and part sea serpent. Bottom: George du Maurier's 1868 Punch cartoon 'A Little Christmas Dream.'

illustration of the Jabberwock is more helpful in understanding the poem that Humpty Dumpty's clever explanation of various words. The Jabberwock is a rather ambiguous figure: seemingly part dragon, part bird, and part sea serpent. Many readers have interpreted the beamish boy as a young knight slaying the dragon, a very different figure of the White Knight that Alice will later encounter.

Michael Hancher has suggested that a prototype for Tenniel's Jabberwock was the 1868 *Punch* cartoon by George du Maurier 'A Little Christmas Dream' but notes that Maurier's creature resembles a mammoth while Tenniel's looks much like a dragon (106). Hancher argues that du Maurier's cartoon was intended a satirical comment on Louis Figuier's *The World Before the Deluge* (1865), a popular illustrated book on palaeontology which features dramatic illustrations by Edouard Riou. In his introduction, Figuier argued that books on natural history were more appropriate reading material for children than fairy tales or fables (Rudwick 1992: 216). But in Du Maurier's cartoon the young boy is frightened as he is being chased by an antediluvian monster coming down the street, a nightmare caused by reading Mr Figuier book instead of fairy tales such as 'Cinderella' and 'Puss in Boots' (272). In *The Tenniel Illustrations to the 'Alice' Books*, Hancher reproduces two of Riou's illustrations including 'Ideal scene of Lias with Ichthyosaur and Plesiosaurus' (107). Martin Rudwich in *Scenes from the Deep: Early Pictorial Representation of the Prehistoric World* has shown that many of the popular illustration of the world before human existence featured oysters and other shellfish, so oysters were understood to be a part of the world of dinosaurs and other extinct creatures (116).

The nineteenth century had an increased interest in the discovery of fossils and the growing fields of geology and palaeontology under the direction of Richard Owen who coined the term 'dinosaur' in 1842. The Ichthyosaurus, or 'the fish lizard', was the first large-scale fossil remains discovered by the 12-year-old Mary Anning in 1811 that initiated her distinguished career as a fossil hunter and palaeontologist. Anning provided important specimens to Richard Owen, William Buckland, and De la Beche and other geologists. Her discovery of the bones of Ichthyosaurus also gave rise to the supposition of the existence of ancient sea serpents. One of Anning's best customers was Thomas Hawkins who

Figure 82. John Martin's illustration from Waterhouse Hawkins's The *Sea-Dragons as They Lived* (1840), which made the connections between dinosaurs and sea serpents.

created one of the most extensive private collections of fossils which he eventually sold to the British Museum. Hawkins published *Memoirs or Icthyosauri and Pleiosauri: Extinct Monsters of the Ancient World* (1834) and his *Book of the Great Sea-Dragons* (1840) luridly illustrated by John Martin made the connection between ichthyosaurs and plesiosaurs and sea serpents. While Richard Owen argued against the belief of sea serpents and their links to extinct reptiles such as Itchthyosaurus or Plesiosaurus, it remained a long-held belief in the popular imagination and fiction as seen in the plot and mock-documentary images that appear in Arthur Conan Doyle's *The Lost World* (1912) (Fallon 2021: 136–147; 154).

The artist and sculptor Waterhouse Hawkins under the direction of Richard Owen would first create small models of dinosaurs and other extinct animals for the Great Exhibition of 1851 in Hyde Park which Carroll visited. He reported in a letter to his sister Elizabeth that the interior of Crystal Park was 'like a sort of fairyland' with its avenues of statues, fountains, and canopies

A VISIT TO THE ANTEDILUVIAN REPTILES AT SYDENHAM—MASTER TOM STRONGLY OBJECTS TO HAVING HIS MIND IMPROVED.

Figures 83 and 84. Top: Waterhouse Hawkins's Crystal Palace was a popular attraction when the Crystal Palace was relocated to Sydenham in 1854. Bottom: John Leech's 1855 *Punch* cartoon 'Visit to the Antediluvian Reptiles of the Crystal Palace Dinosaurs – Master Tom Strongly Objects to Having his Mind Improved.'

(*Letters*: 17). Entering the largest glass-enclosed building in the world which was three times the length of St Paul's Cathedral that housed over 1,300 exhibitors must have seemed like entering into an alternative world just beyond the looking-glass. When Joseph Paxton's Crystal Palace was moved and reassembled in 1854 to Sydenham Park, Hawkins was commissioned to construct thirty-three life-size dinosaurs and other extinct animals. These fanciful Victorian versions of dinosaurs, the Crystal Palace Dinosaurs as they were known by the public, were immensely popular and the construction of these life-size sculptures was widely reported in *Punch* and the *London Illustrated News*. The opening of Charles Dickens's *Bleak House* (1853) makes reference to them within, which in the foggy November weather allows him to imagine a chance encounter with a 40 ft megalosaurus making its way up Holborn Hill (5). I would argue that Tenniel's illustration of the Jabberwock combined elements of Hawkins's the teeth of Ichthyosaurus, the elongated neck of the Plesiosaurus – both sea creatures – and the wings of Pterodactyl. Hawkins was also a popular lecturer and one of his favourite presentations with the public was 'The Age of Dragons' in which he proposed that the pterodactyl, which he felt was a combination of a fish, reptile, and bird, was the original dragon and the basis for the medieval legend of St George and the dragon (Bramwell and Peck: 29). Based on the fossil remains of dinosaurs, Hawkins argued for the possible existence of dragons.

Carroll had originally planned to use the illustration of Jabberwock as the frontispiece for *Looking-Glass* but had concerns that 'it is too terrible a monster, and likely to alarm nervous and imaginative children' (*Handbook* 61) after consulting by circular with a group of thirty mothers, he agreed that the image was too frightening and replaced it with the illustration of Alice and the White Knight. John Leech drew an 1855 *Punch* cartoon of a terrified young boy being forced against his will to visit the Crystal Palace Dinosaurs (8). Nightmares resulting from a visit to the Crystal Palace Dinosaurs were not limited to children, another 1855 *Punch* cartoon features a man summoning up visions of the various monstrous creatures after a hearty dinner (50).

Figures 85 and 86. Top: John Tenniel's 'Hatter in Prison.' Rejected illustration from
Through the Looking-Glass featuring the Hatter in prison with oyster shells on the floor.
The text refers to this illustration on page 463 of the chapter. Bottom: 'The Effects of a
Hearty Dinner after Visiting the Antediluvian Department at the Crystal Palace' a 1855
Punch cartoon 'Visit to the Antediluvian Reptiles of the Crystal Palace Dinosaurs –
Master Tom Strongly Objects to Having His Mind Improved.'

After providing his explanation of various hard words in 'Jabberwocky,' Humpty Dumpty then provides his own fish poem, 'Humpy Dumpty's Song'. Like 'The Walrus and the Carpenter,' in his poem Humpty Dumpty invites the fish not for a walk, but into a kettle of water. Unlike the oysters, these little fish decline Humpty Dumpty's invitation which angers him and then gets a corkscrew to summon them from the beds. Zirker suggests that one can unlock this riddle poem by suggesting that these fish are actually shellfish, or oysters (2018: 95). But unlike 'The Walrus and the Carpenter' the poem ends abruptly before it reaches conclusion. When Alice attempts to explain Humpty Dumpty's poem to the Red and White Queens, she is also cut off abruptly, 'I know what he came for,' said Alice, 'he wanted to punish the fish, because–' (*TTLG*: 225). Just as 'Jabberwocky' reappears in *Looking-Glass*, 'Humpty Dumpty's Song' reappears when Alice is being quizzed by the Red and White Queen. After one of the Red Queen's puzzling statements that reminds Alice of 'a riddle with no answer' (224), White Queen adds new information to 'Humpty Dumpty's Song' by explaining that Humpty Dumpty came to the door with the corkscrew since he was looking for a hippopotamus. This additional detail links the poem to 'The Mad Gardener's Song' in Carroll's *Sylvie and Bruno* in which the banker's clerk descending from a bus is transformed a hippopotamus and raises the fear, 'If this should stay to dine,' he said, 'There won't be much for us' (98). This poem then circles back to 'The Walrus and Carpenter' and the question which of the two characters ate the most oysters. It is worth noting that *Sylvie and Bruno* includes the poem 'The Three Badgers,' which, as Gillian Beer has suggested, may be read as a ruthless revision of 'The Walrus and the Carpenter' (2016: 402) which the naive herrings who wander away from to their homes and in the mouths of the badgers. Alice's understanding of 'Humpty Dumpty's Song' is his desire to punish the fish for their reluctance to be being easily caught, cooked, and eaten. These fish are not quite so gullible as the oysters in 'Walrus and the Carpenter'. As Karl Steel has noted, much premodern writing situated oysters as animal life at its most helpless, and with the inability to move and limited senses placed oysters only slightly above plants and trees (2019: 12). As recent as the publication of *Animal Liberation* (1975), Peter Singer argues the line between ethically significant and ethically insignificant animals lies 'somewhere between a shrimp an oyster', although by 1990, and in the second edition, Singer was still uncertain if oysters are capable of feeling pain but recommended not eating them (1990: 174). The world may be your oyster is inspirational to everyone except oysters. Pity the poor oyster.

'White Queen's Riddle' serves as a prelude to the final riddle of *Looking-Glass*: 'Which Dreamed It?' After promising to recite 'The Walrus and the Carpenter' to Kitty, the black kitten whose ravelling and unravelling the ball of worsted begins the story of *Looking-Glass*, Alice poses the question whether her adventures were simply her dream or part of the Red King's, a conundrum that Tweedledee and Tweedledum raise after their recitation of 'The Walrus and the Carpenter'. Carroll remains silent as on oyster in terms of the riddle's solution and ends *Looking-Glass* with a direct question to the reader 'Who do *you* think it was?' (*TTLG*: 240). But this riddle is fishy in that it is a bit of a trick but has a surprising easy solution. As the 'White Queen's Riddle' suggests it is simple to cook an oyster in a dish, since 'because it is already in it' (Carroll 231). One returns to the first fishy riddle of *Looking-Glass*, 'Jabberwocky', and recalls that Alice discovered it in a book. She re-emphasizes that she read the puzzling poem in a book, in contrast to some of the poetry that was recited to her when Humpty Dumpty asks where she had found such hard poetry. The person who actually dreamed the adventures of *Looking-Glass* and put in in a book for Alice and others to read was either Alice or the Red Queen but Lewis Carroll. Unlike the conclusion of *Wonderland* where Carroll explains away Alice's adventures as part of her dream, in *Looking-Glass* he provides a riddle that credits his creation. So, 'There's glory for you!' (*TTLG*: 186) and the solution to the final fishy riddle of *Looking-Glass*.

Bibliography

Books

Aarsleff, Hans, *The Study of Language in England, 1780–1860* (Princeton: Princeton University Press, 1967).

Abercrombie, John, *Inquiries Concerning the Intellectual Powers and the Investigation of Truth* (Edinburgh: Waugh and Innes, 1832).

Abrams, M. H., *The Mirror and the Lamp: Romantic Theory and the Critical Tradition* (New York: W. W. Norton, 1958).

Ahlberg, Janet, and Allan Ahlberg, *The Jolly Christmas Postman* (London: Puffin Books, 2014).

Ansell-Pearson, Keith, *Viroid Life: Perspectives on Nietzsche and the Transhuman Condition* (London: Routledge, 1997).

Armstrong, Isobel, *Victorian Glassworlds: Glass Culture and the Imagination, 1830–1880* (Oxford: Oxford University Press, 2008).

Ayres, Jackson, *Alan Moore: A Critical Guide* (London: Bloomsbury, 2021).

Bacchilega, Cristina, *Postmodern Fairy Tales* (Philadelphia: University of Pennsylvania Press, 1997).

Bacon, Francis, *Novum Organum, or True Suggestions for the Interpretation of Nature* ([London, 1620], New York: P. F. Collier & Son, 1902).

——, *The Works of Francis Bacon*, 10 vols ([London, 1740], London: J. Johnson, 1803).

——, *Valerius Terminus: Of the Interpretation of Nature* (London, 1734).

Baetens, Jan, and Hugo Frey, *The Graphic Novel: An Introduction* (Cambridge: Cambridge University Press, 2015).

Bartley, William Warren III, ed., *Lewis Carroll's Symbolic Logic* (New York: C. N. Potter, 1977).

Beer, Gillian, *Alice in Space: The Sideways Victorian World of Lewis Carroll* (Chicago: University of Chicago Press, 2016).

Bindman, David, *William Blake: The Complete Illuminated Books* (London: Thames & Hudson, 2001).

Bolter, Jay David, and Richard Grusin, *Remediation: Understanding New Media* (Cambridge, MA: MIT Press, 1999).

Bourgeois, David, *Making Space: The Subversion of Authoritarian Language in Lewis Carroll's Alice Books* (Montreal: McGill University, 2002). MA Thesis.

Bown, Nicola, Carolyn Burdett and Pamela Thurschwell, eds, *The Victorian Supernatural*, (Cambridge: Cambridge University Press, 2004).

Brooker, Will, *Alice's Adventures: Lewis Carroll in Popular Culture* (London: Continuum, 2004).

Buckley, Arabella Burton, *Through Magic Glasses* (London: Edward Stanford, 1890).

Buongiorno, Teresa, *Dizionario della Fiaba* (Rome: Edizioni Lapis, 2014).

Butler, Judith, *Precarious Life: The Powers of Mourning and Violence* (London: Verso, 2004).

Caputo, John D., *The Insistence of God: A Theology of Perhaps* (Bloomington: Indiana University Press, 2013).

Carpenter, Humphrey, *Secret Gardens: A Study of the Golden Age of Children's Literature* (London: Faber and Faber, 2012).

Carroll, Lewis, 'Alice on the Stage', *The Theatre*. April, 1887, reprod. In 'Appendix C', Kelly, Richard, ed., *Alice's Adventures in Wonderland* (Peterborough: Broadview Press, 2011), 223–227.

——, *Alice's Adventures in Wonderland* (London: Hutchinson, 1934).

——, *Alice's Adventures in Wonderland* (London: Hutchinson, 1992).

——, *Alice's Adventures in Wonderland* (London: Macmillan, 1865).

——, *Alice's Adventures in Wonderland and Through the Looking Glass and What Alice Found There* (London: Penguin Classics, 1998).

——, *Alice's Adventures in Wonderland and Through the Looking-Glass*, Hugh Haughton, ed. (New York: Penguin, 1998).

——, *Alice's Adventures in Wonderland and Through the Looking-Glass* (Ware: Wordsworth Editions, 1993).

——, *Alicia En El País De Las Maravillas* [Alice in the Land of Marvels, Spanish translation by Jaime de Ojeda] (Madrid: Alianza Editorial, 1970).

——, *Alicia En El País De Las Maravillas* [Alice in the Land of Marvels, Spanish translation by Juan Gabriel López Guix] (Barcelona: Ediciones B, 2002).

——, *As Aventuras De Alicia No Pais Das Maravillas* [Alice in the Land of Marvels, Galician translation by Teresa Barro e Fernando Pérez-Barreiro] (Vigo: Edicions Xerais de Galicia, 1984).

——, 'Bruno's Revenge', in *Sylvie and Bruno* (London: Macmillan, 1889).

——, *Nursery Alice* (Macmillan: London, 2015 [1890]).

——, *Sylvie and Bruno Concluded* (London: Macmillan, 1893).

——, *Symbolic Logic and the Game of Logic* (New York: Dover, 1958).

——, *The Hunting of the Snark: An Agony in Eight Fits* (London: Macmillan, 1876).

——, *The Wasp in a Wig: A 'Suppressed' Episode of Through the Looking-Glass and What Alice Found There, with a Preface, Introduction and Notes by Martin Gardner* (London: Macmillan, 1977).

——, *Through the Looking-Glass and What Alice Found There* (London: Macmillan, 1871/1872).

——, *Through the Looking-Glass and What Alice Found There* (London: Macmillan, 1881).

——, *Through the Looking-Glass and What Alice Found There* (London: Hutchinson, 1934).

——, and Jan Švankmajer, ill., *Alice's Adventures in Wonderland & Through the Looking Glass* (Prague: Athanor, 2017).

——, and John Vernon Lord, ill., *Through the Looking-Glass* (London: Artists' Choice Editions, 2011).

——, *Through the Looking Glass*, reprod. in Donald J. Gray, ed., *Alice's Adventures in Wonderland* (New York: W. W. Norton, 2013), 105–208.

——, *Through the Looking-Glass and What Alice Found There* (London: Macmillan, 2015).

——, and Maggie Taylor, ill., *Through the Looking-Glass* (San Francisco: Moth House Press, 2018).

——, and Peter Hunt, eds, *Alice's Adventures in Wonderland and Through the Looking-Glass and What Alice Found There* (Oxford: Oxford University Press, 2009).

——, and Ray Dyer, eds, *Sylvie and Bruno with Sylvie and Bruno Concluded: An Annotated Scholar's Edition* (Kibworth: Trouvador, 2015).

Caruth, Cathy, *Explorations in Memory* (Baltimore: The Johns Hopkins University Press, 1995).

Chakrabarty, Dipesh, *Provincializing Europe: Postcolonial Thought and Historical Difference* (Princeton: Princeton University Press, 2000).

Chesterton, G. K., *Orthodoxy* (London and New York: John Lane, 1909).

—— , and Alberto Manguel, ed., *On Lying in Bed & Other Essays* (Calgary: Bayeux Arts, 2014 [1908]).

Chevalier, Jean, and Alain Gheerbrant, *Dicionário de Símbolos* (Rio de Janeiro: José Olympio, 1999).

Cohen, Morton N., *Lewis Carroll: Interviews and Recollections* (London: Macmillan, 1989).

——, *Lewis Carroll: Interviews and Recollections, II* (London: Macmillan, 2005).

——, *Lewis Carroll: A Biography* (London: Macmillan, 1995).

——, *Lewis Carroll: Photographer of Children: Four Nude Studies* (New York: Aperture, 1996).

——, *Reflections in a Looking Glass: A Centennial Celebration of Lewis Carroll, Photographer* (New York: Aperture, 1998).

——, and Anita Gandolfo, eds, *Lewis Carroll and the House of Macmillan* (Cambridge: Cambridge University Press, 1987).

Collier, John, and Malcolm Collier, *Visual Anthropology: Photography as a Research Method* (New Mexico: University of New Mexico Press, 1986).

Collingwood, Stuart Dodgson, ed., *The Lewis Carroll Picture Book* (London: Collins' Clear-Type Press, 1899).

Cooley, Charles Horton, *Human Nature and the Social Order* (New York: C. Scribner's Sons, 1902).

——, *Life and the Student* (New York: Alfred A Knopf, 1927).

Coward, H. and Foshay, T., eds, *Derrida and Negative Theology* (New York: University Press, 1992).

Cox, Brian, and Jeff Forshaw, *The Quantum Universe* (London: Penguin Books, 2011).

Crary, Jonathan, *Techniques of the Observer: On Vision and Modernity in the Nineteenth Century* (Cambridge, MA: MIT Press, 1991).

Darwin, Charles, *The Descent of Man and Selection in Relation to Sex* (New York: D. Appleton and Co., 1871).

De Bono, Edward, *Six Thinking Hats* (London: Penguin, 2016).

De Mauro, Tullio, *Ludwig Wittgenstein: His Place in the Development of Semantics* (Dordrecht: D. Reidel, 1967).

Defoe, Daniel, *A System of Magic; or, a History of the Black Art: Being an Historical Account of Mankind's Most Early Dealing with the Devil; and How the Acquaintance on Both Sides First Began* (Oxford: D. A. Talbots, 1840 [1727]).

Derrida, Jacques, *Copy, Archive, Signature: A Conversation on Photography*, English translation by Jeff Fort (Stanford: Stanford University Press, 2010).

——, *Of Grammatology*, English translation by Gayatri Chakravorty Spivak (Baltimore: Johns Hopkins University Press, 2016).

——, *The Animal That Therefore I Am*, English translation by David Wills, Marie-Louise Mallet., ed. (New York: Fordham University Press, 2008).

Donaldson, Julia, and Axel Scheffler, *Monkey Puzzle* (London: MacMillan Children's Books, 2020).

Dowling, Linda, *Language and Decadence in the Victorian Fin de Siècle* (Princeton: Princeton University Press, 1986).

Eno, Brian, and Peter Schmidt, *Oblique Strategies* (Self-published, 1975). Card deck.

Erikson, Erik H., *Identity, Youth, and Crisis: Youth and Crisis*, 2nd edn (New York: W. W. Norton, 1968).

Ernst, Bruno, *The Magic Mirror of M. C. Escher* (Cologne: Taschen, 2007).

Fallon, Richard, *Reimagining Dinosaurs in Late Victorian and Edwardian Literature* (Cambridge: Cambridge University Press, 2021).

Farrar, Frederic William, *An Essay on the Origin of Language, Based on Modern Researches* (London: J. Murray, 1860).

——, *Chapters on Language* (London: Longman, Green & Co., 1865).

Fludernik, Monika, ed., *Beyond Cognitive Metaphor Theory: Perspectives on Literary Metaphor* (Oxon: Routledge, 2011).

Flusser, Vilém, *Gestures* (Minneapolis, MN: University of Minnesota Press, 2014).

Fort, Ilene Susan, and Tere Arcq with Terri Geis, *In Wonderland: The Surrealist Adventures of Women Artists in Mexico and the United States* (Munich: DelMonico Books, 2012).

Foucault, Michel, *Discipline and Punish: The Birth of the Prison*, English translation by Alan Sheridan (New York: Vintage Books, 1993).

——, *Power/Knowledge*, English translation by Colin Gordon (New York: Pantheon, 1980).

Foulkes, Richard, *Lewis Carroll and the Victorian Stage: Theatricals in a Quiet Life* (Farnham: Ashgate, 2005/2017/2019).

Gableman, Josephine, *A Theology of Nonsense* (Eugene, OR: Pickwick Publications, 2016).

Gardner, Martin, ed., *The Annotated Alice* (London: Penguin, 1970).

——, *The Annotated Snark* (London: Penguin, 1962).

——, and Mark Burstein, *The Annotated Alice: The 150th Anniversary Deluxe Edition* (New York: W. W. Norton, 2015).

——, *The Annotated Alice: The Definitive Edition: Alice's Adventures in Wonderland and Through the Looking-Glass, and What Alice Found There* (London: Penguin, 2001).

Genette, Gérard, *Paratexts: Thresholds of Interpretation*, English translation by Jane E. Lewin (Cambridge: Cambridge University Press, 1997).

Godwin, Malcolm, *The Lucid Dreamer* (New York: Simon & Schuster, 1994).

Griffith, David L., *George MacDonald's Lilith A: A Transcription* (Blacksburg: Virginia Polytechnic Institute and State University, 2001). MA Thesis.

Guilford, Joy Paul, *The Nature of Human Intelligence* (New York: McGraw-Hill, 1967).

Guite, Malcolm, *Faith, Hope and Poetry* (Oxford: Ashgate, 2012).

Hadamard, Jacques S., *A Mathematician's Mind, Testimonial for An Essay on the Psychology of Invention in the Mathematical Field* (Princeton: Princeton University Press, 1945).

Halliwell, James Orchard, ed., *Popular Rhymes and Nursery Tales: A Sequel to the Nursery Rhymes of England* (London: John Russell Smith, 1849).

Hames, Peter, *Dark Alchemy: The Cinema of Švankmajer* (London: Wallflower Press, 1995).

Hancher, Michael, *The Tenniel Illustrations to the 'Alice' Books* (Columbus: Ohio State University Press, 1985).

Hanks, Patrick, *Lexical Analysis: Norms and Exploitations* (Cambridge, MA: MIT Press, 2013).

Hanson, Christopher, *Game Time: Understanding Temporality in Video Games* (Bloomington: Indiana University Press, 2018).

Haraway, Donna, *Simians, Cyborgs and Women: The Reinvention of Nature* (New York: Routledge, 1991).

Harkness, Deborah, *John Dee's Conversations with Angels: Cabala, Alchemy, and the End of Nature* (Cambridge: Cambridge University Press, 1999).

Harrison, Peter, *The Fall of Man and the Foundations of Science* (Cambridge: Cambridge University Press, 2007).

Hirshfield, Jane, *Ten Windows: How Great Poems Transform the World* (New York: Alfred A. Knopf, 2015).

Hovan, Marcie, *Happily Ever After? Ambiguous Closure in Modernist Children's Literature* (Pittsburgh: Duquesne University, 2016). PhD Thesis.

Hunt, Robert, *The Poetry of Science: Or the Studies of the Physical Phenomena of Nature* (Boston: Gould, Kendall, and Lincoln, 1850 [1848]).

Hutcheon, Linda, *A Theory of Adaptation* (Abingdon: Routledge, 2006).

Hutchings, David, and James Ungereanu, *Of Popes and Unicorns: Science, Christianity, and How the Conflict Thesis Fooled the World* (Oxford: Oxford University Press, 2021).

Jacob, François, *The Statue Within: An Autobiography* (New York: Cold Spring Harbor Laboratory Press, 1988).

Jacques, Zoe, *Children's Literature and the Posthuman* (New York: Routledge, 2015).

James, Henry, William Veeder, and Susan M. Griffin, eds, *The Art of Criticism: Henry James on the Theory and the Practice of Fiction* (Chicago: University of Chicago Press, 1986).

Jameson, Fredric, *The Prison-House of Language* (Princeton, NJ: Princeton University Press, 1975).

Jaques, Zoe, and Eugene Giddens, *Lewis Carroll's Alice's Adventures in Wonderland and Through the Looking-Glass: A Publishing History* (New York: Routledge, 2016).

Johnson, Steven, *Where Good Ideas Come From: The Seven Patterns of Innovation* (London: Penguin, 2010).

Jones, Bence, *The Life and Letters of Michael Faraday* (Philadelphia: J. B. Lippincott, 1870).

Julia Kuehn and Paul Smethurst, eds, *Travel Writing, Form, and Empire: The Poetics and Politics of Mobility* (Abingdon-on-Thames: Taylor & Francis, 2008).

Kaku, Michio, *Parallel Worlds: A Journey through Creation, Higher Dimensions, and the Future of the Cosmos* (New York: Doubleday, 2004).

Keene, Melanie, *Science in Wonderland* (Oxford: Oxford University Press, 2015).

Keller, James R., *V for Vendetta as Cultural Pastiche: A Critical Study of the Graphic Novel and Film* (London: McFarland, 2008).

Keller, Marjorie, *The Untutored Eye: Childhood in the Films of Cocteau, Cornell, and Brakhage* (Rutherford: Fairleigh Dickinson University Press, 1986).

Ketner, Joseph, *Andy Warhol* (London: Phaidon Focus, 2013).

Knoepflmacher, Ulrich, *Ventures into Childland: Victorians, Fairy Tales, and Femininity* (Chicago: University of Chicago Press, 1998).

Kohlt, Franziska E., 'More than a figment of scientific fancy': Dreams and Visions in Victorian Psychology and Fantastic Literature, 1858–1900* (University of Oxford, 2019). DPhil Thesis. <https://ora.ox.ac.uk/objects/uuid:48e38bf1-1092-451f-95f1-6b1c69b32e7a>.

Kuhn, Thomas, *The Structure of Scientific Revolutions* (Chicago: University of Chicago Press, 1966).

Lakoff, George and Mark Johnson, *Metaphors We Live by* (Chicago: University of Chicago Press, 1980).

Lastoria, Amanda, *The Material Evolution of Alice's Adventures in Wonderland: How Book Design and Production Values Impact the Markets for and the Meanings of the Text* (Burnaby: Simon Fraser University, 2019). PhD Thesis.

Lear, Edward, *Nonsense Botany and Nonsense Alphabets* (London: British Library Publishing, 2006).

Lecercle, Jean-Jacques, *Philosophy of Nonsense : The Intuitions of Victorian Nonsense Literature* (New York: Routledge, 1994).

Lee, Suzy, *Alice in Wonderland* (San Francisco: Last Gasp, 2003).

——, *Mirror* (New York: Seven Footer Press, 2010).

——, *The Border Trilogy* (Milan: Corraini, 2018).

Lewes, George Henry, *Problems of Life and Mind*, II (Boston: James R. Osgood, 1875).

Lewis, C. S., *The Last Battle* (New York: Macmillan, 1966).

Lightman, Bernard, *Victorian Popularizers of Science: Designing Nature for New Audiences* (Chicago: University of Chicago Press, 2007).

Lilly, William, *An Introduction to Astrology: With Numerous Emendations, Adapted to the Improved State of the Science in the Present Day: A Grammar of Astrology, and Tables for Calculating Nativities by Zadkiel* (London: Bell, 1878 [1647]).

Lin, Grace, *Where the Mountain Meets the Moon* (New York: Hachette, 2009).

Lindseth, Jon, Alan Tannenbaum, and Warren Weaver, *Alice in a World of Wonderlands: The Translations of Lewis Carroll's Masterpiece*, 3 vols (New Castle: Oak Knoll Press, 2015).

Louvel, Liliane, *Poetics of the Iconotext*, English translation by Laurence Petit (Farnham: Ashgate, 2011).

Lovett, Charles, *Alice on Stage* (Westport: Meckler, 1990).

——, *Lewis Carroll and the Press* (London: Oak Knoll Press, 1999).

——, *Lewis Carroll among His Books* (London: McFarland, 2005).

——, *Lewis Carroll: Formed by Faith* (University of Virginia Press, 2022).

Lubac, Henri de, *Paradoxes of Faith* (San Francisco: Ignatius Press, 1987).

MacDonald, George, *A Dish of Orts* (London: Sampson Low Marston & Company, 1893).

——, *Lilith* (Grand Rapids: William B. Eerdmans Publishing Company, 1981).

——, *Lilith: A Romance* (New York: Dodd, Mead and Company, 1895).

——, *The Poetical Works of George MacDonald* (Moscow: Dodo Press, 2007 [1919]).

——, *Unspoken Sermons* (London: Longmans, Green, 1987).

——, *Unspoken Sermons: Third Series* (London and New York: Longmans, Green, 1889).

Margoliouth, Herschel M., and Pierre Legouis, eds, *The Complete Poems of Andrew Marvell* (Oxford: Oxford University Press, 1971 [1681]).

Maurice, Frederick D., *The Friendship of Books* (London: MacMillan, 1874).

McCorristine, Shane, *Spectres of the Self: Thinking about Ghosts and Ghost-Seeing in England, 1750–1920* (Cambridge: Cambridge University Press, 2010).

McGrath, Alister, *The Dawkins Delusion?: Atheist Fundamentalism and the Denial of the Divine* (London: SPCK Publishing, 2007).

McGrath, Rita, *Seeing around Corners* (Boston: Houghton Mifflin Harcourt, 2019).

McHale, Brian, *The Cambridge Introduction to Postmodernism* (Cambridge: Cambridge University Press, 2015).

McLeish, Tom, *Faith and Wisdom in Science* (Oxford: Oxford University Press, 2014).

——, *The Poetry and Music of Science*, Rev. edn (Oxford: Oxford University Press, 2019).

Melchior-Bonnet, Sabine, *The Mirror: A History* (Oxon: Routledge, 1994).

Miller, Jonathan, *On Reflection* (London: National Gallery Publications Limited, 1998).

Mitchell, Kirsty, *Wonderland* (Surrey: Kirsty Mitchell Photography, 2016).

Moffett, Thomas, *The Silkewormes, and Their Flies* (London: Nicholas Ling, 1599).

Moore, Alan, and Melinda Gebbie, *Lost Girls* (Marietta, GA: Top Shelf Productions, 2006).

Moretti, Franco, *Distant Reading* (London: Verso, 2013).

——, *Graphs Maps Trees* (London: Verso, 2005).

Morris, Jeremy, *F.D. Maurice and the Crisis of Christian Authority* (Oxford: OUP, 2008).

Morris, Rosalind, ed., *Can the Subaltern Speak?* (New York: Columbia University Press, 2009).

Müller, Friedrich Max, *Lectures on the Science of Language* (London: Longman and Todd, 1866).

Nietzsche, Friedrich, *Thus Spoke Zarathustra*, English translation by Thomas Common (Ware: Wordsworth Editions Limited, 1997).

Nikolajeva, Maria, Power, *Voice, and Subjectivity in Literature for Young Readers* (New York: Routledge, 2010).

O'Connor, Ralph, *The Earth on Show: Fossils and the Poetics of Popular Science, 1802–1856* (Chicago: Chicago University Press, 2008).

Oppenheim, Janet, *The Other World: Spiritualism and Psychical Research in England 1850–1914* (Cambridge: Cambridge University Press, 1985).

Ortiz-Hartman, Kimberley, *Principles of Sociology: Societal Issues and Behavior* (New York: Salem Press, 2018).

Otto, Elizabeth, and Patrick Rössler, *Bauhaus Women: A Global Perspective* (London: Herbert Press, 2019).

Parker, John W., ed., *Essays and Reviews* (London: John W. Parker and Son, 1860).

Parker, Rozsika, and Griselda Pollock, *Old Mistresses: Women, Art and Ideology* (London: Pandora Press, 1981).

Paxman, Adam, *It Came from the Glass Curtain!* (Print-on-Demand: Independently Published via Amazon, 2021).

Peliano, Adriana, *Alice and the 7 Keys* (Kissimmee: Underline Publishing, 2021).

Piehler, Liana F., *Spatial Dynamics and Female Development in Victorian Art and Novels: Creating a Woman's Space* (New York: Peter Lang, 2003).

Poincaré, Henri, 'Mathematical Creation', in *The Foundations of Science*, English translation by George Bruce Halsted (Lancaster, PA: The Science Press, 1915).

Popper, Karl, *The Logic of Scientific Discovery* (London: Routledge, 2002 [1934]).

Potter, Jonathan, *Discourses of Vision in Nineteenth-Century Britain* (London: Palgrave Macmillan, 2018).

Pseudo-Dionysius, *Pseudo-Dionysius: The Complete Works*, Colm Luibhéid and Paul Rorem, eds (New York: Paulist Press, 1987).

Quist-Adade, Charles, *Symbolic Interactionism: The Basics* (Wilmington: Vernon Press, 2019).

Ray, Satyajit, ed., *The Select Nonsense of Sukumar Ray*, English translation by Sukanta Chaudhuri (Oxford: Oxford University Press, 1997).

Rees, Rosemary, *A. Longman History Studies in Depth: Britain 1815–1851* (London: Longman, 1998).

Reichertz, Ronald, *The Making of the Alice Books: Lewis Carroll's Uses of Earlier Children's Literature* (Ithaca: McGill-Queen's University Press, 1997).

Reynolds, Kimberley, *Radical Children's Literature: Future Visions and Aesthetic* (London: Palgrave Macmillan, 2007).

Robinson, David, Stephen Herbert, and Richard Crangle, eds, *Encyclopaedia of the Magic Lantern* (London: Magic Lantern Society, 2001).

Robson, Robert, *Ideas and Institutions of Victorian Britain* (London: G. Bell and Sons, 1967).

Rose, Gillian, *Visual Methodologies: An Introduction to the Interpretations of Visual Materials* (London: SAGE Publications, 2012).

Rose, Jacqueline, *The Case of Peter Pan, or the Impossibility of Children's Fiction* (London: Macmillan, 1994).

Saussure, Ferdinand de, *Course in General Linguistics* (Chicago: Open Court, 1995).

Schwab, Gabriele, *The Mirror and the Killer-Queen: Otherness in Literary Language* (Bloomington: Indiana University Press, 1996).

Shulz, Christopher, and Gavin Delahunty, *Alice in Wonderland through the Visual Arts* (London: Tate, 2011). Exhibition Catalogue.

Shuttleworth, Sally, and Geoffrey Cantor, eds, *Science Serialised* (Cambridge, MA: MIT Press, 2004).

Simmons, John, *Rossetti's Wombat: Pre-raphaelites and Australian Animals in Victorian London* (London: Middlesex University Press, 2008).

——, *The Tiger That Swallowed the Boy: Exotic Animals in Victorian England* (Faringdon: Libri Publishing, 2012).

Sliwinska, Basia, *The Female Body in the Looking Glass: Contemporary Art, Aesthetics and Genderland* (London: I. B. Tauris, 2016).

Smith, Lindsay, *Lewis Carroll: Photography on the Move* (Islington: Reaktion Books, 2016).

Stein, Gertrude, *Picasso* (New York: Dover Publications, 1984).

——, *The Gertrude Stein First Reader and Three Plays* (Boston: Houghton, 1948).

——, *The World is Round* (New York: Harper Design, 2013).

——, *To Do: A Book of Alphabets and Birthdays* (New Haven: Yale University Press, 2011).

Stern, Jeffrey, *Lewis Carroll's Library: A Facsimile Edition of the Catalogue of the Auction Sale Following C. L. Dodgson's Death in 1898, with Facsimiles of Three Subsequent Bookseller's Catalogues Offering Books from Dodgson's Library* (New York: Lewis Carroll Society of North America, 1981).

Stewart, Susan, *On Longing: Narratives of the Miniature, the Gigantic, the Souvenir, the Collection* (Durham: Duke University Press, 1993).

Sundmark, Björn, *Alice in the Oral-Literary Continuum* (Lund: Lund University Press, 1999).

Susina, Jan, *The Place of Lewis Carroll in Children's Literature* (New York: Routledge, 2010).

Sutherland, Robert D., *Language and Lewis Carroll* (Paris: Mouton, 1970).

Talairach-Vielmas, Laurence, *Animals, Museum Culture and Children's Literature in Nineteenth-Century Britain: Curious Beasties* (London: Palgrave Macmillan, 2021).

——, *Fairy Tales, Natural History and Victorian Culture* (Basingstoke and New York: Palgrave Macmillan, 2014).

Tennyson, Alfred, and Christopher Ricks, eds, *A Selected Edition* (New York: Routledge, 2014).

Thornton, Sarah, *33 Artists in 3 Acts* (New York: W. W. Norton, 2013).

Tigges, Wim, *An Anatomy of Literary Nonsense* (Amsterdam: Rodopi, 1988).

Trench, Richard Chenevix, *On the Study of Words* (London: Macmillan, 1874).

Turner, Frank Miller, *The Greek heritage in Victorian Britain* (New Haven, CT: Yale University Press, 1981).

Turner, Victor, *The Ritual Process: Structure and Anti-structure* (Chicago: Aldine Publishing, 1969).

Ungureanu, *James, Science, Religion, and the Protestant Tradition: Retracing the Origins of Conflict* (Pittsburgh: University of Pittsburgh Press, 2019).

Vacklavik, Kiera, *Fashioning Alice: The Career of Lewis Carroll's Icon, 1860–1901* (London: Bloomsbury, 2018).

VanderMeer, Jeff, *Acceptance* (London: Fourth Estate, 2015).

Wakeling, Edward, *Lewis Carroll, Photographer* (Oxford: Oxford University Press, 2002).

——, *Lewis Carroll: The Man and His Circle* (London: I. B. Tauris, 2015).

——, *Lewis Carroll, William Allingham and Their Friends* (Oxford: Oxford University Press, 1991).

——, *The Lewis Carroll Handbook* (Oxford: Oxford University Press, 1979).

——, and August A. Imholtz, Jr, *Lewis Carroll's Alice: An Annotated Checklist of the Lovett Collection, 1965–2005* (Oxford: Oxford University Press, 2006).

Wakely-Mulroney, Katherine and Louise Joy, *The Aesthetics of Children's Poetry: A Study of Children's Verse in English* (Abingdon: Routledge, 2017), 74–93.

Warren-Crow, Heather, *Girlhood and the Plastic Image* (Hanover: Dartmouth College Press, 2014).

Weaver, Warren, *Alice in Many Tongues: The Translations of Alice in Wonderland* (Madison: University of Wisconsin Press, 1964).

White, Laura, *The Alice Books and the Contested Ground of the Natural World* (Abingdon: Routledge, 2017).

Willis, Martin, *Vision, Science and Literature, 1870–1920: Ocular Horizons* (Abingdon: Routledge, 2011).

Winter, Alison, *Mesmerized: Powers of Mind in Victorian Britain* (Chicago: University of Chicago Press, 1998).

Wittgenstein, Ludwig, *Philosophische Untersuchungen/Philosophical Investigations*, English translation by G. E. M. Anscombe, P. M. S. Hacker, and Joachim Schulte, 4th edn (Oxford: Blackwell Publishing, 2009).

Woolf, Virginia, *Nurse Lugton's Curtain* (London: Harcourt Brace Jovanovich, 1991).

——, *The Widow and the Parrot* (London: Harcourt Brace Jovanovich, 1988).

——, and Quentin Bell, eds, *Quentin, Charleston Bulletin Supplements* (London: The British Library, 2013).

Wright, Thomas, *Narratives of Sorcery and Magic, from the Most Authentic Sources*, 2 vols (London: Richard Bentley, 1851).

Yaguello, Marina, *Language through the Looking Glass: Exploring Language and Linguistics* (Oxford: Oxford University Press, 1998).

Yates, Frances A., *The Art of Memory* (Harmondsworth: Penguin, 1969 [1966]).

——, *The Rosicrucian Enlightenment* (London: Routledge, 2008 [1972]).

Articles in Journals and Book Chapters

Apter, Emily, 'Untranslatables: A World-System', *Against World Literature: On the Politics of Untranslatability*, 39 (2008), 581–598.

Arnavas, Francesca, 'Alice in the Glassworld: Carroll's Unconventional Heroine Escaping the Frame', *The Carrollian*, 35–36 (2021), 102–112.

——, 'Come into the Garden Alice: Rude Flowers, Dream-Rushes, Aphasic Woods and Other Plants in Lewis Carroll's Nonsense Worlds', in Melanie Duckworth and Lykke Guanaio-Uluru, eds, *Plants in Children and YA Literature* (Oxon: Routledge, 2021), 59–73.

Brandt, Per Aage, 'Curiouser and Curiouser – A Brief Analysis of Alice's Adventures in Wonderland', in Rachel Fordyce and Carla Marello, eds, *Semiotics and Linguistics in Alice's Worlds* (Berlin: De Gruyter, 1994), 26–33.

Bravo, Eduardo, 'Benjamin Lacombe ilustración para aprender a ser adultos', *Visual: magazine de diseño, creatividad gráfica y comunicación*, 25 January 2018. <visual.gi/benjamin-lacombe-ilustracion-para-aprender-a-ser-adultos/>, accessed 12 April 2022.

Brown, Celia, 'Paranormale Phänomene und Dees Spiegel' and 'Kausalität von Socrates bis Bacon', in Celia Brown, ed., *Alice hinter den Mythen: Der Sinn in Carrolls Nonsens* (Paderborn: Fink, 2015), 75–89.

Brown, Melissa Shani, and Jude Roberts, ' "Orgies in the Garden of Heaven": The Pornographic Playground of Alan Moore and Melinda Gebbie's Lost Girls', *Culture, Theory and Critique*, 62/3 (2021), 223–248.

Burstein, Mark, 'To Catch a Bandersnatch', *The Lewis Carroll Society of North America* (1970/2004),<https://www.lewiscarroll.org/wp-content/uploads/2010/03/ToCatchaBandersnatch.pdf>, accessed 1 October 2022.

Burstein, Sandor, 'The Alice in Wonderland Syndrome, an Update', *Jabberwocky, the Journal of the Lewis Carroll Society*, 27 (1994), 23–31.

Campbell, Stuart, Elizabeth Healey, Yaroslav Kuzmin, and Michael D. Glascock, 'The Mirror, the Magus and More: Reflections on John Dee's Obsidian Mirror', *Antiquity: A Review of World Archaeology*, 95/384 (2021), 1–18.

Carroll, Lewis, 'An Easter Greeting to Every Child Who Loves "Alice"', in *Through the Looking-Glass* (London: Macmillan, 1976).

——, 'Bruno's Revenge', *Aunt Judy's May-Day Volume for Young People* (1868), 56–68.

——, 'Some Popular Fallacies about Vivisection', *Fortnightly Review*, 23 (1 June 1875).

Cass, Richard, 'Which Came First: The Siege Gun or the Egg? Notes on the Career of Humpty Dumpty', *The Carrollian*, 35–36 (2021), 55–64.

Chaparro Martinez, Alba, 'Translating the Untranslatable: Carroll, Carner and Alícia en Terra Catalana?', *Journal of Iberian and Latin American Studies*, 6/1 (2000), 19–28.

Conger, Rand D., and M. Brent Donnellan, 'An Interactionist Perspective on the Socioeconomic Context of Human Development', *Annual Review of Psychology*, 58/1 (2007), 175–199.

Dawson, Gowan, 'Science and its Popularisation', *The Cambridge Companion to English Literature, 1830–1914* (Cambridge: Cambridge University Press, 2010).

de Rijke, Victoria, 'Modernist and Avant-Garde Children's Books', *Revista de Letras Norte@mentos*, 13 (2020), 197–217.

Demo, David, 'Self-Esteem of Children and Adolescents', in Timothy Owens, Sheldon Stryker, and Norman Goodman, eds, *Extending Self-Esteem Theory and Research Sociological and Psychological Currents* (Cambridge: The Press Syndicate of the University, 2001), 135–156.

Derfus, Pamela, Patrick Maggitti, Curtis Grimm, and Ken Smith, 'The Red Queen Effect: Competitive Actions and Firm Performance', *The Academy of Management Journal*, 51/1 (2008), 61–80.

Diamond, Hugh Welch, 'On the Application of Photography to the Physiognomic and Mental Phenomena of Insanity', in Sander Gilman, ed., *Face of Madness* (New York: Brunner/Mazel, 1976).

Dupee, F. W., 'General Introduction', in Gertrude Stein, ed., *Selected Writings of Gertrude Stein* (New York: Vintage Books, 1990), ix–xvii.

Evangelia, Moula, 'Graphic Novels as Self-Conscious Contemplative Metatexts: Redefining Comics and Participating in Theoretical Discourse', *Journal of Literature and Art Studies*, 8/2 (2018), 181–189.

Foucault, Michel, 'Dream, Imagination and Existence', in Keith Hoeller, ed., English translation by Forrest Williams, *Dream and Existence, Review of Existential Psychological & Psychiatry*, 19 (1986), 29–78.

Freud, Sigmund, 'On Narcisism: An Introduction', in James Strachey, ed., *The Standard Edition of the Complete Psychological Works of Sigmund Freud*, vol. 14 (1914), 67–102.

——, 'The Interpretation of Dreams (Second Part) and On Dreams', in James Strachey, ed., *The Standard Edition of the Complete Psychological Works of Sigmund Freud*, vol. V (1900–1901), 629–686.

Fyfe, Aileen, 'Reading Children's Books in Late Eighteenth-Century Dissenting Families', *The Historical Journal*, 43/2 (2000), 453–473.

Gerlach, Eric, 'Aristotle's Categories & the Order of Wonderland', *Knight Letter*, 3/4/104 (2020), 15–20.

Goethe, Johann Wolfgang, 'Goethe on Morphology', in Erich Trunz, ed., *Hamburger Ausgabe: Werke Hamburger Ausgabe in 14 Bänden* (Hamburg: Chr. Wegner, 1948–1960; Reprinted, C. H. Beck, 1981).

Goodman, Lizbeth, 'Literature and Gender', in Lizbeth Goodman, ed., *Literature and Gender* (New York: Routledge, 1996), 1–41.

Gourlay, Lesley, 'Threshold Practices: Becoming a Student through Academic Literacies', *London Review of Education*, 7/2 (2009), 181–192.

Grenby, M. O., 'The Origins of Children's Literature', in M. O. Greby and Andrea Immel, eds, *The Cambridge Companion to Children's Literature* (New York: Cambridge University Press, 2009).

Grice, Paul, 'Logic and Conversation', in Paul Grice, ed., *Studies in the Way of Words* (Cambridge, MA: Harvard University Press, 1989), 22–41.

Hacht, Anne Marie, 'Major Works', in Anne Marie Hacht and Margaret Brantley, eds, *Literary Themes for Students: The American Dream* (Detroit: Gale, 2007), 453–466.

Hancher, Michael, 'Humpty Dumpty and Verbal Meaning', *The Journal of Aesthetics and Art Criticism*, 40/1 (1981), 49–58.

Hanich, Julian, 'Reflecting on Reflections: Cinema's Complex Mirror Shots', in Martine Beugnet, Allan Cameron and Arild Fetveit, eds, *Indefinite Visions: Cinema and the Attractions of Uncertainty* (Edinburgh: Edinburgh University Press, 2017), 131–156.

Holquist, Michael, 'What Is Boojum? Nonsense and Modernism', *Yale French Studies*, 43 (1999), 100–117.

Huber, Irmtraud, 'Another Poetry of Science: Tom McLeish (2019) in Comparison with Robert Hunt (1848)', *Interdisciplinary Science Reviews*, 45/1 (2020), 23–29.

Hunt, Peter, 'Introduction', in *Alice's Adventures in Wonderland and through the Looking-Glass and What Alice Found There* (New York: Oxford University Press, 2009), vi–xliii.

Kérchy, Anna, 'Picturebooks Challenging Sexual Politics: Pro-porn Feminist Comics and the Case of Melinda Gebbie and Alan Moore's "Lost Girls"', *Hungarian Journal of English and American Studies*, 20/2 (2014), 121–142.

Kincaid, James R., 'Alice's Invasion of Wonderland', *PMLA*, 88 (1973), 92–99.

Kind, Amy L., 'Wittgenstein, Lewis Carroll and the Philosophical Puzzlement of Language', *Episteme*, 1 (1990), 33–42.

Kingsley, Charles, 'The Study of Natural History', in *Scientific Lectures and Essays* (London: Macmillan, 1890), 181–182.

Kohlt, Franziska E., '"The Stupidest Tea-Party in All My Life": Lewis Carroll and Victorian Psychiatric Practice', *Journal of Victorian Culture*, 21/2 (2016), 147–167.

Koustinoudi, Anna. '"In Friendly Chat with Bird or Beast ... Mixing Together Things Grave and Gay": Desireful Animals and Humans in Alice's Adventures in Wonderland and Through the Looking Glass', in Brenda Ayres and Sarah Elizabeth Maier, eds, *Animals and their Children in Victorian Culture*, (London: Routledge, 2020), 50–65.

Lakoff, Robin Tolmach, 'Lewis Carroll: Subversive Pragmatist', *Pragmatics*, 3/4 (1993), 367–385.

Lastoria, Amanda. 'Lewis Carroll, Art Director: Recovering the Design and Production Rationales for Victorian Editions of Alice's Adventures in Wonderland', *Book History*, 22/1 (2019), 196–225.

Larner, Andrew, 'The neurology of "Alice"', *Advances in Clinical Neuroscience & Rehabilitation*, 4/6 (2005), 35–36.

Lecercle, Jean-Jacques, 'Nonsense and Politics' in Elisabetta Tarantino and Carlo Caruso, eds, *Nonsense and Other Senses* (Newcastle: Cambridge Scholars Publishing, 2009), 357–380.

——, 'The Pragmatics of Nonsense', in Jean-Jacques Lecercle, ed., *Philosophy of Nonsense: The Intuitions of Victorian Nonsense Literature* (London: Routledge, 1994), 69–111.

Leitch, Thomas, 'Adaptation and Intertextuality, or, What Isn't an Adaptation, and What Does It Matter?', in Deborah Cartmell, ed., *A Companion to Literature, Film, and Adaptation* (Oxford: Wiley-Blackwell, 2012), 87–104.

——, 'Mind the Gap', in Julie Grossman and R. Barton Palmer, eds, *Adaptation in Visual Culture: Images, Texts, and Their Multiple Worlds* (London: Palgrave Macmillan, 2017), 53–72.

Lilienfeld, Scott, and Hal Arkowitz, 'Are All Psychotherapies Created Equal?', *Scientific American Mind*, 23/4 (2012), 68–69.

Lindseth, Jon, 'A Note on Savile Clarke's Alice in Wonderland: A Dream Play for Children, Including a Newly Identified Third Edition', *The Carrollian*, 22 (2008), 25–30.

Lippman, Caro, 'Certain Hallucinations Peculiar to Migraine', *Journal of Nervous and Mental Disease*, 116 (1952), 346–351.

Lopez Guix, Juan Gabriel, 'The Translator in Aliceland: On Translating Alice in Wonderland into Spanish', in Susan Bassnett and Peter Bush, eds, *The Translator as Writer* (New York: Continuum, 2006).

Lovell-Smith, Rose, 'Eggs and Serpents: Natural History Reference in Lewis Carroll's Scene of Alice and the Pigeon', *Children's Literature*, 35 (2007), 27–53.

——, 'The Animals of Wonderland: Tenniel as Carroll's Reader', *Criticism*, 45/4 (2003), 383–415.

MacDonald, George, 'The Imagination, Its Function and Its Culture' [1893], in *A Dish of Orts* (Lexington: Editora Griffo, 2015), 6–182.

——, 'The Mirrors of the Lord', *Unspoken Sermons: Series I, II, and III*, Project Gutenberg <http://www.gutenberg.org/cache/epub/9057/pg9057-images.html>, accessed 20 November 2022.

Maslow, Abraham H., 'Theory of Human Motivation', *Psychological Review*, 50 (1943), 370–396.

Mayer, Jed, '"Come Buy, Come Buy": Christina Rossetti and the Victorian Animal Market', in Laurence W. Mazzeno and Ronald D. Morrison, eds, *Animals in Victorian Literature and Culture: Contexts for Criticisms* (London: Palgrave Macmillan, 2017), 213–231.

——, 'The Vivisection of the Snark', *Victorian Poetry* 47/2 (2009), 429–448.

McLeish, Tom, 'Emotion and Reason in Scientific Creation', in *The Poetry and Music of Science: Comparing Creativity in Science and Art* (Oxford: Oxford University Press, 2022).

Millán-Varela, María del Carmen, '(G)Alicia in Wonderland: Some Insights', *Fragmentos*, 16 (1999), 97–117.

Moretti, Franco, 'Conjectures on World Literature', *New Left Review*, 1 (2000), 54–68.

Morris, Jeremy, 'The Text as Sacrament: Victorian Broad Church Philology', *Studies in Church History*, 38, 365–374.

Müller, Friedrich Max, 'Comparative Philology', *Edinburgh Review*, 94 (1851).

Myrone, Martin, 'Prudery, Pornography, and the Victorian Nude (Or, What Do We Think the Butler Saw?)', in Alison Smith, ed., *Exposed: The Victorian Nude* (New York: Watson-Guptill Publications, 2001), 23–35.

Paxman, Adam, 'Separating the Rainbow's Egg: Reflection on a Practice-as-Research Investigation Illustrating Themes in George MacDonald's Fairy Tales', *North Wind*, 37 (2018), 56–97.

——, 'The Abandoned Storybook illustration 1', *Burning Zebra* (2013), <https://burning-zebra.blogspot.com/>, accessed 19 October 2022.

Pitcher, George, 'Wittgenstein, Nonsense, and Lewis Carroll', *The Massachusetts Review*, 6/3 (1965), 591–611.

Polhemus, Robert M., 'Lewis Carroll and the Child in Victorian Fiction', in John Richetti, ed., *The Columbia History of the British Novel* (New York: Columbia University Press, 1994), 579–607.

Poon, Wilson C. K., 'The wound of knowledge: R. S. Thomas' Cruciform Poetics of Science and Religion', in Michael Fuller, ed., *Science and Religion in Western Literature: Critical and Theological Studies* (Abingdon: Routledge, 2022).

Prickett, Stephen, 'F. D. Maurice: The Man Who Re-wrote the Book' (Presidential Address given at the 2002 Annual General Meeting of the MacDonald Society), *North Wind*, 21 (2002), 1–14.

Rhys Morus, Iwan, 'Seeing and Believing Science', *Isis*, 97/1 (2006), 101–110.

Richards, Catherine, 'Blue-Bell in Fairyland: An Alice Imitation', *Knight Letter*, 105/3/5 (2020), 24–30.

——, 'What Is Missing from Henry Savile Clarke's Musical Dream-play, Alice in Wonderland', *Theatre Notebook*, 76/3 (2022), 154–173.

Richards, Mark, 'Charles Dodgson's Work for God', in Snezana Lawrence and Mark McCarthy, eds, *Mathematicians and their Gods: Interactions between Mathematics and Religious Beliefs* (Oxford: Oxford University Press, 2015).

Rivero, Silvia, 'Representations in Linguistics and Literature: An Analysis of Ferdinand de Saussure's and Lewis Carroll's Construction of the Object Language', *Invenio*, 13/24 (2010), 13–26.

Schmahmann, Brenda, 'Introduction', in Brenda Schmahmann, ed., *Iconic Works of Art by Feminists and Gender Activists* (New York: Routledge, 2021), 1–20.

Secord, James, 'Newton in the Nursery: Tom Telescope and the Philosophy of Tops and Balls, 1761–1838', *History of Science*, 23/2 (1985), 127–151.

Sewell, Elizabeth, 'Is Flannery O'Connor a Nonsense Writer?' in Wim Tigges, ed., *Explorations in the Field of Nonsense* (Amsterdam: Rodopi, 1987), 183–214.

Shi, Flair Donglai, 'Alice's Adventures in Wonderland as an Anti-feminist Text: Historical, Psychoanalytical and Postcolonial Perspectives', *Women: A Cultural Review*, 27 (2016), 177–201.

Shires, Linda M., 'Fantasy, Nonsense, Parody, and the Status of the Real: The Example of Carroll', *Victorian Poetry*, 26 (1988), 267–283.

Shuttleworth, Sally, 'Spiritual Pathology: Priests, Physicians, and *The Way of All Flesh*', *Victorian Studies*, 54/4 (2012), 625–653.

Siljanovska, Liljana, and Stefani Stojcevska, 'A Critical Analysis of Interpersonal Communication in Modern Times of the Concept "Looking-Glass Self (1902)" by Charles Horton Cooley', *SEEU Review*, 13 (2018), 62–74.

Smith, Roger, 'The Physiology of the Will: Mind, Body and Psychology in the Periodical Literature, 1855–1875', in Geoffrey Cantor and Sally Shuttleworth, eds,

Science Serialised: Representations of the Sciences in Nineteenth Century Periodicals (Cambridge, MA: MIT Press, 2004).

Spector, Jill, 'Sculpture in Around: A Believe In', in Diana Thater, ed., *Drawling, Stretching and Fainting in Coils* (Munich: Bayerische Staatsoper, 2007), 38–40.

Stone, Olive M., 'The Status of Women in Great Britain', *The American Journal of Comparative Law*, 20/4 (1972), 592–621.

Stonebanks, Christopher, and Melanie Stonebanks, 'Religious Identity in the Classroom and the Looking-Glass Self', *Counterpoints* (2010), 229–241.

Sundmark, Björn, 'Some Uffish Thoughts on the Swedish Translations of "Jabberwocky"', *European Journal of Humour*, 5/3 (2017), 43–56.

Tannir, Sophia, Mike Dupin, Manila Austin, and Christina Stahlkopf, 'From Captive to Captivating: The New Customer Journey Model for Companies', *Applied Marketing Analytics*, 7 (2022), 4–18.

Thater, Diana, 'Off with Their Heads!', in Diana Thater, ed., *Drawling, Stretching and Fainting in Coils* (Munich: Bayerische Staatsoper, 2007), 78–81.

Todd, John, 'The Syndrome of Alice in Wonderland', *Canadian Medical Association Journal*, 73 (1955), 701–704.

Topham, Jonathan, 'Publishing "Popular Science" in Early Nineteenth-Century Britain', in Bernard Lightman and Aileen Fyfe, eds, *Science in the Marketplace: Nineteenth-Century Sites and Experiences* (Chicago: University of Chicago Press, 2007), 135–168.

——, 'Periodicals and the Making of Reading Audiences for Science in Early Nineteenth-Century Britain: The Youth's Magazine', 1828–1837, in Louise Henson, Geoffrey Cantor, Gowan Dawson, Richard Noakes, Sally Shuttleworth, Jonathan R. Topham, eds, *Culture and Science in the Nineteenth-Century Media* (Oxford: Routledge, 2004).

Turing, Alan, 'Intelligent Machinery, a Heretical Theory', *Turing Archive* (2012), <https://rauterberg.employee.id.tue.nl/lecturenotes/DDM110%20CAS/Turing/Turing-1951%20Intelligent%20Machinery-a%20Heretical%20Theory.pdf>, accessed 1 May 2022.

Turner, Beatrice, '"Which is to be Master?": Language as Power in Alice in Wonderland and Through the Looking Glass', *Children's Literature Association Quarterly*, 35 (2010), 243–254.

Vande Kemp, Hendrika, 'The Dream in Periodical Literature', *Journal of the History of the Behavioural Sciences*, 17 (1981), 88–113.

Wade, Nicholas J., 'Toying with Science', *Perception*, 33 (2004), 1025–1032.

Walker, Adam, 'Objects of Nonsense, Anarchy, and Order: Romantic Theology in Lewis Carroll's and George MacDonald's Nonsense Literature', *North Wind*, 37 (2018), 11–27.

Weaver, Sarah, 'Philology and the Metaphors of Language', *Literature Compass*, 12/ 7 (2015), 333–343.

Weaver, Warren, 'The Mathematical Manuscripts of Lewis Carroll', *American Philosophy Society*, 98/5 (1954), 337–381.

Weber, Dawson, 'Well! I've Often Seen a Cat without a Grin, But a Grin without a Cat! It's the Most Curious Thing I Ever Saw', in Diana Thater, ed., *Drawling, Stretching and Fainting in Coils* (Munich: Bayerische Staatsoper, 2007), 46–49.

Williams, James A., 'Lewis Carroll and the Private Life of Words', *The Review of English Studies, New Series*, 64/266 (2012), 651–671.

Woitkowski, Felix, and Murat Recai Sezi, 'The Technologized Creation: The Mythological Foundation of Posthumanism in EX MACHINA', *Zeitschrift für Fantastikforschung*, 7/2 (2020), <https://zff.openlibhums.org/article/id/2888/>, accessed 21 January 2023.

Woolf, Virginia, 'Lewis Carroll', *The Moment and Other Essays* (2015), <https:// gutenberg.net.au/ebooks15/1500221h.html>, accessed 10 April 2022.

Wulfman, Clifford, 'The Plot of the Plot', *The Journal of Modern Periodical Studies*, 5/1 (2014), 94–109.

Yanai, Itai, and Martin Lercher, 'The Two Languages of Science', *Genome Biology*, 21 (2020), 147.

Letters, Diaries, Reminiscences, Poems and Scores

Abele, Francine F., ed., *The Political Pamphlets and Letters of Charles Lutwidge Dodgson* (Charlottesville: Virginia Press, 2001).

Anon, *Penny Illustrated*, 29 December 1900, 3.

——, *St Nicholas*, January 1888, 186.

——, *The Court Circular*, 1 January 1887, 5–6.

——, *The Dundee Courier*, 29 March 1910, 7.

——, *The Evening Standard* [London], 21 December 1906, 8.

——, *The Kent and Sussex Courier*, 1 January 1926, 11.

——, *The Manchester Courier and Lancashire General Advertiser*, 16 December 1915, 4.

——, *The Morning Post*, 28 December 1898, 6.

——, *The Stage*, 11 April 1929, 6.

——, *The Stage*, 30 December 1915, 25.

——, *The Times*, 20 December 1900, 4.

——, *The Worcester Chronicle*, 7 May 1887, 4.

——, *Truth*, 26 December 1906, 22–23.

Butler, Samuel, 'Hudibras Part II, Canto III' [1684], *All Poetry* (Undated), <https://allpoetry.com/Hudibras:-Part-2---Canto-III>, accessed 28 April 2022.

Cavendish, Margaret, 'A World Made by Atomes' [1653], *Emory Women Writers' Project* (2016), <http://womenwriters.digitalscholarship.emory.edu/toc.php?id=atomic>, accessed 18 February 2021.

Cohen, Morton N., and Roger Lancelyn Green, eds, *The Letters of Lewis Carroll*, 2 vols (London: Macmillan, 1979).

Collingwood, Stuart Dodgson, ed., *The Life and Letters of Lewis Carroll* (London: Fisher Unwin, 1898; reprinted New York: Century, 1967).

Green, Roger Lancelyn, ed. *The Diaries of Lewis Carroll*, vol. 1 (London: Cassell, 1953).

MacDonald, George, *Lilith B*, MSS 46187 B (London: The British Library, 1895(?)).

Royal Court Theatre Souvenir, *Alice in Wonderland* (London: Christmas, 1909), 9.

Savile Clarke, Henry, *Alice in Wonderland*, 1st edn (London: Court Circular Office, 1886). Libretto.

——, *Alice in Wonderland*, 2nd edn, believed printed 18 January 1887 (London: Court Circular Office, 1886). Libretto.

——, *Alice in Wonderland*, 3rd edn, believed printed 25 January 1887 and reprinted subsequently (London: Court Circular Office, 1886). Libretto.

——, *Alice in Wonderland*, 4th edn (London: Court Circular Office, 1888). Libretto.

——, and Walter Slaughter, *Alice in Wonderland a Dream Play for Children* (London [1898]). Song words only.

The Letters of Charles Lutwidge Dodgson to Henry Savile Clarke. Manuscript letters of Alfred C. Berol Collection, New York University.

Wakeling, Edward, ed., *Lewis Carroll's Diaries* (Herefordshire: The Lewis Carroll Society, 1993–2008).

Newspaper Articles, Reviews, Interviews, and Blog Posts

Butsova, Hilda, 'Interview', in *Oral History Archive, Dance Collection* (New York Public Library, recorded 5 July 1975), 25–26.

Coates, Nick, 'Through the Emotion Looking-Glass', *LinkedIn* (2020), <www.linkedin.com/pulse/through-emotion-looking-glass-dr-nick-coates>, accessed 29 April 2022.

Connealy, Leigh Erin, 'The Mad Hatter Syndrome: Mercury and Biological Toxicity', *Natural News* (2006), <http://www.naturalnews.com/amalgams.html>, accessed 12 April 2016.

Danesi, Marcel, 'The Doublet Puzzle: A Masterpiece from the Pen of Lewis Carroll', psychologytoday.com, 17 August 2009. <https://www.psychologytoday.com/us/blog/brain-workout/200908/the-doublet-puzzle-masterpiece-the-pen-lewis-carroll>, accessed 20 May 2022.

Dickinson, Peter, 'A Defence of Rubbish', *Peter Dickinson Books* (2018), <https://www.peterdickinson.com/defenseofrubbish>, accessed 10 May 2022.

'Fractal foundation', <https://fractalfoundation.org>, accessed 15 February 2021.

Gopnik, Adam, 'Understanding Steinese', *The New Yorker* (2013). <https://www.newyorker.com/books/page-turner/understanding-steinese>, accessed 13 December 2021.

Grumbine, Robert, 'Science Jabberwocky', *More Grumbine Science* (2009), <http://moregrumbinescience.blogspot.com/2009/08/science-jabberwocky.html>, accessed 27 November 2022.

Gubar, Susan, 'The Jabberwocky in a Cancer Lab', *The New York Times* (2018), <https://www.nytimes.com/2018/05/17/well/live/the-jabberwocky-in-a-cancer-lab.html>, accessed 17 October 2022.

Iker, Gil, 'Making Visible the Invisible: Iker Gil Interviews George Legrady', *MAS Context: Journal of Architecture*, 7 (2010), <https://mascontext.com/issues/information/making-visible-the-invisible>, accessed 20 October 2021.

Lupi, Giorgia, 'Data Humanism, the Revolution Will Be Visualized', *Print* (2017), <https://www.printmag.com/article/data-humanism-future-of-data-visualization/>, accessed 30 October 2021.

Mitchell, Kirsty, 'The Story Behind Wonderland', *Kirsty Mitchell Photography* (2018), <www.kirstymitchellphotography.com/galleries/wonderland/the-story-behind-wonderland/>, accessed 12 April 2022.

Overbye, Dennis, 'John A. Wheeler, Physicist Who Coined the Term "Black Hole," Is Dead at 96', 14 April 2008. <https://www.nytimes.com/2008/04/14/science/14wheeler.html>, accessed 20 May 2022.

Schulz, Kathryn, 'What Is Distant Reading?', *The New York Times* (2011), <https://www.nytimes.com/2011/06/26/books/review/the-mechanic-muse-what-is-distant-reading.html>, accessed 15 October 2021.

Schwarzbach, F. S., 'The Lady of Shalott in the Victorian Novel (review)', *The Henry James Review*, 7/1 (1985), 51–52.

Tantimedh, Adi, 'Finding the "Lost Girls" with Alan Moore', *Comic Book Resources* (2006), <https://www.cbr.com/finding-the-lost-girls-with-alan-moore-part-1-of-3/>, accessed 19 April 2022.

Wakely-Mulroney, Katherine, 'Reflections and Transparencies: Through the Looking-Glass and *Sylvie and Bruno*', *Through the Looking-Glass: A Sesquicentenary Conference*, 4 November 2021, <https://throughthelookingglasssesq uicentenary.wordpress.com/video-talks/>.

Encyclopaedia, Dictionary, References Book, and Database Entries

'Charles Horton Cooley', *American Sociological Association* (2021), <https://www. asanet.org/about/governance-and-leadership/council/presidents/charles-h-cooley>, accessed 14 January 2022.
Hanks, William, 'Deixis', in David Herman, Manfred Jahn, and Marie-Laure Ryan, eds, *The Routledge Encyclopedia of Narrative Theory* (Oxon: Routledge), 99–100.
'Savile Clarke Alice Productions', *Lewis Carroll Resources* (2022), <https://lewisc arrollresources.net/savileclarke/index.html>, accessed 21 October 2022.

Films and Video Material

Feynman, Richard, 'Nobel Lecture' [1965], *YouTube* (undated), <https://www.yout ube.com/watch?v=5tvzmuUPpNw>, accessed 20 October 2021.
Garland, Alex, dir., *Ex Machina* (Los Angeles: Universal Pictures, 2015).
Geronimi Clyde, Wilfred Jackson, and Hamilton Luske, dirs, *Alice in Wonderland* (Los Angeles: Walt Disney Animations Studios, 1951).
Mitchell, Kirsty, dir., *The Wonderland Book* (London: Kirsty Mitchell Photography, 2017).
Wachowski, Lana, dir., *The Matrix Resurrections* (Burbank: Warner Bros., 2021).
——, and Lilly Wachowski, dirs, *The Matrix* (Burbank: Warner Bros., 1999).
——, *The Matrix Reloaded* (Burbank: Warner Bros., 2003a).
——, *The Matrix Revolutions* (Burbank: Warner Bros., 2003b).

Poetry

Notes on Contributors

BRITTANI ALLEN is a PhD student in English Literature at Cardiff University. Her areas of interest are Victorian studies and children's literature, particularly environmental literature for children. Her thesis offers critical commentary about how a selection of nineteenth-century literature for children describes fantasy worlds in which unconventional features and behaviours occur providing lessons about humans, nonhumans, and other organisms cohabit to promote sustainability and futurity rather than exploitation.

FRANCESCA ARNAVAS is Research Fellow and Lecturer in Comparative Literature and Literary Theory at the University of Tartu. She works within the research group on Narrative, Culture, and Cognition. She has researched and published on Victorian literature, cognitive narratology, and literary Victorian and postmodern fairy tales. She is the author of *Lewis Carroll's 'Alice' and Cognitive Narratology: Author, Reader and Characters* (De Gruyter, 2021). Her second monograph, titled *Uncanny Fairy Tales: Hybrid Wonders in the Mirror*, has been published in 2024. She is the curator of the international art exhibition "Transforming Literary Places", part of the cultural programme of Tartu 2024 European Capital of Culture.

REBECCA BEVINGTON is completing a PhD in the University of York's Department of English and Related Literature, funded by the White Rose College of Arts and Humanities. Rebecca's thesis focuses on refugee women's literature and contemporary trauma writing, with a particular interest in testimonial and semi-testimonial representations of forced displacement, exile, and exception. She is also interested in dystopian literature, post-capitalist futures, accelerationism, and artificial intelligence.

CELIA BROWN was born in Cambridge, UK. After reading Human Sciences at Lady Margaret Hall, Oxford (1973–1976) she was awarded her

PhD in Sociology at the LSE London in 1982. She moved to Germany in 1980 to study painting at the State Academy for Fine Arts – Städelschule – in Frankfurt am Main (1980–1985). Celia now lives and works as an artist and independent scholar in Freiburg in the Black Forest, where she exhibits regularly at Galerie G. Images and conundrums inspired by her Alice research are often incorporated into her artworks. Her reflections on the mythological and historical influences on the Alice books were published in *Alice hinter den Mythen* (Wilhelm Fink, 2015). An art-science project at Freiburg and Oxford universities culminated in a book *Alice im Spiegelland* (transcript, 2012), with Alice playing the leading role in the lecture performances.

BRIGID CHERRY is an independent scholar who retired from the post of Research Fellow in Screen Media at St Mary's University, Twickenham. Her research is focused on the Gothic and horror in film and popular culture. Recent publications include work on the use of memes as fan discourse and fan art in *Twin Peaks* fandom and in *Doctor Who* fandom, on graphic novel adaptations of *Alice in Wonderland* and of *The Shadow over Innsmouth*, representations of real-world serial killers in crime drama, and Gothic aesthetics in the films of Tobe Hooper. She is the author of the books *Cult Media, Fandom and Textiles* (2018), and *Lost* (2021), and co-editor of *Doctor Who – New Dawn: Essays on the Jodie Whittaker Era* (2021).

NICK COATES (C Space) narrowly escaped a career in academia, writing his PhD – *Gardens in the Sands* – on space and the Francophone Caribbean novel, before deciding to apply his research skills elsewhere. Nick now leads C Space's global consulting efforts, helping make innovation more human, and humans more innovative. He is proud to have had a hand in Spotify's mood search, new luxury cruise brand Explora Journeys, the airport in Abu Dhabi, and more. But he is also a big advocate of curiosity, creativity, and co-creation, a subject he has published extensively on (including in the *European Business Review*). Even more curiously, he is working on a book project looking at the Beatles & Lewis Carroll, codenamed *Alice & The Eggmen*. He lives in East London with his family, nine cats, a bearded dragon, and a collection of ninety-four musical instruments – at last count.

NED COLVILLE entered the world of marketing, branding, and innovation with a somewhat tangential degree in Spanish and Linguistics (including a year spent teaching in Buenos Aires) and an enthusiastic helping of optimism that a job blending commerce and creativity was indeed a viable career choice. That hope has certainly been fulfilled on the pathway to his current role as Global Director of Human Truths at Interbrand, which was recently described by *The Financial Times* as the world's leading brand consultancy. He's delved into multiple thorny challenges of how to help brands grow over the years, including scooping into the world of ice cream as part of the team that created the indulgence paradox that is Unilever's Magnum Mini and navigating global cultural nuances of socializing on the move to contribute to the development of Diageo's Pocket Scotch. He rejects the outdated notion of making things and then trying to figure out how to make people want them (advertising in other words) and instead champions the cause of understanding what people want and then making those things, more commonly known as human-centred design. An occasional land-artist, shed-dweller, and proponent of the powers of introversion in an extroverted world, he lives in the Oxfordshire countryside with his wife and three children.

AMY DE NOBRIGA is Course Leader on the BA (Hons) Illustration programme at Leeds Arts University. She is an illustrator, researcher, and academic. She holds a BA (Hons) in Graphic Arts specializing in Illustration from Liverpool John Moore's University, a PGCE in Post Compulsory Education and Training from Edge Hill University, and an MA with distinction in Illustration and Graphic Design from Liverpool John Moore's University. Their practice-led research focuses on exploring unseen abstract narratives from literature through unorthodox methodologies, including data visualization, distance reading, and shape-based topologies.

MATTHEW DEMAKOS has been writing about the life and works of Lewis Carroll for over twenty years. His papers include 'Hiawatha Annotating,' an in-depth look into Carroll's poem 'Hiawatha's Photographing'; 'Alice's Adventures from *Under Ground* to *Wonderland*,' an exploration into the differences between the two works; 'Children through the Ages,' a study into the true ages of Carroll's so-called 'child-friends'; and 'The Authentic Wasp,' a look into the authorship of 'The Wasp in a Wig' episode. In a more comic bent, Demakos wrote 'Alice's Ups and Downs: A Pedantic Approach to Exactify Ambiguity in Wonderland' and its sequel 'Bounding Brooks and Hopping Hedges: Looking-Glass Chess For Beginners'. The first retells *Wonderland* with a keen eye on Alice's ever-changing height, and the second retells *Looking-Glass* while scrutinizing the chess moves made by the characters. He has also written on Carroll's shyness in 'Accountably and Unaccountably Shy,' and has two as-yet unpublished annotated versions of Carroll's poems 'The Walrus and the Carpenter' and 'A-sitting on a Gate'. He has also written five works related to John Tenniel. He is retired and lives in Chatham, NJ, USA, with his wife and three children.

JADE DILLON CRAIG Associate Professor of Children's Literature at the Norwegian University of Science and Technology, Norway. She is the author of *From How to Catch a Star to Now: Theorising Oliver Jeffers' Picturebooks* (forthcoming, Routledge) and co-editor of *Family in Children's and Young Adult Literature* (Routledge, 2023). She has published several book chapters and articles related to children's literature, Alice studies, fairy tales, and visual texts for young readers. She is co-editor of *Children's Literature in English Language Education*. Jade co-founded the Children's Literature Education and Research (CLEAR) research group at NTNU and is a founding board member of the Association for Research on Children's Literature in English in Norway (ARCLEN).

PAUL FAGAN is an Irish Research Council Postdoctoral Fellow at Maynooth University, where he is working on the project 'Celibacy in Irish Women's Writing, 1860s–1950s' (GOIPD/2022/634). He is a co-founder of the International Flann O'Brien Society, a founding general editor of the *Journal of Flann O'Brien Studies*, and an elected member of the International James Joyce Foundation Board of Trustees. Paul is the co-editor of *Finnegans Wake: Human and Nonhuman Histories* (2024), *Irish Modernisms: Gaps, Conjectures, Possibilities* (2021) and *Stage Irish: Performance, Identity, Cultural Circulation* (2021), as well as five edited volumes on Flann O'Brien – the most recent of being *Flann O'Brien and the Nonhuman: Animals, Environments, Machines* (Routledge, 2024). He is currently finalizing a monograph on Irish Literary Hoaxes.

HAYLEY FLYNN is an ECR whose PhD addressed 'The Dream Debate and the Periodical in the 1860s'. Her research interests include nineteenth-century dream interpretation guides and portrayals of the unconscious in literature and science in Victorian periodicals. She is currently working on an article about women and dream in the 1860s periodicals.

JOSEPHINE GABELMAN is an independent scholar who completed her PhD at the University of St Andrews in 2013. Her first monograph, *A Theology of Nonsense* with a foreword by John Milbank (Cambridge: Lutterworth Press, 2017) explores the connection between Lewis Carroll's literary nonsense and the Christian imagination. She is currently working on a new book, which challenges the theology of sanitation, offering instead a compostable approach to iniquity and holiness. It is tentatively titled: *Holy Shit: The Fertility of Sin*.

KAREN GARDINER has a multidisciplinary background, with a doctorate in Theology and Literature from Nottingham University on 'The Influence of F. D. Maurice on the Imaginative Works of Lewis Carroll', and an MA in Psychology of Religion from London University. She is a Church of England Parish Priest in North Yorkshire and is fascinated by the literary and psychological links between fantasy and theology.

ERIC GERLACH has taught courses in the history of philosophy and human thought at Berkeley City College for the past sixteen years, including Greek, Indian, Chinese, Islamic, French, German, and British philosophy, logic, and ethics. He is currently studying the work of Poe, Carroll, and Wittgenstein, and what they can show us about how thought, logic, and meaning work in abstract and concrete situations.

REBECCA GIBSON is Assistant Professor in the Anthropology Unit of the School of World Studies at Virginia Commonwealth University. She holds a PhD in biological anthropology from American University. Recent publications include *The Corseted Skeleton: A Bioarchaeology of Binding* (2020) and *Global Perspectives on the Liminality of the Supernatural: From Animus to Zombi* (2022). Her research interests are many and varied, ranging from robot/human sexual interactions, to gender and the supernatural, to corsets and skeletons. When not writing or teaching, she can be found reading mystery novels on a pile of stuffed animals, with a warm cup of tea.

JUSTINE HOUYAUX is a translator and translations studies PhD student at the Centre Interdisciplinaire de Recherche en Traduction et en Interprétation (CIRTI) of ULiège (Belgium). Her research focuses on the translation of cultural elements in the French translations of *Alice's Adventures in Wonderland* from 1869 to 2019, and she regularly strays away from it to go down various rabbit holes, including but not limited to Louis Aragon's contribution – the French reception of Carroll, the Surrealists, and the Interwar period. Her first book, a critical edition of René Bour's 1937 translation of *Alice's Adventures in Wonderland* (Presses Universitaires de Liège, 2023), dives into those incidental points of interest.

CLARE IMHOLTZ is an independent researcher from Beltsville, Maryland. She is currently preparing an edition of Lewis Carroll's letters to *Alice* playwright Henry Savile Clarke. A former secretary of the Lewis Carroll Society of North America, she has published several articles and edited two books about Lewis Carroll. Her research on Carroll-Macmillan relations has been published in *Papers of the Bibliographic Society of America*, *The Book Collector*, and elsewhere. By profession, she is a retired librarian.

CHRISTOPHER (KIT) KELEN is a poet and painter, resident of Worimi lands, in the Myall Lakes of New South Wales. Published widely since the 1970s, he has more than a dozen full-length collections in English as well as translated books of poetry. An Anne Elder and ABC/Bicentennial Award winner in the distant past, in 2017, Kit was shortlisted twice for the Montreal Poetry Prize and won the Local Award in the Newcastle Poetry Prize. In 2019 and 2020 Kit won the Hunter Writers' Centre award in the NPP. He was also shortlisted for the ACU prize in 2020. In 2021 he won the bronze medal in the Newcastle Poetry Prize. As a visual artist, over the last fifteen years, Kit has had ten solo painting and drawing exhibitions in Australia, Portugal, Spain, Sweden, and Macao. Emeritus Professor of English at the University of Macau, where he taught for many years, Kit Kelen is also a Conjoint Professor at the University of Newcastle. In his scholarly writing, Kit has produced a string of books about poetry, the most recent of which is Poetics and Ethics of Anthropomorphism – children, animals, and poetry, published by Routledge in 2022. In 2017, Kit was awarded an honorary doctorate by the University of Malmo, in Sweden. You can follow Kit's work-in-progress at the Daily Kit – <https://thedailykitkelen.blogspot.com/>.

ANNA KÉRCHY is Full Professor of English Literature at the University of Szeged, Hungary. She is interested in interfacing Victorian and postmodern fantastic imagination, gender/body studies, humanimal studies, children's/YA literature, and intermedial dynamics. Her publications include the monograph *Alice in Transmedia Wonderland* (2016) which won the HUSSE book award, 'The Acoustics of Nonsense in Lewis Carroll's Alice Tales' (*IRCL*, 2020), 'Alice's Non-Anthropocentric Ethics' (CVE, 2018), and a forthcoming anthology of 'Jabberwocky's' translations co-edited with Björn Sundmark, Kit Kelen, and Michael Everson.

AFRINUL HAQUE KHAN is Assistant Professor and Head in the Department of English at Nirmala College, Ranchi, India. Her papers have been published in several reputed national and international journals and books. She has done her doctoral research on the works of V. S. Naipaul and her thesis is titled 'Displacement and Migration: Major

Themes in the Works of V. S. Naipaul'. Her areas of research include nineteenth- and twentieth-century British Literature, Postcolonial Literature, Dalit Literature, Film Studies, Gender Studies, etc. Her recent publications include 'V. S. Naipaul and Jhumpa Lahiri: The Politics of Identity and the Performance of Exoticism', in *Representing the Exotic and the Familiar: Politics and Perception in Literature* (Bharat and Grover, 2019), '"Masculinizing" the Women: Strategic De/Reconstruction of Gender in the Fiction of South Asian Women Writers', in *Development, Governance and Gender in South Asia: Perspectives, Issues and Challenges* (Rahman and Tiwari, 2021) and 'Shaping the Culture of Tolerance: A Study of Forster's Humanism in Howard's End and A Passage to India' in *Polish Journal of English Studies*.

FRANZISKA E. KOHLT is an author, broadcaster, and researcher in History of Science, Comparative Literature, and Science Communication. She holds a DPhil from the University of Oxford, where she investigated the intertwined histories of the nascent science of Psychology and fantasy literature in Victorian Britain. She is currently a Leverhulme Research Fellow at the University of Leeds and the Inaugural Carrollian Fellow of the University of Southern California. She is the author of *The Folklore of Dreams* (Audible, 2022) and *Alice Through the Wonderglass* (Reaktion, 2025). Her research interests include childhood culture, history of psychology, education, and entomology. She is also a former translator for Marvel Comics.

PIERFRANCESCO LA MURA is a mathematician, poet, and translator. He received a PhD from Stanford University in 2001, and between 2001 and 2003, he was Fellow of the Institute for Advanced Studies at the Hebrew University of Jerusalem. Since 2003 Piero has been Professor at the HHL Leipzig Graduate School of Management, where he holds the Chair of Economics and Information Systems. In 1986 he won the 'Premio Nazionale di Poesia Ciro Coppola'. He also translated several classical and contemporary poets, including Sappho, L. Carroll, A. Ginsberg, and E. Ostashevsky.

AMANDA LASTORIA holds North America's first PhD in Publishing. She has more than a decade of professional experience in the publishing industry, most significantly in the area of book production. Amanda developed the standard lists of titles for Sir John Tenniel's *Wonderland* and *Looking-Glass* illustrations and is the former Editor of *Lewis Carroll Review*. She teaches histories of publishing with an emphasis on materiality at Simon Fraser University and histories of print practice at Emily Carr University of Art + Design in Vancouver, Canada.

GUILHERME MAGRI DA ROCHA holds a doctoral degree in Letters from the São Paulo State University (UNESP). His research focuses on Modernist Anglo-American children's literature. He has received funding for his research from The São Paulo Research Foundation – FAPESP and has conducted research at various universities and institutions. He has experience teaching English language, literature, and culture in various educational settings. He has also organized academic and cultural events and worked on various research projects.

ANN MARTIN is Associate Professor in the Department of English, University of Saskatchewan. In addition to articles on Canadian, British, and American modernisms, her publications include the monograph *Red Riding Hood and the Wolf in Bed: Modernism's Fairy Tales*, *Interdisciplinary/Multidisciplinary Woolf* co-edited with Kathryn Holland, and *Virginia Woolf in the Modern Machine Age*, a special issue of the *Virginia Woolf Miscellany*. With Christopher Townsend, she is currently co-editing the essay collection *Modernity Must Drive: The Motor Car, Material Cultures, and British Modernisms*.

TOM MCLEISH, FRS, was a soft matter physicist and Professor of Natural Philosophy at the University of York, where he was also a member of the Centre for Medieval Studies and Humanities Research Centre. He led the UK 'Physics for Life' Network, and co-led the 'Ordered Universe' project. He was Canon Scientist at St Alban's Cathedral, author of *Faith and Wisdom in Science* (OUP, 2014) and *The Poetry and Music of Science* (OUP, 2019), and was Chair of the Royal Society's Education Committee.

Tom was passionate about radical interdisciplinary thinking, contributing to several national reports on interdisciplinary research. Tom passed away in February 2023 and is greatly missed.

ADAM PAXMAN is Academic Skills Advisor in the Student Engagement Team at Edge Hill University (EHU). Adam has contributed a chapter on EHU's postgraduate online pre-arrival induction platform to a Staff and Educational Development Association (SEDA) book due for publication by Routledge in 2023. He previously lectured in FE, HE, and HE-in-FE, specializing in Contextual Studies for various design programmes. Adam has also previously worked as a freelance illustrator. He has presented papers informed by speculative fiction and illustration practice-as-research on Arthur Rackham, Lewis Carroll, George MacDonald and *Through the Looking-Glass, and What Alice Found There* at symposia and conferences. Adam's research has appeared in the *Journal of Illustration* and *North Wind: A Journal of George MacDonald Studies*. He contributed an abstract about fictional research satirizing pre-school TV favourite *Paw Patrol* to the *Journal of Imaginary Research*. Adam also independently publishes fiction and poetry books via Amazon.

ADRIANA PELIANO is a visual artist, designer, illustrator, writer, and Alice hunter. Her work travels on different media through objects, collages, assemblages, and installations, dialoguing with literature, video, music, theatre, and fashion. She graduated in Communication at UnB (University of Brasília, 1999), accomplished an MA in New Media Arts at KIAD (Maidstone, UK, 2003) and received a Master's degree in Aesthetics and Art History at USP (São Paulo, 2012). She has illustrated both *Alices* twice, translated the *Underground* Manuscript into Portuguese recreating Carroll's graphic design, founded the Lewis Carroll Society of Brazil, and published articles and books both in Portuguese and English such as *Alice and the Seven Keys* (Underline, 2021).

NILCE M. PEREIRA is a lecturer in English Literature at the State University of São Paulo, Brazil, where she teaches at both undergraduate and graduate levels. Her primary research interests include translation and intercultural studies; Shakespeare studies; Victorian literature and culture; (the translation of) children's literature; comics and graphic narratives; and the association of the verbal and the visual in illustrated publications.

CLEIDE ANTONIA RAPUCCI holds a doctoral degree in Letters from the São Paulo State University (UNESP). She is a retired professor at the School of Sciences, Languages, and Humanities, where she taught from 1990 to 2023 and retired as a lecturer in the Department of Modern Languages. She has experience in English Literature, with emphasis on Angela Carter, literary translation, feminist criticism, and female character. She has published a book *Mulher e Deusa: a construção do feminino em Fireworks de Angela Carter* and is a certified translator in the English language. She is a member of the ANPOLL GT, 'Vertentes do insólito ficcional'.

JOSHUA RAWLEIGH is a PhD candidate in English literature at Indiana University, Bloomington, and received his MSt by Research in Victorian Literature from the University of Edinburgh. His research focuses on the roles that literary form, religious contexts, and the past play in shaping British literature during the long nineteenth century. His doctoral dissertation focuses on prophecy as a mode of address that enabled the creation of otherwise inaccessible social visions in the long nineteenth century. His recent work has appeared in *The Journal of Scottish and Irish Studies* and *Reading Religion*.

CATHERINE RICHARDS is an independent scholar and researcher of the life, works, and legacy of Charles Lutwidge Dodgson, better known as 'Lewis Carroll'. She is co-editor of the research website *Lewis Carroll Resources* and serves on the editorial board of *The Snarkologist*, a journal dedicated to Lewis Carroll's epic nonsense poem, *The Hunting of the Snark*. Current research interests include parody, early theatre productions, and 'Alice' as a symbol of Britishness.

ADAM ROBERTS is Professor of Nineteenth-Century Literature at Royal Holloway, University of London. He is the author of twenty-four novels and many non-fiction and academic works, including *History of Science Fiction* (2nd edn 2016) and *H. G. Wells: a Literary Life* (2019). His most recent novel is *The This* (Gollancz, 2022). He was born exactly 100 years after the publication of *Alice's Adventures in Wonderland* and presently lives a little way west of London.

BAS SAVENIJE graduated in Philosophy in 1977. Since then, he has held a range of positions at Utrecht University, amongst them as university librarian. From June 2009 until January 2015, he was Director General of the Koninklijke Bibliotheek, National Library of the Netherlands. Since January 2015, he is an independent advisor with a particular interest in the free and unlimited accessibility of scholarly publications (Open Access). Also he is the chairman of the Dutch Lewis Carroll Society (www.lewi scarrollgenootschap.nl). For more information: www.bassavenije.nl.

ELLEN (ELLIE) SCHAEFER-SALINS is a third-generation collector of Lewis Carroll books and related items. The Schaefer collection started in the 1890s and is the oldest collection still in private hands. Dr Schaefer-Salins also claims to have the largest collection of Wonderland teapots in the world with over 230 teapots. As an Associate Professor of Social Work at Salisbury University (Maryland, USA), she teaches courses in clinical social work, diversity issues, deaf studies, and disability studies. She is fluent in American Sign Language and has worked as a social worker and mental health therapist in the deaf community in the Washington, DC area for over thirty-five years. Her work continues with deaf clients in a small mental health private practice in addition to her full-time university responsibilities. The chapter blends her interests in Lewis Carroll and clinical social work/psychology.

NICHOLAS SCHILERO graduated from Ohio State University in 2015. He studied Philosophy, Logic, and Linguistics. He is a blogger, an aspiring horror movie maker, and children's book author. Check out his upcoming projects at his website WarpedMindsMedia.com.

BJÖRN SUNDMARK is Professor of English Literature at Malmö University (Sweden), where he teaches English literature and children's literature. He is the author of the study *Alice in the Oral-Literary Continuum* (Lund UP, 1999), and the co-editor of four essay collections: *Translating and Transmediating Children's Literature* (Palgrave Macmillan, 2020), *The Nation in Children's Literature* (Routledge, 2013), *Child Autonomy and Child Governance in Children's Literature: Where Children Rule* (Routledge, 2016), and *Silence and Silencing in Children's Literature* (Makadam, 2021). He was the editor of *Bookbird – Journal of International Children's Literature* 2015–2018, served on the Swedish Arts Council 2013–2016, and was Chair of the Swedish August Jury 2016–2019.

JAN SUSINA is Professor of English at Illinois State University, where he offers courses in Children's Literature and Victorian Studies. He is the author of *The Place of Lewis Carroll in Children's Literature* (Routledge 2010).

LAURENCE TALAIRACH is Professor of English Literature at the University of Toulouse Jean Jaurès and Associate Researcher at the Alexandre-Koyré Center for the History of Science and Technology. Her research interests cover medicine, life sciences, and English literature in the long nineteenth century. Her most recent monograph is *Animals, Museum Culture and Children's Literature in Nineteenth-Century Britain: Curious Beasties* (Palgrave Macmillan, 2021). She is the author of five monographs, nine edited volumes, over seventy articles, and a series of twenty-seven children's books (Enquêtes au museum), which deal with biodiversity and conservation and take place in natural history museums.

MICHELLE WITEN is Junior Professor of English and Irish Literature at the Europa-Universität Flensburg (Germany) as well as Director of the EUF Centre for Irish Studies. She obtained her DPhil from the University of Oxford and is the author of *James Joyce and Absolute Music* (Bloomsbury 2018) and co-editor of *Modernism in Wonderland* (Bloomsbury 2023/ 2024). Recent publications include articles on *Darby O'Gill and the*

Little People and Stage Irishness, the Ladybird Books and Brexit, *Dracula* and the Irish Question, and a co-edited special issue of the *James Joyce Quarterly* on 'Joyce and the Nonhuman'.

LUXIN YIN won a full scholarship on the Erasmus+ program in Children's Literature, Media, and Culture, and graduated from the University of Glasgow in 2022. She joined The Ohio State University in 2022 to study Medical Humanities and Social Sciences. Her research explores youth health, doctor–patient relationships, and the health decisions and negotiations of people with disabilities and chronic illness.

Index

Genre Fiction and Film Companions

Series Editor: Simon Bacon

The *Genre Fiction and Film Companions* provide accessible introductions to key texts within the most popular genres of our time. Written by leading scholars in the field, brief essays on individual texts offer innovative ways of understanding, interpreting and reading the topics in question. Invaluable for students, teachers and fans alike, these surveys offer new insights into the most important literary works, films, music, events and more within genre fiction and film.

We welcome proposals for edited collections on new genres and topics. Please contact baconetti@googlemail.com or oxford@peterlang.com.

Published Volumes

The Gothic
Edited by Simon Bacon

Cli-Fi
Edited by Axel Goodbody and Adeline Johns-Putra

Horror
Edited by Simon Bacon

Sci-Fi
Edited by Jack Fennell

Monsters
Edited by Simon Bacon

Transmedia Cultures
Edited by Simon Bacon

Shirley Jackson
Edited by Kristopher Woofter